Mr Shakespeare's Whore

by

Lizzie Jones

**Grosvenor House
Publishing Limited**

This book is published by
Grosvenor House Publishing Ltd
28-30 High Street, Guildford, Surrey, GU1 3HY.
www.grosvenorhousepublishing.co.uk

A CIP record for this book
is available from the British Library

ISBN 978-1-907652-62-2

All the known facts about the life of Aemilia Bassano are incorporated in the novel. All the characters in the novel, with the exception of Vincenzo Albinoni, are real historical personages.

Dedicated to all those who like to hear me talk about the 16th & 17th centuries and whose interest has been my inspiration.

"This above all, to thine own self be true,"
William Shakespeare.

PRELUDE

As I waited for him to come to me my heart was thumping painfully and seeming as loud as a playhouse drum in the silence. I had to admit to being afraid as I wondered what this first night would be like. I had fancied myself as worldly-wise but now my eighteen years seemed too few for I had no experience in the arts of love and he was sixty-three. Images were whirling around in my mind but they must have been plucked from imagination and literature for I hadn't dared to tell anyone or ask advice. Neither was there the sanction and support of solemn church vows as there had been with my sister Angela. I felt completely on my own in these unfamiliar surroundings and for once my self-confidence deserted me in the full realisation that I had put myself at his disposal.

A young maidservant had brought my supper on silver plates, capon and sallets aureate with marigold flowers, and a glass decanter of dark ruby wine. Seated in solitary splendour in a high-backed ornately carved chair at the head of the table, I had only toyed with the food, for nervousness had taken away my appetite. But I filled and re-filled the fragile crystal goblet with the rich pungent liquor until its musky sweetness made my head whirl and my throat feel parchment dry. The panelled walls of dark burnished oak shed a lambent warmth in the glow from the branched candelabra overhead, lulling me into a dreamlike trance. Through the open doorway

I could see into the bedchamber which was dominated by the enormous tester bed hung with drapes of gold damask, the matching counterpane turned back in readiness to reveal the pristine sheen of silk sheets, and my fears began to plague me again, my thoughts dancing as restlessly as the flickering sequins of candlelight on the polished surface of the table and the silverware.

The maid returned to take away the remnants of my half-eaten meal then when she had cleared away, in silence and with lowered eyes, she spoke in her soft country accent, "I will help you get ready."

Her words took me by surprise as I immediately thought, Am I not ready dressed in my finest embroidered gown. Then I realised the significance of what she meant as she took from one of the chests in the dressing chamber a shift fashioned from such fine lawn as to make it almost transparent, the sleeves and neck edged with costly cobweb lace. The temptation to change my mind and run from the room surged within me as I realised the inevitability of my situation. Yet despite my qualms, something stayed my steps more than her deft unlacing of my bodice and corset, the untying of my petticoat and the removal of my linen shift. Then she was brushing my hair, struggling with the recalcitrant curls until it hung to my waist in a black rippling cloud. "His Lordship will be with you shortly," she murmured and after dropping a brief curtsey she closed the door behind her, leaving me alone again. I shivered. I was accustomed to my nightshift of plain coarse linen and I felt naked and exposed beneath the gossamer covering. Returning to the dressing room I found the chest in which I had seen an array of cloaks and robes and took out a sleeveless mantle of azure blue velvet, the colour of a midsummer sky. Wrapping

2

it around me, I crossed into the parlour and looked through the leaded window panes at the murky river, the encroaching night folding its shadows around the busy traffic but a barge or wherry occasionally illumined by a sudden shaft of gold as the sunset struggled to keep its radiance a little longer. The familiar scene brought with it memories of home and safety and suddenly I was filled with a great longing to wait for a young man of my own age whom I loved and really wished to give myself to. I closed my eyes as the vision of Robert Devereux intruded. For a moment I fought against a feeling of panic but when I opened my eyes again I relished the luxury of my surroundings, deep padded seats, silver candlesticks, embroidered drapes and tapestry hangings with mildly erotic scenes to titillate the senses. The fleeting regret vanished for this was what I was getting in exchange for giving myself to a man I scarcely knew, a man forty-five years older than I was. This was the royal palace of Whitehall. This was the entree into the life I had always wanted, that I had aspired to and was determined to have. I was nervous and I felt vulnerable but I had no wish to return to my old life at any cost.

My lute was one of the few possessions I had brought with me and I took it from where it lay on a padded settle of cobalt velvet. Its familiarity soothed me as I fingered it lovingly, caressing the neck of polished cedarwood and plucking the strings haphazardly, then because music always calmed me I began to play some of my father's favourite tunes. He always came into my mind when I was happy or sad, pensive or just playing music, and the lilting notes carried the cadences of his voice to my ears - "I am afraid a musician's daughter has not the status ever to be a great lady." I wondered what he would think if he could see me now. After all it was he who had first introduced me to the Queen's kinsman at Kenilworth castle when I was seven years old. I wondered if he would be disappointed or proud of me. He would not be shocked, not my father with his unconventional spirit, but I could not be certain he would be pleased that the life I had chosen for myself was that of a paramour.

CHAPTER 1

OVERTURE

The memories I have of my father are of music and laughter, wine-breathed kisses, long slender fingers caressing my hair, stories told in a language I seemed always to have understood, and again, always, music. My memories are out of all proportion to the time I knew him because his joyful spirit coloured all my early life, his inheritance bequeathed me the passion and rich culture of his native land, and the music which flowed in his veins became inseparable from my existence.

One of my last memories of him was the great celebration at Kenilworth Castle, fourteen days of entertainment for Queen Elizabeth orchestrated by the Earl of Leicester as the finale of that year's elaborate progress through the midland shires. He was one of the musicians providing the entertainment and I thought I was going to miss his presence at home once again until he made the suggestion that was to change my life.

"Don't be foolish, Battista, it's quite out of the question that you should take Aemilia to Warwick."

I was almost asleep on the settle when I was roused by my mother's words, her speech always sounding sharp and impatient in contrast to my father's gently harmonious tones with their rhythmic cadences and lilting Italian vowels. "Who would care for her while you were working, where would she stay, and besides it is too long a journey for a child of seven years."

I pressed myself deeper into the soft cushions of the oak settle, which ran almost the length of the wall to the left of the big stone fireplace, trying to make myself invisible so that no movement might make them aware of my listening.

"We are to be lodged in citizens' houses, there will be a truckle bed for her. She can sit and listen while I play as she often does, she will not stray far from my sight. And on the journey she can ride in front of me and if it should rain there will be room in the covered wagon that is to convey our instruments and our baggage." As usual my father sounded amused by the thought of difficulties and I could imagine his brown eyes sparkling in his long dark face.

"You take it upon yourself to presume the agreement of others to your plans without asking their opinion. Has it occurred to you that your fellows might not welcome the addition of a child to your company?"

"Dai, we are all kin, they love Aemilia. There will be no discordance on that score. Come, Meg, think what a wonderful experience it will be for her. This is to be an entertainment such as the Court has never seen before. And all the sights of the journey too, the child has never before left London. She will be in the open countryside instead of in the stink and heat of the city, prey to all the dangers of disease and miasma in the heat of summer."

Holding my breath I didn't realise that this was the argument most likely to sway my mother whose fear of London's plague months was well justified, having suffered the loss of my two young brothers. As she did not demur further, my father continued, "Think how splendid the entertainment at Kenilworth will be. They say Lord Robert has spared no expense to provide an unsurpassed spectacle for the Queen."

"They say it is all an attempt to win her hand in marriage," sniffed my mother disparagingly but I could sense by her tone of voice that her objections were lessening, as they usually did to my father's persuasions once she had made known her dissatisfaction.

"Dai, he has tried too long and too often for that and the Queen is now past forty," my father laughed. "Besides the rumour goes that he is now ensnared by the Earl of Essex's widow, the beautiful Lettice, wild, willing - and young!" I pricked up my ears, especially when my mother snorted disapprovingly. "But the money he is eager to expend on the project is beyond our wildest imaginations. So, Meg, will you give your consent to Aemilia coming with me. I will take good care of her as you know."

From where I was curled on the settle I couldn't see my parents' faces but I knew that my mother's expression would have hardened as she said tartly, "It would really make little difference what I said. You always go your own way, Battista." My father didn't reply and once again I was aware of some discord between my parents that I did not understand. "And what about Angela?" my mother continued. "It doesn't seem fair to exclude her. She is the elder and by right any favour should go to her." I held my breath, lifting my head a little from the cushion's velvet folds in order to see my father's reaction. I had thought I was safe but this was a new objection and could be more dangerous.

"Angela is nearly fourteen, not a suitable age to take in a party of men and courtiers, most of them careless and some of them licentious. Besides Angela is not so fond of music as is Aemilia."

The danger was over and I smiled secretly to myself. I had always known that I was my father's favourite.

He tried not to make distinctions but I knew and I loved him for it. I resembled him. Angela was always considered prettier with the same rosy complexion and wide blue eyes as our mother and silky brown hair that stayed obediently where it had been brushed. My skin was sallow, my eyes dark as bugle beads and my black hair curly, thick and unruly. People called me "la piccola Italiana." I knew I wasn't complimented like Angela and I was very conscious of the mole in the base of my throat, but I was my father's favourite and that was all that mattered. Like him I loved music above all things and quickly grasped what he taught me, already in his estimation performing well on the lute and the recorder he had bought for me. I was like him in other ways too but I didn't know it then.

"I suppose the presence of the child might inhibit your philandering," my mother muttered as her final contribution to the discussion but I didn't understand the significance of the words. I was exhilarated with joy that not only was I to be part of the Court for two weeks, to be in the presence of the Queen herself, to be going on a long exciting journey, but all this in company with my father.

The visit to Kenilworth Castle was to remain the most vivid of all my childhood recollections. The short time I knew my father was full of happy memories, of holding his hand and meeting the Queen in the Palace of Whitehall, of watching a play in the Blackfriars when he was part of the music and afterwards being taken to speak with the actors, of perching on his shoulders while we watched a water pageant on the Thames, of sitting in the garden on fine summer evenings or beside the big fireplace in the parlour on cold winter nights while he told me stories of Italy or played music to me or taught me to play the lute and the recorder. But those summer days in the year 1575 were emblazoned for ever in my memory as the high-rising sun by day and the thousands of candles by night illuminated the sparkling costumes and jewels of the Queen and the Court like the celestial vision in Dante's Paradiso.

The journey to Warwickshire had been full of strange sights for me who had never been out of London. At first I had been overwhelmed by the sheer expanse of fields of pasture or waving grain, wooded hills and endless sky, and was glad of my father's strong arms around me as we rode and the laughter and singing of the procession of musicians. I had seen fields in London but not such endless vistas and most of the time I was accustomed to narrow streets crowded with bustling throngs and hemmed in by tall close-packed buildings where it was almost impossible to see the sky. Here in this unfamiliar landscape animals were more plentiful than people with only field-labourers and shepherds or groups of milkmaids to stare at us between scattered villages, though sometimes we passed farm carts loaded with produce or a pedlar bent double under his loaded pack.

But when we arrived at Kenilworth I thought I had reached the land of faerie, a place of enchantment that I knew from my father's tales of knights and damsels, nymphs and sorcerers. I caught my breath in amazement as in the distance I saw its towering battlements rising from the heat haze, the castle seeming to float above the mass of water surrounding it. As we rode closer I could see the encircling moat spreading out into a pool and then into the great lake which spanned two sides of the huge medieval castle. Then we were riding across the wooden bridge which traversed the moat and where workmen were busy erecting posts all along its length, ready to hang the banners and heraldic emblems celebrating the Queen's majesty, my father explained. Across the moat we passed through a splendid new gatehouse where my father pointed out to me the initials carved in the stone, R.D. for Robert Dudley, Earl of Leicester, who had received the castle as a gift from the Queen and then spent a fortune rebuilding, renovating and creating new apartments. Once through the gatehouse the gardens stretched ahead. To the right was a formal intricately designed pleasure garden with imaginatively contrived fountains, some cascading water in rainbow hues, beds of flowers in a riot of colour and hedges cut into fantastic shapes. To the left informal parks and pathways, crowded now with a vivid tapestry of strolling courtiers, led into the distant hunting grounds. Still we had to pass through another gatehouse, this time the old four-square Norman keep, and then we found ourselves in the inner court of the castle itself, flanked on two sides by the medieval Great Hall which Lord Leicester had restored to its original magnificence and to which he had added imposing buildings recently constructed with all new-fashioned comforts.

"Fit for a Queen indeed," my father commented, his eyebrows rising in speculation at the opulence of the new constructions.

"Fit for a King perhaps," laughed Alfonso Ferrabosco, his friend and fellow musician in the Queen's Musick. "Perhaps we were mistaken about Lord Robert's ambitions."

I listened intently. My father spoke carelessly with his friends and I liked to listen to the conversation of the musicians who were familiar with the gossip of the Court.

We went first to the Great Hall where the musicians were often to play although much of the entertainment was planned for outdoors if the fine weather held. The hall was high and vast with a vaulted roof soaring upwards supported by carved stone pillars. Tall arched windows with stone tracery of fruit and foliage filled the huge space with light, and between the windows on one side an enormous ornately carved marble fireplace spread its bulk. At either end of the hall a dais had been prepared, one draped in purple velvet and cloth of gold on which stood a gold throne for the Queen, the other red-curtained and with stools for the performers. Every room we passed through was rich with colour - hangings and tapestries with stories on them that I wanted to stop and study, carved chairs and tables inlaid with ivory and mother-of-pearl, gold and silver plate, rainbow hued Venetian glass, and burnished mirrors to reflect the myriad tints of sun-touched gems by day and the thousands of candles which would glow in the candelabra and wall sconces by night. I had never seen anything so wonderful in all my life, not even on my one visit to the Palace of Whitehall, and I had to keep blinking my eyes to make sure I wasn't dreaming while my father, his hand holding mine, smiled contentedly at my delight.

"Here comes Lord Robert, Earl of Leicester," he whispered, and instinctively I hid in the background as Robert Dudley came to welcome the musicians and make his wants known to them. While they talked I had time to study him carefully - tall and handsome but with a florid face and tending towards stoutness, not much younger than my father but moustached whereas my father was always clean shaven. He was splendidly dressed in a tightly laced amber velvet doublet pricked and slashed with gold, the high collar surmounted by a double-tiered ruff that made his head look separate from his body, and a black velvet hat embellished with curling red feathers sat jauntily atop his thinning brown hair. I had heard my father say that he and the Queen had loved each other for many years and it was thought at one time that they would wed. I wondered what he had looked like then when he was young. He must have been very handsome. Now there were whispers that he was planning to marry the beautiful widow of the Earl of Essex. She had a young family and I wondered what would happen to them now that the Queen's favourite was to be their new father. A loud peal of laughter interrupted my musings and I saw that it was my father enjoying some private merriment with the Earl who was punching him playfully in the ribs as he made some jocund remark. Then he was taking me into his care again though I noticed a smile played around his lips as if he were still recalling some pleasant memory.

We were lodged, together with most people who were not of the nobility, in inns and citizens' houses in Warwick, an hour's ride on horseback. I couldn't wait to go back to the faerie castle and hardly slept that night for excitement, constantly rising from my narrow truckle bed in the chamber cramped with sleeping bodies to look for signs of the dawn, and as soon as rose ribbons streaked the sky I was ready dressed. Perhaps it won't be there, I thought fearfully, perhaps it will have vanished in the night as in one of King Arthur's adventures, but then far in the distance I saw its nebulous shape rising out of the early morning mist.

The musicians were to welcome the Queen in the inner courtyard and my father perched me on one of the walls to watch. I was not able to see the first part of her arrival where the Lady of the Lake appeared floating on the water to the accompaniment of a speech of welcome delivered by an actor on the bridge, but when she appeared through the gatehouse into the inner courtyard, despite the great press of people, I was able to see her clearly. I caught my breath in amazement because even from the distance I was entranced by this faerie queen sparkling with gems, her bejewelled white dress dazzling the eyes, the sun fingering her red hair with sparks of gold. This was the Queen of England, our Queen, and I, Aemilia Bassano, was part of that great crowd who worshipped her.

The week passed all too quickly in a flurry of musical concerts, plays, water pageants, masques, fireworks on the lake, all amidst a throng of lavishly garbed courtiers and their ladies, each trying to outdo the others in the richness of their costumes and jewels. And always in the centre reigned the Queen - Queen of the Castle, Lady of the Lake, Mistress of all mens' hearts. I felt so proud that my father's music was part of this splendour. Within the castle walls or outside in the balmy air his recorder, sweet and nimble, darted like quicksilver amongst the consorts of recorders, viols and lutes, as the best musicians in England made music divine as the heavenly spheres. During the water pageant the musicians were concealed inside the body of a gigantic dolphin, then during the firework display they played on barges where beneath them, under the surface of the lake, fireworks magically burned without being extinguished. For me the enchantment never stopped.

My father wasn't always in attendance. On some days the Queen went hunting when it was said Lord Robert provided all manner of diversions for her; on two days there was rain so the Queen took her rest; while on another day the people of Coventry provided their own entertainment for their Sovereign. On those days my father kept me beside him and we explored the gardens, the water meadows and the deer parks, when he explained everything to me and told me stories about people we met. Sometimes we watched the entertainments together, one day seeing an Italian acrobat who performed such incredible feats with his body that his limbs seemed to be made of lute strings, and afterwards my father talked with him about their native land for a long time. He knew so many people, so many courtiers, and always they stopped to talk to him. I thought the ladies especially liked to talk and laugh with him. One such golden lady in a glowing satin gown of buttercup yellow with huge padded sleeves of gold and white stripes, her auburn curls peeping beneath her cap of gold mesh, kissed him on the lips and pouting petulantly asked, "Why did you bring the child, Battista?"

My father replied, "Perhaps it was to protect myself from too much temptation," before returning her kiss and whispering in her ear something that made her tremble with laughter.

On another occasion we encountered a richly dressed courtier before whom my father removed his hat and made a deep bow. Surprisingly the man did not continue on his way but after a brief nod of the head in return asked, "And who is your delightful companion this time, Signor Bassano? With her striking looks she must of necessity be your daughter."

"My daughter Aemilia, my Lord."

"A beautiful child." The man put his hand lightly on my head and I gazed solemnly up at him. No-one had ever called me beautiful before except my father. He was of my father's age, nearing fifty years old, and the same build, tall and spare, with a long face adorned by a small pointed beard and deep-set appraising grey eyes. But where my father wore the Royal livery, he was dressed in a padded black silk doublet slashed with gold and lavishly decorated with gold braid, and his reddish brown hair peeped beneath a stiff high-crowned hat of black velvet embellished with several jewelled brooches. He put his hand beneath my chin and smiled down at me and though I smiled shyly back at him I felt no intimation of the significance of the encounter, not even the fluttering of a butterfly's wing that can eventually bring about a tempest.

After he had gone my father said, "That was Lord Hunsdon, the Queen's cousin and one of the highest nobles in the kingdom. You are greatly honoured that he should take note of you, tesoro."

There were so many great lords and ladies surrounding the Queen but always she drew mens' eyes. Her gowns she changed several times a day but they were always blindingly brilliant with gold, silver, precious stones and jewelled embroidery, her ruffs of fine lace and tulle floating behind her like gossamer clouds, her vivid red hair on top of which sat the aeriest confections of gold wire and gems.

I had last seen her at the Yuletide festivities but then only briefly. My father had presented her with a Venetian lute as his New Year gift, a custom followed by all her servants from the greatest to the lowest. He had made one of his periodic visits to Italy that year, to his home town of Bassano del Grappa where he was born and where the family still held property, then on to Venice where he and his brothers had been reared as their father made musical instruments for the Doge. From his father's own workshop now operated by his brother Giacomo, the only one of his five brothers not to seek his fortune in England, he had brought back a beautiful instrument inlaid with ivory and with thirty one ribs. The Queen loved all things Italian - fashions, literature, music - and spoke always with Italians in their own tongue. She had been so delighted with the gift that she granted him the privilege of presenting his family to her. So my mother, Angela, and myself, all in our best clothes and accompanied by my father, waited one January morning in the Presence Chamber. I was agog with excitement though holding onto my father's hand in the splendour of our surroundings. The lofty tapestry-hung hall was thronged each morning by all those who had permission to be at Court and hoped to be singled out for the Queen's special attention as, preceded by a procession of noble lords with the Lord Chancellor bearing the seals of state and two gentlemen carrying the royal sceptre and sword, accompanied by her ladies-in-waiting all dressed in white, and guarded by the Gentlemen Pensioners in red damask and carrying gold battleaxes, she made her way into the Privy Chamber where only the most privileged persons might enter. My mother only accompanied my father to concerts at Court on the rarest of occasions and she stood now, uncomfortable in her best padded gown of grey brocade trimmed with fur and paralysed with fear at the thought of having to speak with the Queen. Angela had caught her nervousness like an ague and stood with lowered eyes but I was bubbling with excitement, taking everything in and unable to keep still despite my mother's severe looks. As the Queen passed she stopped before us, greeted my father then spoke a brief word with my mother, smiling at Angela and me as we curtseyed low, before continuing on her daily round. I remember thinking then that I wanted to be part of this glorious company myself, participating in the life of the Court with all its splendour, mixing with rich and important people.

Now after fourteen magical days at Kenilworth my imagination was fired the more. I knew that what I wanted from life was to be a great lady and I told my father this as we made the long journey homeward, tired now but still buoyed with exhilaration. "When I am grown I want to be a Court lady and serve the Queen and wear beautiful gowns and jewels," I said confidently as I nestled against him, trying to alleviate the discomfort of the long hours on horseback and sated now with the tedium of the monotonous countryside.

For once he was solemn as he replied, "I don't think there is much chance of that, tesoro. I'm afraid a musician's daughter has not the status ever to be a great lady. Now if you were a boy you could be a musician like me, like your uncles' sons are, and so share in some measure the life of the Court. But unfortunately you are only a little girl, piccola mia, and that is not possible." He felt the heaving of my shoulders and added encouragingly, "You could perhaps teach music in a noble household and no doubt you are likely to marry a musician. Unless perhaps you could attract some wealthy merchant, a goldsmith perhaps, and then you could wear gold and fine clothes."

"You once told me that women can be musicians in Italy," I said.

"That is so. In Italy there are women singers and musicians who play in concerts and all the nobles of Venice come to listen to them. There are also women who are poets and writers and are equal with the men. But this is England not Italy and things are different here. Listen, when you are older I will take you with me to Venice and who knows what will happen."

This new promise made my homecoming less disappointing. I had not wanted to go back to our dark house in Bishopsgate, to sit with Angela practising the needlework I so hated or listening to my mother read the psalms or one of the books of moral fables she loved. But my father's promise of taking me to Venice inspired me to work harder at my music and at the reading, writing, and French I learnt from Madame La Motte, the widow of a French Huguenot weaver who earned her living by teaching young boys and girls in a little school she had set up in her house near us. However my dreams of going to Italy with my father were shortlived for a few months later he was dead.

I remember my uncle Giovanni, one of my father's brothers, running in from the street without knocking and into the reception room on the ground floor where we were accustomed to eat. This room had wooden rafters and yellow plastered walls with some plain chairs and stools set about. The floor was stone flagged and the window on the back wall, which looked out over our small vegetable and herb garden, had a blue linen curtain which could be drawn to keep out the cold at night as there was no fireplace and we had to rely on the heat from the adjoining kitchen. The table was a board on trestles which could be dismantled when more space was required. Our maid Phoebe was bringing the bowls of soup from the kitchen next door and Angela and I were already sitting on our stools at the table while our mother hovered over us pouring the ale into our pewter mugs when uncle Giovanni, with the most serious expression I had ever seen on his face, burst into the room and taking her arm he whispered something we could not hear as he led her up the stairs to the parlour on the first floor. Ignoring Angela's admonitions I followed them and heard my mother screech, "Oh Jesu, has someone killed him? I warned him time and time again."

My uncle's voice was unsteady as he replied, "No Meg, no-one tried to kill him this time. He died naturally, of a seizure. We had just finished rehearsing for Sunday's church service when he said he was tired and must sit down. Then he just fell to the floor and when we reached him he was………Santa Maria, he was the youngest of us all," his voice crumpled as his brother's body had done.

I flung the door open and rushed into the room, tugging at the rain-soaked sleeve of my uncle's doublet and screaming, "What has happened to my father?"

Giovanni swept me up into his arms, crushing my body against him as his tears dropped on my head, murmuring "povera piccola" over and over, and I was aware of my mother standing stiffly with her hand on the wall and making great gulping sounds. Angela appeared in the doorway, unease etched on her pretty face, with the wide-eyed Phoebe behind her, wiping her hands nervously on her brown canvas apron. Soon, as the tragic news unfolded with the details of Battista Bassano's sudden death, everyone was sobbing together.

The rest of the day passed in a maelstrom of confusion. My father's body was brought home and laid in the parlour on the trestle table which had been dismantled and carried up from the reception room, and a steady stream of visitors came to offer their condolences and pay their respects to his body. Angela was put to helping Phoebe in the kitchen provide refreshments for the visitors while my mother with her customary constraint dealt with relatives, neighbours and fellow musicians, her eyes dry after the first outburst of tears. I was sent around the neighbourhood with messages, more to get me out of the way than to be usefully employed for the news had travelled fast. I was glad to be out of the house for that familiar place had suddenly become strange and unreal, no longer the comfortable centre of my universe but a dark empty cavern of fear with my father's dead body filling the chasm with despair. I couldn't believe that Bishopsgate could look so normal with everyone going about their ordinary business, street cryers with their wares, market stalls, delivery carts, busy housewives haggling over prices, apprentices quarrelling and tormenting hapless passers-by, masters roaring their commands, maids wasting time on their errands to dally with would-be gallants. I wanted to stand in the middle of the crowded street and cry out, "Do you not know that my father has died and the world is ended."

That night I lay as usual besides Angela in the big bed we shared in the smaller of the two chambers on the third floor. Sometimes, for example if we were ill, the maid Phoebe would sleep on a truckle bed beside us though usually she slept on a palliasse in the kitchen. Mother and father occupied the big bedchamber next to us though tonight mother slept alone in the tester bed as she sometimes did when father did not come home saying his work had kept him late.

The house was a tall narrow building of wood and plaster, bulging a little at the front with a rather crooked window in the overhanging upper storey but tightly wedged between a Flemish wool merchant's on one side and a Huguenot tire-maker's on the other, as if they were supporting a tipsy companion. It wasn't a large house, comprising the reception room and kitchen at ground level, the parlour on the first floor and two bedchambers on the second, but was a considerable house for a musician, owned and paid for by my father and well furnished. It was situated in one of the better districts of the city, though in Bishopsgate Street without, on the far side of the gate in London's city wall and close to Bedlam hospital. Because it was outside the jurisdiction of the city proper it was well populated with foreigners like us, many of them Dutch and French artisans.

When Angela had finally snuffled herself to sleep I lay awake in the dark, too full of despair to cry. It was as if I were being crushed to pieces as I had seen Phoebe grind peppercorns with the pestle and mortar. I could not imagine what life would be like without him, Battista Bassano, Queen's musician, my father and centre of my universe. I slid silently from beneath the linen sheets and the warm wool counterpane which my mother had embroidered in crewel work and crept as quietly as I could down the narrow creaking staircase to the next floor and the parlour. I must look at him, I must talk to him and ask him why he didn't wait to see me grow up and take me to Venice. Lying on the table the shrouded figure was dimly visible, shadowed in the moon's pale beams filtering through the leaden panes of the uncurtained casement and making the dust motes on the polished wooden boards look like a sprinkling of flower pollen. I slowly drew away the sheet. But he wasn't there. This lifeless figure, still as a statue, wasn't my father. He looked much older, his long nose bony and pinched, his laughing dark eyes shuttered, his lips pulled sternly together instead of curved into his habitual smile. It was no use trying to talk to my father because he had gone away to play his music with the angels. I knew the angels played music because in the paintings they nearly always held musical instruments. My father had gone to play his music with them and left me behind. I had depended on him so much, teaching me music, taking me to court, giving me dreams and promises. Whatever would I do without him.

Chapter 2

CHORALE

"I have a proposition for Aemilia," said Stephen Vaughn, his dry voice betraying an unusual eagerness, and I pricked up my ears though I was supposed to be reading and paying no attention to the conversation between my mother and our neighbour seated together in the parlour. Master Vaughn lived nearby with his wife Judith, though in Bishopsgate Street within, on the other side of the gate in the city itself. Here there were many fine houses belonging to rich merchants, amongst them that of the Lord Mayor himself. The Vaughns lived in an extensive stone-built residence with three gables and an oak studded door, which my mother told us had been one of the old monastic properties appropriated by King Henry and given to them because Stephen's father had served the King as a merchant ambassador in the Low Countries. The childless couple had been close friends of my mother for as long as I could remember and now he was sitting in our parlour in earnest conversation with her whilst I was supposedly concentrating on a psalm in French which Madame La Motte had set me to learn by heart. Master Vaughn was tall and thin with stooping shoulders and sparse grey hair receding from a high forehead, making him look older than he was. His face was long with carved cheekbones and deep-set eyes and he had always seemed like an old man to me though I suppose he was only in his fortieth year. I listened intently to what he was saying though outwardly concentrating on my book and showing no sign of interest.

"I think I could arrange for her to be taken into the household of Susan Bertie, or the Dowager Countess of Kent as I should rightly say," he announced proudly and waited for my mother to be suitably impressed.

"For what reason?" My mother wasted words no more than she wasted anything else, in contrast to the passionate outpourings which had always been my father's mode of speech, but the coolness of her tone disappointed Master Vaughn who regarded her with some impatience.

He sighed heavily then said, "Come Margaret, surely you acknowledge that Aemilia needs careful guidance now that she has been deprived of a father, though you know I always had reservations about Battista's supervision, allowing her into the company of his loose companions and taking her off to Kenilworth. If she comes under the influence of the Bassanos there will be little moral example and I feel that without careful nurturing some of her father's characteristics could easily flower in her, the seeds are there, she is more Italian than English. And there is also the influence of the Romish religion. I know Battista outwardly conformed to the English church but privately he kept his old ways and the rest of the family are all Papists." My mother was well aware that he had only made his statutory appearances at the Parish church of St. Botolph in order to appease her and the law, though actually the Queen exempted foreign musicians and artists from the penalties of Catholocism, so she said nothing.

Taking her silence for agreement Stephen continued, "My family's connections with the Duchess of Suffolk and therefore with her daughter the Countess of Kent could secure such a placement once the circumstances were known. Since her widowhood the Countess has much time on her hands and being childless would find great satisfaction in being responsible for the little girl's moral and spiritual education."

"I admit the suggestion has much to recommend it," my mother reluctantly acknowledged, "but I am myself quite capable of providing moral and spiritual instruction for my children and I have no intention of allowing Aemilia to come under the influence of the Bassanos."

"But you could not provide her with an education such as the Countess could offer," persisted Stephen Vaughn, "an education not generally available to girls of Aemilia's class."

"And of what use would such an education be to Aemilia?" my mother demanded. "It is enough that she learns to read and write, which is provided by Madame La Motte's little school. The only other skills necessary are household skills which I myself can provide, as I have already done with Angela."

"On one level I agree with you," replied Master Vaughn, "but you must know that education for all, men and women alike, has always been a priority in our Reformist beliefs. It is the most effective way to spread the Protestant religion and counter Romish heresies. An educated woman ensures an educated and godly household and a fit helpmeet for a devout husband, the sort of union you must wish for your daughter surely".

It seemed as if he wished to say more but I sensed my mother stiffen as she replied quickly, "Yet even with such obvious advantages I am loath to have Aemilia taken from me."

"The Countess's house in the Minories is but a half hour walk from here, Margaret. There would be many visits to and fro for you both, why 'tis no more than if she were at a board school."

The two were talking as if I weren't there, as elders always did despite my sitting amongst them. My father had never done that but had always talked to me and included me in his conversations with others. I couldn't help myself and cried, "But I like Madame La Motte's school."

Master Vaughn looked shocked as he said, "You see what I mean, the child is a natural rebel," while my mother with a pained expression on her face said, "How dare you interrupt. Go upstairs to your chamber."

I left the room reluctantly but stayed outside the door straining to hear what might be said further. All was silent but then my mother suddenly flung the door open and seeing the look on her face I fled up the narrow stairs, tripping on my kirtle as I did so. I sat sulkily on the bed musing on what had been said and trying to understand the situation. I was angry at the way Master Vaughn had criticised my father and the way he seemed to be taking it upon himself to order my life now that father was dead. I had always been aware of the antagonism between him and my father and knew that my mother's close friendship with the Vaughns had been the cause of many disagreements between my parents, especially when my mother became increasingly influenced by the Vaughn's religious views and strict observances. Stephen and Judith Vaughn were of the reform religion and his sister Anne had published a translation of the sermons of John Calvin, which was my mother's preferred reading. I did not like the suggestion of moral and spiritual education which sounded very unpleasant. Yet on the other hand the two women mentioned were obviously great ladies - a Duchess and a Countess - and I couldn't help feeling excited by the fact that they might be interested in me. They could be the means by which I could attain my ambition of being a great lady myself. If I were to live with them they would take me to Court and I would meet many important people. Moral and spiritual education might be tolerable under the circumstances and I was eager to learn more. However when I was called down for supper Master Vaughn had gone and to my disappointment my mother never made mention of the matter and I knew I dare not ask.

I continued to ponder the mystery in my thoughts but when after a few days no further talk was forthcoming I forgot about it, especially when Angela regaled me with some news of her own.

"I am to be married," she said, rushing to meet me at the door when I returned from the Dame School, her rosy face more flushed than ever.

"But you are only fourteen." I was shocked by this new turn of events.

"Well not this year, but next year when I am turned fifteen. Master Vaughn has arranged a match for me with a merchant acquaintance of his, Master Joseph Holland, a partner in a company that imports fine wines." She smiled in a show of self-importance, and pirouetted around the room.

"Meddling, interfering Master Vaughn again," I burst out angrily. "What right has he to run our lives in this way." I was filled with fury and cried, "Father wouldn't have let you be married so soon."

"But I like the idea," Angela rippled happily. "Master Holland is a gentleman with a fair house and a thriving business and I shall be well maintained."

"Then he must be an old man," I said suspiciously.

"He is thirty five," my sister responded defiantly, tightening her small rosebud mouth.

"But that is as old as mother." I was even more horrified and said with revulsion, "How can you bear to be loved by such an old man."

"He is handsome enough and kind and well mannered. I would much prefer to be the mistress of my own house than have to live here with mother, the house is so dreary now that father has gone. I shall be able to please myself instead of always having to do what she says."

"You will just have to do what your husband says instead. All wives must," I retorted. "I shall never marry unless I marry a great lord and then I shall be able to please myself because great ladies do."

My sister laughed her rippling laugh but I sensed the mockery in it and feeling hurt I said pathetically, "Anyway I shall miss you, I don't want you to go away, I have only you for my friend."

Angela looked at me quizzically because we often quarrelled and there was too much difference in our ages to share much in common, (we had lost the brother who had arrived between us), but she put her arm around my shoulders saying, "But you are going away too. Master Vaughn says you are going to live with the Countess of Kent for a time in the Minories."

"No-one has told me" I muttered, resentful again at being excluded from matters that concerned me. "I hate Master Vaughn."

"That's wicked of you, Aemilia. He is very kind and is trying to do the best for us now that father has died. I think you are lucky going to live in a noble household."

"Shall I be a servant?" I asked suspiciously.

"I don't think so. Master Vaughn says you are to be educated by the Countess herself. That is a far greater honour than being taught by Madame La Motte. And you like learning things. You aren't like me, I hate learning and only want to do embroidery and make simples and cook, all the things I shall be able to do when I am married."

"Did Master Vaughn tell you anything else?" I fished, but she shook her head. Then on a sudden intuition I said, "Mother is going to be lonely when we are both gone."

"Neither of us is going far, you will only be a mile away and I less than that." Then thinking about it for a moment Angela added, "I suppose she will marry again, most widows do. She isn't old, and with both of us taken care of she might have a better opportunity. Perhaps that is what Master Vaughn was thinking about, no doubt he will find a husband for her too."

I bit back the retort that sprang to my lips but I did not like the idea of my mother marrying someone else and me being forced to have a stepfather after my real father. For a moment I thought about the Earl of Essex's young family having Robert Dudley as their stepfather and wondered how they would like it. Perhaps it was as well I were to go away because I could not forbear watching another man pay court to my mother.

Later that afternoon she called me privately into the parlour and explained what had been arranged for Angela and me. The parlour was the best room in our house with a white plaster ceiling on which were worked graceful scrolls and flourishes like the finish of someone's signature. The walls were of linenfold panelling and there was a big stone fireplace with heraldic carvings that my father had bought from an old house that was being dismantled and had it transferred here. With its iron firedogs and a pair of large bellows it was really too large for our parlour and sat a little crookedly but the room was always warm in winter. There was a long settle with velvet cushions along one wall, a carved wooden chair with arms and another one without, two joint stools, a long low coffer with two lids and a tree of life carved on the front, and a court cupboard with three inset panels, each with a carved and painted Tudor rose, in which the few pieces of silver plate were kept. On one wall hung one of our most precious possessions, a painting of the flight into Egypt in a gilded wooden frame, which my father had brought back from Italy. It was a dark room because the casement window overlooking the street had small leaded panes, but to me it always seemed cosy, especially at night when the candles in their pewter candlesticks were lit. My mother seated herself on the chair and I sat on a stool beside her.

"You are going to live with the Countess of Kent for a while in her London house although the family also has a country seat in Lincolnshire. You are very fortunate, Aemilia, because you will receive an education that girls of your status are not normally entitled to but I warrant you will benefit by it, you have a quick mind and the Protestant faith believes that the education of the mind makes us better servants of God. However I must warn you that you are to be sober, conscientious and give thought to spiritual things. The family of the Countess are of strong religious beliefs of a firm reformist conviction. I have told you before how the family of Master Vaughn crossed the sea to Geneva when Mary Tudor was Queen because they could not bear to accept a Papist Sovereign and knew that they would be persecuted. Well the Duchess of Suffolk and her husband were of that same company. They fled the country with their daughter Susan, who is now Dowager Countess of Kent, facing poverty and persecution for their Protestant faith, a story which John Foxe told in his Book of Martyrs, a book which your father would never allow you to read but which I shall give to you now."

Now that my fate had been definitely decided I gave much thought to what my new life would be like. I liked the idea of living in a noble household and meeting the kind of people I had seen at Kenilworth. I liked the thought of being able to learn new things, especially the sort of things that noble ladies learnt. I found the story of their travels exciting, how they had faced danger in foreign lands, leaving behind all their friends and possessions, a story which my mother had now told me in more detail. But I was not so sure about these ladies themselves. The Dowager Duchess of Suffolk and the Dowager Countess of Kent sounded like old women - strictly religious, inflexible in their beliefs, hard faced and dressed in unadorned black - and I did not suppose I should find much amusement there. It was with trepidation that I prepared to meet them and begin my new life.

My mother and I were dressed in our best gowns, she in her padded grey brocade with her ruff and winged coif newly starched and I in my yellow mockado with white satin kirtle and matching cap, as Stephen Vaughn accompanied us to their house in the Minories. This was the street running behind the looming white mass of the Tower towards Aldgate, an area occupied by many of the reformists because, like our Bishopsgate without, it was in the Liberties outside the city walls and therefore beyond the jurisdiction of the city authorities with their strict regulations for religious observances. The house was similar in style to the Vaughn's but much larger, four-storeyed with many gables and chimneys and huge leaded windows. The stone frontispiece was ornately carved with heraldic bearings, those above the arched studded door finished in gold. I was not surprised by the palatial appearance because I had been told that the Dowager Duchess of Suffolk was the widow of Charles Brandon who had first been married to the Princess Mary Rose, one time Queen of France, sister to King Henry and aunt to Queen Elizabeth. In such a magnificent family I was prepared to be nervous but then I reminded myself that I had met the Queen herself as well as other nobles at Kenilworth. However the Duchess herself was not in residence and it was her daughter, the Dowager Countess of Suffolk, into whose presence we were led. With wide eyes I took in every detail of the splendid rooms through which we were ushered, noting rich furnishings of carved and polished oak, damask curtained windows, tables with vividly-coloured turkey carpets, gold and silver many-branched candelabra. But when the steward of the household opened the last door my eyes fell to the ground as I heard Master Vaughn make his courtesies and a soft voice reply in welcome to him and my mother.

"This is Aemilia," said Master Vaughn and prompting me, "Make your reverence to the Countess."

I curtsied deeply, trying not to wobble, then looked up. I had been expecting an elderly lady and to my surprise I saw a very young woman whom I was later told was twenty-one years old. Susan Bertie, recently widowed, was indeed dressed in a simple closed gown of black velvet but her ruff was of gossamer tulle and a double string necklace of large pearls shone milky white against the blackness. She was not beautiful. Her light brown hair was drawn severely from her face and mainly covered by a black widow's cap and veil, and her face was too square and pale. But her mouth was wide and full, curving upwards in an indication of good humour and in the velvet brown eyes was the reflection of some deeper quality within. I sensed it as kindness and immediately warmed to her. Later when I was older and knew her better I realised it was serenity, a manifestation of ease with herself and with the world.

She smiled at me. "Welcome to my house, Aemilia. I hope you will be happy here." Her voice was soft and low.

My initial impression of Susan Bertie, Dowager Countess of Kent, did not alter in the five years I spent as a member of her household though my position remained always ambiguous. I usually ate with the servants but the higher servants like Master Glover the steward and Mistress Roper the housekeeper in whose care I was for much of the time. I was not expected to do any manual work but it was part of my education to help Mistress Roper with the spice cupboard and the best linen, to learn the skills of the stillroom and to understand the household accounts. But I spent many hours with Lady Susan herself. She taught me French and allowed me to read fables and poems as well as Bible translations and religious treatises. She worked with me at needlework, enlivening an occupation I hated by reading to me, and arranged for me to practice music with Nicholas Lanier, one of the Queen's French musicians, who came to play music with her from time to time. I told Cecily Prink, with whom I shared a bedchamber, that I would have liked one of my uncles to have taught me. Cecily at fourteen was the youngest of the Countess's ladies though too proud of the fact to make possible any friendship between us and she said dismissively, "Oh they wouldn't have wanted that. The Bassanos are Papists whereas the Laniers were Huguenots." However Nicholas Lanier had married my cousin Lucrezia, my uncle Antonio's daughter, so he was still a link with my father's family, though I found his manner rather cold and distant in contrast to the spontaneity of the Bassanos. Lady Susan also taught me etiquette and deportment, showing me how to walk and move gracefully though I still ran about in my hoydenish manner when I was at my own liberty. Occasionally I was set to dine with them so I understood the rituals of ceremony and how to converse politely with strangers. Later, when she realised how quickly I assimilated languages, she arranged for me to learn Latin with one of her clergyman friends and as I loved to play with the words, making logical patterns with the sequence of ideas, I earned the praise of the serious young pastor who proceeded to teach me a little Greek. But chiefly the Countess's instruction to me was of religion. She read the Bible and books of spiritual guidance to me and explained the doctrines of theology, especially those of John Calvin, warning me of the evils of the Papist religion with its idolatry and heathen practices and reasoning that the only true faith was the reformed Protestant faith with its reliance on revealed truth and personal salvation. I didn't mind the Bible stories, especially the Old Testament with its violent happenings and vendettas and its strong women like Judith, Susannah, Deborah and Esther. I didn't mind the spiritual treatises if they were in French and I could practise my skill with the language. I enjoyed the gory tales of the Protestant martyrs and I liked to hear Lady Susan tell of her family's adventurous voyages across the sea when she and her brother were only children. Even when her teaching was of religion her manner was never dictatorial but always gentle and persuasive. But in actual fact I paid no deep attention to the substance of her discourses which washed over me as lightly as summer rain on the cobbles which are dry again within moments and leave no trace behind. I must confess that in this respect I was a great disappointment to her. She bought my clothes and at first I had hoped them to be of rich materials and decoration, but instead they were of plain though expensive wool with simple ruffs at neck and cuffs. She must have seen my disappointment because she said, "Never think too much of your appearance, Aemilia. Beauty lies in the soul and not in fine outward garments. Also you must remember it is not fitting for a girl of your status to be gowned in silks and satins as the nobility are, this is why there are the sumptuary laws."

Another time she said, "A virtuous woman is a price far beyond rubies. Always remember that, Aemilia. A good man will seek a virtuous wife, not one whose attraction lies in fine clothes and jewels and who will waste his substance while the larder lies empty."

Sometimes in a fit of rebellion I would complain to myself about her own stock of jewels and the fact that once her period of mourning was over her gowns were of sumptuous materials and colours, her brown hair laced with pearls and fine nets. But in honesty, as I grew older I had to admit that the Countess followed her own precepts and her affluent appearance was the expected representation of her status not of any worldly vanity, and the wealth expended on personal luxury was equal to that which she bestowed on charitable works. She never flaunted herself nor appeared coquettish in the presence of men even though as a wealthy young widow she was a considerable prize, and whilst keeping her dignity she never treated those of lesser rank, including her servants, with anything less than kind respect. Although I ignored much of what she told me in the matter of religion and though I sometimes felt resentment that I was never allowed to be, nor never expected to be, of the same social class, I did admire Lady Susan and was grateful for what she gave me.

Occasionally the Dowager Duchess of Suffolk visited the house and then I always had to be on my best behaviour because she terrified me. She tested me mercilessly on the precepts of religion and I had to keep my wits about me to answer her correctly. Her personality seemed too big for her small frame, her voice was sharp and loud, her eyes little and bright as a bird's. She was almost sixty years old but her energy and quick movements belied her age and she seemed to be in a constant state of motion - overseeing, controlling, ordering - nothing escaped her sharp observation and her tongue mercilessly lashed anyone who fell short of her exacting standards. Her skin was sallow, her hair still raven black with only a few silver threads, and I remembered that her mother had been a Spanish lady-in-waiting to King Henry's first wife, Catherine of Aragon. Her father, Baron Willoughby, had been a great favourite of the King's and when he died his only child Catherine, named after the Queen, inherited his vast fortune. Because of her great wealth she had been married off as a young girl to the King's brother-in-law, the widower Charles Brandon Duke of Suffolk, thirty years her senior.

"She has had such a romantic life," Cecily Prink once told me when she was in one of her unusually communicative moods. "At fifteen she was one of the noblest ladies in the land because her old husband was first married to the Princess Mary Rose. Then when the Duke of Suffolk died and she was still only a young woman she became passionately enamoured of Richard Bertie, the steward at their country seat Grimsthorpe Castle, and married him despite all the opposition to such an unacceptable match. Susan and her brother

Peregrine are their children. Then when they were persecuted for their Protestant faith under Mary Tudor they fled the country. They arrived in Holland late at night on a freezing Christmas Eve with no money and nowhere to stay. They were sheltering in the lee of the church porch when the kindly pastor saw them and gave them hospitality."

With her strength and indomitability I could well believe the stories of their adventures as they wandered penniless across Europe, but I found it difficult to reconcile the romance of passionate love with the bossy old woman of my acquaintance.

"She really is only Mistress Bertie now but she continues to call herself Duchess of Suffolk," said Cecily scornfully. "She apparently didn't love him enough to take on his lowly status." Privately I thought that if I were a noble lady I would never marry beneath me and I could understand why she was unwilling to give up such a renowned title. "She has been trying for years to get her father's title of Lord Willoughby granted to Richard Bertie," continued Cecily, "but the Queen won't hear of it. She has no particular liking for the Duchess with her reformist beliefs and the fact that she is related, even if only through marriage, to the detested Grey family." I knew of the executed Lady Jane Grey, nine days Queen of England, and her unfortunate younger sister Lady Catherine Grey, locked up in the Tower for marrying secretly without the Queen's permission and dying there. "The Duchess's step-grandchildren," said Cecily knowingly, her small eyes almost disappearing in her weasel face. She didn't often favour me with her conversation, considering me both her junior and her inferior, but sometimes she took delight in airing her superior knowledge of worldly affairs, especially as I grew older, and though I didn't like her airs and graces which I uncharitably considered an attempt to compensate for her plain face, I was always eager for gossip.

In spite of the Duchess of Suffolk's dictatorial manner she was kind to me, encouraging my studies and pleased when I showed progress. Despite my awe of her I nonetheless had to admit a grudging admiration for the old harridan as I secretly called her, not least because she inspired in me the belief that women should be educated equally with men, an opinion shared by her friends like Mildred Cecil, wife to the Lord Chancellor Burghley. One evening she took me with her to dine at the Burghley's London house in the Strand. The house was ostentatiously furnished but when we sat at the enormous table in the great hall I was amazed to find that the company included all the members of the large extended household of scholars and poor writers who lodged with Lord Burghley, as well as many of the servants. William Cecil was a long-standing friend of the Duchess, somewhat younger than she but grey-haired and stooping a little with a strong-featured face and shrewd appraising eyes. He took a kindly interest in me, telling me about his garden at his country house Theobalds and the improvements he was making there as he had a passion for botany and architecture.

"I met the Queen once or twice with my father and I saw her for a whole week at Kenilworth castle," I confided to him, warmed by his easy manner.

His eyes twinkled but he said seriously, "She has so many rare gifts. She is wise beyond all the princes of Europe and I have dedicated the whole of my life to serving her."

In that moment I wished again that I had been born a boy and could serve her as a musician as my father had. If only women could be musicians at the English court as my father had said they were in Venice. I was about to confide my longings to Lord Burghley when he found a boy near my own age, for he also included amongst his household the wards and young noblemen who were in his care to be educated, and he introduced me to Robert Devereux, the young Earl of Essex. At thirteen years old he was tall and athletic with auburn curls, blue eyes and a ready smile. As he took my hand and looked into my eyes my heart fluttered in my chest like a bird trying to break free and for the first time in my life I knew what it was to be in love for I had read many poems and classical stories. My loins tingled and my throat felt dry and I was overcome with shyness. I didn't know what to say but remembering my father's gossip I stammered, "I met your stepfather at Kenilworth castle once."

"Oh yes, Leicester," he said offhandedly. "He does well enough by me, though the Queen made me Burghley's ward. Why were you at Kenilworth? I've never seen you before."

"My father was a musician there, Battista Bassano."

"I know the Bassano musicians, but not your father."

"He's dead."

"I'm sorry. My father's dead too."

For a moment there was a bond between us. Then he moved away and and as my eyes followed him my heart went with him. I no longer wanted to be a boy and for the first time I felt unreservedly glad to be a girl with the burgeoning realisation of how a handsome boy could satisfy undefined longings. I fantasised that the next time we met I would be sumptuously dressed instead of wearing a plain dress of grey wool with a lawn ruff because I was determined to see him again. Burghley's own son, Robert Cecil, was away but I had heard that, though a very clever boy, he was small and mis-shapen with a large head and crooked back because his nurse had dropped him when a baby. I thought how hard it must be for him to spend so much time in the company of the strikingly handsome Robert Devereux. The desire to see him again stayed with me but the only other time I was taken to the Cecils he was away at the University in Cambridge.

I loved being part of this lively throng. Talk was non-stop on all subjects under the sun, often interspersed with laughter though everyone behaved with decorum and there was no heavy drinking though the food was rich and plentiful. I did not feel awkward or unwelcome as a dependant of the Suffolks because there were so many in like circumstances, receiving education or patronage. Lady Burghley drew me into conversation, showing a great interest in my studies and particularly eager to know about my progress in the Latin language and I warmed towards this clever woman with her plain face and kindly disposition.

The stimulating company of educated women became an integral part of my life in the grand house in the Minories. One of Susan Bertie's closest friends was Margaret Russell, daughter of the Earl of Bedford. She was also of the Reformist religion for her father had been a companion of the Duchess of Suffolk when he too had fled to Geneva during the reign of Mary Tudor. Margaret was due to marry George Clifford, Earl of Westmorland, who for many years had been a ward of her father, though she was rather a plain girl with a square face and eyes that were set unevenly. Later she was to cross my path in a most surprising way. She was a lady-in-waiting to the Queen and Susan herself spent some time in the Queen's service though it was no secret the Queen had no love for the reformists, or Puritans as they were being named. ("She prefers Papists," I once heard Stephen Vaughn say bitterly. "We have been most disappointed in her in the matter of religion."). Sometimes when her friends were visiting, Susan would include me in the company and take delight in demonstrating to them my knowledge, especially of religious matters. I preened myself in the acquaintance of such noble young ladies, enjoying reading to them or sometimes playing music, as Lady Susan commanded. I also envied them with their high birth, their position at court and the noble marriages they had contracted though they were seldom great beauties. I often wondered why Susan with her intelligence, charm, and wealth had never remarried and once I had made bold to ask her.

"Our lives are predestined by God," she replied. "If it is His plan that I should marry again then he will provide a husband for me in His good time. In the meantime there are many ways in which I may serve Him, not least by training you in his precepts."

It was on a visit to the family country estate, Grimsthorpe Castle in Lincolnshire, that God's design manifested himself to Lady Susan and gave me the opportunity to meet with the most learned lady of my acquaintance though I did not recognise either at the time. The name had not sounded pleasing to me and I did not look forward to my visit, imagining an eerie windswept edifice high on a crag with looming towers and dark cellar prisons, so that I had considered feigning illness. However the Duchess of Suffolk insisted the change of scene would benefit me and I was pleasantly surprised on our arrival for Grimsthorpe was a comfortable sumptuously furnished house with all modern refinements though its turrets, small windows and gatehouse revealed its original purpose. It was set on a low ridge surrounded by flat fields with the great Lincolnshire forest hovering nearby but despite its grandeur there was a general air of isolation.

For me there was little of interest apart from the large library and a fine set of virginals. I did not ride and did not wish to learn, having a fear of horses, and when the Duchess commanded a walk through the woods I hated the contrast to a stroll through the busy London streets where there was always someone to talk to or some spectacle to watch. If you travelled any distance from the castle the landscape became flatter and even more monotonous with deep ditches beside the lanes to absorb the flood water. I buried myself in books, taking advantage of the wide selection of volumes, for there was no-one in the vicinity to call on and visitors to Grimsthorpe were few and usually elderly. One such was the Countess of Shrewsbury, who had a house close by. Another intimidating old lady of the same ilk as the Duchess with whom she shared a long acquaintance, the Lady Elizabeth Talbot was tall and erect with small pale blue inquisitive eyes in a stern uncompromising face that looked as if it were chiselled out of stone. She was severely garbed in black that showed to advantage the long rows of splendid pearls, and a black cap and veil almost completely covered her faded auburn hair. She had in her charge her six year old orphaned granddaughter Arbella, a chubby solemn-faced child with wide apprehensive blue eyes and frizzed auburn hair, looking like a miniature court lady in her stiff boned purple farthingale and ruff. I had ignored the child from my superior years, chafing at having to spend time with old women and babies, although my interest had been aroused by her purple gown for the colour was forbidden to all except those of royal descent But as I was almost twelve years old the little Arbella seemed hardly worthy of attention. Then her grandmother commanded, "Arbella, converse in French with Aemilia."

The child looked startled, not knowing what to say, then began hesitantly, "Je m'appelle Arbella Stuart et j'ai six ans."

I replied in like manner and soon, to my amazement, we were chattering away together easily about French poetry. The Countess of Shrewsbury permitted herself a thin smile saying, "Arbella is much advanced for her age and has the accomplishments of a much older child. I myself have only the rudiments of education - reading, writing and accounts - though," (with a pointed look at Catherine Bertie), "this has not prevented me from making my way in the world. However I am having Arbella educated to be the most learned lady of her time, as Queen Elizabeth is. Fit to be such a queen herself." No comment was made on this statement by the Duchess or Lady Susan and at the time I did not understand its relevance.

"Converse in Italian now," she commanded the child. "Then recite to Aemilia some of the verses you have made." Once again I was amazed by the child's precocity though there was little sign of affection in Lady Shrewsbury's manner towards her. I felt pity for the little Arbella, orphaned and committed to the care of such a stern guardian as her grandmother, living in such inhospitable surroundings. I wished I could have been her friend and taken her back to London with me, and I thought longingly of the happy childhood I had known when my father was alive.

One visitor to Grimsthorpe however was not old. Sir John Wingfield, a nephew of Lady Shrewbury, was reasonably young and personable though of a somewhat solemn disposition. He contrived to spend time alone with Lady Susan and when he left I noticed she was more than usually animated and her pale face had a healthy rosy flush.

For myself I was not sorry to leave Grimsthorpe. I didn't like the countryside. There were too many fields and trees and not enough people. I belonged in London and I liked the city with its noise and bustle and crowds. I liked to be amongst people, especially people who were rich and well dressed and had tales to tell. It was Cecily Prink of course who told me the tale of Arbella Stuart, gloating over the fact that I had been compelled to go to Grimsthorpe while she had stayed in the Minories.

"Many people think she will be our next Queen. Her mother was the Countess of Shrewsbury's daughter but her father was Charles Stuart, Earl of Lennox, grandson of King Henry's eldest sister Margaret. Arbella's parents married without the Queen's permission and she was so angry that she put them all in the Tower, including old Lady Shrewsbury. Some people think the rightful heir is Mary Stuart but she is a prisoner and likely to remain one and besides England will never tolerate another Catholic Queen. Mary does have a little son but he is weak and sickly and not likely to live, and he is himself a prisoner of the feuding Scottish lords. So Arbella Stuart, who is his cousin and the only other descendant of both the Tudor and Stuart kings, is the most likely heir when Queen Elizabeth dies."

I felt a little thrill of excitement at the knowledge that I had met the next Queen of England in that little precocious child and hoped she would remember me in the future, another step towards my ambition to be a part of courtly life. But the days on the whole were routine during my stay in the Suffolk household and visits to noble houses, which I loved, were rare.

One day in 1580 when I was twelve years old I was making my way back to the house in the Minories after paying a visit to my mother when my attention was caught by a bill posted on a wall. Drawing closer to read it I realised it was a playbill advertising the comedy 'Ralph Roister Doister' to be performed by the Earl of Leicester's Players at The Theatre on the following day at three of the clock. I had heard about these new playhouses, called The Theatre and The Curtain, which had recently been built near Finsbury fields off the public road from Bishopsgate to Shoreditch, not too far from either my home or the Minories. I decided I would love to go and see what it was like, especially because the actors were those patronised by the Earl of Leicester. I had once watched a private theatrical performance when my father had been playing with the musicians and he had sometimes taken me to see interludes in the street on festival days, but I had no idea what these new public playhouses were. I knew they were considered immoral by many people, especially the Puritans and also the city council which was why they had to be built outside their jurisdiction, so it was no use asking for official permission. I also thought I had better not venture alone but I did not know who might be willing to accompany me in such a risky enterprise. I put my mind to finding a stratagem and eventually sought out Tom Dancy, one of the kitchen scullions, and put my proposition to him. A cheeky irrepressible boy with a round freckled face and an impish grin revealing more spaces than teeth, he was tall and gangly for his fourteen years, mischievous and always ready for a prank such as this.

The following day we successfully sneaked away from the house in the lull following dinner. I wasn't prepared for the vast crowds of people hurrying along the Shoreditch road, many of them the vulgar sort laughing and cavorting rowdily, though there was a fair smattering of merchants and their well-dressed wives and some apprentices obviously evading their masters. Gentlemen also passed on horseback, carelessly splattering the walkers with mire for the road was rough and muddy with great potholes. The houses were generally mean and tumbledown, some of them not much more than hovels with a patch of garden, though as we neared our destination there were clusters of timber and thatch buildings. As the road broadened into fields we came across a horse pond where the riders left their mounts to be looked after by urchins eager for a penny and there were stalls selling trinkets and gingerbread. From here we could see The Theatre and we gazed in amazement for it was like no building I had seen before. It was a strange looking octagonal structure in wood and plaster painted white, with a thatch roof on top of which was a hut with a flag flying aloft. Around the side of the building were several doors through which the crowds were now pouring and after standing hesitantly for a time we followed them to one of the entrances. In a booth a man sat taking money.

"I'll pay," I said to Tom who looked momentarily disconcerted.

"Standing or sitting," said the man without looking up.

"How much is it?"

"A penny to stand, two pence for a seat in the galleries, three pence for the best seats with a cushion. "

"Standing please. Two persons."

The gatherer took my money then lifting his head studied me earnestly saying, "Keep tight hold of your purse in your hand, Mistress, or you soon won't have it."

I did as he said, clutching it tight as we were pushed inside by the flow. We found ourselves in a huge circular space only partly covered by the thatch roof for in the middle it was open to the sky. The floor was covered in rushes though soon obscured from view as the crowds poured in, filling every inch of the standing area. Projecting out into the space was the wooden stage, half of which was covered by the roof of the hut whose underside was a blue painted canopy spangled with gold stars like the sky and supported by two huge wooden pillars ornamented to look like marble. At the back of the stage were two great doors for the actors to make their entrances, and in the middle of them was a recess draped with vividly painted curtains and surmounted by a balcony for the musicians. I looked around in wonder. Around three sides of the stage rose three tiers of galleries with seating benches, filling now at a steady rate. The standing spectators were pushing frantically trying to get as close to the stage as they could and Tom and I wriggled our way amongst them, holding hands so as not to be separated in the crush. There was a stink of unwashed clothes and sour breath, a strong smell of drink, and I felt mens' hands touch me familiarly. Amongst the audience strolled fruit sellers and ale vendors and painted women with garish clothes and bare breasts that Tom said were whores. I wasn't sure what he meant but I could see how they laughed with the men who fondled them. But when the trumpets sounded and the first actors in their bright costumes strutted through the doors at the back of the stage all else was forgotten in the excitement of the performance. Tom and I had managed to squirm and wriggle our way until we were standing by the stage itself and could actually rest our arms on it though we couldn't move an inch and were almost squashed as flat as boards by the crowd. I had never expected to see so many people and reckoned there must have been more than a thousand all together. But the previously clamorous crowd had fallen remarkably silent once the actors began to speak, following the plot attentively, laughing raucously and sometimes shouting encouragement to the characters who for the space of two hours carried us into another world. Tom and I were so engrossed that we felt no fatigue standing, and afterwards our exhilaration carried us nearly home before we began to think about what the repercussions of our escapade might be. We became more and more nervous as we approached the big house but to our tremendous relief we managed to sneak in by the back entrance to the surprised realisation that we had not been missed.

Because our misdemeanour had gone unnoticed and we had so enjoyed the experience we dared to go again the following week to see 'The Blacksmith's Daughter.' I was now completely engrossed in the world of the theatre and beginning to feel at home there, but on our third visit to watch 'Gammer Gurton's Needle' our luck changed. When we returned in a mood of misplaced optimism it was to find a furious red-faced cook waiting for Tom with a threatening metal poker in his hand whilst I was ordered to Lady Susan's parlour.

"I am ashamed of you, Aemilia," she said in her calm voice, her ruby damask gown swishing from side to side as she walked up and down before me. "I cannot believe that you have left the house without permission, and in company with one of the lowest servants who should have been at his work. That alone is a matter of great shame. But to visit a public playhouse," she paused to emphasize her revulsion, "that is beyond belief. The playhouses are places of sin and iniquity, an encouragement to the basest of human thoughts and behaviour."

I was enboldened to insist, "It was but a simple comedy to make people laugh, not at all lewd or immoral. I once watched a play with you, my lady."

"A private performance of a classical epic for a family's education, Aemilia, carefully chosen for its edifying content to instruct and inspire. A public playhouse is entirely different, a nest of undesirable folk - thieves, cutpurses, drunkards, bullyboys, women of ill repute - who go only to prey on others and afterwards to brawl and fight in public disorder on the highway. A playhouse is never the place for a lady or a person of morals."

"There were merchants' wives there in the galleries, they weren't all the lower sort. And also many lords and gallants."

"A man's life is different to ours, Aemilia. They have more freedom, as is their right. Never think to compare your behaviour with that of a man." She sighed again, seating herself with her hands clasped loosely on her lap. "I sometimes think I have failed with you, Aemilia. You have learnt Latin and French, you have appreciated literature and music, you have studied logic and philosophy. But," she paused again, "I really do not know how effective your moral and spiritual understanding is."

I knew I ought to say, "I am sorry I have disappointed you," but no words came. I was grateful for all the tuition I had received, understanding how fortunate I had been to be given such a privilege. But I couldn't help being a rebel at heart and knowledge had given me confidence. Why should I have to subscribe to their moral precepts, to their idea of what God expects from us. How could they be so sure that this was the life God required. My father believed in God and the Saints but he loved music and plays, wine and lively company and,

I suspect, beautiful women. I also felt resentful that they believed I was not of their class. Now that I had been educated like a noblewoman I did not believe that these aristocratic ladies were superior to me because they happened to be born in a lord's bed instead of a musician's. And why should I not consider myself equal to a man? Queen Elizabeth did!

My rebellious musings were interrupted by Lady Susan saying, "In any case, Aemilia, it is now time for you to leave us." Her words concentrated my attention again. "You are twelve years old now and it is time for you to return to your mother and prepare yourself for marriage. Your learning should make you a valuable helpmeet for a merchant or lawyer and a good mother to your children. Also I am going away because I am to be married myself after seven years of widowhood." She smiled and it was as if a lamp glowed beneath her serene features. "He is Sir John Wingfield, whom I met at Grimsthorpe through the acquaintance of Lady Shrewsbury."

"I am very glad for you, my lady," I said sincerely. "I hope you will be very happy."

"And you too, Aemilia," she said, rising and taking my hand in hers. "Remember God has ordained your life and predestined you for salvation if you will keep His precepts and seek His will."

Her words fell on deaf ears. I had other thoughts on my mind than religion. I was wondering what would become of me now that I was being dismissed from this noble household, my education at an end as was my fragile link with the Court. I did not know what I had expected from my long sojourn with the Suffolks but I had never imagined being cast back into my former life with no further end in view. I had anticipated forging connections in high places, being offered a position in one of the noble houses perhaps, at least being retained as an attendant to Lady Susan with entree to aristocratic life. What opportunity was there now for me to renew my acquaintance with the Earl of Essex or any other young noblemen. I was devastated by this sudden turn of events but of one thing I was certain, I was determined to put my experiences to better use than being a partner to a merchant and in time a good mother.

CHAPTER 3

RONDO

My home in Bishopsgate seemed very small after the Suffolks' great houses and I found it unbearably confining. The four rooms stifled me, all together not much bigger than Lady Susan's drawing room. My restlessness and ill temper were increased by the resentment I felt at being turned away, if not exactly from Paradise then from the gate to a better life, without having achieved what I had hoped. Why couldn't Lady Susan have kept me with her as one of her ladies like Cecily Prink, whose learning and intelligence were greatly inferior to mine. In such a great household I could probably have attracted the attention of important people as I grew older. But after a few days of frustration my youthful optimism reasserted itself. I was twelve years old and there was time to achieve my ambitions if I put my mind to it, while at the moment came the intoxicating realisation that I was free - free from the constraints of constant study, free from the trammels of rules and regulations, free from persistent supervision, free to wander at will through the streets and courts of London. My mother had got used to being without me and her custodial instincts grown slack. She had never remarried, never shown any inclination to do so despite Stephen Vaughn's continual attempts to bring suitable suitors to her notice, enjoying the freedom of a widow's state as I soon realised. My father had left her satisfactorily provided for. She had a modest but comfortably furnished house, a small annuity, and regular rent from three other properties, two that my father had purchased for investment and another that had belonged to her own family. She was not wealthy but the prospect of a rich husband was not sufficient inducement for her to exchange her liberty as a widow for the repression of a wife, perhaps also with the burden of a second family. She expected me to fulfil my tasks in the house, to help Phoebe with light duties, to sew and mend, to make salves and sweet potions, to lend a hand with the cooking, but the work was not onerous. The running of errands and shopping were a delight to me when I could wander to my heart's content, talking with those I met on the way from idle apprentices to gossiping goodwives who knew all the London news. And once these obligations were fulfilled my time was my own as my mother visited her friends and made her regular forays to the markets or services at the many City churches, all equal in her interest.

But one thing I needed was money. My father had left me a hundred pounds but that could not be touched until I was twenty-one or married, whichever was the sooner, and that chafed me. I needed money to go to the playhouses which I was now at liberty to frequent. Also I wished to fancify my clothes with braids and ribbons for they were too plain for my liking. Neither of these needs came within my mother's remit and indeed I preferred her to be ignorant of them. One day I was passing Madame La Motte's house in a Huguenot enclave off Silver Street when an idea wormed itself into my mind and impulsively I knocked at her door. She did not recognise me at first then smiled welcomingly and invited me inside. I told her all about my education at the hands of the Countess of Kent and seeing that she was impressed, especially with my command of Latin and French, I asked if I might help her with some teaching. She considered for some time then admitting that her little enterprise was thriving and that sometimes she had too many pupils she agreed for me to help her on one or two days a week. I was ecstatic for though I had no intention of running a Dame school it was satisfying to be earning money by my own efforts, money to spend on whatever I wanted, and for the moment I felt important and mature, a fact confirmed by the first appearance of my monthly flux.

"I am glad to see you occupied in a useful way, Aemilia, putting to good use what you have been privileged to learn from the Countess," said Stephen Vaughn one evening when he was supping at our house with his wife Judith. "And the money will go to helping your mother with your maintenance now that you are back home again." I stared at him blankly, hoping that my mother would not divulge how little I gave her. I never made any attempt to hide my dislike or indifference to him because I hadn't then learnt how to charm with smiles and sweet words even those I loathed if they were important or in line to grant me favours. "Naturally we shall be looking for a suitable husband for you now so it will only be temporary," he continued, with his usual disregard for any response I might wish to make.

"She is yet too young, Stephen," his wife Judith gently admonished him. Judith Vaughn was more sympathetic than her husband but she reminded me of a plump pheasant with her small stature and heavy bosom. Her grey hair was tucked tight beneath her coif and her pale blue eyes and small round mouth were set in a plain dough-coloured face which exhibited a permanent air of resignation.

"Nonsense," he said roundly, "Angela was but her age when we first began to sound out Master Holland and look how successful that match has been."

I had to admit that Angela seemed happy enough but it was not the life I envisaged for myself. I often went to visit my sister who lived in Leadenhall Street above the premises where her husband stocked and sold wine. The apartments were far more spacious than ours and finely appointed. The parlour had two large windows - one overlooking the busy street and the other a well-stocked herb garden and orchard beyond - and boasted several armed tall-backed chairs, an emblazoned turkey carpet on the polished oak table, a carved court cupboard with the beginnings of a collection of silver plate and many candlesticks. The kitchen had a new-fashioned oven where their own baking could be done instead of having to send to the baker's as we did, and the main bedchamber a frescoed wall and tapestry hangings with a bed hung in red velvet. Angela was immensely proud of the house and never tired of pointing out to me the latest acquisition. But her talk consisted of nothing but household stuff and prices, or her little son Philip who was nearly a year old. She had now been married three years but her first child had died and this little survivor, named after our brother who had died as an infant, had taken over her whole life. She mooned over him as if he were the only child in the world, pointing out continually all his clever ways and his latest achievement, he had just started to toddle and lisp. He was a handsome enough child and seemed to have taken a fondness for me but I hated his sticky hands on my gown or his wet slobbering kisses on my face and I didn't like his smell. I knew that

I didn't want to be burdened with children so young. Angela was only eighteen but already she was grown fat and her pleasant face seemed to have set into a mask of complacency that sometimes seemed idiotic. She looked so different from the radiant young bride of three years previously in her gown of pale pink silk covered in rosebuds, when I had almost envied her in her importance as she strewed flowers and sweetmeats to the admiring spectators in the churchyard. I knew she was happy, she loved her husband who appeared to treat her well and doted on her child, but I was adamant that I wanted something better from my life. I didn't know exactly what, nor indeed how to attain it away from the Suffolks. But in my heart I knew that I must find it and the immediate step was to forestall all attempts to find a suitor for me.

"Bring Aemilia to supper tomorrow evening, there is someone I would like you both to meet," Stephen Vaughn would say to my mother. Then the events would acquire a regular predictability. He might be a merchant, a lawyer, a silversmith, a printer, but always a Puritan who would talk avidly to Stephen and Judith Vaughn and my mother whilst looking me up and down like a piece of merchandise and offering me only banal politeness to which I responded with deliberate indifference. Sometimes he would be the son of an acquaintance, a student at the Inns of Court, an apprentice who had almost finished his indentures and was due to share in the business, or perhaps a clerk. They were rarely handsome or interesting so I decided to amuse myself by pretending to be acting in a play, wearing my gayest clothes, acting coquettishly and shamelessly exploiting their gaucherie and timidity, so that I could at least enjoy the evening. Afterwards back at home my mother would chide me but not as severely as I had expected and I realised she was in no great haste to see me wed, either because she had become accustomed to my company or because she herself was appreciating the benefits of a single life against a married woman's duties.

One day I dared say to her, "I shall only be interested in someone like the Earl of Essex, Robert Devereux. I met him once when I was with the Duchess of Suffolk at Lord Burghley's house. He was so handsome, tall, spirited, intelligent - and rich."

"You may as well forget these vain dreams now, Aemilia, for that is what they are, foolish idle dreams that will bring you nothing but discontent and bitterness," she said sharply. "It is useless to look for a husband above your station. The nobility live in a different world to ours."

But he remained my dream lover and one day I encountered him. I went as often as I could to the playhouses in Shoreditch, though keeping it a secret from my mother whose opinion was no less condemnatory than Lady Susan's had been. I also discovered that some of the inns allowed the theatre companies to use their yards for performances. The layout was not so different from the playhouses as the inns had galleries built around a courtyard where a stage of wooden trestles could be erected, and while the poorer sort filled the yard in front of the stage the better classes watched from the galleries where benches had been set for them. One afternoon I had gone to the Black Bull Inn in Bishopsgate, not far from home, to see 'Robin of the Greenwood' performed by the Earl of Leicester's Players. I was standing as usual and the play was almost done before I noticed Robert Devereux seated in the first gallery with a company of other young gallants. I caught my breath in excitement and watched him surreptitiously because I did not want him to see me amongst the groundlings. But when the performance had finished I waited with thumping heart, putting myself deliberately into his line of vision. I did not know if he would remember me but he did and saluting me courteously stopped to talk for a while.

"Aemilia Bassano. What a long time since we met at Lord Burghley's house. I have been studying at the University since then. Are you still sojourning with the Duchess of Suffolk.?" I considered he must be about seventeen now and he was more handsome than ever, tall and broad, his chestnut hair curling on the top of his ruff, dressed in the latest fashion but with still the same warm smile and easy manner.

I told him that I had finished my education but was suitably vague about my present position and he seemed not to notice. "I wanted to go on the voyage to Virginia that Walter Raleigh has organised but the Queen says I am too young and would not give her permission," he said regretfully.

I murmured my sympathies and he seemed in no hurry to depart. I praised the actors of his stepfathers's company and we turned to discussing the play, my tongue loosening effortlessly as I felt his attraction. When at our parting he kissed my hand I experienced the same sensations as when I had first met him at Lord Burghley's house. Only afterwards did I wonder about the impression I must have made on his companions, a young girl unaccompanied at an inn with my hair uncovered and without collar or ruff, only a black ribbon covering the mole on my throat, but I didn't care. I waited only for our next encounter and continued to go to the playhouses.

I did not see him again for a long time but one day watching a play at the Black Bull Inn in Bishopsgate I encountered my uncle Alvise who was one of the musicians playing for the performance. I did not recognise him at first because I had seen none of my Bassano relatives since my father's death due to my mother's reluctance to carry on the association, but he had seen me standing by the stage and afterwards came to greet me. "Aemilia, it is really you. How goes it with you, cara? What a long time since we have seen you." His voice with its lilting cadences and exaggerated vowels reminded me of my father and I smiled happily in recognition. "Ehi, Aemilia, how you have grown, and grown to resemble your father too, though more handsome than ever he was," his eyes were twinkling now.

Alvise was the second eldest of the six musician brothers and the one responsible for bringing the rest of his family to England to find work at the court of King Henry. He had always been the one closest to my father who had named one of my dead brothers after him. He was an old man now, over seventy years of age with long thinning white hair and a face as brown and lined as a walnut, though with an upright carriage and still practising as a musician. He wrapped his arms around me, almost weeping with emotion and I felt the warmth of my father's personality emanating from him. When we parted he said, "I shall not let you disappear again, cara, be sure of that."

He was as good as his word for a short time later he arrived at our house in Bishopsgate to my mother's surprise. However she greeted him civilly enough and after taking a cup of ale and asking politely about our present circumstances he made known the reason for his visit. "We are having a family festa in my daughter Laura's house and I have been sent to invite all my brother Battista's family," he said. "We do hope you will be able to come, Meg, and also Aemilia whom we have not seen for some time. Angela too and her husband if her domestic duties can spare her." But his still-sharp eyes were fixed upon me.

I turned impulsively to my mother, "Oh may we go, please say yes."

If the message had been delivered it would probably have been returned with a polite excuse but I knew she would find it difficult to refuse the old man personally, now adding further pleas to mine, and so was forced to compromise as he knew she must. " Aemilia may attend, provided you will be responsible for her, Alvise, and see that she is escorted safely home at a reasonable hour. But I'm afraid I must decline. I am past the age for such revels and it would bring back too many memories," she finished lamely.

Alvise shrugged his shoulders, his hands rising in resignation, and I felt that he understood her real reasons and was sorry for them. All that mattered to me was that I had her witnessed permission to go and visit my Bassano relatives where they all lived close together in Mark Lane in the Liberties not far from the Tower.

The evening stayed in my memory long after it was over as being full of laughter and noise, music and wine, an exuberant gathering such as I had not known since my father's death. There were so many people, so much talking all at once in a mixture of Italian and English illustrated and complemented by rapid hand movements, cups of wine constantly replenished, loud bursts of laughter and always someone with a musical instrument in his hand, often accompanied by song and sometimes dancing. My father's brothers - Alvise, Jaspero, Giovanni and Antonio - all seemed much older than when I had last seen them but my father had been the youngest. Now however there was a new generation of cousins some of whom had children of their own. The boys were particularly wild and boisterous, especially the grandsons of Alvise and Antonio, both about twelve years old. Alvise's daughter Laura had married a Jewish Italian musician called Joseph Lupo and their son Thomas lived up to his name by wolfing down all the food he could lay his hands on. Antonio's daughter Lucrezia had married the French musician Nicholas Lanier who had sometimes given me musical tuition during my time with the Countess of Kent, and their eldest son Alfonso left his playmates for a time to approach me with a show of friendliness.

"I'm pleased to meet you cousin Aemilia and I have a present for you," he said with his wide innocent smile and dancing brown eyes, and he pressed something into my hand. I screamed as the slimy object touched my palm and dropped the little frog onto the floor with a baleful glare.

"Horrible boy," I yelled, while his father who had seen the exchange clipped him around the ear. But at that first encounter I had no premonition of the trouble Alfonso Lanier was to cause in my life. Later in the evening the two boys were pressed into playing a duet on their recorders and the devils were suddenly transformed into angels by the sweetness and skill of their playing.

I loved the evening and was loath to leave at the early hour my mother had ordered but I was exhilarated by the realisation that I was back in my father's circle, the circle of Court musicians that my mother and her Puritan friends had tried to distance me from. This meant that my connection with the Court was revived, albeit on the fringes, because sometimes my aunts and cousins would invite me to accompany them when the families of the musicians were allowed to join the audience at Court performances or civic commemorations on special days like Shrove Tuesday, St. George's Day, Accession Day or the Lord Mayor's Parade, when music would play such an important part. I loved to hear my kinsfolk play, sometimes imagining my father was still with them, and basked in their reflected glory when important people praised them. But I always wished I could be playing myself and though I no longer wished I were a boy so that I could be apprenticed like my male cousins, I could see no reason why women could not be musicians as they were in Venice.

One Accession Day I went with my uncle Giovanni's grandson, Mark, to the tiltyard at Whitehall to watch the annual joust in the Queen's honour. The celebrations were open for spectators because the Queen wished everyone to commemorate her accession to the throne but at a price of twelve pence for a seat the cost was too high for most ordinary people. Mark was eighteen and an apprentice luthier but because his elder brother Sebastian was one of the trumpeters he had been fortunate to secure a good place on the stands not too far away from the Privy Gallery from where the Queen and the nobles would watch the proceedings. However most of the younger nobles took part in the jousting, tilting in pairs on horseback with lances and swords then on foot with pikes, all in splendid clothes and shining armour and accompanied by a retinue of gentlemen, pages and trumpeters. All the courtiers tried to outdo each other not only in their prowess but in the magnificence of their appearance and the size of their retinue, each one trying to gain the exclusive favour of the Queen. I was excitedly trying to recognise the participants and Mark and I were exchanging bets but it was my cousin who pointed out to me Sir Philip Sidney.

"He will be the winner, he's the most popular contestant this year," he said confidently and I looked towards the handsome young man in spectacular blue and gold armour, accompanied by attendants dressed all in silver and gold. "He's in love with Penelope Devereux, the Earl of Essex's sister," Mark continued. "Have you read any of the sonnets he's written about her?" When I shook my head he continued, "They've been circulating privately around the Court and the literati, Sidney wouldn't stoop to anything so vulgar as having them published. 'Astrophel and Stella' they're called, Penelope being the star and he the starlover, a neat conceit."

We saw him effortlessly take the prize of the tournament and then the Queen's glove as a mark of her favour and Mark claimed his winnings from me, a penny and a kiss. I studied Philip Sidney anew, his tall athletic figure, his classical head of short brown curls (his blemished skin not discernible from a distance), and wished he were writing sonnets about me. I thought how exciting it must be to have people read poems about you. "What is Penelope Devereux like? Have you seen her?" I asked Mark, feeling a spark of interest in this girl who was Essex's sister and could inspire a popular courtier to write poems in her praise.

"You can't miss her," he laughed, his brown eyes sparkling. "She is the most beautiful girl I have ever seen." I felt a pang of envy. How fortunate I considered Penelope Devereux, blessed with beauty, noble birth, the Earl of Essex for her brother and Philip Sidney her sworn admirer. I longed to see her.

After the jousting came the comedy when a company of actors performed a burlesque of the rituals. Drawn in a carriage with horses disguised to look like elephants they addressed the Queen in comic verse before enacting their own version of the aristocratic combat. Laughing and clapping my hands I was not aware of being studied by a nobleman sitting at the

Queen's right hand in the Privy Gallery until Mark said, "You have caught the attention of an important courtier, Aemilia."

"Is it the Earl of Essex?" I couldn't help asking, for I had looked for him unsuccessfully.

Mark looked at me quizzically as he replied, "No, Essex isn't here. He's sulking because the Queen wouldn't let him joust. It's his great-uncle, his grandmother's brother, the Lord Chamberlain."

I looked up and perused the long narrow face, the amused intelligent eyes, the fading red hair just visible beneath his black velvet hat, and realised it was Lord Hunsdon who had called me beautiful at Kenilworth seven years ago when I was only a child. He was an old man, old enough to be my grandfather, but he was a very important man and a relative of the Earl of Essex and he had called me beautiful. I was sorry not to be wearing anything better than my blue wool cloak but it was November and chilly. I tilted my head and smiled at him. He didn't return my smile but he nodded his head slightly and held my gaze until I dropped my eyes in embarrassment.

"I do not like you spending so much time with the Bassanos, wasting time on plays and music in the company of entertainers," my mother said to me later. "They are not the best associates for a fatherless girl and could harm your reputation."

"You have relatives who are musicians," I retorted. Several of my mother's family, the Johnsons, were musicians and Edward Johnson stood high in the Queen's favour after composing a song for her entitled 'Eliza is the Fairest Queen.' It was through this connection that my mother had first made the acquaintance of my father but under the influence of her Puritan friends her links with the musical world had slackened. The Puritans did not condemn secular music and often played and sang in their own homes as I had often witnessed in the household of the Countess of Kent. But professional musicians they viewed with distaste particularly as they often performed in the playhouses, which they hated with a venom verging on obsessional, and often shared the same kind of louche lifestyle as the actors. Also most of the foreign musicians, who comprised the majority of the Queen's Musick, were Catholics. Puritans disapproved of sacred music as being a remnant and constant reminder of Papist ceremonies. They were not pleased that the Queen encouraged musicians like Thomas Tallis and William Byrd to write anthems for church services and that she greeted foreign ambassadors with religious compositions, believing that religious themes were ill served by musical adaptation while the church should be concerned only with prayer and preaching and the seductive lure of beautiful sound distracted from spiritual concentration.

"At least the Johnsons are Protestants," she said. "Be careful you are not lured into the Papist circle of the Bassanos, Aemilia. England is a dangerous place for Catholics at this time due to the strong penalties the Queen has ordered in the wake of so many plots to assassinate her and make Mary Stuart our Queen." I recognised the note of satisfaction in my mother's voice for the recent harsh legislation pleased the Puritans who considered the Queen had always been too lenient towards the Catholic faith.

"Musicians and artists are immune from persecution," I countered.

"But not if they are converts," my mother insisted.

"William Byrd is, and the Queen turns a blind eye," I replied.

"It is exceedingly dangerous to be involved in any way with the Papist religion," she insisted. "Your father's recklessness almost caused his death at one time. No," she continued as I started to question her, "I have no intention of opening up that episode. Sufficient to say that sharing a musician's bed is not a comfortable experience." I caught the note of bitterness in her voice as she clamped her lips shut.

"Well I have no intention of becoming a Catholic," I retorted sulkily, angry that she would not elaborate on an intriguing episode in my father's life. And definitely not a Puritan, I said to myself. I gave no thought to theological considerations which would no doubt grieve the Countess of Kent, now Lady Wingfield. It would also grieve my mother which is why I never prolonged any conversation with her on religious matters although I had noticed that her preoccupation with religion was becoming stronger of late, though I was unsure whether that was because of my increasing rebelliousness or the fact that she seemed to be ailing. She never complained about any particular indisposition but she began to lose weight, to be constantly tired, and her rosy face acquired an unhealthy pallor. However because her lack of energy often kept her within doors I surmised that all she needed was fresh air so on the fine nights of Spring I would persuade her to take a walk to Moor fields. With my youthful optimism I thought the exercise would do her good though it only succeeded in making her more tired.

One evening Stephen and Judith Vaughn had supped with us but when my mother excused herself and retired to bed they did not leave immediately. "I have something of import to say to you, Aemilia," Stephen began in the tone of voice that prepared me for one of his homilies and I groaned inwardly. "Now that you are sixteen I think you should seriously consider letting us arrange a suitable marriage for you."

"I am not in any haste to be wed," I insisted, wondering how long this was going to last and how I could be rid of their company without showing too much discourtesy.

He remained silent for a time then nodded to his wife who continued seriously, "We do not want to alarm you, Aemilia, but I do not know if you are aware how sick your mother is. Neither she, nor your friends, would wish to see you alone in the world. It would be well to give some thought to your future."

They did not say any more and made their farewells, leaving me deep in consideration of this new possibility. I did feel frightened for a time but then with the optimism of youth I soon began to think that Stephen Vaughn was exaggerating for his own ends and my mother would soon recover her strength. However with the approach of summer she did not improve as I had expected but neither did she worsen as the year progressed so my fears lessened.

One afternoon I decided to go to the private Blackfriars theatre, rooms in the old monastery beside the river where the boy companies performed. I didn't care for the boy actors as much as the professionals and the plays were not so much to my taste but it had rained all week so there had been no performances at Shoreditch or at any of the inns whereas the Blackfriars was an indoor space. It wasn't a private theatre in any real sense, except for the higher admission prices which regulated the audience, but was so called because it was reserved for performances by the children of the Chapel Royal and not available to the professional actors. I got Jack Milmay to accompany me for now I was a young lady it was unacceptable to attend performances alone.

There was always someone willing, one of our neighbouring artisan families, a servant with a few hours to spare, someone from the wide circle of musicians of my acquaintance, depending on the venue and the cost. Jack was the son of one of the sackbutt players in the Queen's Musick, a lad of about my own age and an apprentice musician himself whose plain round face and shock of unruly hair disguised a quick wit and a ready tongue. He was complaining vociferously about the weather as we splashed our way through the filth and slush of the streets, the kennels overflowing with refuse as the water blocked the drains and we were sodden when we arrived at the Blackfriars. "Oh stop moaning, at least we will we warm and dry inside," I reproved him, excited as usual because I was going to watch a play, even though my cloak was soaked and my shoes and stockings and the lower part of my gown were all begrimed with mud. The theatre was part of the old refectory of the monastery, a spacious rectangular area with a curtained dais at one end and all the spectators seated on benches with some chairs at the front for important nobles. We paid our admission and found a place on a bench near the back of the hall with its lofty high-beamed ceiling. The play was an adaptation of the classical myth of Echo and Narcissus written by one of the University scholars and had neither the blood and gore nor the rumbustious buffoonery of the public playhouses being chiefly a vehicle to display the excellent voices of the boys to good effect. "I've seen better," I remarked dryly to Jack afterwards. "I don't know why the actors fear the competition of the boy companies. Did you not think it was worth our getting wet after all?"

"On the contrary I found the music excellent and the boys skilfully trained," he replied. "And look at the audience. No riff-raff here. What would the players give for such discerning observers."

"But that's just the point, Jack, they are observers. At the public performances the audience shout and jeer, encourage the actors, give themselves wholeheartedly to what is happening on the stage believing it to be real. This is what the actors need, this reciprocity, this involvement." I laughed half ashamedly at Jack's quizzical look.

"If you were a boy I think you would be a player yourself," he mocked and I felt too embarrassed to admit to it. I would love to have been a player, or at least one of the musicians. But his words about the audience were true, they were all well dressed and circumspect with many of the highest class and none of the meaner sort. They were also clean and dry, indicating that they had arrived in coaches. Then to my astonishment I saw Lord Hunsdon approaching me from his chair near the stage. He was accompanied by a tall voluptuous woman splendidly dressed in a farthingale of rose coloured silk with a kirtle of a paler shade embroidered in silver thread. Her curlicued ruff had silver thread woven in the fine cambric and a tall crowned hat of pale grey felt sat atop her abundant chestnut hair. She looked to be almost forty years old, her face rouged and finely chiselled but hard, her grey eyes cold with disdain as she surveyed us.

"Mistress Bassano." Lord Hunsdon saluted me courteously, his eyes sweeping swiftly over Jack. "I believe you are inammorata of the theatre." I could sense something akin to amusement in his gaze as he registered my somewhat bedraggled state, my curls springing waywardly with the damp.

"Oh yes, my Lord, I am," I replied, flustered that he should find me here looking less than my best.

"I believe you are often seen in the playhouses." His eyes held an inscrutable expression, part amusement but part challenging as if daring me to question how he knew so much about me and what might be my justification for such unladylike behaviour. I dropped my eyes, feeling suddenly embarrassed and not knowing what to say. He leaned closer towards me and lowered his voice so that only I could hear his words. "Give my name to the gatherers, Aemilia, and they will find you one of the best seats at no charge. I will arrange it." Then he made his salutations again and departed, making no attempt to introduce his companion nor ask about mine.

"God's bones, Aemilia, it would seem the Lord Chamberlain has a fancy for you," Jack murmured when he had gone. He was looking both amused and taken aback.

The encounter had shaken me somewhat but I was now recovering my composure and I snapped, "Don't be so ridiculous. He knew my father. In fact I first met him with my father when I was a child. Why he is about the same age my father would have been had he lived."

"Apparently, from what I hear, that does not prevent him from being attracted to beautiful young women. He has much of his father in him I think." Seeing my look of bemusement he added, "King Henry".

"His father was William Carey, husband of Mary Boleyn. He is the Queen's cousin."

Jack laughed. "The official story. Nearly everyone believes he is the son of Mary Boleyn and King Henry, and therefore the Queen's half-brother. Why do you think she favours him so much. And notice the red hair!"

It took me a few moments to digest this. "And the woman, was she his wife?"

Jack roared with laughter. "No. Lady Hunsdon would never be seen at the theatre of an afternoon. The woman was probably one of his light 'o loves. It is said he has several mistresses and a few by-blows, and his wife bore him twelve children, though not all of them lived."

"Twelve children? And he still keeps mistresses! But he is old," I cried.

"Apparently he has quite a reputation," Jack laughed again, leaving no doubt as to his meaning. "And from the way he looked at you I think he might be harbouring some fantasies about you. So if you want to keep your good name I should beware. Though you could do worse," and he nudged me suggestively.

"I won't let you accompany me again, Jack Milmay, if you don't amend your speech," I retorted angrily. "And don't you dare say anything of this to anyone else."

But when I got home I began to feel a little excited. I had no intention of putting myself in the way of an old philanderer like Lord Hunsdon and it was fortunate my path hardly ever crossed his. But on the other hand it was flattering to be singled out by such a powerful noble. I took the Venetian gilded mirror my father had once given me and looked at my reflection. I was different. I still didn't think of myself as beautiful but my hair was an intense black, thick and glossy with curls that had grown gentler over the years instead of the unruly mop of my childhood. My dark eyes were fringed with thick curving lashes, my skin though dark hued was unblemished, (apart from the mole on my throat which I always tried to cover;) my teeth perfect, their whiteness emphasized by the tint of red Spanish leather I rubbed on my lips, and my figure tall and slender, my small waist defined by the tight boned bodices I wore. When I was younger I didn't like to be different but now

I did, different to all the red-haired white-skinned copies of the Queen that proliferated everywhere by dint of henna and white lead. I knew now at seventeen that I had power to attract a man. If someone as rich and noble as Lord Hunsdon noticed me perhaps it was not without the bounds of possibility to find a young husband for myself from a class above me. Perhaps I might even be able to attract the Earl of Essex. It was a dream, but a pleasant one.

Lord Hunsdon kept his word with regard to theatre performances and the gatherers just smiled knowingly when I approached and directed me to the best seats, the first gallery of the inns, the second gallery of the playhouses with a cushion to sit on. At first I felt self-conscious to be seated amongst the better classes and the recipient of speculative glances but then I began to enjoy the attention and found no shortage of partners to accompany me. I never encountered the Lord Chamberlain again but occasionally I would catch sight of him from a distance.

The next year my mother's health worsened steadily and as 1586 progressed she often did not rise from her bed and if she did it was only to lie on the settle in the parlour supported by cushions. Her frame was mere skin and bone, her blue eyes dull and sunken, her once-rosy complexion had faded to a grey hue, and although she never complained I knew she was in constant pain so that I had to continuously give her draughts from the apothecary I always seemed to be visiting. I spent as much time as I could with her, feeling guilty that I had never really done so and we had never established a close rapport together. I had always seemed to be disagreeing with her or at least ignoring her admonitions, even as a child seeking my father's company while she showed a distinct preference for the meek and obedient Angela. Now when I feared I was soon to lose her I tried to compensate for my past indifference by spending time reading to her or just holding her hand for company while she dozed fitfully, my one-time impatience transmuted into compassion tinged with remorse and anxiety. When I wasn't at home with her I was often at the house of my sister Angela who was expecting another child and suffering from severe morning sickness that rendered her incapable for half the day.

It was a terrible year. England had joined with the States of the Dutch Republic in declaring war against Spain who were occupying the Netherlands and preparing an army there to invade England in support of Mary Stuart. The Earl of Leicester was sent to command the English force accompanied by his nephew Philip Sidney and his young stepson the Earl of Essex on his first military campaign and I listened for news avidly. The news that came shocked the whole of London for at the Battle of Zutphen Philip Sidney had been mortally wounded and subsequently died. The glorious golden hero Philip Sidney, soldier, poet, courtier, patriot, beloved by the Queen and England's darling, was dead. I remembered seeing him at the Accession Day tilt and I wondered what Essex's sister Penelope was thinking. Despite his adoration of her and everyone's expectations, they had not married, whether from personal choice or family pressure I didn't know. She had married the Earl of Warwick and he had married Sir Francis Walsingham's daughter, but he had made her name immortal as Helen's by his poetry and their names would always be joined together by his sonnets. Londoners couldn't believe the news until the Earl of Leicester brought his body home in a ship with black sails and a great state funeral was held in St. Paul's church, the largest and most important of London's two hundred churches, attended by the whole city cursing the name of Spain.

Then a plot was discovered for a combined force of France and Spain to invade England and assassinate the Queen, sanctioned by the signature of Mary Stuart. The agent who carried the messages, Anthony Babington, was hanged, drawn and quartered in front of a large cheering crowd of Londoners. Mary Stuart was found guilty of treason and finally after twenty years' imprisonment ordered to be put to death. And my mother was dying too.

One day I was surprised by our maid Phoebe presenting me with a letter fastened by a strange intricate seal which, in some awe, she said had been handed to her at the door by a man in nobleman's livery. Opening it with trepidation I saw it was headed from the palace of Whitehall. It was an invitation to a private performance of 'The Arraignment of Paris' by the playwright and actor George Peele, to be acted by the Lord Admiral's Men at the behest of Lord Hunsdon. A note was added to the effect that a coach would call for me at the appointed time and signed by Henry Carey himself. I read and reread the note, excited and afraid in equal measure, unsure of the implications. Contradictory interpretations bounced around in my head. Lord Hunsdon knew I loved plays and perhaps there was no more to it than that. Then the recollection of how he looked at me sent a shiver down my spine. Why should he send me a personal invitation to the Court when I was only a musician's daughter living in modest circumstances? Was there some ulterior motive behind this exceptional honour? There was no invitation for anyone to accompany me. I needed someone to talk to but there was no-one suitable, not my mother or her friends or my sister. Yet finally I acknowledged that I could not possibly refuse, for this distinction from such a great nobleman was nothing less than a command. I accepted the inevitable and once the balls stopped spinning I felt the thrill of anticipation though the dizziness did not abate. I had visited the palace before but always with my father or the musicians. Now I was being invited in my own right. Aemilia Bassano was going to the Palace of Whitehall at the personal invitation of the Lord Chamberlain himself, the highest Court official and effective head of the entire Court. It was the beginning of my dream and who knew where it might lead, perhaps to the Earl of Essex, Lord Hunsdon's great-nephew.

On the appointed day, the hours lagging laboriously and untidily like the stitches in my embroidery frame, I thought of nothing but what I could wear and wished I had something more splendid than my best blue taffeta. The gown itself was a deep vibrant blue which set off my dark looks and I had recently replaced the old sleeves by a new set in green satin with a matching kirtle inside the open front of the skirt. I had wanted the new additions to be a dramatic crimson but my mother would in no way give her consent claiming that I would "look like a whore," so I had to be content with red laces tying the sleeves into the bodice and fastening it at the back. My ruff was small and simple with a narrow edging of lace and a veil covered my loose hair. My best cloak was only wool, blue with a grey lining, but I could discard it at the earliest opportunity.

I had only very occasionally travelled in a coach when I was living with the Countess of Kent, and never alone, and for an hour before the due time I kept surreptitious watch from the parlour casement, relieved my mother was asleep in bed. However when my conveyance arrived it was one of the new sedan chairs accompanied by link boys. The swaying motion did nothing to improve the nausea caused by my nervousness and apprehension and my head ached with. anxiety about what I should do when I reached my destination. I both wanted the terrible journey to end and at the same time to go on for ever so that I need not face the consequences. However my worries were needless because on arrival at the Whitehall Palace stairs one of the bearers led me confidently along the road which led directly to the chapel and the Great Hall as if he had been given detailed instructions. This enormous space with its high arch-beamed roof and walls covered with vivid Flemish tapestries of classical scenes was where the Queen often allowed musical and dramatic performances to be held and was set with chairs and benches facing a raised curtained dais. Immediately I found Lord Hunsdon at my side, richly garbed in black velvet braided with gold and with his gold chain of office as Lord Chamberlain responsible, amongst his other duties, for all Court entertainments and also the music of the Chapel.

"I am pleased that you could come, Aemilia, and I want this to be a very happy evening for you. I know how you enjoy plays and the Lord Admiral's Company are the best company of actors in London. Do you know their chief player, Edward Alleyn?" His tone was smooth and polite with no suggestion other than that of a considerate host welcoming an invited guest and I began to relax.

"I have seen him once or twice. He is truly excellent," I replied. Edward Alleyn was the son of a Bishopsgate innkeeper whose inn had often been used for performances, and at only twenty two years of age was already making a name for himself as the most popular actor n London. Relieved by Lord Hunsdon's formal composure, my nervousness began to diminish now that I was on a subject dear to my heart.

"I have found you a place near to some people who knew your father and here is Master John Dowland whom you must know as a musician." He escorted me to a seat in the middle of the hall then left me in the attentive company of a fair-haired sturdy young man wearing a plain though well-fitting doublet and hose of a blue that matched the colour of his eyes. He was about twenty five years of age but already well known as a composer of lute songs and I remembered that his first published book had been dedicated to Lord Hunsdon's son, George Carey. I felt at ease with him and when Lord Hunsdon had gone away I found much to talk about as we shared our common interest and acquaintances.

I was delighted by the performance and the Lord Admiral's company were indeed the best actors I had ever seen playing together. I fell in love with the tall and darkly handsome Edward Alleyn with his magnificent musical voice and compelling stage presence. I was so enthralled with him and the play that once it had begun I was scarcely aware of the splendid surroundings of Whitehall nor the elevated company of which I was part, lords and ladies though the Queen herself was not present. Neither had I given further thought to Lord Hunsdon, John Dowland being an easy companion with an appreciation of the performance to match my own. When the play had finished and the actors took their bows to thunderous applause, I was sure that Lord Hunsdon had nothing more in mind than providing me with a treat he knew I would relish, though as I looked around I felt vulnerable in the press of so many splendid strangers and was aware for the first time of curious looks at my modest dress and lack of jewels in the midst of such overall magnificence. My nervousness returned in the wake of uncertainty about what was to happen next and I wanted to know how I should return home, but I soon found Lord Hunsdon at my side again, allaying my anxiety by saying, "I will have you escorted home, Aemilia. Was the performance to your taste?"

"Oh yes, my Lord, it was magnificent. I am truly grateful for your kindness to me," I cried wholeheartedly, relieved at the normality of the conclusion to the evening and wondering how I could ever have suspected otherwise.

He hesitated, his eyes fixed on me, and once again I was aware of his intimate interest as well as the intelligent scrutiny behind the grey pupils and I shivered. "This could be your life, Aemilia, if you wish. Here at Whitehall with all the best that life can offer." His words cracked the surface of normality and I felt unable to reply, not being absolutely sure of his meaning though my blood tingled in my veins and I could feel the warmth suffusing my cheeks. "I want you," he continued calmly though I could sense the underlying excitement in his voice. "I have watched you for a long time, more often than you have known. I have wanted you for a long time but I have waited until you are eighteen, I am a very patient man. But I can't wait any longer. Will you come to me now? I will give you anything you desire."

I couldn't look at him and my throat was dry as I found myself croaking hoarsely and uncertainly the first words that came into my head, "I can't."

"In what way 'cannot'?" He sounded amused rather than displeased.

I couldn't say the words that rose to my mouth. "Because you are past sixty and I am just eighteen.

Because it would be so shocking to my family and all my friends, to Lady Susan and the Vaughns, to all our neighbours in Bishopsgate, even to the Bassanos and no doubt to the Queen herself who did not tolerate sexual laxity in women." Instead I found myself saying frantically, "Because my mother is dying."

I didn't know how he would react, I knew instinctively that Henry Carey was a man not accustomed to being refused anything, but after a pause he said with what I felt was genuine compassion, "I am sorry, my dear, I did not know. You must go home to your mother. But think about what I have said. I shall wait a little longer but that will only increase my desire for you and I shall ask you again at a more suitable time." He did not touch me but the intensity of his emotion pressed upon me like a physical embrace and I felt imprisoned, overcome with a sense of inevitability. Then he turned away to swiftly and efficiently arrange my transport home, this time in a coach with his servants.

I went to bed immediately, trying to still the tumult of my thoughts, but sleep was impossible. So many images and thoughts chased around my brain. All my life since I was seven years old at Kenilworth I had wanted to be part of the Court, to mix with people of noble birth, to wear rich clothes and jewels, to be courted and admired. If I had ever spoken those words aloud it was to be quickly disillusioned, even by my father. There was no way a girl of my class could enter that magical world even though I were as educated, as accomplished, as handsome, as noble women were. Yet here was the opportunity being handed to me! But at what cost? I would lose my reputation and all chance of securing a prestigious marriage. No man worth his salt would ever want me afterwards if my seducer should tire of me quickly or if he should die, he was an old man after all.

And did I really want to squander my first experience of love on an old man, he was sixty three and I had recoiled in revulsion when Angela had been willing to marry a man not yet forty. Yet this was no ordinary man. He was probably the most powerful person in the kingdom after the Queen, the chief officer of her household, her blood relation, immensely rich, educated and cultured, and from my experience courteous and kindly disposed. But he was a married man with several mistresses to his credit and certainly not faithful to any woman. Perhaps he would quickly tire of me once he had taken my virginity and then where would I be. I decided to talk to Angela on the morrow, not the ideal confidante but the best I had.

When I visited my sister the following day she was lying propped up on pillows in the capacious marital bed with a bowl by her side into which she periodically vomited. Her son Philip was at the curate's school in St. Mary's church and her husband was in the shop and storeroom below. I found it difficult to begin the conversation because on my arrival she launched into a long monologue about her debilitating condition, the hardships of childbearing, how there would be no future generations if men had to undergo this suffering and how afterwards she did not think she would let her husband near her.

I broke in with, "Nonsense, Angela, this sickness will pass and you know when the child is born you will consider it all to have been worthwhile as you did with Philip." Then having broken into the conversation I continued as quickly as I could so she would have no time to reply, "Anyway I want to ask your advice about my own life." Then as concisely as I could I related my experience with Lord Hunsdon and his offer to me.

Her first reaction was amazement that such a great lord should even notice me, Aemilia Bassano. Then this was followed by shock and disgust that I should even be considering the proposition. "Fornication is a sin, Aemilia, and to fornicate with a married man is a double sin." There was no answer to this and she continued, "It would kill our mother and what would everyone say, our whole family would be disgraced and ostracised. What would happen to my husband's business if it were known his wife was the sister of a whore."

"If I were Lord Hunsdon's whore his business could greatly increase," I couldn't resist saying, to which remark her lamentations were renewed.

"You have always been a rebel, Aemilia, Master Vaughn was right. But your education at the hands of the Countess of Kent has obviously done you no good at all."

"My education fitted me for the life of a noblewoman, Angela, not for the life of a merchant's wife in Leadenhall Street. Lord Hunsdon has offered me whatever I want. He's rich and powerful and kin to the Queen, whether her cousin or her brother as many folk think."

"But for how long? And when he tires of you what then? Who will marry you? You are only eighteen and could lose all chance of finding a good husband for yourself."

This was my main consideration. Henry Carey had had several mistresses according to popular report. Well I would have to make sure he didn't tire of me and if he did there might possibly be other younger lords who would take me on the same basis. What was marriage anyway but a life of slavery for a woman. A mistress was under fewer restraints and with careful manipulation could forge her own independence. But Angela's warnings were all of the same ilk interspersed with dire prophecies of my eternal damnation so I made my farewells as soon as I could, leaving her somewhat hard-heartedly to her vomiting.

This did not cease at the expected time however and I began to think I had been severe on her as her pregnancy continued to be full of problems. But I had problems of my own to solve and I realised I could only solve them for myself. It was my life and I had to make my own decisions so I was not too frustrated at having to spend so much time by my mother's side especially while she dozed as it gave me the opportunity to reflect, to let my heart and mind come to terms with what I felt was my destiny. The Countess of Kent may have tried to instil into me her belief that God predestined our lives but I believed we made our own choices and the education that had been gifted to me was not to be wasted on a man of middling class. I was destined to be a lady and if the only path to such a status was as a great nobleman's mistress then so be it.

Lord Hunsdon left me alone but he did not forget me. Every now and then a gift would arrive - a diamond clip, a single string of pearls, a sapphire bracelet - nothing too extravagant but always delicately worked and always with a simple greeting accompanied by his flamboyant signature. If it hadn't been for these tokens of remembrance I might have suspected I had dreamt it all, my deep-felt desires taking to themselves the shape of sleep-induced fancies.

It was early one morning, scarcely dawn, when one of Master Joseph Holland's apprentices brought a message urging me to come at once as Angela's labour had begun. When I arrived I could see that all was not well and the maidservants and the midwife were looking progressively alarmed as Angela's screams intensified, her body tossing and arching in agony on the matrimonial bed. The nightmare scenario continued for several hours as I bathed her sweat-drenched face and spoke soothingly to her, while the midwife tried in vain to reach the struggling child so eager to be born. It was all in vain. Towards noon my sister and her child were both dead.

The shock was too much for my mother's frail body. She struggled to attend the funeral of her elder daughter on an April morning when fluffy white clouds sped across a blue-washed sky and a pale sun fingered purple and yellow crocuses, a day cruelly bright with all the promise of spring, but could not make it over the threshold. I stood beside a distraught Joseph Holland and his young son Philip as the coffin of my twenty five year old sister was lowered into the ground.

Two months later the ritual was repeated for my mother. It was a year shadowed by death for in February Mary Stuart had been beheaded at Fotheringay castle and the removal of the greatest Papist threat to Queen Elizabeth had given great satisfaction to my mother in her last weeks. Now she herself was being buried on top of my father in St. Botolph's churchyard, close beside the graves of my two brothers and my only sister on a mild June day when roses blossomed in profusion. I was eighteen years old and I was now the only survivor of my family. I had never felt so alone in my life as I realised that those closest to me had all gone and I regretted how I had not truly appreciated them. As the condolences of Stephen and Judith Vaughn, my Bassano and Johnson kin and our neighbours in Bishopsgate, flowed in a seemingly unending stream through my consciousness I was aware of my own mortality. For the first time I realised the uncertainty of life, the uncompromising truth that youth and beauty fade, carpe diem. But I was still alive and fearful that chances do not always come twice I acknowledged the prompting of my spirit. The sun suddenly edged away the louring clouds to reveal a rim of silver on the flat grey canopy that was shading now to a pale azure, and a warm summer breeze brushed my cheek.

The day after my mother's funeral a parcel arrived at our house. Inside was a beautiful gown of black velvet studded with seed pearls. A single word was written on the note – 'Well?'

I agonised no more and returned a simple answer. 'Yes.'

Chapter 4

TOCCATA

I had no idea what would happen next but I had no spare time to let fear or regret overtake me for I was kept busy in the aftermath of my mother's death. She had made me the executrix of her will leaving me everything she had, except for the lease on one of her properties which was to go to Angela's widower Joseph Holland and their son Philip, on the understanding I was first to clear any debts. The only other bequest was her most valuable ring, a Johnson family heirloom, which she left not to me but to Judith Vaughn, a sure testament of her friendship with these people I had never really liked. Stephen Vaughn and my brother-in-law Joseph were to help me fulfil all the conditions of the will which took some time and left me little opportunity to consider my own position. Naturally everyone wondered what this was to be. Our friends and acquaintances took it for granted that I would lease our house and move in with the Hollands to help care for my young nephew until I should undertake a convenient marriage, and I did indeed feel strong pangs of guilt that I had no intention of doing so when my help and support might be needed. I had heard nothing further from Lord Hunsdon and did not know what his plans entailed but even if I had never made his acquaintance I would not have relinquished my own house. This now offered me some form of independence and though my circumstances were still modest I had at least enough money to pay my way. This might have satisfied me apart from the grand ambitions I had always nurtured. However, predictably, everyone was shocked. "You cannot possibly live on your own, a single woman of just eighteen with only a maid for company. This is quite unacceptable behaviour for someone of your class." This was the universal sentiment, uttered with only slight variations, and it angered me. Everyone accepted without question that women must always be under the control of a man - father, brother, husband, protector, even brother-in-law. And why always this emphasis on my class. The nobility of course had more freedom, but so did the poor whom no-one cared about.

I procrastinated by saying I must sort out all our belongings if I were to lease the house, realising I might have to do this anyhow when Lord Hunsdon sent for me. My thoughts were a maelstrom of confusion. "I want you," he had said. "Will you come to me?" But I was uncertain as to what exactly he had meant? Did he just want to make love to me or would he set me up permanently as his mistress?

The turbulence of my thoughts and emotions were paralleled by the confusion in the country at large. The execution of Mary Stuart had not been the final solution to Papist interference in English affairs but had given further provocation to Spain, smarting under English attacks on their shipping and Francis Drake's recent burning of the flotilla in Cadiz harbour, and they were preparing a great armada to invade England, the largest fleet ever to set sail it was said. No-one was really sure what was happening, London alert to every new rumour.

In the streets, shops, and churches, an invasion was the main topic of conversation while the playhouses were revelling in the popularity of patriotic plays. My acquaintances seized on the possibility of imminent war as a further reason why I could not possibly live in the house alone and I made a pretence of listening to them.

In the midst of all this activity a letter was delivered to me by a liveried page. Would I attend the Lord Hunsdon at his apartments at Whitehall on the following day when a servant would escort me to the embarcation at White Swan on the river and from there a barge would convey me to the Privy Stairs at Whitehall. I felt a momentary panic as I wondered if I had made an irrevocable decision. Was there now no turning back?

I dressed with care in the new gown I had recently purchased for such an eventuality. It was simple as I did not want to draw too much unfavourable attention to myself - a light summer-weight cream linen embroidered with blackwork, with tightly fitting sleeves of a buttercup yellow. The outfit was completed by a small ruff and a yellow cap on which I had fastened a gold and pearl pin, one of Lord Hunsdon's gifts. But I felt nervous and conspicuous as I walked down Bishopsgate to the Thames with a liveried servant in attendance. "Take hold of yourself, Aemilia," I chided myself sternly, "all the gentry walk the streets in the company of a liveried attendant. Isn't this something you have always wanted." But my nervousness did not abate when we reached White Swan stairs and I was handed into Lord Hunsdon's waiting barge with many curious eyes fixed upon me. It was a strange experience to be seated in the luxury of a private barge upholstered with crimson and gold velvet cushions with a canopy overhead to protect from the weather instead of in a normal wooden-benched ferry boat, but despite my apprehension I couldn't help enjoying the sight of the river's busy traffic from this unaccustomed vantage point as we sped swiftly down towards Whitehall. Yet my heart was thumping uncomfortably as we disembarked, not at the accessible Whitehall Palace Stairs as last time but at the privileged Privy Stairs, and I wondered what was to happen next. However everything was accomplished smoothly with no hesitation nor lack of courtesy so that it seemed a perfectly normal occurrence to be escorted thus into the palace of Whitehall as if I had every right to be there. As I was led through a confusing warren of corridors, galleries and ante-rooms I remembered having been told that there were more than two thousand rooms in Whitehall and indeed the walk seemed endless as we passed attentive servants and strolling courtiers who saluted me. At last my attendant stopped at the door of Lord Hunsdon's private apartments and once the door was opened I was left alone with him.

"Welcome Aemilia," he smiled encouragingly then kissed me gently on the cheek. "You look more beautiful than ever."

His obvious approval and composure gave me confidence and I smiled at him. "Thank you my Lord."

He took my hand and seated me in one of the carved chairs whilst he talked generally, commiserating about my loss and querying what I had been doing. I didn't like to be gazing round like a doting fool but I noticed the room was comfortable rather than grand - of modest proportions, wood panelled, a wall of book shelves, a desk with more books and maps, a large globe and several pipes with a tobacco jar - a man's room. I had seen many luxurious rooms during my stay with the Suffolks and at Kenilworth but Lord Hunsdon had no need to display his wealth or influence. Finally he said,

"Now I want to show you something." He led me a little further along the passage and opened another door. A small hallway led into a parlour that was one of the most beautiful small rooms I had ever seen. It was hung with tapestries of classical scenes, some of them mildly erotic, and had a large leaded window overlooking the river. There were two carved chairs cushioned in blue and gold velvet with a matching settle and foot stool, a carved oak coffer on which sat a Venetian glass bowl of rose petals, and a side table inlaid with ivory on which some books were set. He opened another door into a small dining room, oak panelled this time but with a crystal candelabra above the polished table around which were set four tall-backed chairs. Against one wall was a court cupboard full of silver plate. Another door led into a bedroom almost completely filled by an enormous tester bed hung with gold brocade drapes and a counterpane of the same stuff turned down to reveal silken sheets. Gold candlesticks shimmered on a polished chest with more candles on wrought iron stands. Gold brocade hangings covered the walls. I couldn't help the gasp which escaped from my lips but he was opening yet another door into a dressing room with pegs and tenterhooks, clothes presses and a marble stand with a ewer and basin of glazed porcelain besides which stood jars of unguents and perfumes. To one side stood a circular marble bath tub with a mound of fine linen drying cloths and Castille soaps. He opened one of the chests to show me a supply of the finest cambric shifts and other linen, and another press to reveal what appeared to be a selection of velvet cloaks and mantles, saying, "I have not chosen gowns for you because I thought you would like to select your own. A tailor will attend you at your earliest convenience and you may go to any merchant and select stuffs and materials, trimmings and head tires, with no regard to cost, anything you want you may have. I will choose your jewels. I want your beauty to have the best setting."

He led me back through the rooms. "These apartments are yours as soon as you wish, Aemilia."

I was overcome by amazement and my head was whirling with a mixture of exhilaration and trepidation. It was all too much, I had never expected anything like this.

"My apartments are close by and sometimes you will come to me, dine with me, spend time with me. Other times I will come to you but otherwise your time will be your own to do as you please. I shall not always be here. I have other residences as you must know but I am often in attendance at Court and there will be much entertainment for you to enjoy. A maid will attend you and see to all your personal needs and you will have the use of my own servants to convey you to places or take messages or indeed anything that you have need of. Your meals will be provided here from the palace kitchens. Is this arrangement satisfactory to you, Aemilia?"

During the short time since the death of my mother I had found myself sometimes wondering whether I wanted to relinquish our little house in Bishopsgate and my new-found freedom in order to put myself under the control of a man. But this man was offering me a life such as I had only dreamt of, the sort of life I had always wanted. The cost might be high, I had the uncomfortable feeling I was being purchased like a desired piece of merchandise, and I did not know how long it would all last but I had considered all that. In any case this threat of war and invasion by Spain might put an end to life as we knew it. There really was no decision to make. However I did not intend to let him see how overwhelmed I was. For his generosity he was getting much in return - Aemilia Bassano, aged eighteen, worthy to be a lady, in his estimation beautiful, and also a virgin.

"It is quite satisfactory, my Lord," I replied, hoping my voice didn't waver.

A smile hovered at the corner of his mouth. "Then come at your own convenience. But do not let it be too long. A week perhaps?"

"I have several things to complete. But no longer than a week, I promise."

The most difficult thing was to explain my absence to family and friends.

"I have decided to lease the house. Perhaps you could arrange it," I said to Master Vaughn.

"I am glad you have seen the wisdom of this. I take it you are going to live with the Hollands?" he replied with a self-satisfied smile and I had an urge to take it off his face.

"The truth is I have received an offer of a place at Whitehall, as a lady's maid," I proclaimed.

"How is this? Why have we not been told before? Who has arranged it?" He was spluttering with frustration.

"I do have friends at Court as you know, Master Vaughn. In fact some of them were first introduced to me by yourself."

"Is this someone of Lady Wingfield's acquaintance then? I do not understand why I haven't heard anything before."

"Oh it is someone I met through a friend of hers," I replied vaguely, enjoying his discomfiture but realising I was digging a hole for myself.

"What is this lady's name?" he asked in his peremptory manner.

Then I had a sudden inspiration. I knew that Lord Hunsdon had a daughter Philadelphia who was a great favourite of the Queen. The name had stuck in my memory because it was such an unusual one. "Lady Philadelphia Carey," I lied unashamedly. He was impressed and temporarily silenced. By the time he had discovered otherwise it would be too late.

But I knew I would have to act swiftly now so it was less than a week before I was ready to go. I decided to let our house furnished, for I had no intention of ever returning here, taking with me only my personal possessions and our most valuable acquisitions including plate and the Venetian painting. Once the word had gone about that I had received a position at Court it was no surprise that a coach came to collect me after I had sent word to Lord Hunsdon. As I locked the door of the house in Bishopsgate I felt a momentary regret at leaving my family home where I had spent a happy childhood, secure in the knowledge that I would never live there again. But then I turned eagerly to my new life and the realisation that my new abode was going to be as splendid as anything I had ever dreamt of.

This time Lord Hunsdon was not waiting for me and a serious young woman called Bess helped me to put away my belongings. She was about ten years older than I was, small and dumpy in her blue wool gown with a plain round country face indented with smallpox scars and brown hair just visible beneath her starched white linen coif but her movements were deft and quick and she exuded an air of general competence. I soon felt that she was honest and trustworthy and would be a great asset to me. "His Lordship said he will be with you after supper," she informed me in her country brogue. "You are to eat alone and I am to fetch it for you. In the meantime is there anything you would like me to do?"

"No thankyou, I shall play some music and perhaps read until supper time."

A short time later Bess came with my supper, capon and sallets beautifully arranged on pewter plates with marigold flowers, and rich ruby wine in a decanter of Venetian glass with a matching goblet. I drank it all and began to feel light-headed though most of my meal remained untouched.

I moved into the parlour and because music always calmed me I took my lute and began to play some of my father's favourite tunes. "I wonder what he would think if he could see me now," I mused, recalling the time he had first introduced me to Lord Hunsdon at Kenilworth. I did not think he would be shocked, it was not in his nature, but I did not know if he would be pleased at the choice I had made. I think he would rather I had married a musician and remained in his world. When I put the instrument down I began to walk around the apartments, sitting on all the chairs, touching everything, reassuring myself with my own books, my mirror, my trinkets, looking out of the window and watching the busy traffic on the river until I began to feel at home in the rooms. I wandered into the bedroom and lay on the bed. The counterpane had been turned down and as I felt the soft sheets and pillows beneath me I tried to imagine what the night would be like, my heart thumping uncomfortably. What would it be like to have him make love to me, he was after all an old man and I thought fleetingly of Robert Devereux. If only it could have been him who had given me all this then it would indeed have been paradise.

My fears and doubts returned as I sat alone in the small room, feeling almost a prisoner as the evening sky drew a black shutter over the window. Then Bess returned and when she had cleared away the remains of the meal she said, "I will help you to get ready."

What is wrong with my best embroidered gown I thought involuntarily, then immediately chided myself for my innocence. There was only one reason he was coming to me after supper. Bess took from one of the chests a beautiful shift of such fine lawn it was almost transparent, the sleeves and neck deep edged with costly lace, then she brushed my hair until the curls were tamed and fell to my waist in rippling waves. When she had gone I found in one of the chests a loose sleeveless mantle of deep blue velvet, the colour of a midsummer sky, and slipped it over the shift to hide my near-nakedness. Then to still my racing heart I took my lute again and began to play until a light knock on the door made me lay it down and I rose expectantly. The door opened and Lord Hunsdon stood there clothed in a loose gown of black silk, his red hair diffused with grey and looking more sparse now he was bareheaded. He stayed looking at me for a long instant saying irreverently, "You look like the Virgin in one of your Italian paintings." I could sense his subdued excitement then he moved towards me taking me in his arms and kissing me passionately as he murmured, "I worship you, my dear."

I closed my eyes, frantically summoning up an image of the Earl of Essex as he led me to the bed and began to disrobe us both. But surprisingly Robert Devereux soon began to fade from my thoughts. Henry Carey was an experienced lover with many years' experimentation in the arts of love. Respecting my nervousness he made no attempt to force himself on me but instead pleasured me and encouraged my desire until I was ready to give myself to him. He was strong and well made, for many years a soldier, and as I began to feel comfortable with him I responded to his virility. He did not seem like an old man, though I had to admit I had nothing with which to compare it. But his joy in me was sublime, his adoration induced surrender and he pleasured me in a way I had not anticipated. I enjoyed his lovemaking as much as I enjoyed every other part of the life he gave me and everything I ever did with later lovers I learnt from him. At the end of that long near-sleepless night I emerged a different person, my innocence gone for ever and aware now of what he expected from me, though not displeased by it. I came to realise that power and admiration can be aphrodisiacs and although I never felt love for him I grew to admire him and relished the great power he wielded. He was effectively the head of the entire Court responsible for all its administration - the supervision of servants, the welcoming of guests and foreign representatives as well as arranging all Court entertainments - and had under him a huge staff of ushers, porters, grooms and some three score musicians. This together with his idolisation of me was enough for me to find pleasure in our physical union and I always counted myself fortunate to have received my first experience of lovemaking from such an assured and skilled practitioner.

Afterwards he said, "Thankyou my darling girl, thank you for coming to me. I shall care for you and treasure you."

"Thankyou my Lord. You have given me so much already," I said, still overwhelmed at how I had been rewarded.

"My name is Henry Carey. My friends call me Harry."

The next morning when he had left I found beside my pillow a gold necklace and pendant with an intarsia design of a sapphire and diamond cross within the encircling initials of my name, the most precious jewel I had ever been given in return for what I had given him - the precious gift of my virginity.

CHAPTER 5

FANTASIA

"You have many of the traits of your father," Lord Hunsdon said to me one evening when he had come to me. I was lying naked, only partly covered by the sheet, and raising myself on one elbow I looked at him questioningly. He sat on the edge of the bed saying playfully, "You are an excellent musician." He loved to hear me play the lute or the virginals which he had bought me and had been surprised at my skill. He was very fond of music and had commissioned from the popular miniaturist Nicholas Hilliard a portrait of the Queen playing a lute.

"I learnt first from my father," I said, "but you don't only mean in music do you? Did my father have lovers?"

"He had a sensuous nature," he replied evasively, removing the covering from my body. "The hot blood of the Italians coursed in his veins."

"When he died my mother thought he had been murdered," I reminisced, remembering her anguished cry, "Has someone killed him?" when news came of his death, and also her aborted comment later that an attempt had once been made on his life.

"I doubt that would have been a jealous lover," he replied. "Your father had other strings to his lute. On his visits to Italy he picked up items of news that were sometimes of use to Sir Francis Walsingham. It is quite usual for musicians and artists who travel to other countries to be used by the State in this way. But as a foreigner with Catholic connections he also had opportunities to infiltrate radical groups here in the city and pass on information and this sometimes can lead to dangerous misunderstandings. An attempt was once made to kill him, some years before you were born, by three reformist activists who mistakenly believed he was a Papist spy working for the Pope. Fortunately the malefactors were apprehended, whipped and pilloried and had their ears clipped." I looked at him in amazement, realising how little I had known of my father. "He enjoyed the spice of danger," Lord Hunsdon said, his hands exploring my body.

"And do you think I am like that?"

"I do not think you are set for a quiet life, sweetheart, despite your upbringing with the Berties," he laughed as he began to divest himself of his elegant clothes. "Many men will crave you because you are passionate and sensuous and made to tantalise men with your dark unscrutable nature." One time he had made the ambiguous comment that his aunt, Anne Boleyn, had a mole on her throat as I did, adding, "She was a dark lady like you." Partly undressed now he began to caress me in earnest as he said, "I am an old man and perhaps my time with you is short but you must have no-one else while you are with me. I have seen the young men of the Court cast longing glances upon you but you are mine, Aemilia, only mine, remember that." His voice had grown hoarse with desire but there was also an unmistakeable warning in it as he clasped his arms possessively around my body. I began to surrender myself to him, involuntarily responding to him as he caressed me, my own desire rising in anticipation of the pleasure to come, but once again I was aware that I was his property and the truth was that he had bought me.

However most of the time I closed my mind to such uncomfortable thoughts, enjoying all aspects of my new life.

Much of my time during the day was my own and I spent hours in the mercers and haberdashers in Cheapside, the Exchange, or on London Bridge, admiring the latest wares and fingering the luxury goods. I was always accompanied by Bess and one of Lord Hunsdon's liveried menservants and this ensured immediate attention. "We have a new selection of silks recently arrived from France, Mistress Bassano. May we show you the latest colours and designs." The goods were always collected by one of Lord Hunsdon's servants and the accounts paid by him, always on time which made him a valued client. I especially loved the haberdashers' shops where I could pore over laces and ribbons, gold and silver trimmings, embroidered braids. I never tired of the long sessions with the tailor, prinking and posing before the mirror, suggesting alterations and refinements. Then there were visits to the tire-makers to choose hats and head-dressings, experimenting with various styles - small round hats decorated with brooches or tall crowned felts with curving brims, and for Court wear elaborate fantastical confections of gold and silver wire, tulle and semi- precious stones. I was made ostentatiously welcome in all the establishments, partly because of Lord Hunsdon and partly because my unusual looks presented a challenge for the tradespeople to create something special with no limit on cost and I gloried in their attention. I soon began to realise what suited me best - bold vibrant colours of deep blue and yellow and red, tight boned bodices to display my tall slim figure and low decolletage because modesty was not a consideration in the circumstances.

I was soon well known in the city and in the Court, gossip travels fast. Men ogled me and women envied or scorned me. Many of my old acquaintances were exaggeratedly fulsome to me, obviously hoping for favours. The Bassanos and other Court musicians treated me as they had always done and considered me very fortunate. But one day I saw the Vaughns in the street and they ostentatiously turned down an alley. I must admit I hoped never to meet Lady Wingfield but I knew she was not enamoured of Court life. At Court no-one dared treat me with anything but exaggerated politeness when I was in the company of Lord Hunsdon, but if I were on my own some of the ladies would ignore me. It was the same with the Queen. Alone, she was often sharp with me, "Your gown is cut too low Aemilia Bassano. I am not in favour of immodesty at Court." Then sometimes she would say curtly, "But since you are here, girl, you might make yourself useful and play something on the virginals for me."

If I had been the mistress of any other courtier I would have received short shrift and would not even have been allowed in her presence. But her kinsman, whether cousin or half-brother, was one of the few people really close to her. She loved and trusted Henry Carey to a degree no-one else, with the possible exception of Robert Dudley, ever achieved. Since the beginning of her reign he had been her most trusted adviser, councillor and supporter. Now Lord Chamberlain of the Royal Household he had been Captain-General of her forces at the time of the Northern rebellion, was a Privy councillor and in his younger days had been captain of her personal bodyguard. She knew his nature, made allowances for his needs, and excused his peccadillos as she had her father. So if he was by my side I could bask in her acceptance, if not exactly approval.

With him I enjoyed most of the Court festivities, music and entertainment and special celebrations for feast days or the welcoming of some foreign representative. He liked to have me beside him for he was proud of me and flaunted his possession of me, especially in the presence of younger courtiers. He would take my hand to dance one of the stately dances like the Pavane then would sit and watch admiringly while one of the young gallants accompanied me in the more lively galliards or the Volta but his attention would be alerted for any liberties. He liked to have me beautifully dressed, constantly telling me that my beauty deserved the best that money could buy, but even though I was not blind to the realities of our relationship I was determined not to be merely his plaything. I left him in no doubt as to the excellence of my education and accomplishments and as time went on and I spent much time in his company he began to appreciate my conversation and opinions. Educated and cultured himself, he began to value my views on new poetry and music and plays we had seen and began to share his thoughts with me about the current political situation. I enjoyed his conversation and eased myself into his life as companion as well as paramour. I knew that this was comparable to the Venetian whores who were sought after as much for their education and accomplishments as for their amatory skills and this was the role I aspired to for I did not want to follow in the path of his more transitory amours.

I now had the money to buy new books, and at the playhouses which I visited avidly I could demand the best seats and fawning attention from those who hoped for my influence over the Lord Chamberlain, responsible for all entertainment at Court. A new theatre called The Rose had recently been built on the South Bank of the river, a new departure from the site of the other two theatres in Finsbury fields, but Bankside was a popular area of recreation with gardens and several bear and bull baiting rings, easily accessible from the city either by the bridge across the river or the hundreds of boats that ferried people across for a penny charge, and still out of the jurisdiction of the city authorities, being in the liberty of the Clink. I took a private barge there as soon as I could and as we neared the South Bank I could see the building quite clearly, almost identical in style and shape to The Theatre and The Curtain though even bigger, as I discovered when I went inside. I had been informed by Lord Hunsdon, with his usual knowledge of affairs, that it had been built by Philip Henslowe, a well-known investor in commercial enterprises, who with the growing popularity of theatrical performances had considered a playhouse to be a profitable undertaking, though as well as renting out the building to the various theatre companies he intended to use it also for the even more profitable activities of bear baiting and dog and cock fighting. We disembarked at the Paris Garden stairs, the crowded ferry boats giving us respectful preference, though many of the eager playgoers walked across the bridge and through Southwark with its notorious narrow alleys crammed with hovels, unsavoury inns and brothels in the proximity of the Clink gaol, an area I later came to know well. The painted Rose was clearly visible on the front of the white plastered building and Lord Hunsdon's manservant, keeping close by my side, said, "There used to be a rose garden here but it is also in honour of the Tudor rose of our dear Queen."

Overhearing him a rough-looking individual with a patch over one eye laughed raucously saying, "Common name for a punk more likely, there's no shortage of them round here."

The gatherers recognised me and we were escorted to cushioned seats in the second gallery in the company of the richest spectators, our presence affording some pre-performance entertainment to the groundlings who were enjoying their pies and ale in the standing space below us. The playhouse was crammed to the fill with what I estimated to be more than two thousand spectators but once the trumpets sounded and the Prologue appeared from the curtained alcove at the back of the stage all attention was concentrated on the action. The company today were the popular Lord Admiral's Men and my interest had already been captured by the promise of a new play entitled 'Tamburlaine' by an author I had never heard of - Christopher Marlowe.

On my return to Whitehall I described it enthusiastically to Lord Hunsdon. "It was the most incredible play I have ever seen. I've never seen a character like this on the stage before, so powerful, so ruthless and wicked yet so compelling, played by Ned Alleyn so he had the audience completely under his spell. It was a very brutal play, composed almost entirely of butchery and torture and there was one scene where Tamburlaine enters in a chariot drawn by the kings he has reduced to slavery." Lord Hunsdon was shaking his head in amusement as I went on, "Yet the most striking aspect of the play was the language. I have never heard language like this on the stage, sweeping you along with its force and strong rhythms, listen!" I-struck a dramatic pose and imitating Alley declaimed, "Is it not passing brave to be a king, and ride in triumph through Persepolis."

"You really ought to be a player Aemilia," he laughed.

"You must come and see this play, Harry, it is amazing."

"Better than that, my dear, I shall arrange for them to give a private performance. You have whetted my appetite. And the story of great military achievements will not go amiss in this time of ever increasing threats from Spain."

I flung my arms around him. "But who is this Christopher Marlowe? I have never heard of him before and I know most of the playwrights."

"He is the son of a country shoemaker, though a University man. And he is just twenty two years old." My eyes widened in surprise, though I was accustomed to his knowledge of topical affairs. "There are rumours that he is tainted with some……..radical opinions, which is why I dare not suggest a presentation at Court yet. But I am sure that Lord Howard would arrange a private performance with his company. Young Master Marlowe has stirred up a measure of interest in more ways than one."

The second time I saw 'Tamburlaine', performed in the Lord Admiral's London house, lacked the spectacular stage effects which were only possible in a playhouse but this gave more prominence to the force and momentum of the language, an outpouring of words that was spellbinding. It also gave me a sight of Christopher Marlowe himself. I couldn't take my eyes from the tall and slender young man, finding it hard to believe that he could write so skilfully and passionately at twenty-two years of age. I thought he was exceptionally well dressed for a playwright, especially such a young one with a modest background, in an extravagant slashed doublet of tawny velvet and satin with a score of silver buttons, matching hose on his well-shaped legs and with a yellow velvet cap perched rakishly on his head. His thick brown hair curved to chin length, a small moustache emphasized the cynical curve of his mouth and his dark brown eyes gave the impression of seeing everything but revealing nothing. He never smiled all evening and there was a wariness in his demeanour. Once he caught me looking at him and he returned my glance but though he held it for a long time there was nothing of the admiration, or even awareness, I was used to receiving and a shiver tingled my spine at his impassivity.

"My dear Aemilia, how I love your country of Italy, some of my happiest times have been my travels there, especially in Venice." My reverie was broken by the Earl of Oxford bending to kiss my hand.

"My country is England, my Lord, I have never been to Italy," I smiled.

Edward de Vere was almost forty years old now and his career at court had been chequered by alternate favour and disgrace. He had angered the Queen on a number of occasions by his violent and rash behaviour but had also been favoured by her for his elegance, his courtly speech, his skill as a dancer, a poet, a linguist. Once a ward of Lord Burghley he had married his daughter and then angered the Lord Chancellor by being openly unfaithful to her. He had squandered his inheritance by extravagant living yet much of it had gone on patronising men of letters and he also gave his name to a company of players. "Then one day you must go there because you are a true child of your country, so dark, so beautiful. Italy is a country of beautiful things. Do you know I brought to England the Italian fashion for perfumed gloves, a pair of which I presented to the Queen." He sniffed his own embroidered leather gloves ostentatiously. He then regaled me with a torrent of Italian. He made an absurd figure with his paned and padded trunk hose and jewelled codpiece, clocked stockings with embroidered panels, and red shoes with enormous rosettes. His corseted doublet of green silk was both slashed and prinked, his ruff so stiff that he couldn't move his head and a tiny round hat with an ostrich feather perched precariously on his greying hair. I thought to myself how fortunate I was not to have to rely on the favour of the Earl of Oxford and couldn't help casting a glance to where Lord Hunsdon stood, tall, composed, restrainedly elegant in black silk and gold lace. But since the Earl clearly sought my company I might as well bask in his attention and decided to make use of him to sound his knowledge and opinions of Venice. I found his reminiscences interesting especially when he began to tell me of his visits to the literary salon of a poet called Domenico Venier where poets and writers read and discussed their work.

"There was a most beautiful courtesan there," he said with a knowing look at me. "She played the lute and the virginals, could discuss politics and philosophy as well as any man, was extremely knowledgeable about poetry, both of the ancients and the new writers, and she wrote poetry herself. She was treated equally with the men in her company. Her name was Veronica Franco."

I remembered how my father used to tell me there were more opportunities in Italy for women to share the artistic life of men and I wished again that he had been spared long enough to take me there. Perhaps I could have built a life for myself on the pattern of this courtesan. I had been given the chance to taste something of this existence now but only to a certain degree. My life was totally dependent on my lover, my opportunities circumscribed by him. I was not independent in my own right like Veronica Franco. But I could learn much from these Venetian courtesans who were not content to merely satisfy men's physical needs and I was determined not to go the way of some of Lord Hunsdon's other fleeting amours.

My lover now came towards me and I knew he considered the Earl had monopolised my attention long enough as he said, "Lord Oxford, I must take Mistress Bassano to meet a cousin of yours, Lord Strange." I was beginning to realise how closely interwoven were the nobility, a tight-knit elite that suffered no breach by anyone outside their rank. No matter how careful Lord Hunsdon was of my presence and how many of the nobility I was introduced to, I was always conscious that I was but his paramour, a "kept woman." However if I could hold him and become a permanent fixture in his life I might be able to increase my influence and this was my ambition. It was a pity he was not a younger man.

Lord Strange, Ferdinando Stanley heir to Lord Derby, was one of the most handsome and accomplished of the courtiers and a distant relative of Lord Hunsdon being the great-grandson of the Princess Mary Rose. In his late twenties he was of medium height with an intelligent mobile face, lively grey eyes and thick auburn hair curling on his shoulders, an emerald ear-ring visible below the curls. A moustache and small pointed beard emphasized his firm chin and his nose was almost aquiline. People talked openly about him being always in debt to his tailor and he was dressed expensively in the height of fashion, but tastefully, unlike Oxford's self-indulgence. Recognised as a skilled musician and poet himself, he had been supporting theatrical performers since he was a student at the University. Beginning with a troupe of acrobats and jugglers he had now been the patron of a company of actors for several years and recently they had amalgamated with Lord Leicester's company due to the increasing ill health of the Earl. The enlarged Lord Strange's company was now becoming recognised as one of the finest in London, set to rival the Lord Admiral's Men so he had been particularly interested in this evening's performance. He was an attractive unpretentious personality and Lord Hunsdon knew that I would enjoy his company and that he would be happy to talk to me about the theatre. He was enthusiastic about the new-discovered talents of the young Christopher Marlowe saying, "If he continues in this way he will revolutionise the writing of plays. Unfortunately the Lord Admiral's Men seem to have secured his services. I only wish we could find such a promising new playwright for ourselves."

Lord Hunsdon returned with me to my apartments and I reflected on what a perfect evening it had been, comprising all the things I loved best - noble company, a theatrical performance, actors, writers, interesting conversation and admiration by important courtiers.

"What did you think of the play?" I asked him.

"Inclined to be repetitious," he replied. "The second hour was but a repeat of the first and privately I began to tire of the orgy of brutality. It was obviously the work of a young man. However the language redeemed it. I must admit I have never heard such powerful inventive language on the stage before. If young Marlowe continues in this vein then London has a writer of great note."

Then conversation ended because although he liked to talk with me he had other things in mind and the evening finished with my indulging his passion.

Ever since I had first gone to him the fear of an invasion by Spain had hung like a threatening storm cloud over

England. However over Yuletide thoughts of war had been buried beneath the merriment of the season's elaborate festivities. The only disappointment had been the obviously low spirits of the Queen who was upset by the absence through sickness of the Earl of Leicester, the first time for thirty years that he had not been at Court at Christmas but whose health had been deteriorating steadily since his return from the war in the Low Countries. However once the jollity of Twelfth Night had passed the cold rainy weather brought a sudden jolt back to reality. All around the Court and the town there was only one topic of conversation. There was no doubt that King Philip of Spain had assembled a large fleet and was preparing to sail against England in the spring. In part retaliation for the execution of Mary Stuart, in part revenge for Drake's daring raids on Spanish shipping, but mainly because His Most Christian Majesty was impelled by a genuine religious fervour to turn England back to the one true faith, Philip was ready to move into action. England was put on a state of alert. Beacons were ready on high ground, the militia exercised and defences prepared.

"I shall be greatly occupied with the Queen and the council so I shall have to neglect you for a time," Lord Hunsdon told me. "Her Majesty has made me Principal Captain and Governor of the Army to defend London. Leicester is Lieutenant-General but he is not well so more responsibility will be put upon me. Lord Howard as Lord Admiral is in charge of the fleet together with Drake and Hawkins, but if they cannot hold off this armada and there is an invasion by the Spaniards then I will be in charge."

I was thrilled by the power invested in him. Despite his age his reputation for courage was well known and he was greatly esteemed by the soldiers. I basked in the glow of his high authority but I was also not a little afraid of the imminent dangers though he reassured me by saying, "I really do not think it will come to an invasion, I have much confidence in our ships and our sailors."

"They say our ships are fewer in number and much smaller than the enemy's," I reported what was hearsay amongst the general public. "Francis Drake has seen the fleet in Cadiz harbour." He had also burnt several of the ships standing there.

"That is not necessarily a disadvantage, my dear," Henry Carey replied. "Drake has much experience in harrying Spanish ships, he can move faster and with more agility than they can, and our admirals are more familiar with the currents of the Channel and the waters around our coasts. However finally we must put our trust in God and the rightness of our cause."

Despite the cold wet weather it was as if we were waiting for a summer storm to break, the air charged with the oppressive anticipation that comes just before the first lightning cleaves the skies. People continued to go about their daily work, I visited the shops and the playhouses, but it seemed as if everyone was holding their breath. My own feelings swung like a pendulum between a fear of the unknown and a recklessness to make the most of every minute in case the life that I knew might soon come to an end. I felt excessively proud to be the mistress of one of the most important men responsible for England's defences and, I must admit, showed no small degree of arrogance in making the fact known to all and sundry, mentioning his name whenever I got the opportunity. Although our time together was sparse, our brief sexual encounters had been spiced with the ingredient of uncertainty as the country continued to wait throughout the spring.

On May Day the Queen, determined to keep her usual schedules, ordered the customary picnic to Epsom fields with ladies and courtiers on horseback and in coaches, accompanied by carts loaded with hampers of food, linen and plate. Lord Hunsdon was too occupied but through his influence I had been included in the company as he thoughtfully considered it would be a pleasant diversion for me. We set off shortly after dawn so the maids could sprinkle themselves with dew and dream that night of their lovers, gathering branches of may blossom as we rode along and stopping to watch the countryfolk dancing around their maypoles as the day progressed for this was a national holiday in which all cares could be forgotten. Often the Queen stopped to give her greetings and assure her lowly subjects that all was well. Once we reached our destination the coaches were unloaded, cloths spread on the ground and a feast as sumptuous as any in a great hall was enjoyed in the pretence of a country picnic while musicians played and sang. I did not find favour with all the women. One of the Queen's most beloved ladies-in-waiting was Philadelphia Carey and she always pointedly ignored me but I suppose I might have done the same with one of my father's lovers. Such examples of coldness were compensated for by the attentions of the men and I never lacked a companion when Lord Hunsdon was absent from my side. I was aware that my situation as a paramour encouraged their free behaviour and their conduct veered between respect for Lord Hunsdon and liberties towards me. I had to be careful not to be too responsive for this would have displeased my lover, though he was proud to see me admired. It vexed me that I was considered wanton when he was my only lover but had enough wit to realise that the inference was understandable so I revelled in the attention paid to me and cocked a snook at ladies who were offended or envious. Since I had come to Court I had often seen the Earl of Essex. The first time we met I felt embarrassed when he grinned and said, "I see my great-uncle has taken the prize," but he appeared not to judge me and always showed me friendliness. He was beside the Queen on this day and greeted me courteously then a short time later he returned in company with his sister. I had seen Penelope, now Lady Rich, from afar and I had been fascinated by her ever since I had known about the poems written about her, so I welcomed the opportunity to be acquainted. At twenty-six, four years older than her brother, she truly lived up to her reputation and was indeed one of the most beautiful girls I had ever seen with her mass of red-gold curls, perfect features complemented by an habitual sunny smile and her slender graceful carriage. She was universally admired for her beauty but also for her skill in dancing and music, literature and languages, and was constantly having poems and music dedicated to her. I envied her more than ever.

"Penelope is especially fond of Italian music and literature and speaks the language fluently so I am sure she would appreciate the opportunity to speak with you," her brother said, holding her hand as he introduced me to her.

Penelope smiled warmly saying, "Un piacere," and when Essex left us alone together we spent a pleasant interlude talking about our many shared interests. Although I envied Penelope her illustrious family and the abundance of gifts she had been showered with, it was impossible to feel resentment in the face of her natural sweet disposition.

"Lady Rich showed me kind attention today," I told Lord Hunsdon afterwards.

A fleeting smile crossed his face as he said, "No doubt young Essex introduced you to her." When I admitted it he continued, "He likes to provoke the Queen. He considers she treats his mother and Penelope badly."

"But Lettice is her cousin and Leicester's wife."

"Enough reason for hostility. That ten year old betrayal has never been forgiven."

"And Penelope?"

"Enough that she is her mother's daughter. And rumour says she is not faithful to Lord Rich, the two statements not entirely unconnected," he said dryly. My interest in Penelope Rich increased.

It was only a few days after our May Day excursion that we heard the great Armada had at last set sail. It had been delayed by Drake capturing many small coastal craft laden with supplies for the Spanish ships and burning thousands of barrels and barrel staves, which increased his heroic status in the eyes of the general populace. Lord Hunsdon informed me that another factor was the sudden death of Philip's most trusted and experienced commander Santa Cruz. His replacement was the Duke of Medina Sidonia who they said had never before been on a ship, a fact which made our sea captains laugh.

Now that it was known that the fleet was actually on its way the mood in England changed to one of spirited optimism. Young men boasted they couldn't wait to tackle the dagos, and householders set about fortifying their houses with sticks and staves, reinforcing their doors and windows. The Queen composed a special prayer to be read in all the churches. But the Armada didn't arrive and Londoners were puzzled and frustrated by the delay. Later we learnt that they had had to stop at Coruna to be revictualled and reconditioned because much of the food was rotten and the water polluted as, thanks to Drake, there weren't enough barrels for storage. So England continued to wait in a state of bewildered inactivity.

Lord Hunsdon was busy with the defences around London. I liked to go down to the river with crowds of other curious people to watch the work taking place and knowing he was responsible for it. Nine gun batteries had been placed along the river at strategic points, usually where there was a bend except where the ground was too marshy. An attempt was made to block the whole of the river by constructing a boom from Gravesend to Tilbury, a string of barges across the river reinforced by stakes and covered by a floating battery, an idea Lord Hunsdon had got from the defences of Antwerp in the war in the Spanish Netherlands. I was very proud of his achievements and when sometimes people recognised who I was and nudged each other I would salute them graciously for he was popular amongst the Londoners.

By July it was known that the Spanish fleet were actually on their way and war fever increased. Our fleet under the command of Lord Howard, Drake, and Hawkins, was on the alert at Plymouth. Our army in the Low Countries was ready to impede the Duke of Parma should he attempt an invasion of England in support of the Armada. Leicester's place as General of the English troops there had been taken by none other than Peregrine Bertie, Lady Susan's brother, now at last granted the title of Lord Willoughby. After the Duchess of Suffolk's prolonged and fruitless attempts to get her father's title renewed for her husband Richard Bertie, the Queen had at last compromised by awarding it to their son. Despite her antipathy towards his mother, the Queen liked Peregrine Bertie and had favoured him with the position as Leicester's replacement, an office he had gratefully accepted for despite the Queen's approval he was no more enamoured of Court life than was his sister.

However the next news we heard was that the Armada had been scattered by a great storm and once again we waited with baited breath. "When is all this going to end? The suspense is driving everyone crazy," I voiced my worries to Lord Hunsdon on one of the rare occasions when we were together, he having sought me out to comfort his own great anxieties.

"I do not know, my dear," he replied. "Everyone is wishing for action. It is difficult to keep our morale high when every day we are expecting news and we are disappointed. Come play some music for me then we will go to bed, I have need of you to take my mind from matters of state for a while." I used all my skills to divert him, glad of his need of me.

It was an interminable three weeks more before the information came that the Spanish fleet had managed to reform but our own fleet was now grounded in Plymouth Sound by bad weather. Everyone was on tenterhooks, crazed by continual anticipation and weary with the fluctuations of alarms and relief and could settle to nothing, the only topic of conversation everywhere being, "Where is the Armada now?" It was a sultry August day when at last the "Invincible Armada" was sighted just off the Lizard, coming into the English Channel. Beacons were lit across the country and the mood changed now to resolution as everyone stood in readiness. The ailing Earl of Leicester was with an army at Tilbury, waiting to repel an invasion from the Netherlands should the Duke of Parma move. The Earl of Essex, despite his youth, had been put in charge of the Queen's personal safety with a troop of horse equipped at his personal expense in his own orange livery. Lord Hunsdon had offered to arrange for me to go into the country but despite the possible danger I did not want to leave the city. The combination of fear and excitement was a heady mix and there was a strong spirit of fellowship abroad as all London, rich and poor, great and mean, united in one of their few shared experiences.

Only afterwards did we know the full story and Lord Hunsdon was able to tell me most of it. How our fleet were trapped in Plymouth by the weather, sitting ducks not able to move out to sea and face the enemy. How the Armada didn't attack them because they had been ordered to move in unison and they were still waiting for stragglers and for support from the Duke of Parma who did not as yet have the necessary resources. Hence the delay gave the weather time to change so that our admirals were able at last to move the English fleet out. How they then sent fireships amongst the Spanish ships, causing chaos in their formation and they had to retire to Calais for a time to regroup.

We all rejoiced, thinking the conflict over but our joy was shortlived for unfortunately no great damage had been inflicted and they returned. For another anxious nine days the conflict raged with the outcome always in doubt. The Queen went to Tilbury to encourage the soldiers there, wearing a breastplate and swearing to die with them as they overwhelmed her with their protestations of love and loyalty. Lord Hunsdon remained fully in charge in London and occasionally came to me to find solace from his problems often saying, "I am so glad you did not wish to leave the city, Aemilia, for you have been a great comfort to me." But I was afraid and one night I awoke from a nightmare with the words Salve Deus Rex Judeaorum imprinted in my mind though I had no idea where the phrase had come from and I couldn't remember my dream. Then finally a great storm completed the English battery of the great ships, over-balanced and outmanoeuvered as they were. Scattered and helpless they were blown off course around the coasts of England for nearly two months more, losing more than half their ships and more than twenty thousand men.

The whole of England was ecstatic. "Our small island has defeated the most powerful nation in Europe," Lord Hunsdon exulted. "I count it one of the greatest privilege of my life to have participated in this historic event," a sentiment shared by all Londoners. I was prouder than ever to be the mistress of such an important statesman and commander and as I joined in the great thanksgiving service held in St. Paul's church I was thrilled to see him in attendance on the Queen when she arrived in a coach drawn by white horses, with a gilded canopy and a crown atop. It was an exhilarating time to be alive, especially to be young and, by virtue of Lord Hunsdon, to be in the centre of things. Street celebrations raged for weeks in consort with all the Court celebrations and so many poems and eulogies were printed that the presses never stopped. Medals were struck and portraits of the Queen painted, copied and distributed everywhere, representing her as Queen of the Sea and the greatest sovereign in Europe. "As you are of Venetian stock, my dear, I am sure it will please you to know that the Venetian ambassador has proclaimed the Queen, "the great Queen of England and Queen of the Sea," of considerable import as this is Venice's own title," said Lord Hunsdon. I had become closer to him after the fears and worries of the last few months and he never ceased telling me how I had helped to support him during this time. One day he gave to me a gold brooch in the shape of a Spanish galleon, a companion gift to the gold necklace of scallop shells which he had given to the Queen, all the nobleman vying with each other to present her with a topical reminder of this historic event. The Queen's triumph however was tinged with personal sadness. Robert Dudley had been by her side constantly during the danger, escorting her to Tilbury and dining nightly with her. His gift to her had been a necklace of six hundred magnificent pearls which she so treasured that she had worn it in the great commemorative portrait. But he was ill and exhausted and a few weeks later he died. In September, sooner than anyone had anticipated, a second great memorial service was held in St. Paul's, the two hundred yards long nave crammed with the most important in the land. The Queen was heartbroken for this man who had shared so much of her life, in middle-age becoming her "brother and best friend" rather than the would-be lover of her youth. But this now left a great gap in her life and everyone was pondering on who would now fill it, some suggesting Leicester's stepson the Earl of Essex, others the new favourite Walter Raleigh.

I had now passed a year with my lover. It had been a momentous year in the history of England and in my life when many of my dreams had come true - life at Court, wearing rich clothes and jewels, my own sumptuous apartments, achieving a certain independence, and a certain notoriety. I can keep him, I thought confidently. In the first weeks of our relationship I was constantly plagued by the fear that he would soon tire of me and this fabled existence would be as transitory as a dream. But as time elapsed I had become more confident. I had learnt how to please him in bed having read Aretino's erotic manual that he had given me, but I had also proved that I could keep him interested by my conversation and my knowledge, despite my youth and his maturity, so that he genuinely enjoyed my company, and during the eventful months of the Armada I had made myself indispensible to him. I was constantly refining my skills on the pattern of the Venetian courtesans and was determined to make him so dependent on me that he would keep me until he died and by that time, hopefully, my position would be unassailable.

CHAPTER 6

RITORNELLO

Christopher Marlowe had been arrested and put into Newgate gaol for being involved in a fight in Cripplegate, an insalubrious area but where a lot of theatre folk lived, in which one of the three participants had been killed. I heard as much from Lord Hunsdon and reacted to the news with no great surprise for I could not forget the chill I had felt in his presence and the sensation of something sinister beneath his impassive gaze. But I felt regretful for the premature end of this gifted young playwright for the only way out of Newgate, the prison for crimes of murder, was the short journey to the nearby gallows at Tyburn. The episode also confirmed the opinion of the Puritans that all players and playwrights were dissolute and by adding Marlowe to the company of George Peele and Robert Greene fuelled opposition against the theatres. Then surprisingly I heard on my next visit to The Rose that Marlowe had been released, to the great relief of Philip Henslowe and the Lord Admiral's Men, to whom he was a commercial asset, and to the eager playgoers awaiting his next play.

Although I hadn't cared for Marlowe himself I was glad at the news. Just before his imprisonment he had written another play which had supplied great excitement for the theatre-goers and much profit for The Rose's owner. 'The Jew of Malta,' which I had gone to watch at the earliest opportunity, was again full of the evil and cruelty which seemed to be the chief ingredients of his plays, but certainly pleased the groundlings. "He's too valuable to lose and too young to die," I said to Lord Hunsdon, "but it's a strange occurrence, I would have thought him in danger of the noose."

"It would appear he has powerful protectors," Lord Hunsdon replied laconically. I thought he was going to elaborate but after a pause he continued, "Marlowe is too reckless and playing with fire might burn more than his fingers one day."

I recalled again his inscrutable face and wondered about the truth of this strange affair and what activities he might be involved in beside the writing of plays. Despite admiring the powerful writing I hadn't enjoyed 'The Jew of Malta.' But I was forced to admit that my unease came mostly from the rabid animosity the play had aroused in the spectators, not only against Jews but also against all foreigners. There had been a steadily growing antagonism in London towards foreigners pouring into the city for work, mainly French, Dutch and Flemish, whom the Londoners believed were stealing their own trade and employment, and the play had stirred up further resentment against them. The abuse vented against the Jew touched the foreign part of my heritage while my cousin Laura's husband, the musician Joseph Lupo, was a Jew. Also having lived outside the city walls I was acquainted with a lot of foreign workers, like my old teacher Madame LaMotte, and knew them to be honest and hardworking. But I seemed to be alone in my dislike of the play and I salved my unease by saying, "Barabbas had no more semblance to a real person than the Vice in the old morality plays that I once or twice watched with my father when they were performed in the street."

It was coincidence that shortly afterwards I saw a poster advertising a performance of 'The Seven Deadly Sins'. These old morality plays were now out of favour because of their association with the Catholic religion but were occasionally revived, in very modified forms, when the theatre companies were short of something to enact for new plays were in short supply. This particular one had obviously been greatly modified for it was described as 'a most playful comedy' to be acted by the Lord Strange's Men at The Theatre. I didn't expect a play of any worth but Lord Strange's company was beginning to be recognised as one of the best in London and had recently amalgamated with the Queens' Men, a popular touring company, when they had been forced to disband due to lack of financial support after one of their actors had been killed in a brawl. So having met Lord Strange and being interested to see how his new enlarged company performed I took one of Lord Hunsdon's coaches out to Shoreditch. His coach was recognised and people stopped to stare as I swept into the theatre conspicuous in my gown of dark red velvet and matching hat and it was James Burbage, builder and owner of the playhouse, who greeted me before I was shown to one of the best seats in the second gallery. "We are always graced by your presence, Mistress Bassano, and this afternoon will see the first appearance on stage of my younger son Richard. We hope you will be pleased with his performance."

Later back at Whitehall when I was enthusing about the talents of the new young actor, Lord Hunsdon interrupted with mock severity, "Does this mean you are about to transfer your loyalties from Edward Alleyn?"

"They are different. Ned Alleyn is elegant and suave with a musical voice that he uses to its full range like a well tuned lute. Young Richard Burbage is muscular, not so tall, with rugged features and a head of chestnut curls. Neither elegant nor musical he has a powerful voice and a fiery projection that is unique, especially in one so young, he is only twenty years old."

"Well it would seem that Lord Strange's Men now have an actor to rival their strongest competitors," laughed Lord Hunsdon when I had finished describing how his performance had lifted a banal script into an enthralling drama. "All they need now is a playwright to rival Marlowe."

Visits to the playhouses continued to be my favoured form of recreation, especially on the rare occasions when Lord Hunsdon accompanied me and I could bask in his eminence. But although The Rose had provided another purpose-built venue there were still only three playhouses so the many companies had to resort for most of the time to using inn yards - the Cross Keys, the Bull, the Belsavage. One day at the Cross Keys in Gracechurch Street, an inn used most often by Strange's Men if there wasn't a playhouse vacant, I watched a new play of 'King Henry VI' which had apparently been written by a recent recruit to the company, one of the actors from the disbanded Queen's Men. It was a stirring history play with some very dramatic scenes and rhetorical language similar to Marlowe's but I had never heard of the writer and his name slipped my memory.

Lord Strange's Men and the Lord Admiral's Company were now acknowledged as the best actors in London and competed against each other for the favour of the playgoers. Occasionally they combined their talents, especially for Court performances, and they did so when they entertained the Queen at the Twelfth Night revels. The Yuletide festivities were particularly exuberant as England continued to bask in the glory of Armada year, though the Queen was still noticeably melancholy in the aftermath of Leicester's death. To everyone's surprise she seemed to have chosen for her new favourite the handsome self-confident Walter Raleigh, a West Country squire who had attracted her attention through his exceptional good looks and charming manners, but even his attentive presence could not compensate for the loss of her old love. However most nobles had left their country houses to be present at the Court festivities and all the great lords were in attendance with their ladies, one of the few occasions the Queen welcomed wives. Lord Hunsdon's sons and daughters were well represented and his wife was also present. Lady Ann Carey, who had married Lord Hunsdon nearly fifty years ago when they were both just matured, was now a stout woman in her sixties though her ageing face still showed traces of former beauty. She was richly dressed in a black velvet farthingale with a lattice pattern of gold thread, and a French hood of black velvet and jewels covered her grey hair. I stayed well away from the family for I knew better than to flaunt myself in their presence. I had also dressed myself with reasonable restraint, my gown an apple-green taffeta with kirtle and padded sleeves of a darker green studded with tiny pearls. My ruff was of lace and tulle, wired to make a frame for my black hair which was fastened into a silver net scattered with pearl beads. The only jewellery I wore was a small pearl necklace. I knew Lord Hunsdon would appreciate my temperance for I would be carefully scrutinised, but I missed being in his company. When he escorted me I was always sure to receive respect and I met important and interesting people. Most of the men who paid court to me were this night in company with their ladies so I kept mainly to the society of my musician relatives who were performing, including some of my Bassano cousins together with Joseph Lupo and John Lanier, Nicholas Lanier's eldest son by his first wife. I wished I could be performing with them so that I could be openly admired for my own sake, important in my own right. It was at times like these when I realised how much of an outsider I was in this aristocratic society. It would be different if I were married to a great lord instead of being merely his paramour. However Lord Burghley spoke briefly to me and Lady Mildred asked if I still continued my Latin studies, Peregrine Bertie, now Lord Willoughby, was courteous enough to acknowledge me, the recently widowed Earl of Oxford flirted with me and many others of my acquaintance gave me a covert smile though inhibited from discourse by the presence of their wives.

"Aemilia Bassano, what a pleasant surprise," the lilting voice interrupted my discontent and I recognised Penelope Rich, her golden hair a corollary to the splendour of her white and gold brocade gown. "I always find great delight in listening to the music of your family."

We talked for a time about music, knowing we had a common interest. "The galliard that Master John Dowland has composed in your honour is much complimented, "I commented mischievously. "He once escorted me to a performance at Court but he never ventured to write a dance for me."

Penelope laughed casually with the nonchalance of one accustomed to having poems, music and dances composed for her. "Perhaps we might play some music together one day, Aemilia," she suggested.

"That would be a great honour for me, and a great joy," I replied eagerly and we were making plans how to arrange this when we were interrupted by the arrival of her brother. Essex greeted me courteously and seemed pleased that his sister liked me, then he said, "Come Pen, it is time for us to make our salutations to the Queen."

"You go alone, Rob, there are still things I wish to say to Aemilia."

"No, you must come with me," he insisted, taking hold of her arm. Penelope looked uneasy but she allowed him to lead her away. As he turned I could smell the wine on his breath, although the sight of him was still enough to make my heart beat faster.

Even though I was far from the Queen her angry words carried clearly across the Great Hall, "How dare you bring that woman into my presence."

The next words were inaudible then Essex shouted, "All this is on account of that knave Raleigh."

Everyone had now frozen and conversation stopped, though the music still played on, as all eyes turned towards the group on the dais - the Queen with her face like a mask of stone, Essex flushed with anger, Penelope clearly distressed and Walter Raleigh, resplendent in crimson and gold, with a smirk on his handsome features. Essex seized his sister by the hand and turned away from the Queen. "Do you dare to turn your back on me," she cried. Robert Devereux continued to stride down the Hall, impervious to her command of, "Come back here you insolent boy. Alone!"

The two disappeared through the door and a tremor of shocked disbelief rumbled through the audience. The Queen's mask tightened, her eyes narrowed, a sure sign of a tempest to come, and everyone waited in nervous expectation. Then to unanimous relief one of her quicksilver changes of mood wrought a transformation of her features as she turned flirtatiously to Raleigh, laying a hand on his arm and whispering into his ear something that made him laugh. Conversation resumed at a heightened pitch, excitement plucking the chords of discussion. How fragile is my own position when someone like Penelope Rich can be so humiliated I thought. Yet I had the feeling that Essex had engineered the public confrontation and though ignorant of all the issues involved I guessed it touched on the rivalry between him and Raleigh and he had used his sister as a pawn. I looked across the Great Hall to where Lord Hunsdon stood in talk with Ferdinando Stanley and he turned and caught my glance, his eyebrows rising eloquently. Standing with them was one of the actors, a young man in his mid-twenties, and I frowned as I tried to place him in my memory. He was of no particularly distinguished appearance, only of medium height with collar-length brown hair beginning already to recede at the temples. But he had a pleasant lightly-bearded face with high forehead and intelligent brown eyes and I suddenly recognised him as the recent recruit to Strange's Men, the actor who had written the play 'King Henry VI'.

Although I had been deprived of my protector's company all evening he came to me later that night though I hadn't been expecting him. "I thought you would have stayed with Lady Hunsdon seeing she is at Court," I ventured to say.

"Watching you across the room and not being able to be with you whetted my appetite even more," he confessed.

"I missed your company," I said.

He looked pleased. "I do not expect you to love me, Aemilia, but it is gratifying to know that you find some pleasure in our association as well as the rewards you receive. Oh do not be so dismayed," he continued as I babbled my insistence, "it has only been too common with the women I have known."

"What did you think of the Earl of Essex's outburst?" I asked him later when I had satisfied him and he lay langourously contented.

"He takes risks, presuming too much on the Queen's partiality for him. He knew full well that she has forbidden Penelope in her presence though perhaps the Queen is wrong in this and Essex has both strong family loyalties and a pride that will not brook censure. He expected to take Leicester's place in her affections, having been groomed for this by his stepfather, but now he seems to have been supplanted by Raleigh. The Queen is probably teaching him a lesson because she has a great affection for him, not least because he is Leicester's stepson, but Leicester always knew his place and Robert Devereux doesn't. One day he will go too far. And this enmity between him and Raleigh bodes no good at all."

"I was sorry to see Penelope so humiliated. It was hardly her fault."

"She is too beautiful for her own good. No-one ever believed she could remain faithful to the staid Lord Rich. And it isn't in the blood."

I remained silent, wondering if he were thinking of her mother, Lettice Knollys the Queen's hated rival for Leicester's affections, or her great-grandmother Mary Boleyn, Lord Hunsdon's own mother. "I saw you talking to the actor who wrote the play of Henry VI," I said changing the subject.

"His name is William Shakespeare. Lord Strange was generous in his praise and confided to me that he thinks he may have found his company's answer to Christopher Marlowe. He joined them from the Queen's Men when they disbanded. Like many of the players he was expected to turn his hand to adapting old plays or with a group cobbling together new ones, and he seems to have shown some skill so that he was encouraged to write a play of his own. I think Strange seems to have been impressed largely because the play flattered his ancestors, both the Earls of Derby and the Cliffords. But we shall have to see. One swallow does not make a summer and I myself doubt he will pose a threat to Marlowe. He is not a University man, nor a Londoner. I think Strange said he comes from Warwick shire or somewhere similar."

The next news I heard of Robert Devereux was that he had sent a challenge to Raleigh to fight a duel but on the hearing of it the Privy Council had forbidden it and given him a formal reprimand. The Queen renewed her anger towards him for this latest disgrace and continued to favour Walter Raleigh. She knighted him, rewarded him with lands, estates, monopolies and made him captain of her personal bodyguard, a position once held by Lord Hunsdon. From being a poor country gentleman he had risen to be one of the wealthiest courtiers, rumour said he had spent six thousand pounds on a pair of shoes. Robert Devereux in contrast was one of the poorest, despite being a noble born and probably with royal blood in his veins. There was no doubt where my sympathies lay. Most of the courtiers hated Raleigh for his arrogance, calling him "Jack the upstart" and fearing his influence over the Queen, but if it hadn't been for my attraction to Essex I might have admired him. By virtue of his good looks, his boldness and his plausible tongue he had risen from nowhere to become one of the most powerful people in the country, the sort of person I favoured, the sort of person I would like to be, someone who had knocked a hole in the stout wall that was the nobility. Yet I had to admit to doubts that he really had accomplished this. The antagonism he attracted only served to confirm my belief that no outsider could breach the fortress of the aristocracy.

Raleigh however was a man of many talents and interests - travel and exploration, science and experiment, poetry and literature. Ferdinando Stanley was one of his friends amongst the nobility for they shared many interests and Christopher Marlowe was also a close companion, which brought to my mind Lord Hunsdon's remark that Marlowe had influential contacts. One night I was present with Lord Hunsdon at a reading of 'The Faerie Queen' by the poet Edmund Spenser whom Raleigh had become acquainted with when he was given an estate in Ireland that adjoined Spenser's property there. He had been impressed by Spenser's long romance and had encouraged him to come to London where he introduced him to the Queen. There was a large appreciative audience in the Great Hall as Spenser, a tall slender elegant man in his thirties, discreetly attired in black, read his verse. Amongst the audience I noticed Lord Strange's vivacious wife Alice, another imperious red-haired imitator of the Queen. She and her sister Elizabeth, married to one of Lord Hunsdon's sons, had already been lavishly praised in earlier poems of Spenser, who claimed some distant relationship with them, and once again I found myself envying these ladies who inspired poets to immortalise them in verse. How I wished a poet would write something to me but I knew there was little possibility. Men wrote poems about conventional beauties, not unusual dark ladies, and generally only those who were able to reward them either by gifts or by the prestige of their position in life. In fact most poetry, like 'The Faerie Queen', was written in praise of Queen Elizabeth. Even Raleigh, with all his faults, had composed excellent verse in her honour. But an idea was born out of my disappointment. I had always loved words, from my earliest infancy when my father's outpourings in his own language had been my first music, then my studies of Latin and French with Susan Bertie, and Spenser's musical language, its fantasy and inventive allegory excited me. If I couldn't have poems written about me why shouldn't I put some of my thoughts and feelings into verse myself, I had often composed little melodies for my own amusement.

The idea took hold of me and on my next foray into the city I called at a bookseller's in St. Paul's churchyard. The vast area around the church proliferated with shops, especially book shops, printers and stationers, and there I bought some parchment, ink and a set of goose quills. Most of my first attempts were failures as I crossed and re-crossed words and obliterated lines, ruining fine parchment in a manner I would not have been able to if I had had to purchase it myself. But the exercise gave me a sense of independence, if only in my private thoughts, putting me on a level with men. Some few women did write poetry, one such being Philip Sidney's sister the Countess of Pembroke. However this was viewed as an aristocratic accomplishment, their compositions only to be read in private circles and never printed for public consumption or for gain. What if I could publish poetry for a general public, like Veronica Franco. I fantasised - "The poems of Aemilia Bassano, Lord Hunsdon's whore", patronised by His Lordship himself. I looked at another sheet in disgust and destroyed the offending paper.

Everyone was glad when Robert Devereux and Walter Raleigh made a truce in their hostilities, obviously realising that they were in danger of angering the

Queen. Essex reinstated himself in the Queen's favour more than ever and their intimacy was renewed. He was constantly at her side, riding with her, dancing with her, playing cards with her late into the night, amusing her with his witty conversation, delighting her with his excellent manners and constant attentions so that Raleigh had been relegated into the background again.

"At last he has found his niche as Leicester's replacement," Lord Hunsdon had said with satisfaction. "Let us hope he will be content with this."

Hopes however were short-lived for soon relations between him and the Queen were as bad as ever for the simple reason that he had found himself a wife and compounded the offence by marrying secretly. The Queen's favourites were not allowed to marry. She never forgave Leicester for marrying Essex's mother, and Christopher Hatton and Walter Raleigh had both wisely remained bachelors. What was worse than to undertake a marriage was to marry in secret and without her permission. The Queen was furious. She refused to have anything to do with him, consoling herself with Raleigh, and he was ordered never to bring his wife to Court but to keep her in retirement at her mother's house. Others beside the Queen were astounded by this latest indiscretion and puzzled by his choice. The Earl of Essex was one of the greatest nobles in the land with a pedigree from King Henry, and a prospective wife was expected to be of equal rank. Instead he had married Frances Walsingham, daughter of the recently deceased spymaster, widow of Sir Philip Sidney and already mother of two children.

I was shocked and felt as hurt as the Queen, especially because there had never been any indication that his affections lay in any particular place. I couldn't understand it because she was neither beautiful, wealthy, virginal nor of noble birth. I had always been deterred from making advances to him by the difference in our status even though I had been enamoured of him and I knew he had not been impervious to my charms. I wished now that I had tried harder to captivate him for I was in every way equal to Frances Walsingham. I could have been an ideal wife for him, giving him satisfaction in every way as I did to Lord Hunsdon. A consuming jealousy overwhelmed me, making me search for ulterior motives in this strange marriage. I knew Philip Sidney had been his hero and he had been thrilled when Leicester had handed onto him his nephew's sword after his death, implying that Essex was to succeed him as England's champion of anti-Spanish patriotism. I couldn't rid myself of the disloyal suspicion that in taking Sidney's wife also he was making a public avowal to step into his shoes as a great soldier, a noted patriot and a popular leader, using her as a pawn in his ambitions as he had used Penelope. I felt a confusion of jealousy, disappointment and disillusion and I couldn't help voicing my thoughts to Lord Hunsdon.

"God forbid!" he exclaimed. "Essex has neither the wisdom nor the self-control for a leader. Pray God that any fantasies he might harbour do not correspond to his ambitions."

But I suspected he was ambitious enough to consider such a possibility. His loss made a chasm in my heart, especially painful because there had been no preparation for such an event. My emotions felt raw and bruised, as if they had been abraded with sand. There was a strange element of contrivance in the affair. Sidney had been in love with Penelope Devereux but had married Frances Walsingham who had then married Penelope's brother. It was like a play in the theatre. But I knew I had to put him from my mind and bask in the admiration I received from many of the courtiers though none dared pay me too intimate attention knowing I was Lord Hunsdon's property.

Besides making the acquaintance of many young gallants at Court I also saw them often at the playhouses where they were only too happy to escort me. The theatre companies were thriving as never before. Christopher Marlowe had written another great success for the Lord Admiral's Men, although it shocked many people by its amorality and its hints of atheism. Some said Dr. Faustus who sold his soul to the Devil was a homage to Marlowe's friend Walter Raleigh and his associates. Marlowe himself was a member of this group who met for discussion and experimentation but had been termed "the School of Night" because it was rumoured they dabbled in black magic, promoted religious scepticism and indulged in homosexuality, and according to Lord Hunsdon were under secret surveillance by the State. Nonetheless playgoers flocked to the play with its spectacular effects culminating in a fearsome finale where Faustus was carried by devils down into Hell Mouth to the accompaniment of flames, thunder and lightning. Henslowe had expended much money on the special effects and The Rose was well equipped with trap doors beneath the stage and lowering mechanism in the hut above. I saw it several times because with Edward Alleyn in the title role it was truly spectacular.

"I can't see Lord Strange's protégée being able to match Marlowe," I confessed to Lord Hunsdon after I had watched two other plays William Shakespeare had written for his company - a sequel to 'King Henry VI' followed by 'Richard III'. "He seems to be stuck with history and his King Richard owes much to

Marlowe's villains, though I must admit he writes some wonderfully dramatic scenes."

"History plays are always popular," said Lord Hunsdon, "and perhaps it is better that Master Shakespeare eschews the somewhat dangerous ground Marlowe treads."

One afternoon I went to see yet another sequel to Shakespeare's saga of King Henry VI at The Black Bull on Bishopsgate. Whenever I visited my old habitat I armed myself with an air of self-assurance and swept into the inn in my striking gown of cobalt blue velvet with a matching hat. My escort and I were immediately directed to one of the best seats in the first gallery directly overlooking the stage, in company with other rich spectators, and though I was aware of some of my one-time neighbours studying me I was soon immersed in the play. I always enjoyed talking with writers and actors whenever I could so when the performance was over and I saw Master Shakespeare helping to clear the stage with the other players I approached him at the trestles. "I have enjoyed all your history plays," I said. "You have a way with words and you know how to find all the dramatic possibilities in a story," trying not to sound condescending because I was sincere in my opinion. "I loved the scene in 'Richard III' where the King wooed the Lady Anne over the bier of her dead husband."

He looked pleased and studied me carefully. "I hope I shall get better. I drag a long way behind Marlowe," he said. "You're Mistress Aemilia Bassano aren't you? I know several of your family, they play for us sometimes. And I have lodgings in Gracechurch Street off Bishopsgate so I often encounter them in the streets and the taverns."

And no doubt you know of me as Lord Hunsdon's paramour I thought. I would like to have known why he had left Warwick shire to join a troupe of actors, most of them London born and bred and often inter-related, because he seemed to lack the ebullience of a player, but I curbed my curiosity for another time.

Later when I was describing the performance to Lord Hunsdon I said, "I think this man Shakespeare could be a prolific writer even though he isn't yet equal to Marlowe."

"That young man dices with danger and he had better watch his game," he remarked cryptically.

When we heard that Marlowe had been arrested again I was none too surprised, being well acquainted with my protector's extensive knowledge of London affairs. This time he had been thrown into gaol on charges of writing subversive material, in company with a fellow playwright Thomas Kydd with whom he shared a room. Yet despite the serious indictment he was soon set free upon a caution, even more surprising when his friend was kept incarcerated and later died of injuries he had received during torture.

"Why is Marlowe always freed and his companions not?" I enquired of Lord Hunsdon but he would say nothing, though I suspected he was party to some information. Other actors and musicians knew nothing further when I asked around, only venturing the information that the young playwright was busy writing a drama about English history. However when 'Edward II' took the stage he did not disappoint his audiences with his propensity to shock as he audaciously portrayed the blatant homosexuality of the king.

I wondered what William Shakespeare would think of the popular playwright's daring venture into the territory of English history that he himself seemed to find most inspiring. But Lord Strange's fledgling writer proved himself full of mettle by changing his scene to ancient Rome, and 'Titus Andronicus' was as shocking as anything Marlowe had produced with its rape, mutilation and cannibalism. Playgoers relished the gory action of the most bloodthirsty play ever seen on a stage as he picked up the gauntlet, his one advantage over Marlowe being the fact that as an actor himself he was closer to the immediacies of theatrical experience. The war between the theatre companies increased in intensity as they sought to find new plays to tempt audiences and new writers abounded as they realised the theatres could be a profitable consideration. Meanwhile Edward Alleyn and Richard Burbage worked to improve their craft as they competed for the favour of the spectators. I was as excited as most playgoers by the unprecedented activity.

Then disaster struck and 1592 became a calamitous year. A group of apprentices who were unable to get into The Rose caused a riot in front of the theatre, an affray which spread beyond the bounds of Bankside as many troublemakers relished the opportunity for a fight, and this resulted in the Privy Council banning all plays for a period of three months. This was followed as spring approached by rumours that cases of the Plague had been discovered and the possibility put the fear of God into people as an unusually hot summer threatened. And at Court the highly successful Walter Raleigh at last made a mistake. At over forty years of age he had committed an indiscretion with Bess Throckmorton, one of the Queen's maids-of-honour, who consequently found herself pregnant, and he was committed to the Tower as the Queen ranted and raged.

And to my horror I found myself pregnant too.

When I had first gone to Lord Hunsdon he had given me the name of a woman skilled in the knowledge of how to avoid such an eventuality. A fat red-faced dame with none too clean clothes and dubious antecedents I had visited her with some trepidation but she was practical and knowledgeable and had given me useful advice. Later I had made use of her once or twice to good, though painful, effect when I had thought myself with child. But this time was different. I had been caught off guard, not noticing the absence of my flowes which had become irregular, presumably on account of interference with the normal order of fertility. Also my mind had been filled with other things, Robert Devereux's marriage, the excitement in the theatres and latterly worry about the plague which had been spreading its virulence throughout the summer. By August it was so bad, especially in the Shoreditch area, that all the theatres had been closed, no plays were to be performed anywhere and the popular annual Bartholomew Fair at Smithfield had been cancelled. Deaths were increasing rapidly and in the midst of a general anxiety I now found myself with a very particular one. Despite having tried all the remedies, I had drunk jugs of rue water, I knew my pregnancy was too far gone for anything but the most drastic solution and though fearful of the consequences I could not find it in myself to put my life at such risk. I knew Lord Hunsdon had several children outside his large family in marriage so I thought he might accept this inevitability after five years of impunity. I waited until a time when we were particularly close then I told him, "I am with child."

"Is this a certainty? Have you tried everything?" he asked after a moment's consideration of the fact..

"I have tried everything. It is too late. I cannot take the ultimate step, my Lord."

He paused for a while then said, "Then we must find a husband for you."

Of all the responses I had imagined from him, and I had gone through them in my mind in order to prepare myself, this was the most unexpected. His words took some time to register then I stammered, "You cannot mean this. You do not mean to cast me off?"

I waited for him to deny this fact but he didn't reply and there was a sick feeling in the pit of my stomach. I strove desperately to keep calm saying, "You have had children with other mistresses, I know this. Your base-born son Valentine Carey served with you in the army at the time of the Armada."

He looked at me directly for he was never one to avoid the truth. "I can't deny that, Aemilia, but I was young then. Now I am appproaching seventy, too old to see to the rearing of another child. I have grandchildren as you know. In Biblical terms I am near my appointed span. I would not have you left alone with a child when I die."

"But you are not old, you may live for many years yet. Are you tired of me? Have you found someone else? Do you no longer find pleasure with me? Is this an excuse to be rid of me?" My words poured out in anguish.

"I need no excuse to be rid of you, Aemilia, if I so wished," his voice was stern. "But there is no-one else, of that be assured. You still pleasure me as much as you always have but despite your protestations I am an old man. All the worry and activity of Armada year took a great toll on me as it did with everyone, look how many of us are dead - Leicester, Christopher Hatton, Francis Walsingham - and Burghley is sick." It was true that of late his energy had begun to slacken and I had to put more invention into arousing him. There were deep pouches beneath his eyes and more grey than red now in his hair and beard. "And because so many of her old trusted councillors are gone the Queen relies on me the more and demands more from me," he continued. "I think you have given me more pleasure than anyone in my life, Aemilia, certainly in this latter part of my life." He sighed deeply. "You have been my last love but it seems that this may be the right time for you to leave me and marry." Seeing the horror on my face he added, "I am thinking practically and sincerely of your welfare and the welfare of your child."

I was aghast, the sickness intensifying as the severity of his words dropped like stones into the well of my misery, each one sounding the end of the life I had enjoyed for five years. "Please don't abandon me," I appealed in desperation, taking hold of his arm. "When I have had the child it can be put into the care of someone if you do not wish to acknowledge it then we can carry on as before."

"And would you really give up your child? I do not think so, your heart is warmer than you are aware," he said gently. "I myself would not be willing to concede my child to an unknown fate."

"I do not want to leave you," I cried piteously, knowing he would realise my truest regrets.

He smiled ruefully. "I must leave you soon, as I have said. Then what would happen to you. No doubt another man would take you up but I would not wish to have you make a life as a whore until you are too old for anyone, you are worth more than that," he said seriously. "This will be the best solution, believe me. I will find a husband for you and I will set him up with enough money to care for you and the child. You may take all the things I have given you, your clothes and your jewels. If you are careful you should be set for life."

"You once said I was not the kind for a quiet life," I murmured somewhat rebelliously.

"Your life will be what you make it. You have had many advantages," he said sternly.

I knew it was no use appealing to him further. Henry Carey, son of Henry Tudor, was not the sort of person you argued with. I had never dreamt he would cast me off, believing I had too much sway over him, and had trusted him to at least acknowledge the child when he knew he was my first and only lover. At the very least I had expected him to set us up independently so that for the rest of my life I would be provided for and could continue to live in the manner to which I had become accustomed, if only for the sake of the child who would have noble, perhaps royal, blood. But although I was devastated my education had given me too much respect to grovel to any man.

He took me in his arms and kissed me but he left me then and when he had gone I burst into tears. My grief overwhelmed me. I could not believe this was to be the end of everything, so suddenly and irrevocably. Although I esteemed Lord Hunsdon and had grown to have a genuine affection for him, enjoying his company, I acknowledged that the sorrow enveloping me was more for the loss of the life I had enjoyed for five years - beautiful clothes and jewels, my apartments and expensive gifts, and the respect I had received from tradespeople and servants through merit of my protector, treated as a lady at least outwardly. Even more than these was the loss to me of all the people I had shared his acquaintance with - poets and actors, patrons and performers, people of intellect and wit. All this would now be a closed book to me. It would be back to Bishopsgate, to the sort of married life Stephen Vaughn had envisaged for me a few years ago and which I had resolutely refused to consider. For what kind of a husband could be found for me. It would definitely not be anyone of high status. And what sort of man could be bought to take on another man's pregnant whore. Another outpouring of tears overwhelmed me at the implications. I would be gossiped about, laughed at and mocked, used as a moral warning - "Aemilia Bassano, abandoned by her rich lover after just five years, such are the wages of sin". I did not feel I could bear such humiliation.

My near hysteria continued for several days compounded of a mix of self-pity, humiliation, fear, and anger with my lover that a man could so easily abandon with impunity a woman he had made use of because she was bearing his child. I refused to leave my apartments, my face blotched and red as it was. I tried to find an alternative to marrying some unknown man whose greed overtopped his integrity and would have a hold over me all my life. I could disregard Lord Hunsdon's warning and try to find myself another lover who would provide for me in the same manner. Many courtiers had shown me obvious favour, but I would have to wait until after the child was born and then farm it out. But some spark of warning flickered on the borders of my consciousness for I had now learnt it was a precarious existence and a mistress could be abandoned on a whim, not necessarily provided for. History was full of examples of discarded mistresses who had found themselves whoring on the streets. I thought of going to Italy. If I could get to Venice I could perhaps make a living for myself as a musician or a writer. But my father had told me enough of the hazardous journeys he had two or three times made to his homeland - across the sea, through strange lands, over the passes of the highest mountains, beset with perils of storm and tempest, ice and snow, brigands and bandits. I could never make the journey alone, especially with a child.

I did not see Lord Hunsdon for several days. Then he came unannounced to my apartments. He looked sharply at my pale face with its swollen lids and blotchy red cheeks but made no comment, kissing me briefly on the lips. Then he said, "I have been giving some thought to a husband for you, Aemilia. What think you of Alfonso Lanier?"

CHAPTER 7

COURANT

"I'll take you, Aemilia, if no-one else will."

The glare I fixed upon Alfonso Lanier would have frozen stone but he didn't regard it. "How much has he paid you?" I demanded truculently.

He didn't reply but shrugged his shoulders with Italian eloquence, a gesture conveying indifference, reticence, embarrassment, all at the same time. Alfonso, the eldest of my cousin Lucrezia's six children by Nicholas Lanier, was now twenty-one, two years younger than I was. He was handsome, tall and slim with short black curly hair, dark skin that was clean shaven, and brown eyes that held the innocence of a child, the same misleading innocence that ten years earlier had tempted me to take his friendly hand only to find a frog in my palm. He cultivated a disarming ingenuousness and this coupled with his ready smile led people to trust him more than his behaviour often warranted. I knew this because we had been acquainted to some extent for a long time through our family relationship. But he was a fine musician and in fact had taken over what had been my father's position in the recorder consort of the Queen's Musick.

The fact that we were to marry was a fait accompli arranged by Lord Hunsdon and in which I had little say, but I decided that in order to keep my dignity he must not be allowed the upper hand over me and now was the time to make the position clear. He was regarding me with interest and a hint of amusement so I said, "Very well, let me make myself plain so that you know the position exactly. Lord Hunsdon has paid you, a considerable sum I would guess, to marry me and I am with child by him. However do not expect me to be grateful to you, Alfonso. I am happy that for my child's sake he will be given a legal name but for myself I would have been quite capable of being an independent woman. No doubt this transaction is in your own interests." (I was well aware that he lived above his income having a taste for fashionable clothes and enjoying gambling with his friends). "But, notwithstanding the money, you are getting no small bargain. I am educated, cultured, and many men desire me."

"But not enough to marry you when, as you say, you have been a man's mistress and are now carrying his child." Before I could reply he put up his hands in appeasement, a gesture I had often seen my father make when trouble approached. "Don't let's quarrel, Amelia. Let us both accept that we are getting a fair bargain. I don't see why it should not work out well. We are not strangers to each other, in fact we are kin, both with Italian blood, and music forms a common attachment between us." A flicker of a smile touched his lips. "And to tell true I find you very attractive, I always have. So I think I shall seal this bargain by kissing my future wife." He seized me in his arms and his kiss had no trace of cousinly affection as his tongue explored my mouth.

I felt uncomfortable. It was strange having to suddenly change my perception of someone I had known in a different relationship for so long. Everything had happened so quickly that I still could not accustom myself to the fact that Alfonso Lanier was to be my husband. I had never thought that by the age of twenty-three I would be marrying a lowly musician. I had to admit that it could have been worse for I could have been coupled with a man I heartily disliked or, worse still, with a man who disliked me and would make me pay for my sins in more ways than one. Alfonso Lanier was at least young and good looking and seemed unlikely to bear me any ill will, being satisfied with the bargain. He was part of a circle I found conducive and which included many of my relatives and acquaintances who would turn a blind eye to the circumstances of our union and would thus save me embarrassment. I was forced to admit that Lord Hunsdon had my interests at heart and had not made a bad choice but I still felt rancour that he had cast me off so summarily together with his child and that for the second time I was being bought like a piece of merchandise.

My leaving the Court was as swift, but far less pleasurable, than my arriving there. Until the wedding could be arranged as quickly as possible I was to live at my cousin Lucrezia's house in Chelsea. I had no intention of returning to Bishopsgate and having to endure humiliating encounters with my old acquaintances but in any case the plague in the city rendered this unwise, even the Queen had gone to Bath, and Chelsea was still relatively safe. I had brought with me clothes and jewels and three chests of valuable belongings. Lord Hunsdon said I might take Bess with me also but although I liked her and had grown to depend on her I considered her presence would be a constant reminder of the life I had lost so suddenly and unexpectedly. My relatives had been characteristically supportive, joyful about the imminent nuptials of two members of the family and tactfully forgetting that the expected child was not a fruit of our union, however I felt I should broach the subject with my cousin Lucrezia, seeing I was to share her household. "I am sorry that it should be like this. I'm sure you wish it could have been otherwise," I forced myself to say honestly.

Lucrezia was the daughter of Antonio, one of my father's older brothers, and was about forty years old. She was Nicholas Lanier's second wife, younger than he, buxom and still comely with dark hair and eyes, bustling like a mother hen over her brood but with an Italian resignation to whatever life might dispense. "Left to his own devices Alfonso would probably have made a more disastrous choice," she said bluntly. "You know he's a madcap and prone to crazy ideas. It's my hope, Aemilia, that this will be a way of him settling down. The money will give him a start in life." She looked me firmly in the eye. "But you must play your part too. Keep an eye on the purse strings and deal fairly with him."

I wasn't quite sure what she had in mind with her warning but I was glad the affair had brought no antagonism in its wake, at least not with her. I knew that Alfonso's father, Nicholas Lanier, disapproved and I kept out of his way as much as possible but I soon discovered that he disapproved of much of what Alfonso did, often comparing him unfavourably with his eldest son John from his first marriage. Lucrezia had offered to prepare a wedding breakfast for us and Alfonso's five younger siblings entered into the proposed festivities with enthusiasm, especially his only sister, seventeen years old Ellen, with whom I shared a bedchamber. She was affianced to the musician Alfonso Ferrabosco, son of my father's old friend, and eagerly looking forward to her own marriage.

On October 18th 1592 Alfonso Lanier and I were married in the Parish church of St. Botolph in Aldgate because this was my parish and where I still held property. It was where I had been baptised and my parents buried. In a whimsical distraction during the ceremony I wondered if they could see from their graves and what they might be thinking. My mother would certainly not be pleased but I had a feeling that my father might be. "You might marry a musician and then you would still have some contact with the Court," he had once said, though at the time I remembered wanting much more than this from my life. During the ceremony I played a part as if I were acting on a stage, as I often did when having to do something I didn't care for, smiling and throwing ribbons and flowers to the spectators for all the world like a happy bride in order to prevent any malicious talk. I wore one of the beautiful gowns Lord Hunsdon had bought me, the apple green taffeta with the dark green sleeves and kirtle, as green was a popular colour for brides, but the laces were wider apart than they had been. Alfonso was as usual dressed in the height of fashion in a finely tailored scarlet doublet and padded black velvet hose with scarlet panes, a short black cape flung across one shoulder with a matching high-crowned hat and finely pleated ruff. In his flamboyance there was no trace of embarrassment. Afterwards there was a plenteous meal of boiled and roasted meats and fowl, pies, fricassees and tarts followed by custards, jellies and sugar pastes - noisy, jolly and companionable as ever. It all seemed like a typical Bassano festa and I found it difficult to remind myself that this was actually my wedding day. Under the circumstances the ritualistic bedding ceremony was dispensed with and finally the guests dispersed, happy with themselves and for us. I caught my new sister-in-law Ellen studying me with a mixture of curiosity and vicarious anticipation in her brown eyes, her wide mouth open a little, and I felt a flutter of unease as I followed Alfonso upstairs. For the first time I joined him in his small chamber, his parents having the main bedchamber, and a sudden wave of depression overcame me as I recalled the first night with Lord Hunsdon, the luxurious surroundings, the draped bed with the expensive sheets, the mix of fear and exhilaration. I drew the linen curtain on the casement and lit the candle on the coffer then stood uncertain.

Alfonso had already undressed to his shirt and sitting on the uncanopied bed he called, "Come on, Aemilia, make haste. No more old men for you, see what a young man can do." He didn't seem to share any of my awkwardness.

I felt uncomfortable at the thought of being intimate with someone I had known in a different relationship for a long time and fumbled clumsily with my clothes, taking a long time with the lacings so that Alfonso came impatiently to my aid. I spoke sternly to myself, hadn't I seriously considered a profession as a whore when it was irrelevant whom I slept with. He pulled me eagerly into his bed and tugged at my shift, tearing some of the delicate lace. I groaned, remembering Lord Hunsdon's finesse. Then he was immediately on top of me. But soon I had to admit a sensation of pleasure in the physical contact, enjoying his youth and virility, feeling the smoothness of his skin and his prompt arousal. His slim body was lithe and supple but strong and firm and I felt the muscles ripple in his back as I held him. However I was determined not to give any evidence of satisfaction and afterwards I said coolly, "Is that it? I'm used to better than this." I enjoyed watching the smirk disappear from his face. I intended to establish my independence from any proprietorial intentions he might be nourishing and to squash any notions of superiority. "I can see I shall have to teach you some things, Alfonso Lanier." He looked abashed but privately I had to admit that it was pleasurable to have a young man make love to me.

The next time he said, "Hey, Aemilia, how did you learn these things?"

I wouldn't admit to my own enjoyment and the surprised realisation that marriage to Alfonso Lanier might have at least one compensation. Instead I couldn't resist saying, "Don't forget I was a whore. And an old man has a lot of experience after all."

Lucrezia wanted us to stay with her until the child was born and I was content to do so. Afterwards we would look for a house but at the moment Chelsea was plague free and I knew I would value her help and extensive experience, having no mother and remembering Angela's tragedy. It also kept me out of the way of my former neighbours and acquaintances in Bishopsgate, none of whom I was eager to meet. The village was too quiet for my liking but I told myself the fresh air was good for my health, and the house itself was always bustling with activity as three of Alfonso's younger brothers, Clement, Jerome and Andrea, as well as Ellen, were still at home, Innocent as an apprentice musician sharing his father's rooms in the city. It was of necessity a large house for Nicholas Lanier had invested his substantial income in property and owned other houses in the suburbs which he rented out, as well as having lodgings near Lincoln's Inn when he was working. There were always household tasks and cooking to be done. Lucrezia encouraged me to take up the dreaded needle and prepare for my baby's arrival while Ellen sought my help in assembling her trousseau for her own approaching marriage. The city was dead anyway with no plays or performances, many of the shops and taverns shut and a general miasma of fear enveloping the streets as the weekly lists of ever-increasing plague victims were posted. I was worried about the future, regretful for the past, and fearful of the ordeal that lay before me, yet as the weeks passed I was overwhelmed by a strange feeling of tranquillity that Lucrezia said was typical of the last months of pregnancy. I felt as if I were living in a dream, disconnected from the realities of life elsewhere and hardly conscious of the days passing. It was like having drunk the poppy juice my mother used to give me if I had toothache, drowsiness dulling the pain that lay within. "It's nature's way of conserving your energy and calming your spirit for the trial that is to come," my cousin said.

Alfonso didn't burden me with his presence and was often away, lodging in the city. Over the Christmas season the musicians accompanied the Queen to Hampton Court where the festivities were held this year instead of Whitehall because of the plague. He didn't show any inclination to sleep with me as my pregnancy increased and with money to spend he preferred to take his pleasures casually with the admirers the musicians attracted to themselves, while I felt indolent and indifferent.

When my time came at last the birth was an easy one, or so Lucrezia and the midwife assured me. Their assurances fell on deaf ears as I cried and sweated despite the wet chill of a February afternoon. My pains had taken me by surprise so I had no time to be already lying in a prepared chamber but Lucrezia had called up her neighbours for encouragement and Ellen watched nervously from a corner of the room. When Alfonso returned from a rehearsal in one of the Westminster taverns the child was lying swaddled in the family's well-used crib beside our bed. The rush of emotion that had overwhelmed me when my son was laid in my arms had come as a shock. I had mocked my sister Angela and always shown a distaste for infants. I hadn't wanted a child, in fact I had considered giving him away, and now this all-consuming possession shook me with its intensity as I held him close. In my womb he had seemed an alien intrusion but now he was born - breathing and crying and moving his tiny fingers and toes - he seemed to me the most precious gift I had ever been given. His wet hair seemed to be reddish brown but his tiny face was too squashed and puckered for me to deduce any resemblance. All I knew was that he was mine, my flesh and blood, no matter who his father was - Henry Carey or Alfonso Lanier. How could I ever thought of giving him away I thought, as tears of relief and weariness dropped on his face and he snuffled at the sensation.

I was unsure what was passing through Alfonso's mind as he stared down at the tiny sleeping figure, in his swaddling clothes nothing visible except his face. "Shall we name him after your father?" he asked at last.

I was tempted but I had already made up my mind. "No, I want to call him Henry."

"Henry Lanier," said Alfonso. He looked steadily at me and I stared him out. He knew the significance of the name, the name of the child's real father because I thought it might matter some day, but he made neither comment nor dissent.

"He is a strong lusty child and likely to thrive," said Lucrezia. Then she turned to her son saying sternly, "It is your duty to rear him now and be a good father to him," and Alfonso looked unusually serious, though I was unaware of his real feelings about this cuckoo in the nest.

When I was alone I picked him from the cradle and held him in my arms again. Henry Lanier, a musician's son but in actual fact kin to the Queen and the Earl of Essex and Penelope Devereux, and who probably bore in his veins the royal blood of the Tudors. I wondered what his destiny would be and in my heightened emotional state I didn't know whether to laugh or cry. But in the turbulence of my feelings I felt pity for my child who had been denied his heritage.

Later at nightfall Alfonso came to see me, though I would lie alone for a few days while he shared his younger brothers' chamber. He said awkwardly, "I am relieved you have survived safely. Henry will be our first child, won't he? We will have other children together won't we?"

"I expect so," I replied.

I recovered quickly, scorning to keep to my chamber for longer than a week despite Lucrezia's admonitions, and the return of my strength was accompanied by a return of my restive spirit. Now the child was born I must think about the future. Somehow I must climb back to the status of being a rich lady again and the only way in sight seemed to be to push Alfonso into some ambition, though I did not entirely discount other means. I had recovered my slender form and many people complimented me on how childbearing had improved my looks. I was longing to be out and about in company again. London however was still in thrall to the plague. Nothing was happening in the city and those who could afford had gone elsewhere while the actors were touring in the country. For Candlemas, Shrovetide and Maundy Thursday, which the Queen normally spent at Whitehall, the ceremonies continued to be held at Hampton Court. Then she went as usual to Windsor for the St. George's Day pageantry of the Knights of the Garter but afterwards had moved to Greenwich earlier than she normally did. Without the

Queen the heart of the city was dead for everyone important had followed her, including Alfonso in company with the Queen's Musick so he was seldom at the family home. Although I was relieved of his constraints I envied his freedom and longed for my former life at Court. Lucrezia was becoming increasingly irritated by my restlessness and my reluctance to settle into domesticity and I escaped from the house as often as I could, sometimes going as far as Westminster where I had taken it into my head to look for a house.

But I was so eager for a sight of the city itself that one bright May day I made an excuse about having to see to my mother's property and leaving the baby in the care of the willing Ellen I took a barge down the river as far as London Bridge. My heart leapt with joy at the sight of the sole bridge across the Thames with its ancient houses and shops teetering precariously along its length, the wooden water wheels pumping water for the citizens from the force engendered by the river rushing through the nineteen arches, and straddling the bridge at the city end the fantastic vividly painted Nonesuch House with its four corner towers, leaded windows and gilded weathervanes. I made my way up Gracechurch Street towards the exit through the city wall into Bishopgate Street without, not sure where I was going but in the direction of our old house, when coming out of a tenement I saw William Shakespeare and remembered him saying he lodged there. It was convenient for the theatres in Shoreditch.

I greeted him then said, "I did not think to see you here in London. I thought all the theatre companies were touring the countryside on account of the plague."

"Yes they are but I did not go with them." He looked distracted. "I beg pardon, Mistress Bassano but my mind is in a whirl. I have just heard the dreadful news about Kit Marlowe."

I looked at him blankly. "What news?"

The actor blinked as if trying to clear his vision and shook his head in apparent bewilderment saying, "It would appear he's been murdered." My face was a study of disbelief and he continued, "In a tavern in Deptford. An argument about paying the bill."

The news was too startling for both of us to comprehend. Christopher Marlowe, the most promising writer of his age, dead before he was thirty years old. And to be killed in such sordidly trivial circumstances. I knew the theatre world was full of drunkenness and quarrels, brawls and even murders and Marlowe had been involved in fights before, but people of his talent couldn't die like this, so prematurely and so senselessly. Not knowing how to respond I murmured foolishly, "I am Mistress Lanier now. I am wed and living in Chelsea."

The actor made an effort to focus on my face. "My pardon again, Mistress. I thought I had not seen you of late."

"Why are you still in the city?" I asked.

"I have been writing," he said simply.

We made our farewells, both still dazed at the news. As I left him I wondered if he was thinking that Marlowe's death, though tragic, had now left the way open for him to reign supreme as London's leading playwright. He was becoming well known. Before his recent death the author Robert Greene had written a bitter invective about him calling him a mere ignorant actor competing with established University men and scholars, an "upstart crow" attempting to write by stealing their ideas. I wondered what he was writing now, important enough for him to stay in London during the plague instead of touring with his fellow actors. But the news about Marlowe had taken the gilt from my excursion.

I remembered his handsome face with the inscrutable eyes and cynical mouth and recalled Lord Hunsdon's reticence about his activities, only saying that he played with fire. I wondered if there was something more to his death than an argument over a reckoning. Lord Hunsdon would know the details and once again I longed to be back at the hub of events. I got as far as Bishopsgate Street within but when I reached the gate itself, originally a Roman construction but rebuilt in later times to be one of the main entrances into the city, I looked up at the stone barbican where decaying heads were stuck on spikes. London was full of death today. I did not pass through the gate into Bishopsgate Street without but retraced my steps and took a boat back to Chelsea.

Still the plague continued through the summer. The death list was creeping towards ten thousand. But I was tired of living in the village of Chelsea and even the novelty of watching my son thrive could not ease my boredom. There were many grand houses and palaces built along the river here, Sir Thomas More had owned a fine mansion, King Henry had built a nursery palace for the rearing of his children and Katherine Parr had lived there, but the sight of these only increased my discontent with the turn my life had taken. At first I had considered it an advantage that Alfonso would be away most of the time with the Queen's Musick and would not burden me overmuch with his presence, but now I found myself missing him in bed and envying his attendance at Court while I was bound to the house. But when I asked if I couldn't accompany him sometimes he was dismissive.

"For what reason? What excuse could I make for your presence? And who would look after Henry? Your place is at home with my mother, looking after your child. At least until the plague is over and things are back to normal again."

I thought of how my father often used to find reasons for me to accompany him. I was aware Alfonso was not celibate while he was so long away and I knew he was taking great delight in spending money, on clothes, gaming and new friendships. I thought I might feel less resentful once I had a house of my own but I knew it would not be wise to look for somewhere else to live at this time. However to still my boredom I would make regular journeys into the city despite the danger of contagion. Wearing a mask and carrying a cloth soaked in vinegar I went to visit my kin, shopped in the depleted markets, browsed in the booksellers. One day visiting The White Greyhound, a bookshop and printers in St. Paul's churchyard, I saw a book of verse entitled 'Venus and Adonis' by William Shakespeare. It was dedicated to Henry Wriothesley, Earl of Southampton. So this was what he had been writing. The book was expensive at six pence but I bought a copy and took it home to read.

As I read it I became more and more enthralled. This was as good as anything that Edmund Spenser had written. William Shakespeare was obviously not merely an actor and playwright. He was a poet. I wondered what connection, if any, did he have with the Earl of Southampton. I had never met Henry Wriothesley but I knew he was a friend of Robert Devereux and like him had been one of Lord Burghley's wards. Not much older than I, he was reputed to be one of the wealthiest nobles and known to be generous in his patronage of authors. I wondered if he had rewarded William Shakespeare for what was an extraordinary offering. Reading and re-reading the narrative verse inspired me to try writing again and helped to while away the time.

One day on one of my visits into the city I was walking down Gracechurch Street when on a sudden whim I knocked on the door of the tenement from where I had seen Master Shakespeare emerge. A woman of middle age, wearing a plain brown linen dress with apron and coif, opened the door and looked at me suspiciously, noting my fine clothes. "Yes?" Her sharp cat's eyes took in every detail of my dark blue silk gown with its boned bodice, pointed stomacher and sleeves slashed with green taffeta, my tulle ruff, my high-crowned hat of green velvet, my black velvet mask.

"Is Master Shakespeare at home? I would like a word with him."

Her eyebrows lifted while her thin lips drooped downwards. Obviously she was not used to callers of my sort and I intuited she was doubtful of my reputation. "Master Shakespeare does not welcome unexpected visitors. He does not like to be disturbed when he is working."

"How do you know I am unexpected?" I countered. "Please ask him if he is at liberty to admit Mistress Aemilia Lanier."

I had got used to speaking with authority when I was kept by Lord Hunsdon and grudgingly she retreated into the house, returning a short time later with a subdued, "Upstairs to the third floor. The door is open."

As I climbed the narrow creaking stairs I felt a sudden qualm at my impetuosity but he was holding the door open for me saying, "Mistress Lanier, this is an unexpected pleasure."

He must know I don't have a reputation to lose, I thought involuntarily but he appeared sincere enough.

I entered the small dark attic room with its open casement, noting the disorder of books and papers scattered on the dusty floorboards and on the bed standing to one side. There was a chair beside a table which was covered with more papers, an inkpot, quills, a pen knife, a sanding pot, the stub of a candle, a tankard. A dusty livery cupboard had books stacked on top together with candleholders and a wine jug with a broken handle. On a small table stood a pewter bowl and ewer with two more tankards beside them and there was another chair hidden beneath a pile of clothing.

"I ought not to have disturbed you," I apologised, realising the impropriety of this intrusion.

"No, really, I am glad of the disturbance," he said eagerly, drawing forward the other chair, removing the assortment of garments and flinging them onto the bed. "At the moment my mind is a blank and at such times it is better to leave off for a while. Actually I was thinking of taking a walk by the river but this is better, unless you would care to accompany me. I'm afraid my quarters are not the most salubrious though much of this is my own fault as I forbid my landlady to tidy anything."

"I just wanted to tell you how excellent I think 'Venus and Adonis' is," I said realising how inadequate the words were and adding lamely, "It was an impulse as I was passing."

"You still venture into the city then?"

"I bought a copy the last time I was here, from The White Greyhound."

"You paid six pence to have a copy," he said in surprise. "You must have a liking to read verse."

"I read whatever I can."

"And how do you think my verse compares to others of a similar nature?"

It was not said in vanity. He seemed to have a genuine desire to know my opinion, though I was not absolutely sure that he was not testing me also. But when I began to talk about Sidney and Spenser, Samuel

Daniel, Peele and Lyly, Petrarch and the Italian poets, he listened avidly and our enthusiasms coalesced. "Do you read Latin?" he asked as we talked of Ovid and Plato, Virgil and Horace, of rhetoric and irony, metre and metaphor.

"Adequately. But I know hardly any Greek."

"Me too," he sighed. "I'm not a University man. But fortunately there are so many translations now."

Our thoughts ran together, keeping pace. We understood without explanation, presumed without pretension, completely in tune with each other. Time left us behind as we talked.

"I'm sorry to have taken up so much of your time," I said at last, at a loss to know how long we had been talking but dimly recollecting how often the many church bells had chimed.

"I am the one to apologise, talking so long about my work like a schoolboy with his first composition. But you surprised me, Mistress Lanier. I haven't met many women like you."

And I haven't met many men with whom I can share such a rapport, I thought to myself and wondered if we would have the opportunity to meet again, though aloud I murmured, "I have cheated you of your walk."

"Not at all, I will accompany you to the wharf."

As we walked to Old Swan stairs he said, "I am writing another verse narrative," and I felt I had been the recipient of a confidence. But I did not feel I should presume by asking the subject and instead I said, "Then I await its publication. Does this mean however that you have finished with the theatre?"

"Oh no, not at all," he replied vehemently. "The theatre is my first love. I can't wait for the plague to end and the playhouses to re-open."

My response was heartfelt. "Amen to that."

But it was a long time before that was to happen. Before it did I had bought a copy of William Shakespeare's 'The Rape of Lucrece' which was an even greater success than his first composition, selling out almost immediately. Once again it was dedicated to the young Earl of Southampton.

Then in the winter the plague at last began to wear itself out leaving in its wake a total of 15,000 dead. The Queen and Court were going to hold the Christmas festivities back at Whitehall and the Players would entertain them. Lord Hunsdon as Lord Chamberlain would be in charge of the entertainment which was to include Lord Strange's Men, and Alfonso would be part of the Queen's Musick. It seemed highly unlikely that I would be there and I contemplated sadly how in a year my life had changed more drastically than I had thought possible.

Chapter 8

MADRIGAL

When it became certain that the plague had definitely reached its conclusion and life began its slow return to normal, I turned my attention to a most pressing matter. "We must start to look for a house of our own," I said to Alfonso.

"What about your property in Bishopsgate?" he asked. "We could live there, or there is my father's house in Blackheath."

"My house is still under lease and Blackheath is too far out of the city," I retorted. I would definitely not go back to my old house in Bishopsgate which I believed I had left for good. It was far too modest for my needs and besides I did not relish the thought of my former neighbours finding diversion in my return to a life I thought I had left behind, even though I was now respectably married and proud of my thriving child. Neither had I any intention of being further away from the city at Blackheath than I was at Chelsea. "I want to live in Westminster," I stated firmly.

"Westminster! Why Westminster? There are only two sorts of properties in Westminster - poor slums and grand houses. I don't want the first and we can't afford the second."

"I'm sure we could find somewhere," I persisted, having given the matter much thought. The number of grand houses with important inhabitants was one of the reasons I was attracted to the area. It had its own palace and was not far from Whitehall, there was the great abbey church with its important school and the chance of making prestigious encounters was high, an important factor if one wanted to get on in the world. The merchants and tradesmen of Bishopsgate were of no use, especially those in the Liberties outside the walls. Besides I wanted to see some investment in a decent property before Alfonso spent all the money he had received from Lord Hunsdon, slipping away alarmingly fast. "It would be very convenient for you," I continued persuasively. "Not far from your family house here in Chelsea but near to Whitehall and with easy access to the Thames for Greenwich and Hampton Court and all the palaces where you perform. Much more convenient for you than being stuck in Bishopsgate without, or Blackheath."

I could see he was struck by the truth of this but I knew he preferred the freedom of his peripatetic life rather than the responsibilities of a householder and he continued to resist saying, "I can always lodge in the city when I am playing, as my father does."

I was riled by his selfishness and retorted sharply, "Hardly fair if you wish us to have a family," at which he shrugged his shoulders. I knew I would have to work hard to persuade him and continued to broach the subject continuously until he tired of my persistence.

"We'll think about it when the Yuletide festivities are done," he temporised at last.

There was always a lull after Twelfth Night before the next round of ceremonies began in late February.

Perhaps because he felt guilty about his lack of co-operation he surprised me by acquiring an invitation for me to the performance of 'The Siege of London' by a combination of the Earl of Pembroke's and Lord Strange's players at Whitehall during one of the twelve days of Christmas. I had learnt to be wary of his manoeuvres and suspected it was a ploy to divert my attention for a time but I was not one to turn down an opportunity in order to spite him. I was excited but also a little nervous at the thought of entering Whitehall again and perhaps encountering previous acquaintances, so with defiant bravado I chose a low-necked closed gown of red embossed satin with sleeves of white and gold brocade. To my disappointment however I was in no position to see and be seen in the immense crush, as being only a musician's wife I was relegated to a bench at the back of the Great Hall. I caught a glimpse of Lord Hunsdon and thought involuntarily how I used to sit beside him in a chair near the dais. I also thought of our child at home and how his father had made no attempt to enquire about him.

However as usual I enjoyed the play which was particularly symbolic since London had been under siege by the plague for so long. I also noted with pleasure that William Shakespeare was part of the cast of actors as he had hoped and knew he would be as happy as I was that the players were back in business. The music was excellent as always and when Alfonso was at last in a position to join me I deliberately flaunted my husband's youth and good looks as I was aware of curious glances directed at us. He was undoubtedly handsome and debonair in his crimson livery but good looks alone would not gain him favour. If I wished to be part of Court life again then I would have to push him into advancing his career in some way.

One move towards that aim was to purchase a suitable house where we could entertain worthily and I finally wore down his objections. We celebrated

Henry's first birthday in our own home in Westminster at the Long Ditch. In times long past this had been a stream dividing the village from the countryside and making Westminster almost an island, but was now a road converging into Kings Street which in turn led to the broad paved Strand where all the great houses of the nobles stood. Beside us was the parish church of Saint Margaret while to the north was the old palace of St. James with the park beyond. The house, like its neighbours on either side, was built of stone with a roof of pantiles and stood on the main thoroughfare away from the many squalid dwellings which crowded the narrow alleyways or jumbled around the square. The row of three had a covered passageway to one side leading to a paved courtyard in which were the stables and a shared guardarobe, and each house had its own garden and orchard. It was a much bigger house than the one in Bishopsgate with a larder and buttery as well as the kitchen on the ground floor, a dining room and two parlours on the first floor, the larger having walls painted in blue and green, four bedchambers on the second and attics under the eaves.

"We can't afford it," Alfonso had said stubbornly when I enthused about its perfection.

But I was determined to have the house and worked to persuade him. "I'll sell the properties that my mother had in rent, I'll get a lawyer to see to it. And I still have the hundred pounds my father left to me entrusted to Uncle Alvise till my marriage so that will furnish it adequately." I also had the collection of valuables in the three chests I had brought from my apartments in Whitehall - plate and table linen, candlesticks, glass, mirrors and pictures. Even so Alfonso complained that the purchase of tables, chairs and beds made a hole in the money he had been given. We also had to employ three maidservants and take advantage of the occasional labour offered by a poor local man to see to the garden and clean the stables because although we had no horses there would be visitors who had. But I was highly satisfied, not least because I saw it as a wise investment of Lord Hunsdon's money which was being squandered.

"I am only a musician, Aemilia, not a lord as you have been accustomed to," Alfonso complained.

"If we have a fine house we can make important contacts. They could put you in the way of patronage or at least arrange private recitals in their homes. And why don't you try to compose some music, I've heard you often making up tunes when you are practicing," I suggested coaxingly.

Alfonso was a very talented musician but he was lazy. For himself he had no ambition and when his scheduled engagements and practice hours were done he was content to carouse and game with his companions, strutting around in his finery and relishing the admiring glances of both sexes. I realised I would have to do much of the planning. But for the moment I was happy in the illusion that I was once again enjoying the life of a fine lady. And with the close proximity of Westminster pier I was able to take a barge upriver with easy convenience.

By Easter The Curtain, The Theatre, and The Rose, were all open for business again. So too were the several city inns licensed for performances. Being within the city itself these were more stringently controlled than the playhouses in the liberties, and a condition of use was that the acting companies had to give a proportion of their revenue to the poor of the parish and they were not allowed to have performances on Sundays. However being within the city they were more accessible for many people and consequently always full to capacity. I had seen a playbill stuck on a post advertising 'The Taming of the Shrew, a new play by William Shakespeare' to be performed by Lord Strange's Men at The Cross Keys. This didn't sound like a history play so I was eager to see what he had produced for his latest offering. Now that we had three maidservants there was no difficulty in leaving Henry to their care and I was no longer concerned about attending performances alone. I was now a married woman though the aura of respectability was undermined somewhat by the fact that musicians, especially foreigners, were never considered entirely reputable in the equivocal position they shared with actors and artists. Added to this most people associated with the playhouses were aware of my past history. I arrived early enough to secure a seat in the first gallery of the inn facing the stage - a construction of strong planks erected in the middle of the courtyard with a painted cloth behind to divide the acting area from a curtained recess that was the tiring room. The fine day with intermittent sunshine and a light breeze trying to disperse the few greyish clouds was ideal for an outdoor performance and was drawing large crowds. There was a continuous flow of people pushing past the gatherers at the entrance until the yard was packed with people standing so close as to inhabit movement, and the noise, laughter, argument and profanation rose upward borne on a stinking wave of unwashed bodies, strong ale, horse sweat and manure. The spectators in the galleries were of a better class and well dressed though still noisy and exuberant, often flushed with wine for the tap room was doing a thriving trade, and enveloped in a fog of tobacco smoke. Occupying the seat next to mine was a middle-aged man with a short corpulent body bursting from the belly-piece of his flame coloured doublet, his red face partially obscured by bushy whiskers, white like the shock of hair protruding from his yellow pancake hat. Mellowed by the ale he had obviously consumed and with his clay pipe in his hand he struck up a conversation, leaning towards me familiarly and hesitating about putting his hand on my knee. I was about to speak sharply to him when my attention was suddenly caught by what he was saying. "What are they going to do now that they have lost their patron?" he asked, nodding towards the stage.

"Lost their patron? Lord Strange? Or should I say Lord Derby? How mean you sir," I replied in surprise. "Has he withdrawn from their patronage now that he has succeeded to the Earldom?"

A year earlier Ferdinando Stanley had taken over the Earldom of Derby on the death of his father and gone to take up residence at the family estate in Lancashire, though his company of players had continued to be called Lord Strange's Men. I found the man's words puzzling for I couldn't believe Ferdinando would suddenly abandon his company after his long-standing support of the theatre.

"Haven't you heard that he's been murdered?" revealed my companion, not without some relish.

I was so startled that my head was reeling with the shock as if I had received a physical blow. I couldn't believe that anyone would want to kill the handsome, popular, generous nobleman with his wit and his courtesy and his great love of the arts.

"They say he's been poisoned." The fat man shook his head in bewilderment, though it was obvious he was enjoying telling the tale. "It's like one of the plays in his own company." He smiled at the analogy which he had obviously overheard and as I didn't react he continued, "He has no sons to inherit and the title will go to his brother so perhaps he will take over the players in his stead, or who knows what will happen to them."

The sounding of the trumpets put an end to further talk but as the musicians began their fanfare, seated in one of the inn's window embrasures directly above the stage, I was still deeply shocked. Hardly a year since the tragic death of Christopher Marlowe was another unexpected, unexplained, death, equally threatening to London's theatrical life. What would happen to Lord Strange's company now? Perhaps they might have to disband as other companies had done before them. Will Shakespeare would no doubt find employment elsewhere as a budding playwright but the actors had been on their way to becoming the best troupe of players in London.

The spectators had now fallen silent, awaiting the appearance of the prologue. However instead of the expected black-cloaked figure they were accosted by a vociferous drunk, an irate landlady and an argument in an inn. The surprised audience were amused to find that the stage and the inn, the spectators and the actors, had merged into one. The play continued to delight the enthusiastic audience, not least with the exuberant performance of Dick Burbage as the hero. Shakespeare, unusually, was playing a comic role as one of the suitors of the gentle sister and in one instance, being forced into teaching the shrew Katherine to play the lute, he made an appearance with his head stuck through the middle of the offending instrument. The audience roared with laughter and I was laughing heartily myself, leaning over the gallery rail, when he looked up and saw me and our eyes met, communicating briefly before he returned to his role in the play.

There was enthusiastic applause for the play and the players as they took their final bow but I was left with a feeling of unease. The girls' father, an unsympathetic character, bore my father's name, and the hero Petruchio, a jaunty braggart, although attracted to Katherine had ostensibly married her because of the money he was being paid to do so. I lingered until nearly all the groundlings had left the courtyard though the tap room was still full and seeing Ellen's betrothed, Alfonso Ferrabosco who had been one of the musicians, I went downstairs and made excuse to talk with him. The players, dressed now in their own clothing, were helping the carpenter and the book-keeper to strike the stage and William Shakespeare saw me. Coming to the edge of the dais he saluted my brother-in-law then turning to me asked, "How did you like the play?"

I shrugged. "Some of the matter I didn't care for. I didn't like the ending."

He looked momentarily taken aback then his expression changed to one of amusement. "I like your honesty, Mistress Lanier. Would you come back to my lodging and perhaps we can talk for a while. I shouldn't be too long here but we must check that all the costumes and properties are safely stored away because tomorrow is a different play, 'The Blacksmith's Daughter'. Look, I'll give you the key, you can let yourself in and wait there for me." He was already fumbling in the leather pouch on his belt and handed it to me. There was no guile in his proposition so I took it and made the short journey further down Gracechurch Street. I let myself in without being seen and made my way up the twisting staircase to his attic room, thinking again how improper it was. However I took the opportunity to pry a little and took up his books - Ovid's Metamorphoses, Chapman's translation of the Iliad, Holinshed's Chronicles, Plutarch's lives of the ancients, Spenser, Marlowe, Samuel Daniel. Then I couldn't help looking at what he was writing, sheets of paper in his sprawling hand with few corrections. Suddenly I heard his feet running lightly up the stairs and put them down hurriedly just as he reached the door.

"First things first," he said, picking up a jar of ale and filling the tankard on his table he quaffed it greedily then refilled it. "The first thing we do after a performance is slake our thirst in the inn, sometimes too much so," he laughed. "I would have asked you to join us and you could have met my friends but I thought we could talk better here." He looked around for another tankard, inspected it in dismay, searched for something to wipe it with, then finding nothing suitable poured some ale into it, swished it around, poured it onto the floor then refilled it and handed it to me. "Sorry about the dust, it might improve the taste."

I laughed out loud and after wiping the chair with my glove I sat down facing him and drank the dusty ale companionably.

"What didn't you like about the play?" he prompted me when he had finished his second tankard.

I felt embarrassed then and murmured, "I was too hasty. It was very amusing, some wonderfully inventive characters and some very beautiful verse." Then I had to be honest and say what was in my mind. "But I didn't like the way Katherine was bullied into obeying her husband. I don't think women should necessarily be subservient to men."

He studied me intently. "Not even when they love each other?"

"All the more reason to respect their equality I would think."

He looked surprised, as if he had not considered the possibility before. His face was open, a pleasant face if not handsome, his brown eyes steady and thoughtful.

Then he smiled. "It was all a fantasy anway. Christopher Sly's fantasy, nothing but a dream. A dream of what men wish women to be."

"Do you?" I countered. "Do you want women to be meek and subservient?"

"No Aemilia." It was the first time he had used my name. "I like women to be intelligent and spirited." Again he looked surprised by the realisation. "And beautiful of course," he added, in a lighter tone. I flushed under his scrutiny then he continued, "But the play was an old one that I rewrote and there is only so much you can do with a reworking. My next play will be more completely mine I promise you, and I will create a heroine more to your taste."

We were completely at ease with each other as we had been on the previous occasion so I took the opportunity to ask about the other matter pressing on my mind. "What will happen to your company now that Ferdinando Stanley is dead? And do you know anything else of the circumstances, seeing that he was your patron?"

"Some talk of poison, some of witchcraft. You know of the regular Papist plots against the Queen. Well it seems some conspirators wished to embroil Ferdinando in one such, Lancashire is a hotbed of Catholic unrest. He chose instead to reveal the information to the Privy Council and in due course the perpetrators were arrested and executed. But it would seem that much rancour was unleashed towards Ferdinando and his death might well be an act of vengeance."

"It's all very tragic. I knew him and I liked him well," I said feelingly. "It would serve as a good plot for a play, Will," his name came out naturally.

"Perhaps a little too sensitive. I doubt the Master of the Revels would licence such. And I have no wish to go the same way as Marlowe. At the moment my mind is tuned towards comedy. The plague is past and my fortunes are shaping themselves. As to your query of what is to happen to our company, well our fortunes are on the rise there also. Our new patron is to be none other than Lord Hunsdon. In future we are to be known as the Lord Chamberlain's Men."

"Lord Hunsdon has agreed to be your patron?"

"Does that not show how highly thought of we are. The best company of players in London and now given Court approval."

A sliver of disappointment pierced my heart in the midst of my joy at the news. I was impressed by Lord Hunsdon's generosity and thought longingly of how I might have benefitted if I were still his mistress. I would have intimate contact with all the players, they would often perform at Court now, and no doubt he would take a personal interest in the company that I could have shared. I rose from my chair and turned my back on him for a moment so that he couldn't see my emotion but I wondered how much he sensed my feelings for he was familiar with my history.

"I'm very glad for you," I said at last, turning around and forcing myself to smile. "None of your admirers would want the company to disband."

He changed the subject deftly. "I have an idea for a new play that I got from a Portuguese romance, in translation of course. But there is also a lot of potential matter in Italian sources. I know a little Italian. I did some secretarial work for the Earl of Southampton last summer and came into contact with John Florio who was one of the Earl's language tutors."

"Yes I know of Florio, he's helped many poets with Italian."

"He's in the process of compiling an Italian dictionary which will be very useful. But perhaps you might be willing to help me with some individual things," he said hesitantly, the steady gaze of his brown eyes inviting me to continue our association.

I felt as if the warmth flooding my heart was suffusing my cheeks as I replied eagerly, "I also know some Italian romances that have never been translated into English and could well serve as ideas for plays, ideas no-one else has used." The thought of being able to share my knowledge with this budding playwright, highly intelligent and well versed in the arts, was exciting and would provide me with a project dear to my heart. But deep in my heart lurked a greater joy that I was unable to define with safety.

"That sounds promising," he said enthusiastically. "So I take it we shall meet again, Aemilia Lanier. And no ill feelings about my 'Taming of the Shrew'? Some man's fantasy that is all." He shrugged then after a pause said deliberately, "My wife can certainly be a shrew at times."

A cold water shower drenched me, extinguishing the fire which had crept into my heart. I desperately hoped he hadn't seen me flinch and said as calmly as I could, "You have a wife? Here in London?"

His gaze was level. "No in Stratford. I left her behind with three children."

I wanted desperately to ask more but I didn't dare. If he wanted me to know more I intuited he would tell me but he remained silent. Our close rapport had been broken and I took my leave.

I had time to think and consider on the journey back to Westminster. It should not matter to me that Will Shakespeare had a wife because he had only asked for my help with his work. He was becoming a friend with whom I liked to talk about literature and the theatre, to some extent as I used to do with Lord Hunsdon except that he was a poet, playwright and actor with more immediate experience. That was all it was, a meeting of minds, a union of intellect. It was obviously so from his point of view because he had gone out of his way to let me know he had a wife while at the same time wanting our association to continue. The fact that he was married was irrelevant for I was married too with a child, it had just never crossed my mind because he was young and lived alone in lodgings.

Yet the information had unsettled my perception of him. I admired his talent as an actor and a writer but I had also judged him to be honest, seeing in his direct appraising eyes the windows of the soul. But now in reality I wondered what kind of man he was to abandon a wife and three young children. I was confused, not least by my own feelings. Despite my denial I understood that my attraction to him was more than intellectual and almost from the beginning there had been a rapport between us, a meeting of minds that I had never experienced with anyone else. Although my desires were set on wealth and status and the cultivation of rich handsome nobles I was drawn like a lodestone to a leather-jerkined travelling player in whose dusty attic room I felt as happy as any place on earth. And the fact that he might not feel the same about me sent a pain through my heart. I had believed I knew what I wanted from life but perhaps I didn't after all. I was jolted with a sudden shock, like riding smoothly in a carriage which suddenly misjudges the edge of the road and rocks lopsidedly off its course.

CHAPTER 9

CANZONE

It was a cold rainy summer. Harvests were bad again, as they had been for several years running, and basic foods were becoming scarce and expensive. Alfonso was constantly complaining about the cost of running our household. And in the theatrical world players and theatre managers were feeling the pinch as many performances in the open-air playhouses and inn yards had to be cancelled because of the weather and the boatmen also lost much of their revenue when there were no entertainments on Bankside. However the weather was good enough for the first performance of Will Shakespeare's new play at The Rose. It was mercifully dry but there was a chill wind rising from the damp ground and I had taken the precaution of wearing my black velvet hooded cloak as I joined the queue for the ferries across to the South Bank. Even though there were more than a thousand boats of one kind or another playing the Thames there were always queues on theatre days. I also wore a black velvet mask for on this particular day I did not want to be recognised.

The lure of a new play and the scarcity of performances over-rode the cool temperatures and the threat of an intermittent shower to guarantee a huge crowd pushing their way along Bankside and into the polygonal building whose flag was flying triumphantly aloft. The standing area in front of the stage was already packed with the groundlings and the three rows of galleries which curved around the stage were also full. I had taken a seat on the end of the first bench in the second gallery, not with the best view of the stage but carefully chosen so that I could see what I wanted, and just before the commencement of the performance I was rewarded. Lord Hunsdon, in a red velvet fur-trimmed mantle and a black hat with brooches, arrived with an entourage and took his seat in a specially curtained area on the other side, one of the so-called 'Gentlemen's rooms.' The patron of the newly named Lord Chamberlain's Men had graced the first performance of a new play with his presence. I had expected no less. I wanted to watch him without being seen but soon 'The Two Gentlemen of Verona' claimed my full interest. Despite both Richard Burbage and Edward Alleyn playing the two heroes, the main attraction was a dog which the comedian Will Kemp unsuccessfully tried to keep under control while the audience laughed uproariously. At the end the applause was deafening and the Lord Chamberlain's Men knew that they had a success. Their new patron also received the cheers of the crowd and turning to acknowledge the galleries his eyes rested on me for a moment. I knew that he realised who I was but he gave no salute and I could not complain, having wanted to remain incognito. But the sight of him, as always, disturbed me and I thought involuntarily of the child I had left at home with the maids, growing handsome and strong, walking now and amusing me with his attempts at speech.

Lord Hunsdon made his way towards the players and I could see him talking to the author. I had now got into the habit of going to Gracechurch Street to wait for Will after a performance at The Curtain or The Theatre or at one of the city inns. But Bishopsgate was too far from Bankside so I made my way to The Angel, a tavern near to The Rose which the players frequented. None of the many taverns on Bankside were particularly salubrious and the taproom was teeming with a wide assortment of the lower classes who had been watching the play, so I asked for a private room upstairs for an hour and left a message for Will. I knew he would be some time for people would want to talk to him, and he would probably slake his thirst with his fellow players who would all be exhilarated by their success. But he burst into the room sooner than I had expected and his excitement was tangible.

"Ah, the dark lady," he laughed.

"You're quicker than I expected."

"We're playing the same again tomorrow which means we didn't have to clear the tiring room or the properties store."

"I don't expect you to leave your friends for me. No doubt you have a lot to talk about."

"I shall go back to them soon enough but first I want to talk to you. What did you think of the play?"

"Excellently done. There is no doubt that everyone considered it a great success and you certainly impressed your new patron. However…," I paused and he waited questioningly. "Don't you think the title is wrong?" He looked perplexed and I said innocently, "Don't you think it should more correctly be called 'The Gentleman of Verona'?"

"How so?"

"Well only Valentine is a gentleman. Proteus certainly isn't. He most definitely wouldn't win my heart after the way he behaved."

He roared with laughter. "'Sblood, Aemilia, one day I will write a play that pleases you. You really are a stern critic."

I laughed too and said enthusiastically, "I liked the dog. How did you know he was going to behave?"

"He didn't did he? But I wanted to create something special for Will Kemp because he's such a skilful comedian. It's a great advantage being part of a regular company because I can write parts that are tailor-made for the actors. Though Kemp often drives me crazy, he likes to improvise and sometimes his performance bears little resemblance to my carefully scripted lines. Lord Hunsdon was greatly taken with the play though and wants us to perform it for the Queen at the Christmas revels at Greenwich palace. God knows what will happen to the dog there. He'll probably piss before Her Most Gracious Majesty."

We laughed together and I said, "I liked the idea of Julia disguising herself as a boy. I know of a similar instance in an Italian romance called 'Gli Inganni', the deceivers. If I remember rightly it tells the story of a girl shipwrecked in a strange place and for safety's sake she takes on the part of a boy and enrols in the service of the Duke. She then falls in love with him but meanwhile the Countess whom the Duke loves falls in love with her, believing her to be a man. Does that sound too confusing?"

"Sounds like something I could work on, you must tell me more. Listen, we have another day at The Rose then we move to The Curtain for four days with 'The Honest Man's Revenge' and 'All is True', then we are at The Cross Keys with Marlowe's 'Jew of Malta.' I don't have much time this afternoon but perhaps you could come to Gracechurch Street on one of those days."

"Does that make Sunday for the 'Jew'?"

"No, Monday. We can't perform on Sundays in the City."

"No of course not. I'll try to come but I'm not supposed to frequent the playhouses more than once a week." We made our farewells then I said, "I think I shall have to borrow your idea and disguise myself as a boy then I could pass myself off as a player."

"You would really like that wouldn't you!"

"I can't see why women can't be players. They are allowed in Italy. My father once saw Francesco Andreini *and* his wife Isabella perform in Venice. I don't acknowledge that theatre and poetry should be men's exclusive domains."

"You are unlike any woman I've ever met, Aemilia." He kissed me on the lips, only briefly but it was the first time he had ever done so and although I felt the urge to return his kiss I resisted and bade him farewell as calmly as I could.

Alfonso was in a complaining mood when I arrived home. "You're never away from the playhouses, Aemilia."

He had arrived home drunk after a rehearsal in a room at one of the city taverns. The Queen was away on her summer progress, this year to Oxford shire and the University, and her musicians were using the time to practice and put together new programmes for the winter. He had an easy-going nature and didn't usually enquire into my activities so I guessed by his peevishness he had been gambling and lost money. He was rarely a successful punter, partly because he usually gamed when he had had too much to drink and partly because he lacked the cunning to recognise cheating.

"Better the playhouses than your usual haunts, taverns and stews."

"Why do I need the stews when I have a whore at home," he retorted, pulling me towards him and trying to free my breasts from the low-necked gown. "Come to bed with me."

"I have to see to Henry," I said, disentangling myself from his clutches.

"That didn't worry you when you went off to the playhouse," he slurred, attempting to undo the laces of my bodice. "You're my wife Aemilia Lanier, so the least you owe me are my marital rights."

"I don't like making love to someone who is drunk."

"I'll show you whether I'm drunk or not."

Alfonso was stronger than he looked and I knew I might as well placate him surmising the outcome, which was as I expected. "I said you were too drunk," I cried triumphantly.

"I can't make love to you not because I'm drunk but because you're too cold towards me. You don't want to have any more children do you, it would clip your wings too much."

It was true. At the moment I didn't want any more children but I knew it was the ale talking so I placated him and left him sleeping. He looked young and vulnerable and for a moment I felt guilty. But he had taken the money and I considered I did as well by him as he did by me, he wasn't faithful but I didn't mind because it salved my own conscience. Generally we fared well enough together and didn't usually enquire into each other's activities during the considerable time we spent apart.

The following Monday I was in the first gallery at The Cross Keys Inn watching yet again Marlowe's 'Jew of Malta' being performed before a raucous audience. Food shortages in the city and high prices always resulted in renewed antagonism towards London's large population of foreign immigrants and the groundlings, mainly the working classes, roughly garbed and noisily vulgar, were once again taking advantage of the play to vent their feelings against foreigners. To do so openly in the streets would be to risk the intervention of the city authorities so this was a safe option, though all plays that encouraged public unrest were frowned upon.

Two hours later I was in Will Shakespeare's attic room waiting for him to appear. When he burst in, his doublet still unbuttoned, it was with an air of excitement that I recognised immediately - the sense of exhilaration when one of his own plays had been performed successfully. Today however he had only been an actor though that was enough to release the outburst of tension that a player's life created, performing a repertory of several dozen plays, changing them almost daily so the strain of remembering lines was considerable, often taking more than one role in a play with quick changes of costume, and having minimal rehearsal time as they rehearsed in the morning and performed in the afternoon.

"What's the good news?" I asked immediately.

"You can read my mind, Aemilia," he said. "But I have indeed received good news. I am to become a sharer in the company. I shall no longer be just a hired man but a permanent member with an interest in the company."

Through my close association with the playhouses I understood the significance. Each theatre company had a membership of about ten or a dozen actors with three or four apprentice boys to play the girls' roles and learn the craft until their voices broke, together with a carpenter, a tireman and a book-keeper who had sole charge of the only complete script and supervised rehearsals. Some of the actors, like Augustine Phillips, could play musical instruments but professional musicians were hired when necessary plus temporary hired actors for large casts. The sharers were a select number of the company who were responsible for the organisation - choice of plays, venues, expenditure, hiring of people, setting the rules.

"Not just an actor's wage now, Aemilia, and a five pound fee for a play, but a share in the profits (or losses if the worse comes to the worst) and most importantly a regular occupation, no longer at the mercy of an employer's whim." I flung my arms around him impulsively, my congratulations adding to his exuberance. "I am a true man of the theatre now. Ever since I joined the Queen's Men when they visited Stratford in '87 I have been plagued by the thought that my employment might not last and I would have to return to be a schoolmaster or a secretary. Now I am a permanent member of the best company of players in London."

There was so much I wanted to ask him but my arms were still around him and he was holding me tight. Then he was kissing me passionately and I was returning his kisses with fervour, drawing his breath into me, the pangs clawing at my loins equating with the hunger in my soul. "I love you, Will," I cried, unable to stop myself. The words came out without hesitation, even though it was the first time in my life that I had ever spoken them.

He sobered suddenly, stopping his kisses and dropping his arms from around me. "I have a wife in Stratford," he said with an effort.

I touched him tentatively as I whispered, "I have a husband in Westminster."

We were looking intensely at each other and I could see the pain cross his face. "I haven't been completely faithful while I've been away but they were casual encounters, taken up and forgotten immediately. This is different, you know that don't you? We mustn't go any further," he said. "Exhilaration at my news has carried me away, made me behave dishonourably."

"No, no," I was pulling him towards me, "don't deny our love, don't cast it away. I love you, Will, and that is the first time I have ever said that to a man in all my life. You love me too don't you, I know it." I was tugging at his doublet and when the sleeves wouldn't come I put my hands inside his shirt, feeling his back hot under my hands. "Make love to me, I need you, I want you and I know you want me." I was pulling him towards the bed but he was making no resistance, except to fling off his doublet.

I pulled his shirt, damp with sweat, over his head and he let me do it, his breath coming in quick gasps. Then I turned for him to unlace my bodice and then the corset, finding him surprisingly deft.

"I often have to help the apprentice boys make quick changes," he said in explanation.

He smiled ruefully and I laughed and suddenly the mood lightened. In a moment all tension had disappeared and we relaxed, feeling at ease with each other as we always had. We were certain now that this was what we both wanted, that this was the natural extension of our closeness. From the beginning we had been one in mind and soul and now there was a deep need to be one in body. The bed was small and hard with the coarse linen sheets unyielding beneath us, the room musty and airless, the pungent smell of our sweat stung our nostrils. But for the first time in my life the act of love was more than physical satisfaction as I gave myself wholly to a man I loved, witholding neither heart, mind nor body in complete and perfect union. It was for me a unique sensation. I had experienced more physical excitement in past encounters but never before this complete renunciation of self into the total absorption of a man I loved with every particle of my being. Will seemed as dazed as I was and afterwards we didn't speak but lay silently in each other's arms for a long time. There was nothing to be said. He was stroking my hair which fell freely over my shoulders and finally he murmured, "I've never see you with your hair loose before. You are so beautiful. Unique. I love you because you are different to other women."

For the first time in my life I felt that beauty only mattered in his opinion, and wealth was inconsequential. This was real wealth - richness of love, richness of being. I knew that I shouldn't break the mood but there was a question I needed to ask even though it might be unwise. "What is your wife like?"

I didn't think he was going to reply. Then he said slowly, almost unwillingly, "Older than I am. A countrywoman who can just read with difficulty but can't write. A Puritan who doesn't care for the theatre. But she is honest, well thought of in Stratford and does well by the children." At my silence and look of enquiry he continued, "Susannah is twelve, intelligent, strong in body and character. Hamnet is ten and his health is poor. His twin Judith is.............is somewhat slow, with difficult moods. Ann has much to do looking after them while I live a life that pleases me here."

I caught the bitterness in his tone and the fleeting shadow of self-disgust that crossed his face and regretted my intrusion into our content. But I had needed to know something of his other life. I kissed him gently, saying, "You must have married young."

"Eighteen. Before I knew what I wanted from life. By misfortune I got a woman with child."

I wasn't going to press any further but he went on, as if he wished now to purge his thoughts, "I was always fascinated with the players, went to all their performances whenever they came to Stratford, knew all the plays. Then in '87 the Queen's Players arrived short of one of their actors who had just been killed in a brawl.

I knew the part and volunteered to step in. They offered me a place in the company and I seized the opportunity. I came to London with them, leaving behind my wife and three children under five years of age. Isn't that the behaviour of a gentleman? Something for a man to be proud of? What do you think of me now?" His bitterness had returned though he continued to hold me close as if he were clutching a lifeline.

"I love you utterly and completely. And I believe your place is here where you give so much delight to so many people as an actor, a playwright, a poet, not in a country town as a schoolmaster or a secretary as you said. You have to follow your destiny even if it brings sadness and sacrifice in its wake. You cannot be held responsible all your life for one mistake you made when you were very young, when in your heart you know you are destined for something more." I held him tight, feeling closer to him than ever.

He didn't respond at first then he said, "Thankyou for understanding me. I really am selfish you know, I think of little but my work and the satisfaction it gives me."

"We are all selfish, it is human nature, the only way to survive."

He never asked about Alfonso but I supposed he knew. I had first met Will when I was Lord Hunsdon's mistress and those in his circle would be well aware of why I was suddenly dismissed into a hasty marriage. He was also acquainted with all the Court musicians including the Bassanos, Johnsons, Laniers and the Ferraboscos, all who played at times for the Lord Chamberlain's Men. But I would have liked him to have asked about my past life so that I could have explained how unique was my love for him and I was not playing the whore again. "You know I love you Will, completely and unreservedly with every part of my being," I spoke my thoughts aloud and hoped he would understand what I meant.

He replied, "My love for you has taken me completely by surprise, unexpected, unlooked for. I have never met a woman like you before. But where can it end?"

"Don't think about the future," I implored, knowing that I didn't want to look beyond the present. "We love each other and we have each other now, no matter what fate has in store for us, and that is all that matters isn't it?"

We lay for a long time together. We didn't make love again because we had given everything and there was no more to give yet. Will's attic room had become my world and I thought of a poem by a young man who often frequented the playhouses and circulated verses among his acquaintances, a dashing handsome gallant always flamboyantly dressed. Will and I had read some of his poems together and I quoted now:

> "Love.....makes one little room an everywhere,
> Let sea-discoverers to new worlds have gone,
> Let maps to other worlds on worlds have shown,
> Let us possess one world, each hath one and is one."

"John Donne has voiced it feelingly," Will acknowledged the other poet. "I wish I had written that for us."

When I left him I didn't remember anything of the journey home, I think I walked on air.

Being Will's lover transformed my life that miserable wet summer when the city streets swam in refuse, huge puddles disguised potholes from the unwary, carriages and carts splashed mud indiscriminately, and in the drenched fields and gardens the grass was a spongy morass while the leaves dripped listlessly from the wan trees. I was surrounded by an aura of invincibility, nothing could touch me, disturb me, anger me. I showered my little son with love, I bent to Alfonso's every whim, I smiled on neighbours and kin, nourished by the great love growing within me and spreading its radiance like Midas's touch on whatever I lighted upon. The greyest day was bright with promise, the chilliest wind fanned the warmth in my heart, the debilitating rain only refreshed the joy of being.

We didn't always make love. We talked as much as we had always done, we read together, often discussing what we had read, I translated Italian for him and he liked to hear me play music. One day he said, "I've written a poem about you, Aemilia," and taking a sheet of paper from the confusion on the table he began to read.

> *"My mistress' eyes are nothing like the sun;*
> *Coral is far more red than her lips' red;*
> *If snow be white, why then her breasts are dun;*
> *If hairs be wires, black wires grow on her head.*
> *I have seen roses damask'd red and white,*
> *But no such roses see I in her cheeks,*
> *And in some perfumes is there more delight*
> *Than in the breath that from my mistress reeks.*
> *I love to hear her speak, yet well I know*
> *That music hath a far more pleasing sound:*
> *I grant I never saw a goddess go;*
> *My mistress when she walks treads on the ground."*

I was silent for a while, disappointment and resentment battling in my breast. I had always wanted someone to write a poem about me and my lover was generally acknowledged to be a fine poet. I had expected something different. I doubted if any of Penelope Rich's admirers would have written thus. "Very amusing, Will. Very diverting," I said in a tight voice. I looked up and he was trying desperately not to laugh, his eyes sparkling with mischief.

"It's a jest, a parody on conventional courtly love poems. Surely you must see that, you with your knowledge of poesy. It's a complete antithesis of what poets usually write to their lovers. I thought you would appreciate the satire on Petrarchan sonnets, I'm disappointed in you."

I had not thought beyond the personal sentiments which I had expected to be flattering hyperboles like other poets wrote to ladies, but with a shock I realised that Will had, and he was more interested in demonstrating his poetic skill than writing about his love for me. He loved to play with words and his plays were full of such paradoxes.

But he was continuing, "Anyway, you must realise it's too short for a sonnet, it lacks a final rhyming couplet. Listen to the ending.

And yet, by heaven, I think my love as rare
As any she belie with false compare."

His face was serious now. "Besides being a deliberate parody it is also a sincere homage to you because you are different. You don't really want to be a conventional beauty and have a conventional ode composed for you in the style of Spenser or Daniel do you? Don't you want something different?"

I was still disappointed but I was forced to smile and had to concede that I had misjudged him.

"But if that does not please you, and I know you are mightily hard to please with my writing, perhaps this will serve." He began to recite this time without a paper.

> *"In the old age black was not counted fair,*
> *Only if it were, it bore not beauty's name;*
> *But now is black, beauty's successive heir,*
> *And beauty slander'd with a bastard shame:*
> *For since each hand hath put on nature's power,*
> *Fairing the foul with art's false borrow'd face,*
> *Sweet beauty hath no name, no holy bower,*
> *But is profan'd, if not lives in disgrace.*
> *Therefore my mistress' eyes are raven black,*
> *Her eyes so suited, and they mourners seem,*
> *At such who, not born fair, no beauty lack,*
> *Sland'ring creation with a false esteem.*
> *Yet so they mourn, becoming of their woe,*
> *That every tongue says beauty should look so."*

He waited, looking for my reaction.

"That's beautiful, Will."

"But still not entirely flattering, I fear you're thinking. I don't need to flatter you do I? I love you, you know my feelings. Anyway these poems are private, personal, not for publication, not for all men's eyes. You don't need to have your name on men's lips do you? We love each other, that's enough isn't it?"

"Yes, Will, that's enough."

He took me in his arms and we made love. Afterwards I lay beside him content. But later making my way home to Long Ditch I pondered, for the first time seriously, on where our love affair was going to lead. We both knew it could go no further than a secret assignation that we could share with no-one. Our two worlds were kept separate, his in the theatre and with his family in Stratford, mine at home in Westminster with my husband Alfonso Lanier and my child. I could never cross into his or he into mine. Penelope Rich had a lover, Charles Blount. It was now known openly that she had borne him two children, as well as the children she had with her husband the Earl of Warwick in whose house she continued to live. Such were the privileges of the nobility. Reactions to an affaire de coeur between an actor and a musician's wife would be quite different. I had to be content with the stolen hours I spent in Will's attic and the satisfaction I got from watching his plays and seeing him on stage, feeling a vicarious pride in the applause he received.

Will was writing prolifically and fast and it pleased me to think his love for me was inspiring him. I was aware that his new play was called 'Love's Labours Lost', and one day he greeted me, "Finished! And now I can tell you that I've written you into it. One of the characters is called Rosaline but I've created her with you in mind, she's a dark lady with an unusual beauty."

"No hidden subtleties?" I asked sceptically.

He put up his hands in surrender, "No satire, no parodies, I swear. A lady-in-waiting to the Princess and loved by one of the Lords. A lot of the men have real life antecedents too, it will be interesting to see how many are recognised."

"When can I see it? How soon will the company put it on?"

He hesitated. "I'm afraid you won't be able to see it yet. It's going to be a private performance at Titchfield, the Earl of Southampton's country house. In fact it was written for him and his friends."

I was disappointed and he said, "It will be put on at one of the playhouses soon enough."

Once again I realised the gulf between the life I had now and the one I had known with Lord Hunsdon. He might even be present at the private performance and I too used to have entree into this inner circle. Now I must wait with the rest of London's citizens for a public showing.

Will had already started writing another play, a history play again, this time about King Richard II. He had also shown interest in an Italian story I had told him about prospective suitors seeking a rich heiress as a wife by having to choose between three caskets and a set of riddles, as well as considering a subject with a Jew as protagonist, intending to better Marlowe. I was amazed at his energy, especially considering he was playing so many roles with the Lord Chamberlain's Men and rehearsing most mornings. The bad weather had curtailed their usual intensive summer schedules but this had meant an increase in private performances. Because Will had no wife to share his lodgings he was spared the necessity of looking after any of the apprentices as the married actors did, but he took his turn with teaching them verse speaking and stage fighting. And although rehearsals were usually conducted by the book-holder, if it was one of his own plays he liked to conduct the rehearsals himself. I considered my time with him to be extra precious.

Rarely did we meet publicly. An exception occurred when Alfonso surprised me by saying that I could accompany him to a musical evening at Lord Burghley's town house. It suited him to offer me these concessions occasionally and in his usual manner he made it sound as if he were granting me a huge favour, though I discovered later that Lady Mildred had made a point of asking him to include me.

"There will be various musical pieces which we are to play but Samuel Daniel is also to read some of his verse and the Lord Chamberlain's Men have been asked to perform some short scenes so you should find it diverting," he said.

I had often attended such evenings when I had been Lord Hunsdon's mistress. Then they had been part of the normal routine of my life and now I realised ruefully that this rare and unexpected event could beget in me such a flurry of excitement. I looked forward to meeting the Cecils again, Will would also be there and there was no knowing who else I might meet. On the appointed evening I dressed with care, choosing one of my finest gowns but not too gaudy, a glowing tawny satin with hanging sleeves, the stomacher and under sleeves of black velvet criss-crossed with gold braid. My maid bound my hair with matching gold braid in the Italian fashion. I knew I looked my best and the admiring glances I received served to confirm my self-satisfaction but it never occurred to Alfonso to flaunt his possession of me as Lord Hunsdon used to. As usual in company he took my presence for granted, seemingly oblivious to attention which had made Lord Hunsdon both proud and possessive, though I appreciated his professionalism in concentrating on his music. Apart from the fact that we slept together, an activity we both enjoyed on a detached physical level, our relationship remained very much as it had always been, as kin with a shared family background.

The years fled away as I found myself once again in the Cecils' great hall, oak panelled and decorated with pictures and tapestries, and I remembered my visit there with the Duchess of Suffolk and my first sight of the young Earl of Essex. This time there was no sign of him but the crookback Robert Cecil was immediately recognisable, his watchful eyes prominent in his long lugubrious face. Once again the guests were a mix of nobles, writers, scholars and dependants, all seemingly at ease and mingling freely with each other, Lord and Lady Burghley making all welcome. I talked with many people I had known at Court for as a respectable married matron I might be saluted safely. Then we were ushered onto our benches for the concert to begin.

I was interested to see Samuel Daniel, the new favourite Court poet, small and dapper with fair curling hair and small pointed beard, and hear him recite from 'The Complaint of Rosamund' and some of his sonnets. He had mastered perfectly the Italian 'dolce stil nuovo' and I only wished I could have caught Will's eye but the actors were preparing for their turn. They performed a scene from 'The Spanish Tragedy', Richard Burbage ranting to perfection as the mad Hieronimo, then a scene from Will's play 'The Comedy of Errors', the atmosphere magically transformed from horror to laughter by the actors' skills. When the concert was finished everyone retired to partake of the supper that had been spread out on trestle tables at the back of the hall, varied and plentiful but without any undue extravagance. To my surprise I found Lady Mildred at my elbow once again and I thought I detected a sparkle of mischief in the shrewd intelligent eyes set in her long equine face. "There is a beautiful set of virginals there, Aemilia. Why don't you try them out while people are eating, quite informally of course. I would like to hear you play again, I once heard you playing for the Queen."

It was well known that Lord Burghley's wife was one of those noblewomen who believed in the right of women to be equal with men in the intellectual and artistic field. There was a moment of complicity between us and I smiled. "I would love to try them, my lady."

I sat down at the instrument and touched it lovingly, caressing the keys and relishing their beauty of tone. I began to play some of Dowland's airs then a pavane composed by my cousin Antonio. I was aware that people were listening and that some came closer but I was completely enraptured by the perfection of the instrument and the way the music seemed to be released almost of its own accord. Only when I had finished and replaced the rosewood lid inlaid with ivory and mother-of-pearl did I realise people were applauding. But Lady Mildred was beside me and thanking me in a clear voice for indulging her, ensuring everyone knew it was at her behest and thus shielding me from impropriety.

"That was excellently performed," Alfonso was generous in his praise when he joined me. "It's pity you're not a man so you could be part of our company."

"Would you like me to be?"

"What do you think?" he grinned and for a moment there was complicity between us, an acknowledgement of the bed pleasure we shared, separate from the cousinly relationship we had always had with each of us striving for mastery over the other. My musician friends were also warm in their endorsement. But I was extremely surprised when Lord Hunsdon, who had only made a late appearance, approached me and complimented me. It was the first time we had met in three years and I felt uncomfortable with him. He looked noticeably older, stooping and his gait slower, his eyes hooded and pouched and with no red now in his grey hair and beard, though he was splendidly dressed as usual.

"Are you well, my lord?" I asked formally, curtseying to him.

"Not as well as I should wish," he replied. "And you? Are you happy?"

From the corner of my eye I caught a glimpse of Will. "Oh yes, my lord, very happy. Very happy indeed." I could feel joy suffuse me and he looked taken aback. I had the feeling he was going to ask more but instead he turned away and I was shocked by the distress on his face.

My eyes had followed Will but he was nowhere to be seen. Only when we were leaving did I find him beside me and while formally saluting me he pressed a piece of paper into my hand. I pushed it down the bodice of my gown but had no opportunity to read it until we arrived home. Then as soon as I could I smoothed it out and with difficulty deciphered the rough scrawl.

> How oft, when thou, my music, music play'st,
> Upon that blessed wood whose motion sounds
> With thy sweet fingers, when thou gently sway'st
> The wiry concord that mine ear confounds,
> Do I envy those jacks that nimble leap
> To kiss the tender inward of thy hand,
> Whilst my poor lips, which should that harvest reap,
> At the wood's boldness by thee blushing stand.
> To be so tickled, they would change their state
> And situation with those dancing chips,
> O'er whom thy fingers walk with gentle gait,
> Making dead wood more blest than living lips.
> Since saucy jacks so happy are in this,
> Give them thy fingers, me thy lips to kiss.

I was amazed. He must have written it during the evening. I retraced all the events in my mind marvelling at what a perfect evening it had been. I had listened to poetry, music and plays, I had been admired and I had actually performed as a musician myself. Not officially like the others it was true, but people had listened and applauded and I knew my father would have been proud. Will too had been there and though we had no opportunity to meet he had written a poem for me, a poem which moreover confirmed his love. I folded it carefully and placed it in my jewellery casket under the locket with the cross which Lord Hunsdon had given me after our first night together, which I never wore but sometimes looked at to remind me of past happiness. Now there was present happiness of a sort unlooked for and Will's poem was worth more to me than the most valuable jewel in the world.

The success of the evening at Lord Burghley's had given me the hope that I might also be allowed to accompany Alfonso to Hampton Court for the Yuletide festivities. The Queen sometimes took a fancy to spending Christmas at the palace there instead of at Whitehall and had commanded her musicians and also the Lord Chamberlain's Men to entertain her for the season. However I was to be disappointed.

"I shall be away for two weeks, it wouldn't be possible for you to come with us, the Queen wouldn't wish it. And we can't both be away from the family celebrations at Christmastide, you must go with Henry to my parents' house," he said but I suspected there would be some ulterior motive to his reluctance. However there was no way I could counter this and on this occasion he had the upper hand. My greatest disappointment was that I would not be able to see Will for this length of time. So I was left to spend the twelve days of Christmas at Chelsea at the house of Nicholas Lanier and Lucrezia, who entertained what remained of their large family. Ellen's new husband was also away with the music but the youngest boys, Jerome, Andrea and Clement, were still at home and Ellen and Innocent arrived for the festivities. For some of the time John Lanier was present and I found a pleasant companion in his wife Frances, daughter of another Italian musician Antonio Galliardello, while their seven year old son Nicholas was a playmate for Henry, who was universally fussed over and accepted as a true member of the family. But I chafed with annoyance imagining Alfonso's circumstances - the opportunities for seduction, the entertainment, feasting, the company of great nobles and the presence of the Queen herself. Will would also be part of that felicity. However the prevalence of good humour and the joyful traditions of Yuletide all helped to while away the time in Chelsea as we decorated the house with garlands of evergreens while the boys brought in the Yule log, constructed a kissing bough together and Ellen and I helped to make the plum porridge. There was constant music and the wassail bowl continuously replenished so that time passed contentedly enough and I enjoyed watching my little son's delighted response to the decorations of holly and ivy and the little gifts he was presented with, cakes, marchpane, a wooden horse and a multicoloured felt ball.

At the end of the twelve days Alfonso came home with many tales to tell and I listened avidly to accounts of the royal festivities (though I suspected I wasn't told everything), as well as the latest gossip and scandals.

"Some of Will Shakespeare's verses were being passed around, sonnets he had apparently written only for private perusal but someone had got hold of manuscript copies."

My heart stopped. "What sort of verses?"

"Sonnets. Love poems. Caused quite a stir."

"Why?" I murmured, my throat dry with apprehension though at the same time I realised Alfonso was being remarkably equable if I had been the subject of them.

"Because they were written to a man."

Whatever answer I was expecting I was not prepared for this. "A man?" I repeated foolishly, thinking I hadn't heard aright.

"Yes to a man. Love poems to a man. To the Earl of Southampton, Henry Wriothesley."

"That can't be true. You're jesting."

"Not at all. Beautiful love poems, *'Shall I compare thee to a summer's day, Thou art more lovely and more temperate.'* Love poems any woman would be pleased to receive. Or what about this,

'A woman's face with nature's own hand painted, Hast thou, the master/mistress of my passion.' It has been rumoured before that he is of Marlowe's inclination but it was quite a shock to read such sentiments in words. No wonder he didn't want them printed. I don't know who's let the cat out of the bag."

The room was reeling around me and I had to hold onto the chair for support. I wanted to cry out, "No! No! it isn't true, I know it isn't true," but I couldn't betray myself. Alfonso was going on with more details and I felt sick inside. "Perhaps it's a jest at his expense, some other poet tricked up in his feathers. Or some jealous rival, God knows he has them, wanting to discredit him," I cried frantically. Alfonso didn't notice the near hysteria in my voice.

"No it's true enough. He admitted his authorship. And why shouldn't he, they're exceptionally well crafted verses."

My mind was racing and my heart beating painfully. All I could think of was that I had to see Will, challenge him personally. I would go to the playhouse at the first opportunity. But it was winter and there were no performances in the playhouses. The actors would be giving private performances, like at Tichfield, Southampton's house. The fact that 'Love's Labours Lost' had been performed there and written for the young lord now assumed a new significance. And I remembered his words when we had first made love, that he had never expected to fall in love, it was unforseen and unlooked for. I would have to go to his house and hope he would be there. I would go tomorrow, I couldn't wait, I couldn't think of anything else and there was a sick feeling in the pit of my stomach. I did not know how I could even wait twelve hours for the truth and the agonizingly long night passed without my being able to sleep at all. I didn't know which was worse, the fear that he didn't love me after all or the horrible visions which I tried to suppress, and I felt I was going mad.

I set off on the morrow as early as I could, yet not so early as to arouse suspicion about the excuse of having to see a lawyer concerning the lease on our house in Bishopsgate, now nearing its expiry. I didn't know what I should do if he wasn't at home and I ran from the wharf to the house in Gracechurch street. The door being on the latch, I ran swiftly up the stairs without ceremony and knocked on the attic door. He opened it immediately, looking amazed at my appearance. "Aemilia, what brings you here so unexpectedly, and so early?" he exclaimed, leading me into the room. I caught my breath as I stepped inside and leaned against the door. Everything seemed so normal - Will in his shirt looking somewhat dishevelled as if he had not been long awake, the bed rumpled, clothes strewn on the floor, the table a mass of paper, drinking vessels perched perilously on dusty surfaces. The familiarity calmed me somewhat. Perhaps it was all a mistake after all but I had to know.

"What about Southampton?" I demanded abruptly without preamble.

"Southampton? Has something happened to him?"

The anxiety in his voice alerted me and I shouted, "About you and Southampton."

He gave a sigh and said, "You've heard about the poems. Alfonso no doubt." There was acquiescence in silence and so he continued, "Lord Burghley wants Southampton, who was a ward of his, to marry his granddaughter, the Earl of Oxford's daughter Elizabeth de Vere. But Henry Wriothesley doesn't want to. So Burghley, encouraged by Southampton's mother, asked me to write some verses pleading with him to do so, appealing to the fact that he is an only son and heir to a great fortune and heritage."

"Sounds far-fetched to me, more like a plot for one of your plays," I said in a tight voice.

"Nonetheless it is true."

"Why you?"

"Because they were impressed with the poems I wrote and dedicated to him."

"According to Alfonso the poems are love poems, he quoted some of them for me."

He hesitated then said, "Yes I suppose they are in a way. Listen and let me try to be honest. I am very fond of Southampton, he has done a lot for me. Not only does he encourage and believe in my work but he has paid me handsomely. Do you know how much he gave me for the poems I dedicated to him?" As I didn't reply he said, "Five hundred pounds."

"Five hundred pounds?" My voice rose uncontrollably in a shriek. The usual gesture for a dedication was from five to ten pounds. "You're jesting surely. That's a fortune."

"Yes I know, but it's true. How else do you think I was able to buy myself into the company, to buy a share in the Lord Chamberlain's Men. I couldn't have done it otherwise."

"But why do you live here with that kind of money?" I asked in amazement, feeling dazed by his disclosure. William Shakespeare must be a very rich man.

He shrugged airily, "It suits me here. And besides I have to send money home to Stratford for my wife and children. And I like to invest some, for a rainy day as we say in the profession." He smiled his disarming smile and I was almost seduced, but not quite.

"So how fond are you of Southampton?" I insisted. "The poems talk about love."

"Yes I do love him if you want the truth. He is beautiful, not handsome but beautiful, with a beauty that moves the senses. He is also intelligent, gifted, witty, kind and incredibly generous to poets and writers. I love him as men can love each other, as Proteus and Valentine in 'The Two Gentlemen of Verona.' But if you mean am I a sodomite the answer is emphatically no. God's bones, you above anyone should know that, Aemilia."

I began to cry, great heaving sobs that dragged from the core of my being relief, regret, trust, uncertainty, hope and fear, all swept up together in a wave of emotion, a great release of the agony of the past hours. His arms were around me, "I'm sorry," but I wasn't sure for what. In his arms I felt calmed but I wanted to go away and think. I felt exhausted after my sleepless night and the wrack of my emotions. His eyes glanced towards the rumpled bed and though I would have liked to have found reassurance in lovemaking there was still too much impairment between us and I extricated myself. "I have to go," I murmured hoping my face didn't show too much signs of weeping.

"When shall I see you again?" There was anxiety in his voice and his eyes were pleading. "I will see you again won't I?"

I hesitated. Then capitulated. "Soon."

I walked home through the city streets instead of taking a boat upriver because I needed time to think and compose myself. I walked heedless of the crowds and carts making passage difficult in the narrow thoroughways, blind to the crowded market stalls and deaf to the raucous cries of street vendors. I believed what Will had told me no matter what the poems might suggest but his disclosure had unsettled me. How could he love me exclusively if, by his own admission, he also loved the Earl of Southampton. Even if there was no impropriety in the relationship I had to share my lover's affections with Henry Wriothesley and it was an uncomfortable sensation. Will had kept much from me, including the vast amount of money he had received and I smiled mirthlessly at how I had always considered him a poor player. The dent in my trust made me wonder if he had also not been honest with me about his relations with his wife and I began to doubt his love for me. Then remembering his assurances, the closeness of our minds, the sweetness of our lovemaking my doubts began to dissolve. I knew him too well to be deceived, I loved him too much to let anything come between us. By the time I returned home I had already forgiven him though I wasn't sure for what. But I was filled with an overwhelming curiosity to know more about Henry Wriothesley

CHAPTER 10

PAVANE AND GALLIARD

"Raleigh's been let out of the Tower to go and look for gold in the Americas," Alfonso announced seemingly offhandedly when we were having supper one evening. He looked up at me then busied himself pushing the meat around with his knife as he said, "I wish I could go with him."

"You wouldn't have enough if you found a goldmine," I retorted dismissively. I was just becoming aware of how fast he was spending our money and was getting worried about our dwindling savings.

He ignored the comment, continuing, "They like musicians with them on long voyages."

"Forget it, Alfonso," I warned him sternly, aware of how he was always looking for new diversions. "It would be foolish to give up your position in the Queen's Musick, we need your wage. Besides you would have to buy a share into the expedition and they don't come cheap."

"He thinks he can find El Dorado. And the Queen appears to have faith in him."

"She is only letting him go because she doesn't know what to do with him," I said sceptically. "She can't keep him in the Tower for ever just for marrying one of her ladies. But she obviously hasn't quite forgiven him. She would never let him go personally on voyages before, he was only allowed to organise and finance them. Well let's hope he finds the mythical kingdom or he will be in bigger trouble than ever."

Alfonso was still lost in his thoughts. "Some day I will travel," he said. "I don't intend to end my life having seen nothing but London and its environs. Some day I'll find a way to go on an expedition."

"What has brought about this sudden urge to leave the Court for danger and uncertainty on the other side of the world? Are you tired of your life as a musician? I rather thought it was a comfortable existence," I implied sarcastically. "If you put your mind to cultivating important connections and weren't such a spendthrift you might get on in the world."

"I'm tired of the tedium, of doing the same thing season after season, year after year. I'm twenty four years old and I don't want to spend the rest of my life just playing music at Court until I am old like the Bassanos."

This was a new turn of thought for Alfonso and I wondered what new scrape he had got himself involved in, or who he had been talking to. No doubt at Court he would have heard much of the voyages of Drake and Hawkins, perhaps hearing tales from the explorers themselves.

"Perhaps when Henry is older we could go to Italy to look at the family property in Bassano del Grappa," I suggested, but he didn't seem enthusiastic. But while he was in a talkative mood I took advantage by asking, "What do you know about the Earl of Southampton?"

"Why?" He regarded me suspiciously at this change of subject.

"Only because I'm thinking of going to see William Shakespeare's play 'Love's Labours Lost' at The Theatre on Sunday and I was told it was written at the behest of the Earl," I replied casually.

"I told you that people say there's more between him and his protégé than writing." He shrugged, "What do you want to know? He's about your age, considered handsome though effeminate, more money than he knows what to do with, a ward of Burghley's and in his bad books because he refused to marry his granddaughter, Elizabeth de Vere."

"Do women consider him handsome?"

He looked at me speculatively with narrowed eyes. "Apparently so. Rumour of some sort is never far from his name. The Queen was very taken with him at one time but recently he's angered her on several accounts, like brawling with one of the other courtiers in the Presence Chamber of all places. But he's very generous to poets and musicians and always willing to give new artists a chance. You seem more than usually curious about him."

"Not really," I shrugged. "You know I'm always eager for Court news and Southampton is one person I've never met. What's the news with Essex these days?"

"Quarrelling with the Queen as usual because she wouldn't let him be part of the expedition to take Brest from the Spanish. She won't let him go where there might be danger and this angers him. She likes to have him near her all the time, taking Leicester's place. But he's bored and his marriage hasn't deterred him from getting one of the maids with child. Incidentally, he and Southampton are thick as thieves, leading the party that's all for outright war with Spain and frustrated by the Queen's reluctance."

I was uncharitable enough to be glad that Robert Devereux's marriage did not seem perfect but I was satisfied with what I had learnt about Henry Wriothesley, some of it confirming what Will had said. Now more than ever I wanted to see him.

On Sunday I made my way to The Theatre to see 'Love's Labours Lost'. Because the playhouses in Shoreditch were out of the jurisdiction of the City council the companies performed there on Sundays, one of the most popular days for the non-working public and the day that drew the most vociferous opposition from the Puritans. As expected, one of the divines had made himself a temporary pulpit from a packing chest outside the playhouse and was noisily haranguing the crowds as they pushed inside, oblivious to his warnings of eternal damnation for so desecrating the Sabbath day. I made my way to a cushioned seat in the centre of the front row of the second gallery with an excellent view over the stage. I was eager to see the character of Rosaline, for which Will said I had been the inspiration. However as the trumpets sounded for the beginning of the play one person claimed my attention more than the King of France who made his entrance with his lords, one of whom was Will. At the same time as the actors progressed from behind the curtains at the rear of the stage three young courtiers climbed the steps at the front and took up their places on stools set to one side. Having spectators on the stage was not a practice the players liked, especially if they talked and competed with the actors for the audience's attention, but they occasionally tolerated the intrusion if they were paid sufficiently for the privilege. No doubt the Earl of Southampton had paid them very well indeed for I knew immediately it was him.

During the King's opening soliloquy my attention was focussed only on the central figure of the three young courtiers, Henry Wriothesley himself. I studied him carefully. He was tall and elegant but well built, richly but restrainedly attired. Besides the peacock finery of his two companions, garish in vivid yellow and turquoise padded doublets, matching paned hose stuffed to extravagant proportions, huge plates of ruffs and tall feathered hats, he wore doublet and hose of black velvet trimmed with silver lace, a gauze standing collar, and black shoes in the new straight-lasted style adorned with ribbon rosettes. His head was uncovered to show his burnished chestnut hair, curling well past his shoulders with a red ribbon tied on one of the long locks. His fingers were very long and slender, a magnificent diamond visible on the index as he toyed with the gold medallion on a long chain around his neck. I studied his face. It was oval, delicately boned, his mouth wide and full, his eyes almond shaped and almost as dark as mine, his nose long and high-bridged. He was more than handsome, he was beautiful as Will had said. All through the play my attention was divided between the action and him. The character of Rosaline claimed my full concentration. Will had repeated many of the sentiments of the sonnet he had composed for me –'*and therefore is she born to make black fair, Her favour turns the fashion of these days,*' - and the lord Berowne, who was played by Will himself, was in love with this dark lady. I had been disappointed by Will's poems but to be a character in a play was an honour not even Penelope Rich had received. However during the long intervals when Rosaline was not part of the action my attention turned time and again to Henry Wriothesley on the stage. He gave the play his rapt attention and if any of his companions spoke he silenced them with his hand. Only once did his gaze move upward to the galleries and seeing me contemplating him he returned my stare for what seemed a long time, considering, not smiling. It disturbed me.

The play did not receive the thunderous applause which always greeted the ever-popular 'Titus Andronicus'. Most of the audience preferred bloodthirsty plots to complicated wordplay and literary allusions and I could understand why Will had written it with Southampton and his coterie in mind. I thought that he would probably be disappointed by the audience's reaction but I knew he had almost finished a new play and had several more ideas in hand, and I had enjoyed it tremendously, especially the music and the seven songs incorporated in the scenario. I waited as usual until the groundlings had pushed their rumbustious way out, then I descended the gallery stairs and was crossing the standing area, picking my way carefully as the rushes were now strewn with debris, when I found the Earl of Southampton in my path. For the first time I realised how tall he was. He had replaced his hat, large and black with an upturned brim, but he now swept it from his head and made a leg in an elaborate bow saying, "Mistress Lanier, Lord Hunsdon's Aemilia. And now I think Will Shakespeare's Aemilia too, or should I say Rosaline."

His smile was mocking, a sardonic curve to his lips, so I answered him with more freedom than I ought to have used to such a great lord, "You are at liberty to think what you like, Sir."

"Would you like to know my thoughts, Aemilia?" His eyes were dark brown with amber flecks, glowing like topaz, and he fixed them on mine with an almost hypnotic intensity. "Might they be pleasing to you?"

Not for a long time had I felt at a disadvantage with a man and I hoped he didn't notice the blush staining my cheeks. Was it because of what he knew about me, or because of what I knew about him and Will, or because

I could feel the power emanating from him like a tangible force?

"I shall be in the Blue Boar in Cheapside on Thursday at noon. I would like you to join me."

He did not wait for any response but swept his hat again in a salutation that I felt carried a hint of mockery, then collecting his minions who had been bandying with the boy apprentices he left the building after a quick nod to Will who had just appeared from the tiring room. He looked disappointed that the Earl had left without speaking but no doubt was well accustomed to his vagaries and I already sensed that Henry Wriothesley liked to toy with his power. He looked enquiringly at me but I mimed that I had to leave and would see him shortly. I felt too disturbed to talk to him at that moment and knew he would sense my discomfiture.

On Thursday at noon I went to the Blue Boar. For three days I had tried to forget the encounter telling myself continually that I had no intention of meeting the Earl of Southampton again. It was disloyal to Will and I had the feeling that it would be very dangerous to entangle myself with Henry Wriothesley. But then I would delude myself that I only wanted to discover what his relationship was with my lover. Yet underneath lay the fact, too shameful for me to admit, that this might be the way to recover the position I had held with Lord Hunsdon. And overall, like a lodestone, was the inescapable pull of his powerful personality that I felt helpless to withstand. He was the most physically attractive man I had ever met yet the aura of danger emanating from him was as strong as a dagger held to the throat. Even from my short acquaintance with him I knew that his angel face held a devil soul. But I walked into the Blue Boar as the bells of St. Mary-le-Bow were chiming noon.

He had taken it for granted that I would come and there was neither surprise nor triumph on his face, merely the acceptance of a fact. "I have a private room upstairs," he said and led the way. The chamber was spacious, oak-panelled and well furnished with high-backed chairs, a table set with refreshment, and a large sumptuously-furbished bed. He seemed at home in the space and I had the impression he often made use of it. There was no preamble. He took me in his arms and began to kiss me, his hand already stroking my thigh above my stocking. He unlaced my bodice deftly and his hands were soon caressing my breasts beneath my thin shift. With a speed born of practice he removed petticoats and stockings so that I was soon completely naked and he followed suit. His body was strong and firm, well exercised, well controlled. He used me as swiftly and efficiently as he would a whore and I responded to him completely and inevitably as he was determined I should. We didn't talk and afterwards there was no exultation.

He leaned on one arm looking at me inscrutably with his dark hypnotic eyes. "When will you see Will Shakespeare again?"

"I don't know."

"When will you see me again?"

"Never."

He laughed with genuine amusement. "Oh yes you will. You are a true whore Aemilia Lanier. Very beautiful in a strange way, very sensuous, and I do desire you, make no doubt about that."

"I shall never see you again." I meant the words sincerely. As I dressed I felt full of shame as he sat silently looking at me, a faint smile on his lips, and it seemed to take for ever. I hastened as quickly as I could though I was forced to ask his help with my lacings. I hurried out without salutations but at the door I was compelled to turn and look at him. His long chestnut hair hung loose over his shirt of fine pleated lawn, open to reveal his muscular chest, and his dark saturnine face had an expression of sardonic amusement, the amber flecks in his eyes glowing like flames. His physical beauty tore at the pit of my stomach like a sword thrust. I shut the door and ran down the stairs. I felt all eyes were upon me as I crossed the crowded taproom and hastened out of the inn into the clamorous street where the market vendors were beginning to pack up their produce. I felt sullied and yet bewitched. I'll make it up to Will, I promised, compensate in some way for this betrayal. With a stab of guilt I reflected that it should have been my husband I was mindful of betraying but I knew Alfonso wasn't faithful to me and although we shared common ties I did not love him. The all-enveloping consuming passion of a lover was reserved for Will.

Alfonso was at home when I returned. He was rehearsing with some of his colleagues in one of the upstairs parlours which he had taken over as a music room. His music and recorders were kept there as well as a couple of lutes and a set of virginals though not so fine as the ones I had played at the Cecils. They often came to our house to rehearse instead of using one of the city taverns and although my hopes of entertaining important people had so far come to nought, at least it was usually filled with musicians and kin playing music and laughing together. I recognised Anthony Holborne's 'Heigh-ho Holiday' and as I looked in I noted with affection that the baby was sitting on the floor, his leading strings tied to the bulbous leg of the large oak table around which the musicians were gathered. He loved listening to music and would sit quietly until he fell asleep. Alfonso had whittled him a rough whistle and, though he was still too young to teach, he liked to hold it in his hand and suck it and if he sometimes inadvertently produced a sound he chortled with glee. I closed the door quietly and went into the best parlour with the painted walls but immediately I stepped into the room I noticed one of the candlesticks was missing from its place on top of the court cupboard. The matching pair of beautifully moulded silver with a relief of fruit and leaves on the base I had brought with me from my Whitehall apartments. I had to restrain myself from dashing immediately to Alfonso and confronting him, but I waited until later when we were alone to challenge him. Then without preamble I demanded, "Where's the candlestick?"

"What candlestick? We have a lot." I knew he was buying time while he thought.

"Don't play games with me, Alfonso, you know the one I mean, one of our most valuable pair."

"Perhaps someone took it."

"Just the one? The only person to take it would be you."

"Aemilia that's not fair." He put on his injured expression. "You make me sound like a thief in my own home." Then seeing my implacable face he said, "I've borrowed it, that's all, I'll have it back in a week, I promise."

"You've taken it to a moneylender?"

"No, not really. Only to Malachi Bembo, he's a friend of Joseph Lupo. I needed some money urgently to pay a debt and he took it as surety. I'll get it back next week you'll see."

He smiled his winning smile of boyish innocence, putting his arm around me. I was filled with fury at his unconcern, at his irresponsibility, at the knowledge that most of our money had gone and at the certainty that

I would never see the candlestick again. But running through my head like a contretemps to my anger was the memory of my time with Southampton. Alfonso had given away one of our most valuable possessions for money but what had I done? In any case the silver had been a reward for fornication. I pushed him away and walked downstairs and down the passage into the back garden. The chill air of early spring washed over me, cooling my thoughts and distilling a faint scent of basil and thyme laced with the pungent smell of damp earth. I bent to pluck one of the pansies brushing my feet, remembering its other name, heart's ease. What a day it had been. For the first time in my life I felt fear for the future. I shivered as a few spatters of rain blew in my face. The drops felt like tears on my face and I cried, "I'm sorry, Will. So sorry." More than ever I wanted him.

But it was a few days before I could see him. Then in his attic room I fell upon him with a hunger I couldn't conceal and he seemed agreeably surprised, returning my ardour with equal fervour. He made no mention of the Earl of Southampton at The Theatre and that gave me hope to think he hadn't seen us talking together. We discussed the play in detail, then he told me about 'Richard II' which was already in rehearsal, and then about a new plot he had in mind. "It's set in Italy again, like 'The Two Gentlemen of Verona', and concerns a feud between two rival families, brought to a climax when Romeo and Juliet from the opposing households fall in love with each other."

"Is it a comedy?"

"Oh no, this is a tragedy. Real weeping stuff. I got the idea from a poem by Arthur Brooke but I'm making a lot of alterations. I think you'll like this one, it's a genuine love story."

I breathed a sigh of relief that my lapse with Henry Wriothesley seemed to have gone undiscovered and swore never to betray him again as our love plumbed a new depth of passion and understanding. One day I felt confident enough to show him a poem that I had written. He was surprised then read it carefully. I sat anxiously while he considered, then he read it again. I began to feel embarrassed, a flush colouring my face at my presumption - women didn't write, and this was William Shakespeare who was beginning to be judged as one of the most able poets on a par with Edmund Spenser, Samuel Daniel and Christopher Marlowe.

"That's good, Aemilia. Very good."

"Honestly? You're not just saying that because you love me and don't want to hurt me?"

"No I'm not. That's excellent. In fact I'm very surprised. I know you are a fine musician and a good judge of other people's verse but I must admit I didn't expect you to be so skilled. It's a pity you're not a man."

Alfonso had said the same about my music, I thought ruefully. Why were the Arts and learning the prerogative of men? Why could a woman not be a musician or a poet, a playwright or even an actor? The boy apprentices worked hard at their craft to be believable heroines, they spoke and sang beautifully, learnt to dance and move gracefully, showed emotion on their painted faces. But how could they feelingly portray the agonies of love, betrayal and loss that only a real woman knows. "I think I shall have to pretend to be a man," I said. "Do you think if I put on doublet and hose you would take me on as a player and I could be a poet too?"

"I prefer you as a woman. Despite what you might have heard," he said, looking me directly in the eyes. Then he added seriously, "Don't give up writing poetry.

It is worth it, if only to empty the heart of the pain that might otherwise kill you."

The cold spring continued, heralding a summer no better than last year's. With the threat of another bad harvest food prices continued to soar and more and more people joined street demonstrations to make their grievances public. Eventually complaint developed into riot as poor people became desperate. They dismantled the hated pillories which were full of rebellious commoners guilty of petty offences or who had dared to accuse the city aldermen, and sent a warning to the Lord Mayor by erecting a makeshift gallows one night outside his Bishopsgate house. In the space of a month there were fourteen riots when shops were broken into and the windows smashed in houses belonging to rich merchants and city officials. It became dangerous to venture into the city as the streets were patrolled by desperate men armed with cudgels and staves and anyone who seemed to be wealthy stood to be attacked and robbed. Apprentices, always prominent in disturbances, seized the markets of Southwark and Billingsgate, forcing honest stall-holders to relinquish their goods then sharing them out among a grasping, battling throng. The authorities had been remarkably patient, understanding the genuine grievances of the poor, but when a thousand apprentices marched together to the gunsmiths' shops on Tower Hill to get themselves arms they took decisive action. By June five of the rebel leaders had been hanged drawn and quartered, and London was placed under martial law.

"All the theatres to be closed," Will announced gloomily. "In summer when we usually perform every day and make most of our money."

"Can't Lord Hunsdon do anything?"

"Not in this instance, no. He can't make exceptions for his own company. Even if we vowed to put on nothing inflammatory, and that's almost impossible in this climate, you know the theatre crowds are the first targets for insurgents and trouble-makers. Nothing is easier than stirring up the groundlings when their emotions have been roused and they've had too much to drink."

"What will you do?"

"We shall have to go on tour, the Burbages are talking about East Anglia. Nobody likes touring, the uncertainty of finding venues and then not knowing whether the Mayor will give us a licence; long walks between bookings, rides if we're lucky; getting ourselves and our costumes wet; sleeping in cheap inns in flea-ridden beds; not to mention the audiences - country folk satisfied with any troupe of unlicensed itinerant players, who can't appreciate our high standards or understand any subtleties. All they want is blood and gore or knockabout comedy with songs and jigs." He groaned.

"At least you will still be performing. What shall I do without you?" I could see the summer dragging miserably away without plays and without my lover.

He was in a melancholy mood, not untouched by some resentment, and he made no effort to answer my question nor say he would miss me. "Depending on where we get to I might hire a horse and go to Stratford. Visit my ill-done-by wife and my neglected children."

I didn't say anything but felt dejected. Our time together had lost its usual contentment and our farewells were muted.

The actors stayed away until August. And while Will was in Suffolk I was sleeping with the Earl of Southampton. I had vowed never to see him again and would have kept my promise but for an unanticipated encounter which caught me unawares. One afternoon I was walking from Long Ditch down Kings Street towards St. James Park, having nothing better to do but flaunt my finery and hope I might meet someone. I had just approached King Henry's Gate with its round-capped towers and Ionic pillars carved with the Tudor rose through which a passage connected the park with the Palace of Whitehall when I encountered someone I was not happy to meet. Henry Wriothesley cantered by on horseback, presumably making for his house in Holborn. His companions continued on their way but he stopped and without dismounting saluted me. "Give you good day Mistress Lanier, I trust you are well and not suffering too much from the absence of our poet."

"Good day to you, my Lord. Now I would be obliged if you would let me pass."

His horse still blocked my way and I had to look up at him, being forced to meet his eyes.

"Not so rash, I find great pleasure in your company. I have looked for you in many places and been unsuccessful. Now we meet by chance I cannot disregard this opportunity." I knew he was lying, he could have found me easily enough, and it was a whim of the moment. But as usual I found myself tongue-tied in his presence and he continued, "On Friday I am holding a musical soiree on my barge, music and poetry. I am sure you would find some delight in the evening. I shall await you there." He wheeled his horse round, doffed his hat and rode off without staying for my response. What arrogance, I thought. He was not much older than I but this assurance was masculinity, power and wealth.

Once again I debated with myself whether or not to go but I knew from the onset that the offer was too tempting - music, poetry, important people. In such company I should have the opportunity to demonstrate my talents and prove to him I was more than an easy bedmate. Also I felt some resentment that Will had not shown more distress at our enforced separation, seeming to care little about my own situation.

On Friday I dressed with care in my blue taffeta gown with black sateen sleeves slashed with silver, the gown open at the front to show the matching black petticoat striped with silver braid. My hair was lightly covered by a silver net threaded with pearl beads and I put on my black velvet cloak with a mask to cover my face. The evening was mild and dry, unusual this summer, as I slipped away from the house taking advantage of Alfonso's absence. There was no transport on the river at this hour so at Whitehall I hired a sedan chair to take me to Temple Bar then slipped down the lane past the Earl of Essex's mansion to where I knew Southampton's large and ostentatious barge was moored near Temple stairs. But when I arrived all was surprisingly quiet, I could hear no sound of music or voices although I could see candles flickering behind the drawn curtains so that the golden silk seemed to dance. I hesitated in some perplexity then I became aware of a shadowy figure lounging on the velvet cushions in the prow and suddenly Henry Wriothesley rose and lifted me, half- resistingly, into the boat. Sensing that I was going to complain he said, "Hush," and opening the curtains into the interior he led me through into the barge's private area. It was spacious and luxurious with gilded benches sumptuously cushioned in red velvet and a table of gilded and painted wood on which were set flagons of wine and two goblets of jewelled Venetian glass. Candles in wall sconces shed a softly enveloping golden glow.

"Where is everyone?" I asked in a disdainful tone of voice that accurately conveyed my thoughts - why didn't I suspect, I wasn't born yesterday.

"Just the two of us, Aemilia, much more rewarding."

"You are a liar."

"Not at all. There is a lute for you to play some music for me and I shall read you some of Will's 'The rape of Lucrece'. And I shall ensure that you find delight in the evening. Music, poetry and entertainment, everything I promised." He was completely unabashed, convinced that no apology was necessary.

"Suppose I were a young innocent girl flattered by your attention?"

"But you aren't. You are a woman of the world familiar with men's stratagems and well acquainted with their desires. Now come, drink some wine, the very best canary, and let us enjoy the evening together."

I played some music for him then he took the lute himself and performed very well. He read some of Will's poetry, mocking me as he read, though his voice was mellifluous with an instinctive feel for the rhythm as he glided sensuously over the erotic verse. We drank a lot of wine then finally we made love, lying on the floor on the thick velvet cushions, the boat swaying gently against its moorings and the water lapping rhythmically against the side. It was like being in a dreamlike trance as I surrendered to the sensuous pleasure of his possession, the candles alternately flickering and leaping with our every movement. Afterwards when we lay still together he said, "You understand why I desire you, Aemilia. A whore could give me satisfaction but you feed my soul as well."

I recognised Marlowe's phrase and thought the reference to Faustus suited him very well. Raising myself on one elbow I looked into his eyes, saying, "The only reason you want me is because I am Will Shakespeare's lover and by taking me you demonstrate your power over him. He loves you."

"Yes I know." He was completely unmoved and still lying on his back began to recite from memory.

"As an imperfect actor on the stage,
Who with his fear is put beside his part,
Or some fierce thing replete with too much rage,
Whose strength's abundance weakens his own heart;
So I, for fear of trust, forget to say
The perfect ceremony of love's right,
And in mine own love's strength seem to decay,
O'ercharged with burden of mine own love's might.
O let my books be then the eloquence
And dumb presagers of my speaking breast,
Who plead for love, and look for recompense,
More than that tongue that more hath more express'd.
O learn to read what silent love hath writ:
To hear with eyes belongs to love's fine wit.

That's very fine you must admit." I felt a surge of envy that Will had never written such sentiments for me but Southampton continued coolly, "But I paid him well for his verse. Burghley and my mother asked him to write some sonnets persuading me to marry Lady Elizabeth de Vere but then he got carried away and our relationship changed somewhat. Anyway she's off my hands now, she's due to marry the new Lord Derby, William Stanley. Good luck to him I say, all the de Veres are shrews. I think I shall arrange for the Lord Chamberlain's Men to perform 'The Taming of the Shrew' for their wedding celebrations. That would be most apt considering they used to be his brother Ferdinando's company."

I couldn't help laughing. Peregrine Bertie had married the Earl of Oxford's sister, Lady Mary de Vere, who was notorious for her caustic speech. It had been said of Peregrine, one of the best swordsmen at Court and known for his bravery in the campaign in the Netherlands, that he had best shown his courage by marrying her.

I had to admit that I had enjoyed my evening with Southampton. He was arrogant, mendacious, faithless, and with a streak of cruelty. But he was clever, witty, talented, generous with his money and with a genuine love of the arts. He was also incredibly handsome and virile. I knew he had caught me in his snare as he had done Will. I now realised however that any vain hopes I had nourished about being able to attract his love and get back some of the life I had known with Lord Hunsdon were undisputably futile. To him I was merely a whore, someone who counted among his pleasurable diversions and would never be part of his public activities. The secrecy was part of his amusement as was the knowledge that he was playing a game with Will. Yet he had an inescapable compulsive attraction for me and although I was ashamed of my dalliance with him and consumed with guilt I felt unable to break free. My love was still reserved for Will, though I had to admit an element of revenge had entered into the picture for what I considered to be his betrayal of our singular love. Such are the vagaries of the heart.

I met Southampton twice more at the Blue Boar for what were no more than sexual encounters, pleasurable but brief. Then in July he retired to Titchfield for the summer as was the custom with all the lords who held country estates. Alfonso was again at Greenwich attending on the Queen as she made her usual move from the insalubrious city to the Palace there at this season. I was surprised how much his absence affected me for there was always music when he was at home and I missed the sounds of the musicians rehearsing. I couldn't even use the opportunity to spend more time with Will. I busied myself with my household tasks, supervising the maids with the annual big wash while the weather was reasonably good, cleaning the house and looking after Henry who, at two years old, was becoming increasingly active. He was a handsome child, tall and strong for his age with an insatiable curiosity and I looked forward to when I would be able to teach him music and his letters. I occupied myself with making recipes and simples and preserving for the winter. I was no great lover of household tasks but I enjoyed distilling flowers for perfumes and scented oils, (skills I had learnt from the Countess of Kent), filling bowls with rose petals and dried flower heads, drying lavender to scent the sheets and aromatic herbs to hang on the walls. I loved the summer when colour filled the house and garden and scents of flowers and herbs pervaded the air, alleviating some of the more unpleasant odours. Westminster had more than its share of poor and destitute cramped in squalid dwellings in narrow dirty alleyways, but Long Ditch and Kings Street were wide paved thoroughfares with fields beyond and the proximity of St. James's park, and the air was fresher than in the city itself, always a stinking fetid miasma in the hot weather. I ventured into the city once to watch Francis Drake and Richard Hawkins in their triumphal procession through the streets, crowded with cheering supporters, before setting off from Plymouth for another attack on the Spanish Main. Big, bluff, red-faced Drake was immensely popular with Londoners because of his fame with the Armada and his piratical raids on Spanish shipping.

Lucrative to himself and also, it was rumoured, to the Queen, the satisfaction to the common folk lay in the debasement of their hated enemy.

But it was August before the disorder in the city had been completely quelled and the theatre companies allowed to return to London. However to my disappointment Will Shakespeare was not with the Lord Chamberlain's Men when I made my way to The Curtain at the earliest opportunity. On making enquiry I was informed he was in Stratford, news which made me dejected as I plagued myself continually with images of him with his wife and children in domestic happiness. I feared that Anne Shakespeare might have recaptured his love, made herself indispensable to him as I would have done and that he would decide to stay there. I worried for two weeks but then by the end of the month I heard that he had returned.

I expected my excitement at seeing him again to be mutual but I was disappointed to find our meeting in an unanticipated low key. He greeted me eagerly enough but seemed unsettled and out of sorts.

"Anne was full of complaints, how I hadn't come home when the fire destroyed so many of the houses in the town and they might have suffered ill, how she hates living in my parents' house, she and my mother don't see eye to eye, and wants a place of her own. Hamnet isn't well, he seems to have got much weaker though Anne assures me he's better than he was. And now my youngest brother Edmond, he's sixteen, has decided that he wants to come to London and be an actor. He thinks there's nothing to it, that he can just learn a part and walk on the stage and expects me to find a place for him in the company. Well he's mistaken because I have no intention of doing so, or of looking after him either."

I sighed and made sympathetic noises, relieved there was no threat from his wife but remembering again how selfish he could be and how protective of his art. "And if that isn't all," he continued furiously, "I get back here and they tell me that the Lord Mayor is demanding we pull down The Theatre and The Curtain because they encourage the disorder we have seen this summer."

"That won't happen," I soothed him. "You have too many powerful friends in high places. Lord Hunsdon would never allow it."

"We hope not but it's another example of the authorities being against us and they can cause us a lot of trouble in many ways, like censoring plays."

"The Master of the Revels does that surely?"

"Edmond Tilney has the final say before licensing a new play, yes. But the authorities can ban certain 'controversial' subjects at given times which means we can perform nothing but mindless domestic comedies - no satire, no contemporary references, no history that does not eulogise the Tudors. My 'Richard II' could never be performed today, even previously we were not allowed to include the deposition scene, they made us cut that out. It may be English history but deposing a monarch is not to be contemplated, even on stage."

"It's been very successful, Will, it's a magnificent play."

His face lightened at the mention of his writing and I saw his ill humour gradually fade.

"My Romeo and Juliet tragedy is finished, going into rehearsal as soon as matters about a theatre are sorted out. We're thinking about The Swan. Another theatre on Bankside is serving us well, four public playhouses now, all outside the jurisdiction of the city's Puritan influences. When I first joined the company there were only two. The inn courtyards are all very well but nothing beats a playhouse." Another investor by the name of Francis Langley had also seen the potential of theatres as commercial enterprises and in choosing to build The Swan on Bankside he had been influenced by the success of Philip Henslowe's Rose. "I've read the play to the other sharers and they're very taken with it," Will continued, "they're sure it's going to be a success." He paused and then said seriously, "This is the first play I've ever written that is a story of love and I think my love for you has helped me to write it."

"I can't wait to see it." I was pleasurably surprised because he rarely spoke of his feelings for me. I thought often of the paradox that he could write such beautiful language expressing deep emotion yet found it difficult to vocalise his own when we were together, even in our most tender moments. Will's poetry was reserved for his pen, not dispensed upon me. But I noted that he had shown no interest in what I had been doing whilst he was away and wondered if any gossip had come to his ears. I decided I had to venture and asked as casually as I could, "Have you seen the Earl of Southampton?"

He remained tantalisingly silent while my heart beat faster, then he replied shortly, "No."

But by the tone of his voice I realised that our thoughts were running on different lines. I had been afraid of what he might have learnt but he was expecting jealous resentment from me. When he saw that I wasn't going to respond he turned on me angrily, as if I were to blame for the omission. "I haven't seen him. Does that please you?"

I didn't feel I could answer as he wished me to and we never managed to recover our rapport. When we parted it was on less than rapturous terms and I felt sad. I had waited for our meeting with such pleasurable anticipation, though with some anxiety, and I had been satisfied on neither account for I was still not wholeheartedly sure that he had not heard something. I chafed and worried and both longed for and dreaded our next meeting.

This however could not have been more different. The first performance of 'The tragedy of Romeo and Juliet' had been a resounding success and he was filled with elation as he related it to me in his room the following day. "We had the audience in the palm of our hands at the end and when John Hemminges gave the epilogue we could hear people weeping. Then there was such cheering and shouting with a gusto we had never seen before. We were all dazed with the success and drank ourselves witless afterwards. Southampton was there and he wants us to do a private performance for him at Titchfield when we finish our season in the theatres, he has a room upstairs which is fitted out as a playhouse. He has also arranged for us to do a private performance of 'Richard II' at Sir Edward Hoby's house in Cannon Row, which means it won't be subject to censorship and we shall be able to include the deposition scene." He was almost levitating with exhilaration and he transferred his happiness to me. We were soon in each other's arms and made love with more passion and profound content than we had known for a long time.

I couldn't wait to see the next performance of the play which was sooner than expected for public enthusiasm demanded a repeat within a few days. In my now habitual place in the third gallery, because it was cheaper than the second, I acknowledged the play fulfilled all the expectations raised by general report. Will had told me he had been uncertain whether to take for himself the part of Romeo's friend Mercutio, to whom he had given a moving death scene, or that of the friar, the lovers' confidant, both important roles.

However finally he had chosen the latter, generously leaving the mesmerising Mercutio to Henry Condell. He was often selfish but never when it concerned the welfare of the Company. The play was the best Will had ever written, the best play I had ever seen and afterwards I told him so.

He was exultant. "I'm glad you have no reservations about this play."

"There is however something that puzzles me, Will. Why did you give Romeo's first love the name of Rosaline again?"

"It was just a name, a name that came into my head."

"She was a dark lady as before."

"No significance intended. It's only a story. If it's poetic it's the more likely to be feigned."

He dismissed the matter carelessly but I was not so sure. Romeo's infatuation with Rosaline causes him great torment and he forgets her when he finds real love. It is true that her rejection of him was because of a vow of chastity but virgin and whore were but two faces of woman, the Madonna and Eve, the feminine duality that intrigued divines and poets, and Will liked word play. Did he suspect something? I told myself I was being foolish, letting my imagination carry me away, but I felt a chill creep across my heart like a cold draught when a shadow covers the sun.

CHAPTER 11

CONTRAPUNTO

It was a year of deaths. Yet it had begun auspiciously. Alfonso had said that I might accompany him to the Court for some of the Yuletide festivities which this year were once again back at Whitehall.

"I think it might cheer you after being confined to the house for so long," he said with unexpected solicitude for I knew he had been disappointed by the miscarriage I had suffered in the autumn. For me however it had come as a relief because I did not know whose child it was - Alfonso's, Will's or Southampton's – and the realisation had brought a deep fear in its wake. But I had been very ill and had seen no-one for several weeks. I had been too ill to care overmuch about our dwindling resources and the steady disappearance of other artefacts from the house, merely existing from day to day and leaving everything to the maids. When I had recovered I still looked so thin and pale that I didn't want Will to see me yet and hoped that absence might increase his longing for me. But as Christmastide approached I had recovered my looks and eagerly anticipated visiting the Court, hopeful that Alfonso would secure me a place for some of the entertainment and willing to forget for a time his regular removal of our valuable belongings, none of which were ever returned despite his assurances. But

I chafed that I was forced to feel grateful to him for the occasional return to what had been my residence for five years. However because he was a royal retainer such visits were at least possible and would not have been an option if Lord Hunsdon had married me off to a merchant or lawyer. But I hated having to be dependent on Alfonso, knowing he could demonstrate his mastery over me by granting or withholding such treats. Nevertheless I buried my resentment and occupied myself with preparing some new gowns. I no longer had money to have new ones made but my stock from my time with Lord Hunsdon was still large and I could alter them beyond recognition by interchanging sleeves and petticoats and purchasing fresh braids and laces.

On Christmas Day the Queen's Musick entertained Her Majesty and a large crowd of courtiers and ladies. I wore my gown of tawny orange satin and black velvet, but without a farthingale as only the Queen and her most important ladies were permitted to wear this style when there was a great crush due to the amount of space taken up by the extravagantly wide skirts on their foundation of willow hoops. My lace ruff was small and neat but with a new edging of jet beads to match my jet ear-rings and my hair was caught up in a snood of gold net. My seat was retired at the back where I was accompanied by my cousin Augustine Bassano's wife, Dorothy, but nonetheless I was noticed and saluted by many courtiers and complimented on my looks. Then to my great surprise I was noted by the Queen and commanded to stand before her. I curtseyed low then stood in trepidation in her presence, as all did. She was now sixty two years old, her face wrinkled beneath the white paint, her nose grown beaked, her teeth blackened, but her eyes were as bright and shrewd as ever as she looked me over.

Her dress, cut low to reveal her breasts, was blindingly bright, the white satin encrusted with jewels, her ruff a foot high with wings on either side, a glittering crown atop her bright red wig.

"Well Mistress Lanier, and how fare you?" she demanded abruptly.

My throat was dry but I was aware of Lord Burghley at her side smiling encouragingly.

"Very well I thank you, Your Majesty."

"I see you have not yet furnished your husband with another son," she said pointedly. "I believe you are too busy gadding around the playhouses, an activity not conducive to either physical or moral welfare. I suggest you attend more to your marital duties and remedy this before it is too late."

"I will try to do so, Your Majesty," I murmured, feeling at a disadvantage and wondering what she knew. Had she heard rumours about me? It was said she knew everything that happened, not only at Court but in her kingdom, though I did not think she would have honoured me by her notice if she suspected any ill conduct. As she turned away and I rose from my curtsey again I noticed Lord Hunsdon's eyes on me but I forbore to smile at him as I saluted him courteously.

Back at home Alfonso was warm in his praise of my conduct and overwhelmed with pride that I had been honoured by the Queen, the substance of her discourse I did not make known to him. We exchanged news that we had gained during the evening and he furnished me with an interesting piece of gossip - Penelope Rich had recently given birth to her lover's fourth child much to her husband's fury. I could imagine what the Queen thought about that.

"The beautiful Penelope must have seven children by now. Why can't you give me another son, you had no trouble with Henry."

"I don't know," I replied as contritely as I could. But I did know, or suspected the answer. I surmised it was because of all the measures I had taken when Lord Hunsdon's mistress. I had heard on good authority that such remedies could make a woman infertile.

"We shall have to try even harder won't we," he grinned. "Let's start now," and he began to lead the way upstairs. I followed him willingly enough, mellowed by the success of my return to the Court and not untouched by a shadow of guilt. He was always easily roused and I rarely found difficulty in responding to his passion for he asked little more than physical gratification and we were both satisfied with that.

Three days later I returned to the Court again for a performance by the Lord Chamberlain's Men of 'The Battle of Alcazar', a patriotic drama by George Peele. The Queen liked the work of Peele, a one-time actor himself, but I knew that Will was a little jealous of him as he had recently written a tribute to the Earl of Southampton. I was excited at the thought of seeing Will again after such a long time though I knew I would as usual be relegated to a seat at the back. Nonetheless I wore my striking gown of red satin, having altered it with new yellow sleeves. My heart lurched when he appeared on the stage, his performance confirming as always the competent and versatile actor he was. However I was unsuccessful in catching his eye and the evening passed disappointingly without having encountered him. Our absence has slackened his love not reanimated it, I thought despairingly. Then as I was making farewells to some of my musician friends a voice behind me whispered, "Thou dost teach the torches to burn bright," and I turned to face him.

"When can I see you?" he said. "I have been too long without you."

"I've been sick."

"Yes I know. I'm sorry but it was impossible to send to you." I raised my eyebrows sceptically at this further example of his selfishness but he rushed on, "'Tis too late for that now. When can you come to me? The sight of you has driven me mad all evening."

I struggled to make some excuse and make him wait a little longer but the sight of his loved face and his gentle brown eyes forced my capitulation. "As soon as I can," I promised.

"We're travelling up to Rutland tomorrow to Sir John Harington's house to give a performance of 'Titus Andronicus' for him and his friends at New Year."

"Rutland! That's a long way for one performance."

"Nigh on a hundred miles. But they are all part of the Earl of Essex's circle so we'll be well paid." And all the same circle as the Earl of Southampton, I thought, but forbore to make comment as I did not want to spoil our new rapprochement. "Will you promise to come to Gracechurch Street as soon as possible after Twelfth Night?" he pleaded.

I promised, and his fingers pressed mine.

So we slipped back into our frequent meetings. Our first coupling was rapturous after our long separation and there was much to talk about. The bed was narrow and hard but set against the wall and we were sitting with our backs to the wall, our arms around each other and still half dressed in shirt and shift, when he said, "Lord Hunsdon has asked me to write a play for the wedding of his grand-daughter Elizabeth Carey to Sir Thomas Berkeley and I'm well on with it as they are to be married in February. The plot is centred around the marriage celebrations of Theseus and Hippolyta but much of the action takes place in an enchanted wood with crossed lovers and fairies. After my visit to Stratford I got to thinking about the Forest of Arden where I grew up and all the old country tales of Robin Goodfellow. I haven't thought of a title for it yet."

"It sounds very different from anything you've done before," I said in surprise. "It's a comedy I take it?"

"Yes, a comedy for a wedding, a story of love, of different sorts of love. But it has its dark side if you've wit enough to comprehend."

"Does love always have its dark side for you, Will?"

He thought for a moment then said, "Yes. Why did you betray me, Aemilia?"

The question came so abruptly and so unexpectedly that it took my breath away. "What do you mean by that?" I replied finally, trying to keep my voice steady.

"Southampton told me that you slept with him." He got up from the bed and began dressing.

"Oh he did, did he?" I took a deep breath. "And you believe him because he said so. Well the Earl of Southampton is a great liar." Will looked uncertain as he lifted his head to look at me so I continued with more confidence, I was used to lying to Alfonso, "You know him better than I. I have only seen him occasionally and spoken to him once at the playhouse, but you must know that he does not set great store by the truth, especially if he wants to create an effect." I warmed to my theme. "He loves the theatre and he is like a player, playing different roles according to his whims and making up the dialogue accordingly."

"I have never found him dishonest." He finished lacing his hose.

"Well time will tell. But you must admit he likes to demonstrate his power." I climbed from the bed and stood in front of him, making him look at me. "Doesn't he like to see you grovel, make you aware of how subservient you are to him?" He winced as if he had been struck and I pressed home my advantage. "He's playing with you, making you doubt me because you love me and it would amuse him to destroy our love and show how much power he has over you." My voice increased in intensity as I seized his shoulders for this was the truth.

"Methinks the lady doth protest too much," he said dryly, moving away to find his doublet. "How is it you know him so well if you have only spoken with him once?"

I wondered if I had given myself away but I replied firmly, "Because of what you have told me about him." I took a chance, "And I have read some of the sonnets that have been circulated." He was buttoning his doublet but again he flinched and I demanded, "Are you going to believe his word against mine? Because that's what it is, Will. Henry Wriothesley is rich and powerful and has been generous to you and others but I find him despicable. So who do you believe, him or me?"

He had moved to sit at the table and I was standing over him. He sighed then said wearily, "I believe you, Aemilia. I'm sorry. Forgive me."

I wasn't sure that I had convinced him and guilt made me lash out at him, "I don't know why you don't write a play about jealousy and suspicion, I'm sure you could do it feelingly."

He apologised again and I felt ashamed at his abjection, at the realisation that I could abase him so wrongfully. I turned away and began to get dressed and nothing more was said on the subject. We talked of other things but afterwards when I left I doubted that he really had believed me. Will was intelligent and perceptive and his writings revealed a deep understanding of the emotions. He said he believed me because that was the way he wanted it but I had the awful presentiment that it was because he needed his trust in Southampton to be inviolate. The subject was never broached again and we continued as if nothing had happened but to me something had died between us.

Francis Drake died at the end of January. Richard Hawkins had died last year at the beginning of the ill-fated voyage to the Spanish main and now Drake had succumbed to dysentery whilst still away. He had been buried at sea, to the accompaniment of drums, cannon and trumpets, by the time the tragic news reached London. A memorial service was held in St. Paul's church with its squat tower a favourite landmark in the city (the spire having been destroyed by lightning thirty years ago), though everyone acknowledged that his most appropriate resting place was the sea that had made him a legend. King Philip of Spain rejoiced and Seville was illuminated. But all England mourned the hero who had shown Spain what Englishmen were made of.

Although Will and I continued to meet regularly something had changed between us, evoked by his mistrust and my guilt. For the first time we were not a perfect union, thinking each other's thoughts, anticipating each other's actions. Sometimes he would be burning with desire for me, other times I would sense a feeling of self-disgust when we had made love. Sometimes he would want to talk about his work, words and ideas pouring from him as if he were drunk with creativity. Other times he would be morose and sullen, my eager questions receiving only monosyllabic replies. Instead of the spontaneity that had always existed between us I began to dread his moods, wondering what humour I would find him in when I opened the door. And yet on the occasions when we were in tune our lovemaking was more complete than it had ever been, spiced with a fierce passion that had grown from our divergence.

After its first private performance at the Blackfriars to celebrate the wedding of Elizabeth Carey, Will's new play, which he had titled 'A Midsummer Night's Dream', was acted at the public playhouses. Although not always possible I tried to see a new play on its first performance so was in my usual place at The Curtain one fine afternoon in early spring. So also was Henry Wriothesley, not seated on the stage this time but in one of the 'gentlemen's rooms' with a company of young gallants, screened from my view by curtains so that I was able to enjoy the play without distraction. It was a complicated story with four plots running concurrently and Will's ability to control the separate threads then intertwine them was masterly. His writing was improving all the time. The audience was enthusiastic, especially during the comedy with the mechanicals and the tragedy they enact before the Duke. Will had said how much the actors enjoyed themselves in this parody of their own art and Dick Burbage's delight as Bottom the weaver, mocking one of his own exuberant roles, was clearly evident.

Afterwards the exultant actors were surrounded by admirers, amongst them the Earl and his companions. I had intended to leave unnoticed but the crush was intense with people heaving and pushing, and making little headway I suddenly felt my arm imprisoned in a strong grip. Expecting it to be some excited playgoer looking to round off his afternoon entertainment with an accessible partner, I turned angrily only to find one of Southampton's young minions beside me. "Mistress Lanier, the Earl of Southampton wishes to speak with you."

I was on the point of making an angry retort but his grasp was strong and he was already leading me towards where the Earl was leaning languidly against the stage and talking with Will so that I had no option but to reluctantly obey. He smiled and saluted me extravagantly, as much as space allowed, saying, "Mistress Lanier, my dear Aemilia, your beauty refuses to be hidden. I am on hand to offer you a passage in my coach. I am sure you would prefer to ride rather than walk along the common highway with the meaner folk, and it is a long way to Westminster."

I glanced briefly at Will but his face was impassive. I had thought of refusing but that would have been a matter of grave insult in public to a man of the Earl's standing and besides common sense urged me it was the more practical choice to a long walk. So after a moment's thought I politely acknowledged my consent. At least he was not alone but in the company of others and surely Will would see all this.

"However firstly I am sure you would wish to join with us all in complimenting our author for an excellent play, and all the players for so ably interpreting it." He gestured towards Will as if giving me permission to talk to him.

"It was unsurpassed. And the players o'er-topped themselves." For the love of God, Will, understand what I am really saying and what I would say if we were alone, I prayed.

"It is easier to write parts for individuals that I know well. That is the virtue of belonging to a company like the Lord Chamberlain's Men. Now if you will pardon me, my Lord, I have much work to do in helping to strike this afternoon's performance, I must play my part with my fellows. Mistress Lanier." He bowed formally and turned away. Southampton looked amused then led me from the building with many curious eyes upon us, including some of the actors though most of them were busy about their work.

His emblazoned coach was waiting outside, parked ostentatiously, but his companions made their way to the horse pond where their horses were being looked after by boys eager to earn a penny and to my dismay I found myself alone with Southampton in the spacious interior of the conveyance.

"I thought your usual mode of transport was on horseback," I remarked tartly.

"You're quite right. I hate coaches - too slow and uncomfortable. But one never knows whom one might pick up at the playhouses." His hand was already on my thigh above my stocking and I moved away from him angrily.

"This is not what I expected," I said frostily, disdaining to address him by his title. "You offered me a passage home and I accepted in good faith."

"Why do you always doubt my word, Aemilia. I am offering you a passage home, with some extras. Surely you didn't expect anything less from me, you know me well enough. The coach is large enough for us to make love in total seclusion."

"Do you honestly think I am a whore?" I asked wearily. "What happened between us was a mistake that I sincerely repent and I meant it when I said I would see you no more in that way. I hope you will not take advantage of me now."

"I never force myself on a woman who is not willing, you may believe me there." He shrugged and moved away from me, taking out his pipe, tobacco and tinder box.

I watched the quick movements of his long elegant fingers then asked, "Why did you tell Will about us?"

"I don't know." I looked at him in amazement and he continued, "Do we always know why we do things? Mischief, boredom, jealousy. I wanted to prise you away from him, I wanted to shatter his illusions about me,

I wanted to demonstrate my power over him, play with him like a cat with a mouse. Sometimes his servility irritates me. You aren't overawed by me. You don't flatter and fawn, in fact you can be insolent. I like you for that." The smoke curled upwards from his pipe and I tried to see his expression through the fug. "Anyway I won't be seeing either of you for a long time, I'm going to Cadiz with Essex."

"Cadiz?"

"An expedition to the Spanish mainland. Drake's dead, Ireland is in arms waiting for Spanish help, King Philip is preparing a new armada, so Essex has persuaded the Queen to let him nip Spanish aggression in the bud by moving against them now. He's got Raleigh to bury old animosities and go with him, thirteen thousand volunteers and nearly a hundred ships. We are to sail from Plymouth by June."

"Does Will know?"

"I've left it for you to tell him."

"Then he'll know we've been together."

"So that gives us grounds for a farewell celebration, the three of us. We could make love together, united in our ties to each other. I'll suggest it to Will."

His face assumed its Machiavellian expression and I wasn't sure whether he was serious or not. I groaned inwardly at what the implications might be. Fortunately we had arrived at the Long Ditch, though in full view of our neighbours. That meant gossip afoot and if it ever came to Alfonso's ears I would have to explain to him how I had accepted the Earl of Southampton's generous offer of a passage from Shoreditch in his carriage, not with the Earl himself of course.

I could not make such a pretence with Will the next time we met. But although cool in his manner towards me he made no mention of what had occurred after the performance, only eager to know what I had thought of the play. Now we were alone I could enthuse without affectation and as always when we talked about his work his spirits came alive.

"Was it really true love though?" I asked. "Theseus subdued Hippolyta by force, Demetrius was made to love Helena by a trick, and Oberon took his revenge on Titania for *supposed* infidelity," I paused significantly, "by making her copulate with a donkey and debasing her in this way, intimating that the act of love itself is beastly. What were you saying Will?"

"Perhaps that love is what we make it - sometimes a power struggle, sometimes an illusion, sometimes a mere animal instinct. I told you it had a dark side, as dreams have."

I looked at him enquiringly, willing him to confess into which category he placed our love but as usual he shied away from expressing his personal feelings. Instead he continued with an effort at lightheartedness, "Finally it is just a play, just something to make the groundlings laugh and the gatherers count our profits. After all Puck excuses it at the end, *'If we shadows have offended, Think but this and all is ended, That you have but slumbered here.'* Anyway I've already started a new play about a Jew as I mentioned to you last year. My Jew however will be a real believable character not an extended Morality Vice like Marlowe's. I've decided to use the Italian story you told me about the three caskets and I've set the scene in Venice in honour of you."

I regarded him sceptically, wondering what concealed references there would be. Then whilst he was in good humour I told him about Southampton. I was not prepared for the extremity of his reaction.

"Is this true?" he cried in disbelief. "Why? Why is he going to Cadiz? He isn't a soldier, he has no experience, he'll get himself killed. How can he waste himself like this, his beauty, his gifts, his generous spirit." His voice was anguished as he sank to the table with his head in his hands repeating the same sentiments over and over while I stood in amazement. Finally he cried, "How can I manage without him, what shall I do if I am never to see him again." There were tears in his eyes and I stood speechless until with a sudden abruptness he turned on me, "How do you know this? When did he tell you? Did you go to his house and make love when he took you home in his coach? How can you both betray me like this?"

"Stop it, Will," I shouted at last. "He took me straight back to Long Ditch. I have no amorous dealings with Southampton, when will you believe me, what do I have to do to convince you. And as a matter of fact he's going off to Cadiz because he's got himself into trouble at Court with a woman, a woman he has fallen in love with and compromised himself because she is not a suitable choice for him. Not me, Will Shakespeare, not me, but a woman called Elizabeth Vernon, a cousin of the Earl of Essex. Alfonso told me this on good authority. The Queen is furious because he refused Burghley's grand-daughter and has now got himself involved with a mere country squire's lass. Your precious Henry Wriothesley is head over heels in love with a woman." I was shouting louder now, all my pent up resentment at his inconstancy rushing out in a flow of rage. "So you have lost him anyway, whether he marries or he dies." Fury and hurt combined to consume me and snatching up my gloves and reticule I stalked from the room slamming the door behind me as I left him weeping.

It was a year of deaths. In the summer Lord Hunsdon died aged seventy. Our son Henry was three. For me it felt like the end of a part of my life because although I had had no contact with him for three years the child we shared continued to be a bond between us and I had never given up hoping that one day he might acknowledge him, especially as he had grown into such a quick and attractive boy. He was given a great state funeral at St. Paul's to which the Queen attended, noticeably grieving. Alfonso was one of the musicians with the full panoply of the Queen's Musick and I took Henry with me into the church and then to watch the long solemn procession pass. I wanted him to know later, though he was too young to realise it now, that he had attended the funeral of his father for I intended to tell him his true parentage when he was of a suitable age. I had wept on hearing of his death, remembering his generosity to me, the way he had followed my path to maturity, his passion in those early days of my youthfulness and the way he had initiated me into the arts of love. I wept also because he had cast me off together with our son, whom I held in my arms as all his numerous family walked openly grieving in the funeral procession. You should be there with your half-brothers and sisters I thought as he waved at the spectacle and looked eagerly for Alfonso amongst the musicians. All London came to pay their final respects for Henry Carey had been a popular Lord, a brave soldier who had helped to keep the peace, a wise councillor who had helped to rule the land and a generous patron who had supported players and playwrights. I wondered what the Lord Chamberlain's Men would do now and knew that they must be worried by the death of their patron.

I told myself this was the reason I wanted to see Will for we had stayed apart since our stormy altercation over

Southampton. I did not know how he would receive me but as soon as he opened the door to me at Gracechurch Street we were in each other's arms, all bitterness forgotten in the solace of our nearness. It was almost two months since the Spanish expedition had sailed and the English force had already succeeded in capturing Cadiz then gone on to harry other ports along the coast and intercept Spanish ships carrying treasure from the Indies. Will made no mention of it and I hoped that now Henry Wriothesley was far away indefinitely we could return to the idyllic days when we had first become lovers, a view he seemingly shared.

"What will happen to you now that Lord Hunsdon has died?" I asked.

"We are to be taken over by the new Lord Chamberlain so our name remains the same."

"That must be a relief to you," I ventured, for not every nobleman was willing to give his name to players and be their patron.

"No, not at all. In fact we are greatly worried. Do you know who the new Lord Chamberlain is? It's Lord Cobham, a Puritan and a hater of the playhouses. He is a close friend of the Lord Mayor who last year was intent on pulling down The Theatre and The Curtain but for the intervention of our good Lord Hunsdon so we are afraid that he might actually support the proposal. Not a happy thought! But for the moment we are out of London, we are due to go on tour into Kent within the next two weeks."

Although the players often left the City in the height of summer it came as an unexpected blow that we were to be separated so soon after our newly-retrieved happiness. But I knew that was a player's life, moving from venue to venue, from Shoreditch to Southwark, to different inns and private houses and touring the countryside even as far as the North of England and beyond, a few years ago some of the Lord Chamberlain's Men had travelled to Denmark. It was the same with the musicians, my father had done it and I knew that Alfonso would be following the Queen again to her summer residence at Greenwich and perhaps even on progress. He had only desisted from attempting to go on the Cadiz expedition on the express command of his father who insisted his place was in the Queen's Musick, but had followed all the news avidly and still felt resentful so I hoped a Progress out of London would cure his restlessness. I settled down to passing the summer months alone once more.

However the players were back sooner than expected and by the end of August the Lord Chamberlain's Men were in London again. I waited eagerly for a sight of Will and as soon as I heard of their first performance, Peele's 'Old Wives' Tale' at The Cross Keys Inn, I was in my usual place in the first gallery overlooking the yard. However there was no sign of him amongst the players. I never usually made myself noticeable amongst the actors though most members of the company suspected a liaison between Will and me. It wasn't uncommon amongst itinerant players and musicians, though, contrary to Puritan report which branded them with low morals, most of the Chamberlain's Men were respectably married with families. But I had to know where Will was and I approached one of his friends, John Hemminges, a leading actor and sharer in the company. The antithesis to the Puritan idea of a typical player, he and his wife Rebecca had a large family as well as sharing their house with several apprentices and giving lodgings to hired men when necessary, and he was active in church affairs in his parish of St. Mary

Aldenbury, whilst being devoted to his art and an excellent character actor.

"Will has gone to Stratford, his son has died. Word was brought to him whilst we were in Faversham," he explained. "It was a great shock to him and he was stricken with grief, especially because it occurred during his absence. He left immediately to arrange the funeral. He will be back but we don't know when."

I thanked him and left, feeling numb. My heart went out to Will, riven with pain as I knew his must be. His only son Hamnet was eleven. I was relieved that Alfonso was not at home because in the privacy of our chamber I wept for Will, feeling the loss as my own. I knew how much he had worried about the boy and how guilt-stricken he had been many times for not being there to help with his rearing. I hugged Henry in my arms, though he struggled to be free from my overwhelming emotion, imagining how I would feel if he were taken from me for at less than four years old he was still in the dangerous age of childhood whereas Hamnet at eleven was considered to be almost safely grown.

Two weeks later Will returned. For the first time ever he sent word to me by a note delivered by the youngest stage hand Gregory, a jack-of-all-trades whose tasks included sticking up playbills around the city so he was familiar with the streets. I went to Gracechurch Street wondering how I was going to console him but sure that he would be in need of the comfort I could give. He was usually waiting at the door when he heard me run up the stairs but this time I had to knock and it was a short while before it opened. He looked at me listlessly, his expressive eyes lifeless, and I noticed his dirty shirt and ink-stained fingers. I was shocked by his haggard appearance but also by the sense of something different about him that I couldn't at first identify. He made no move to embrace me and then I recognised the difference in his demeanour as an aloofness, the distance of a stranger at a first encounter, as if he had put up a protective wall around himself that prevented any close contact. I wanted to touch him but I could sense instinctively that he didn't want me to and I looked at him appealingly as I said, "I'm so sorry."

He brushed my words aside as if he didn't want to hear condolences and when he spoke it was not what I had expected to hear. "I can't see you again."

The brusqueness of the words hit me like a physical blow and I reeled a little. "May I sit down?" I asked weakly and he gestured half-heartedly to a chair standing beside the table. He made no attempt to sit himself but shuffled uncomfortably, his eyes not meeting my gaze.

"I had to tell you personally and not just ignore you."

I felt sick in the pit of my stomach, not understanding this sudden change of heart after we had recovered our earlier happiness before he went away. "Is this because of your grief?" I asked gently, trying to understand.

He sat down then facing me, his elbows resting on the table, hands clasped together. "More than that." His words were staccato, forced out unevenly but with a precision as if he had prepared them. "I think that Hamnet's death is a judgement on me for my sins. God has taken away my posterity, my immortality, because I have neglected my duty as a husband and father for the pleasures of the flesh."

I heaved a sigh but my words came out without hesitation, "It is folly, Will, to think like this. You know your son was never strong and his health has been deteriorating for some time. Nothing that you did or did not do would have made any difference." I made to touch him but he turned away.

"Our love was wrong, Aemilia, for both of us," he said. "It has brought nothing but pain and I can't endure more pain."

His words hurt me and I said vehemently, "And pleasure too, surely it has brought us pleasure. And much more than pleasure - ecstasy of our bodies and harmony of our minds, you know that."

"More pain than pleasure," his voice sounded strangled. "I know you were unfaithful to me with Henry Wriothesley. I tried to believe otherwise but I know your history. And you compounded it by lying to me. Tell me the truth now. For God's sake do me the honour of telling me the truth for once in our relationship."

"I love you, Will, that is the truth." I seized his arm and held it fast, speaking earnestly. "I love you more than I have ever loved anyone in my life, that is the only truth that matters."

"I loved you too, Aemilia," he cried. "But it is over now."

"This is your grief speaking, Will. Give yourself time to recover. You cannot mean this. You cannot turn your back on everything we have been to each other," I cried passionately.

He stood, releasing himself from my grasp and began to pace the room, crushing in his fingers a quill he had picked up from the table. "I do mean it. I have thought about it carefully. I don't want us ever to meet again."

I looked around the room, the bed where we had so often made love, the table where he wrote and we talked, the piles of books, the dust, our room that had been "everywhere" to us. "And you don't want me ever to come here again?" My voice was no more than a strangled whisper.

"No. From now on I shall keep my bed vow. I'm going to buy a house in Stratford for my family, something that I should have done a long time ago instead of leaving them as my parents' responsibility, and I intend to go back there more often for duty's sake. But the only thing that matters to me now is my work, writing and acting will be the two loves in my life."

Two loves. He had always had two loves. For a moment I felt pity for Anne his wife who was excluded. Perhaps she had always known the same agony of loss that I was experiencing now. Because I knew that I had lost him. I knew him too well not to understand that he was implacable in his resolve. I stood to go because I was determined not to abase myself by pleading further with him. I had done that once with Lord Hunsdon to no purpose and I had vowed then that I would never again so humiliate myself with a man. Despite our love, and I did believe that he had loved me, I realised he had not loved me enough and I could never compete in his affections with his work, or with Henry Wriothesley.

"Very well if that is your decision," I forced myself to say. I gathered up my skirts and made for the door then turned. "I am truly sorry about Hamnet and I have shared your pain more than you know. But if you do change your mind when grief has abated somewhat I shall not be here for you. You have made much of my malfeasance with Southampton but you have betrayed me worse. I do not know what your filiation with him is but your heart has always belonged more to him than to me, and your concern was always that I took him away from you rather than that he robbed you of me."

He did not reply as I closed the door behind me and walked slowly down the attic stairs.

It was raining when I stepped outside but I did not know whether it was raindrops or tears that blurred my vision as I looked back at the house where I had spent the happiest hours of my life. Pain consumed me totally.

I did not know how I could continue to exist without the love, the companionship, the intellectual partnership we had shared, the meeting of minds. I recalled his gentleness, his wit, his enthusiasms about his work and his sudden dark moods and melancholies, all of which embodied the man I loved more than I had ever thought possible.

It was a year of deaths - Francis Drake, Lord Hunsdon, Hamnet Shakespeare. And I died a death too. Some flame in my heart expired and life would never be the same again.

CHAPTER 12

BASSE DANCE

I was twenty-eight years old. I had lost my old protector then the love of my life, cast off by both of them. I was unable to give my husband children and we were getting steadily poorer. As the year 1597 dawned I was nearer to despair than at any time of my life. More than ever I missed the companionship I had known with Will Shakespeare, reading poetry and discussing it, analysing the plays I had seen and comparing the merits of new authors. Reading on my own didn't have the same enjoyment and I didn't have the money to attend the playhouses so regularly, as well as finding them painful reminders of Will and the happy times we had spent together. Although Alfonso and I shared a passion for music he was no intellectual companion and his work kept him often away. He was also uncomfortably restless and worried about money.

"We shall have to give up the house, we can't afford it, Aemilia. We must find somewhere smaller to live, perhaps move back into the city," he said once again, these declarations assuming a predictable regularity.

"No we can't give up the house, it would be humiliating. I will sell some more of my things, the rest of my jewels, some more of our plate." I was distressed by the loss of much that I had been given by Lord Hunsdon but anything was better than losing the house.

Alfonso sighed. "I don't know why you are so insistent. The house is far too big for us with only one child."

"Enough, Alfonso," I shouted. Then more calmly, "I do hope we shall have more children, you know that."

"We could sell the house and live with my mother now that Ellen and Innocent both have their own households and Jerome and Clement are apprenticed. With only Andrea at home she would be happy to have us and it would be company for you when I am away performing, and better for Henry too."

"No, I will certainly not give up my own home, how can you ask that of me when I have given you so much and you have wasted it," I shouted furiously. Surprisingly he didn't retaliate so I proffered, "I will dismiss two of the maids and manage with only one of them, though that will be only a small saving, we pay them hardly anything."

"We provide them with accommodation, food and clothes, and prices are rising all the time."

"Very well, I will make small economies whenever I can. And I won't go to the playhouses so much either." I didn't have the same inclination to go now, especially to watch the Lord Chamberlain's Men. It was too painful to see Will or watch one of his plays.

"There's talk of another expedition under Raleigh and Essex," he said casually, though I wasn't deceived by his off-hand manner. "The attack on Cadiz was such a success that it has sparked a lot of interest in a voyage of volunteers to capture Spanish treasure ships in the Azores. Everyone is saying that there is wealth to be got here. They divide the treasure and apparently the gains are vast." He looked at me consideringly from narrowed eyes and as I didn't reply he continued, "If I could find a way to join them I could make our fortune and we could be rich, perhaps richer than you have ever been, Aemilia."

For once his words about travelling did not fall on deaf ears. After five years of marriage I had given up all hope of Alfonso receiving any preferment through his music and I was desperate to solve our financial problems. It was true that Francis Drake had made fortunes for himself and his investors, the Queen amongst them, by his attacks on the Spanish ships sailing from the New World loaded with gold bullion and precious stones of inestimable value. Now Raleigh was planning to emulate him, the previous voyage to Cadiz having been a success. All those who sailed on such voyages partook of the gains and many humble men had enriched themselves beyond expectation, sometimes gaining a knighthood in the bargain. I thought carefully about what he was suggesting. "You would have to buy yourself a share in the expedition first and where could the money come from?" I said consideringly.

Alfonso hesitated then replied, "If we sold the house I would have enough money to do so." Seeing that I was about to interrupt he continued hurriedly, "It would be an investment, can't you see? An investment in a profitable undertaking."

"Let me think about it," I said at last and he knew he had to be satisfied for the time being. The idea was worthy of consideration but I was not willing to sell the house for an enterprise that could be uncertain. There was both risk and danger involved which was why the stakes were so high. It would be catastrophic if we sold the house and then everything was lost. If only I could think of another way to raise some money!

Alfonso continued to broach the subject regularly and I was becoming more enamoured of the project but all the ideas I had considered about raising money I had to abandon for one reason or another.

"If I don't quickly volunteer my name it will be too late, we must come to a decision soon," he complained at my irresolution, but an idea was beginning to form in my mind.

"There is one thing, Alfonso, that perhaps you have not given sufficient thought," I said carefully so as not to offend him. "This is a military expedition. There will be hard fighting and loss of life involved. Raleigh and Essex are military men and most of the volunteers will have had some experience of warfare in the Low Countries and in Ireland. You are a musician, do you think you will be able to cope with mortal combat?"

"I'm not short on courage," he replied stoutly, "and I can use a sword and dagger. You should see me in tavern brawls," he grinned then seeing my expression added, "I'm young and strong and I shall easily learn. They say Essex is a fine leader. I've heard that John Donne the poet is going."

"Very well, if you're sure," I said. "I don't think we should sell the house but I'll see what influence I can summon up. I still know some important people."

He looked at me suspiciously. "Lord Hunsdon is dead. Who else do you know? I'd rather sell the house than have it said my wife bought my share by playing the whore."

"There are times when I hate you, Alfonso Lanier. I have never played the whore since we were wed."

He scrutinised me carefully then said with a hint of bitterness, "You haven't been faithful."

"And have you?"

"It's different for a man."

"Why?" I retorted angrily. "You're married too. Why is it different for a man?"

"Come, Aemilia, don't be stupid. Of course it's different for a man, it's only natural for us to satisfy our physical needs. It's different for a woman because she has to know who is the father of her child and her husband has to be convinced the child is his. Fortunately I have been spared such doubt," he added sarcastically. For once I had to allow him the mastery and remained silent. He sighed then acknowledged my capitulation by saying, "I love Henry as my own son, you know that."

I nodded in agreement. He did spend much time with the child and had begun to teach him to play the recorder as well as getting his cousin Mark the luthier to make a small lute for him.

"Don't mistrust me Alfonso," I said earnestly, "but I have an idea. Just let me do this in my own way."

At first I had thought about the Earl of Essex. I would go to Robert Devereux, be completely honest and for the sake of old acquaintance ask if he would be willing to pay Alfonso's share into the enterprise and divide any ensuing profit. But Essex was not a rich man, everyone knew this. Once one when the Queen was angry with him she had made him pay back all the money she had generously lent to him, an act which had put him into great financial straits. I had heard however that the Earl of Southampton was also to be part of this expedition and Henry Wriothesley was a very rich man.

I dressed in one of my best gowns, a yellow and flame coloured Spanish farthingale, with a red velvet hat styled like a man's with a low crown and shallow brim, of the sort the Queen favoured, and hired a coach in Kings Street to take me the mile and a half or so to Holborn where Southampton's house stood near Gray's Inn. I hoped my journey would not be a fruitless one after the unaccustomed expenditure and I felt a shiver of trepidation as I approached. The coachman was impressed by my destination and followed my commands to wait outside without demur. I walked through the arched gateway with its heraldic emblazons and into the courtyard where I was faced with a three-storey edifice of palatial proportions. I hesitated momentarily, then I recalled our afternoons in the Blue Boar and our evening on his barge and I grasped the brass knocker on the studded oak door with renewed determination. It was opened by an expensively-liveried middle-aged man with a supercilious expression and when I asked to see the Earl he surveyed me with distaste saying, "The Earl of Southampton is not in residence. You may send a message asking for an appointment with him and it will be delivered."

He made to close the door but I stepped forward and with the width of my farthingale between us managed to enter before he could act. He bustled after me in great anxiety, raising his voice as he chided my impudence and that brought other menservants scurrying into the lofty hall. I couldn't resist a quick glance around at the floor of Italian marble and walls hung with Flemish tapestries against which stood rich oak furniture beautifully carved and obviously made by the most skilled craftsmen. But I knew I stood a high chance of being evicted so I drew myself up to my full height, waved my hand imperiously and commanded in a loud voice, "Please inform the Earl of Southampton that Mistress Aemilia Lanier would like to see him."

I did not know what would have happened had not a voice spoken from above, redolent with amusement, and all eyes turned towards the massive central staircase of ornately fashioned polished oak with treads of porphyry-veined marble to match the floor. "Allow the lady entrance," said Henry Wriothesley, surveying us from the top then making his descent. He was wearing a long doublet of white satin embroidered with silver thread, belted at the waist with a jewelled buckle. Beneath his white padded hose were knee-length canions of black velvet then white silk stockings and black leather latchet shoes with the new-fashioned square toes. His chestnut hair hung in waves past his shoulders. He descended slowly and languidly, relishing the effect, then holding out his hand to me he took mine to kiss it saying, "Aemilia, what a pleasant surprise." With a mere raise of his eyebrows he dismissed the servants and I was tempted to favour them with a triumphant smile but judged it not wise to presume too much. He took my hand and led me back up the staircase. I wondered where he was taking me but he ushered me into an oak-panelled study dominated by a huge oriel leaded window overlooking a formal garden, bookshelves completely covering two walls yet otherwise plainly furnished with two desks and comfortable chairs.

"Oh how wonderful to have so many books," I burst out involuntarily, gazing in envy.

"This is where Will Shakespeare used to work," he said, eying me carefully, and I recognised a note of provocation in his tone. He motioned me to a seat then said, "Now, Aemilia, what can I do for you because I am certain the reason for your visit is to ask a favour of some kind."

I felt a flush stain my cheeks but I had never shown humility with him so I answered defiantly, "Yes, my lord, I'm sorry but it is true. Is it so obvious?"

He shrugged carelessly, "I'm used to it. It is what everyone does."

I studied him intently for the first time and noted how bronzed his skin was, how strong and well developed his physique. "You have thrived on the Cadiz expedition,"

I dared to say. "Everyone spoke highly of your military prowess." He shrugged again dismissively and I followed on quickly, "They say you are to be part of the new voyage to the Azores and this concerns my suit. My husband Alfonso Lanier would like to go on the expedition but he does not have the money to buy himself a share and I wondered if you could help him."

"You want to rid yourself of him?" His smile was cynical.

"On the contrary I want him to bring back some money for us."

"Lord Hunsdon's money all gone."

It was a statement rather than a question and I knew he would be aware of all the rumours. However I sensed he was sympathetic so I continued, "Alfonso is young and strong and I have no doubt he would acquit himself well. He is also an excellent musician and I know how valuable musicians are on long voyages."

"Yes, Raleigh, like Drake, enjoys music in the evenings. So Aemilia you want me to buy Alfonso's share into the islands voyage, is that it? And what do I get in return?"

"What do you want?" I asked levelly.

He had been standing and now he reached towards me, pulling me out of the chair and into his arms. His face was close to mine and I could smell his perfume. I waited for his reply, trembling a little. "Nothing," he said at last. "I want nothing." I pulled back a little so that I could study his face. "I could ask you for all sorts of things and no doubt you would give them to me. But I am a reformed character. I have fallen in love and sworn to change my ways. I do not want you or your husband to live with the knowledge that his place was bought by an ignoble transaction. Besides I have used you in the past and I owe you something." I searched his face but there was no sign of mockery. "Rest content I will make sure Alfonso Lanier's name is registered on the list of volunteers and I will see to the account."

He kissed me, but only on the cheek, then he was leading me downstairs and into the hall where two servants were waiting to open the door on his command. I had had no time to thank him but when I turned towards him he gestured with his hand and I knew the transaction was done. It had all happened so swiftly and easily that once in the coach again I felt a sense of disappointment. I had expected more of a struggle - and a reckoning. To my shame I acknowledged that when he took me in his arms I had wanted him.

Alfonso was almost drunk with excitement when I relayed the news to him, though suspicious at first about the means by which it had been achieved.

"I swear to you there was nothing improper," I insisted. "Southampton is famous for his patronage of poets, artists, writers, musicians and so on. He has more money than he knows what to do with. Paying for a musician to entertain him on a long voyage is no more than paying Will Shakespeare for writing some poems for him."

"You know what the rumours are about him and Shakespeare. I hope he doesn't expect the same from me," Alfonso grinned. "Though on such a long voyage with only men present I suppose I'd better learn the skills."

"You had better learn the skills of composing some music for him," I snapped. "The airs that Tom Morley and John Dowland have just published are selling like hot cakes."

"Composing isn't my forte, Aemilia, I leave that to others in our family. My main intention for this voyage is to fight in the action and take some share of the spoils.

But how did you come to know Southampton so well? If I remember rightly you said you were not acquainted with him."

"Not personally no, but we do have many acquaintances in common. He's a close friend of the Earl of Essex as you are aware and I have known Robert Devereux for many years, and he's familiar with many other people I knew at Court when I was with Lord Hunsdon. Also I used to see him often at the playhouses, you might remember he once had me brought home in his coach." I spoke as casually as I could but Alfonso wasn't paying a deal of attention, his mind now consumed with this new project.

The ships were scheduled to depart in June and there was much to do in preparation. Alfonso had to seek the Queen's permission to leave his post for a while, farewell visits had to be made to his numerous relations and friends and many things had to be purchased for the voyage. Warm clothing, wool cloaks, knitted caps and stockings, back and breast armour and a strong chest to carry them, all cost money and we had to resort to selling more of our possessions - some of my best linen from my apartments at Court and one of my finest gowns.

"I hope this voyage is going to be a success and you bring something back," I said feelingly.

"How are you going to manage while I'm away?" he ventured.

"I thought about taking a lodger. A woman," I insisted as I saw his face darken. "There are many widows of merchants, craftsmen, musicians even, who would be glad of rooms in a house such as ours. I could rent one of the parlours and a bedchamber for a goodly sum."

I set about making enquiries in order to soothe his doubts before he departed and he was satisfied by an elderly, soberly dressed, quietly -spoken lady, the recent widow of a scrivener who was only too happy to pay the sum we asked, offering two months in advance.

But when the time came for him to leave for Plymouth I was loath to see him go. After five years of marriage I had got used to having him in my life and was surprised to realise how much I was going to miss his talk, his music, his presence in my bed, even our sparring together. I bade him farewell with genuine regret. "Take good care of yourself, don't put yourself foolishly into danger," I warned, but he was too full of excitement to heed and my unaccustomed solicitude seemed to go unnoticed.

Only with Henry did he show some real emotion about leaving. The child was crying piteously, clinging to him and begging him not to go away. Alfonso hugged him close saying, "I shall come back with so many exciting stories to tell you that every night there will be a different one for you to listen to, and I shall be able to teach you how to fight with a sword, I will make you a wooden one. Now you must promise me that you will practise your recorder every day so that when I come home you can play beautiful music for me." The child nodded tearfully, holding onto him, and I could see tears in Alfonso's eyes too. "Take great care of him, help him to practise with the lute," he ordered me, but he didn't say he would miss me so I kept my feelings to myself.

Instead I said, "Try and make yourself known to Raleigh and Essex so that perhaps they could help you with some preferment when you return. This voyage is to further our ambitions."

He nodded in agreement. But when the time came for us to finally part I held him close, saying seriously,

"If you can bring back some treasure that will be wonderful, but that you come back safe and sound is the only issue that really counts." We had been married for five years and I had never felt so close to him, fearing to lose him as I had lost the other two men in my life. He kissed me but with no real passion, that was always reserved for when he wanted to make love.

"Keep my bed empty," he warned. Then with a final wave he was clattering away somewhat inexpertly on the horse he had hired, his sea chest having already been transported.

After he had gone I felt lonely and unsettled and Henry didn't help by continually lamenting his father. I wondered if he would come back safely or if some harm might befall him, he was after all no soldier. It was going to be a worrisome year with no obvious signs of easement and I longed to be able to see into the future.

I don't know at what point Simon Forman came into my deliberations but I found myself calling to mind how several people at Court, ladies and courtiers both, had visited him for predictions of the future as well as advice on a wide range of subjects. I had seen him several times at The Rose and The Swan because he loved plays and often frequented the playhouses, living close by on Bankside. A striking figure of about forty years of age with strong features and long dark hair, he gave an appearance of being taller than he was in his black gown and black velvet cap. He was a physician and apothecary though he fought a constant battle with the Royal College of Physicians who refused to confirm his status on the grounds that he was not officially qualified, although many people spoke highly of his skills and Sir Francis Walsingham had once intervened to prevent him from being imprisoned. He was however also an alchemist, astrologer and predictor of fate and for that reason he lived on Bankside, out of the jurisdiction of the city and the animosity of his fellow practitioners. Although a little apprehensive I decided I would go and pay him a visit.

I wasn't sure of his house but was certain that once I got to the vicinity of the playhouses someone would direct me and so it fell out. I was surprised by the size of the timber-framed building with two gables and overhanging projections boasting large leaded windows beneath which stood an impressive studded oak door but I knew he worked a thriving business and his fees could be high. Surrounding the house was a large garden of plants and herbs necessary for his profession. I knocked on the door and was admitted into the house by a neatly-presented maidservant and told to wait on a bench in a waiting room as the master was occupied. I waited for what I surmised to be nearly a halfhour then I saw a poorly dressed woman leave with a crying child and soon after the same maidservant led me into Simon Forman's consulting room. I had to lower my head a little into the doorway and as I raised my eyes he was looking at me and saying, "Mistress Aemilia Lanier, I believe. No, not divination," he continued dryly as he noted my surprise, "I have seen you oftimes in the playhouses."

He was tall and straight, not bent as might be expected from poring over books and potions, and he exuded an air of authority. His features were finely cast though I had heard that he came from a poor country family and when I looked into the piercing blue eyes, strangely at odds with the dark hair, I perceived that more than the professional authority emanating from him was a chilling suggestion of mysterious powers. He motioned me to a chair beside a large desk, taking one on the opposite side for himself and saying, "And what might I do for you, Mistress Lanier?"

I was longing to slake my curiosity by looking around the room which I was vaguely aware of being crammed with shelves containing bottles and jars, vials and alembics, volumes of old leather-bound books, with the walls covered with charts and tables of numbers and symbols, but my attention was forced on the figure facing me across a surface of papers, charts and writing materials. I felt momentarily tongue-tied so he continued, "Is it a matter of physic or astrology? No it cannot be your health that is a problem, I surmise you wish to know what the stars foretell for you."

"My husband is gone on the voyage to the Azores. I wish to know what is likely to befall him," I answered directly.

He studied my face but I was overwhelmed by the sensation that he was looking into my soul.

"Do you want to know if he will return safely, or that he will return rich and successful?"

"Both," I answered, feeling it was useless to be anything but truthful.

"Then I must cast charts for both of you and this will take some time." He drew towards him a quill and inkpot and a sheet of paper already half covered in tiny spidery script. "Firstly I need to know everything about your life. To cast a chart requires knowledge of the past as well as the present."

I related to him all the facts of my life including my time with the Suffolks, Lord Hunsdon, and my marriage to Alfonso, because I deduced this was no secret to him yet I also, almost unconsciously, felt myself compelled to reveal my feelings - my resentment at being poor, my desire to be rich and a lady again, my pride in my former noble acquaintances, and my bitterness towards Lord Hunsdon and Alfonso for what I considered their betrayal of me, Henry Carey casting me off and Alfonso wasting all my money. But I mentioned neither Will nor Southampton, either because this was not public knowledge or perhaps from a deep pain and shame that lay beyond excavation. I don't know how long I talked but he wrote it all down using strange symbols. Then he asked me questions about Alfonso and when I had finished he said, "It will take me some time to cast charts for both your husband and yourself. I must calculate the positions of the planets and their ascendant at the time of birth then the position of the planets in the twelve astrological houses to interpret present and future events, I must consult the stars and align the constellations of the zodiac, looking not merely at the future but at the past. Return in a week's time and it will be done."

"How much will it cost?" I asked anxiously as we rose together.

He smiled, a smile that curved his sensuous mouth but did not touch his eyes. "My fee is always contingent with a client's means. A rich gallant does not begrudge four angels but for the poor woman you saw leaving a penny is hard to find." He bent to kiss my hand, his lips lingering longer than was necessary and his tongue moving along my fingers. "No doubt we shall come to a suitable arrangement when it is time."

I left feeling disturbed, both by his words and the sense of latent power emanating from him, and thinking it might be better if I did not return to discover his conclusions. I had heard rumours about him - that he was unmarried and sought favours from women, though the accusation that he dabbled in necromancy was set about by his enemies in the profession of physicians. An icy finger of warning tickled my spine.

However curiosity proved stronger than alarm and I returned the following week at the appointed hour, though not without a shiver of apprehension. This time a middle-aged manservant led me immediately into his presence. He smiled welcomingly at me, holding my hand for what seemed a long time before motioning me to a chair.

"I have good news for you, Mistress Lanier," he said, unfolding a chart which he laid before me. "The auspices are very favourable for your future." He began to explain the symbols, the numbers, the lines of conjunction, finally summarising the interpretation with, "Your husband will return from the expedition rich and with honour, there is a possibility of a knighthood for his services and the indications are that you will be restored to a position of wealth and influence."

This was good news indeed and relief flooded me as beaming with satisfaction I rose asking, "How much do I owe you?"

"Not so fast, Mistress Lanier. There is no haste. Stay and drink a cup of wine with me, I find pleasure in your company." He put his arm around my waist drawing me close and then kissing me on the mouth.

I was afraid to struggle, fearing what power he might exert over me, so gently loosening his arms and smiling appeasingly at him I said, "I shall be pleased to take a cup of wine, Doctor Forman." I extricated myself from his embrace and returned calmly to my chair, continuing to smile encouragingly at him to give the impression I was not averse to his advances but privately wondering how I could get out of the situation if it went any further.

He rose and fetched a wine jug and two earthenware beakers, moving his own chair close to mine so that he could rest his hand on my knee. He touched my foot with his but the width of my gown prevented closer proximity. His hand however moved to caressing my breasts and I thought ruefully how all the men I met considered me a whore. Despite logic assuring me otherwise, I was uncertain of his magical powers and felt wary of rebutting him too harshly. I resigned myself to the knowledge that I had only two options, to leap up and flee as quickly as I could or to succumb to his intentions, when fate itself, in the person of his maidservant, intervened. Knocking at the door she called to her master that he had a visitor of importance who could not wait. I rose without too much unseemly haste, put my half-drunk cup of wine on the table and whilst still moving towards the door I took a silver shilling from my bag and handed it to him saying, "I hope I shall see you again at a more convenient time, Doctor Forman."

The suggested promise seemed to satisfy him for while opening the door for me he said, "Be sure to visit me again, Mistress Lanier. But I know you will."

As I was leaving I saw a richly dressed man preparing to enter and recognised him as Sir Richard Rich, Penelope's husband, who abruptly turned his face away, obviously ashamed to be seen visiting the magician. As I passed the unmarked coach waiting outside I breathed a sigh of relief at my escape. There was a strangely unnerving quality about Simon Forman. He was undoubtedly a lecher but he exuded a charisma that was more than a forceful personality. There was an aura of mystery enveloping him, an uncertainty as to the extent of his powers, that excited speculation. In his presence I was aware of the same kind of fascination emanating from the Earl of Southampton - the manipulation of power, a hint of wickedness, the enticement of the unknown. But whereas with Henry Wriothesley there was overwhelming physical attraction, with Simon Forman it was the compulsion of an inner force. I was determined never to cross his threshold again.

However his favourable predictions sustained me as the weeks after Alfonso's departure dragged interminably. News was passed around but it was already out of date. The expedition had only just left when the ships were forced back to Plymouth by fierce storms and lay in the harbour there for several weeks. It was to be August before they finally made their departure and I could imagine what Alfonso would be doing in the taverns and stews meanwhile. Despite a certain reluctance, I couldn't resist going to see Will's latest play, 'The Merchant of Venice', at The Theatre. Shylock the Jew, played by Richard Burbage, was a full-blooded character as different from Marlowe's protagonist as Will had promised and he had also made use of the story of the three caskets that I had told him. Yet although there was much beautiful verse I was left with a feeling of unease. The hero was called Bassanio who married the rich heiress for her money while his real love was given to his friend Antonio, played by Will himself. I wished I could have discussed it with him and a great longing filled my soul for the little dusty attic in Gracechurch Street. I wondered if he missed me as much as I missed him.

In actual fact I was glad of the company of my lodger, Mistress Wayman. As summer approached I began to feel increasingly unwell. I attributed my general malaise to the hot weather and the stink of the streets but I couldn't eat for a persistent nausea and the cramps in my stomach intensified. It was Mistress Wayman who tentatively asked in her diffident manner, "Do you think there might be a possibility that you are with child Aemilia?"

I was shocked into a realisation that she might be right, the possibility never having crossed my mind. It was hardly a good time to be pregnant with Alfonso away indefinitely, especially as the child was certainly his and I couldn't share the news with him.

I had sworn never to visit Doctor Forman again. But I knew that besides being an astrologer and rumoured magician he was known to be an excellent physician and people spoke highly of his skill. He distilled his own herbs and prepared his own medicines and did not subscribe to the conventional time-worn theories of the College of Physicians which was one reason why they opposed him. However I was determined not to go alone so I asked Mistress Wayman to accompany me, the first time she had ever been on Bankside. She was patently shocked by the squalor of Southwark, holding my arm as vagrants and disreputable-looking characters jostled us in the dirty narrow streets and keeping her eyes averted from the signs of the numerous brothels and insalubrious taverns. The strange edifices of The Rose and The Swan she surveyed in amazement.

"One day I will bring you with me to watch a play," I said with some amusement.

"Oh no, Aemilia, I could not possibly enter into a playhouse," she was visibly shocked. "I have heard of so many crimes committed amongst the spectators and the plays themselves do not encourage a moral way of life."

I assured her that this was not true but I wondered what she would say if she knew the details of my own life. However she relaxed when we reached Simon Forman's house and she saw it was a place of considerable size and dignity. She was told to stay in the waiting room when I was ushered into Doctor Forman's presence.

"You see fit to return, Mistress Lanier," he smiled. "But why the need for a chaperone?"

"Mistress Wayman lodges with me. I felt the need for someone to accompany me because I am not at all well and feared I might not make the journey safely," I replied and proceeded to tell him about my sickness, my head pains, my stomach cramps and my supposition that

I was with child. "I have had difficulty in conceiving and have not been able to bring a child to full term since my firstborn six years ago. It is your advice as a physician I am in need of now."

He nodded in acknowledgement then proceeded to make note of everything I told him, saying at last in a clipped impersonal tone, "I shall have to examine you."

His manner was entirely different to the last time I had visited him and I felt no embarrassment as I undid my laces. He laid his hands on my belly, exerting pressure, then felt my breasts but this time with the concentration of the physician and not the libertine. Then he signalled for me to dress and went to the shelves taking down jars in which were powders which he mixed together and put into two papers. "This mint and camomile will ease your sickness and this of vervain, tansy and knotgrass should help cure the stomach cramps. Dissolve each in a solution of wine and boiled water and drink morning and evening."

"Are you not going to bleed me?" I asked in surprise.

He shook his head saying vehemently, "I do not believe in weakening my patients by blood letting except for one or two particular circumstances, one of the points of contention between the Royal College of Physicians and myself." He paused then said, "I do not think you will keep this child." Then seeing the disappointment on my face he continued, "If it miscarries, as I fear it will, return and I will try to concoct something that will prevent further problems of this nature. Do not pay me now, I am sure I shall see you again." He escorted me to the door and his professional manner disappeared as he kissed me on the lips saying, "You are a beautiful woman. I would like our acquaintance to continue."

"A strange man," Mistress Wayman whispered as we left. "I only caught a glimpse of him but I found him a little intimidating."

"He is a well attested physician," I assured her. "And he is very popular here in Southwark because he treats all the poor, making up his own remedies for them, and does not charge them as much as the apothecaries do. Yet his clients also include some of the wealthiest and most important courtiers."

As we were passing The Swan I saw John Hemminges coming out of the playhouse and stopped to greet him. "Will's back in Stratford for a time," he informed me. "He's made the purchase of a house there, a very fine house from what I hear, the biggest house in Stratford."

This confirmed that he had indeed kept his promise to his family, obviously in a large way, investing some of Southampton's money in a home for them as he said he would. "You must all be feeling happy about the new Lord Chamberlain," I remarked.

"Oh yes," laughed Hemminges. "Lord Cobham was no friend to the players but fortunately his reign was short, though I wouldn't have wished his death. However George Carey, the new Lord Hunsdon, is much more to our taste and should be as good a patron as his father was."

"So matters are going well for the Company?"

He shrugged, "As a matter of fact they could be better. The lease is due to expire on The Theatre and since James Burbage died early this year the landlord is disputing the right to renew it so we are not sure what is to happen. But Will's new play is doing well, 'The Merry Wives of Windsor', have you seen it?" When I shook my head he continued, "I'm surprised about that. You always used to be in the playhouses."

"I haven't been well," I temporised.

"Bring your companion along," Hemminges said with a nod towards Mistress Wayman. "It would be to her taste. It was commissioned by the Queen and written for the New Lord Chamberlain's investiture as a knight of the Garter at Windsor."

"Then I must see it," I assured him as we went our separate ways, thinking how Will Shakespeare's fortunes were continually rising with commissions from the nobility and favour of the Queen herself.

However I was unable to keep my word for some months. In July both the Bankside playhouses were closed by the Privy Council on account of a new play at The Swan which they considered extremely seditious. 'The Isle of Dogs', which lampooned the authorities, was written by a new young playwright called Ben Jonson, a distant relative of my mother's who lived near us in one of the poorer districts of Westminster, though his present habitation was the Marshalsea prison. Such was the precarious existence of playwrights though I didn't think Will would ever find himself in such a position, he was no rebel and content on the whole to entertain rather than satirise. However when the edict was lifted at the end of the summer I did indeed succeed in persuading Mistress Wayman in her first visit to a playhouse and although initially reluctant she found much enjoyment in this domestic comedy about two resourceful housewives and their trickery of the fat philanderer Falstaff. But once again I couldn't help being reminded of my lost life at Court. John Hemminges had said that Will had written the play at the behest of the Queen, who was a great lover of the character of Falstaff, to celebrate the investiture of the new Lord Chamberlain, George Carey, half-brother to my son Henry. The visit to The Rose was not entirely such a pleasant diversion as

I had expected as it engendered too many sad memories, not least seeing Will on stage.

All summer I had been plagued by ill-health and at the end of August I lost the child I was carrying as Doctor Forman had warned. I was full of disappointment, my melancholy increased by my subsequent weakness, and as autumn approached I lamented the loneliness of my life - Will was lost to me and Alfonso was far away with the Earls of Essex and Southampton. The voyage had sailed finally in August after many delays and difficulties and I was filled with a sense of foreboding so strong that I decided I had to visit Simon Forman again to gain his assurance that his prognosis was correct before I had to face the winter. This time I went alone, considering that though Mistress Wayman's company was accordant with a visit to a physician it was not meet for a fortune teller, and reassured by his comportment the last time.

"I lost the child," I told him when I was ushered into his presence.

"I feared it would be so," he replied.

"Why cannot I carry a child to full term?"

"There are many reasons, some of which can be helped. I will prepare a nostrum for you and when your husband returns you must take it every day, hopefully it will hold his seed and you will bear his child successfully."

"If he ever does return," I said morosely. "Are you sure he will come home safely? I am full of foreboding lately."

"This is only a product of your weakness," he assured me. "I foretold his safe return with riches and honour and an increase in your station. But I will prepare a draught to lighten your spirits, many herbs help to comfort melancholy." He put his arm around me and I leant against him, finding solace in his support. It was comforting to feel a man's strength and I laid my head against his shoulder. "The first potion will take some time to prepare. I will bring it to your house on Friday evening," he said.

I knew that he had servants to do these errands for him so I was well aware of the implications behind his words but I felt an indefinable need for his strength, his assurance. In his mesmeric presence I thought no further. "I will prepare some supper for you," I offered and our eyes locked.

He put together a draught of St. John's wort, borage and angelica and gave me the phial saying, "Leave the payment until a later date." This time he did not kiss me as he led the way out.

Afterwards on my way home I wondered why I had done it. But my spirits were low and I had found him supportive. I also had to admit to being bored and ready for some diversion in my life, and I longed for physical contact with a man after being so long alone. I remembered that Lord Hunsdon had said I was not fitted for a quiet life.

On Friday evening I warned Mistress Wayman that I was expecting a guest and she retired early to her chamber. Henry was in bed with our only surviving maidservant Nan on a truckle bed beside him. I prepared a supper of cold meats with a flagon of wine ready set on the table in the parlour and lit the candles for it was already September and the nights growing dark early. I dressed in a simple gown of green cut velvet without underpinnings and with no ruff though as usual I covered the mole on my neck with a velvet ribbon. I listened for his knock at the door and was ready to open it myself, afterwards leading him upstairs to the parlour. Immediately the door was shut behind us he took me in his arms and kissed me.

"I have prepared supper first," I said, knowing the pleasure in anticipation, and he removed his outer gown and velvet cap, laying them on the settle.

"I know your country of Italy well," he said, partaking of the meats laid before him but taking only small quantities of each. "I studied medicine at the University of Padua, a city not too far from your family's home town of Bassano."

I showed my surprise as I said, "But I thought the College of Physicians refused to accept you on the grounds that you were not qualified to practise medicine." "Because I have not studied at the Universities of Oxford or Cambridge."

"Why not?" I asked. "Why go to Padua?"

"Because I had been in prison," he replied. He paused, watching my face, and once again I was roused by the element of mystery that pervaded him. "I was very young and I fell foul of the local landowner for whom my father worked, who had me wrongfully accused and arrested."

I murmured my sympathy and he continued, "I spent a year in prison during which time I learnt to curb my tongue and retaliate with cunning not violence. When I was released I fled the country and made my way to Italy. There I was given the opportunity to study medicine which had always interested me though my family had been too poor to let me pursue my studies beyond the local Grammar school."

Like Will, I thought involuntarily, here was someone else who had made his way in the world without an education from Oxford or Cambridge, a rare occurrence.

"I know much of Venice and the Veneto," he continued, "and my studies in fact make me better qualified than many of the so-called University physicians who have striven to make my life a misery." He left his seat and stood behind my chair, his hands stroking my bare shoulders, his face nuzzling my neck. "So you see we are very much alike, Aemilia. We both come from humble origins but we have ambitions to be equal with those better born and with the natural advantages of their class. Because we are as good as they, we know it and we will use any means to succeed." He began to unbind my hair so that it fell loose on my shoulders then he pulled me from my chair into his arms and I felt his strong body pressing into mine. "We are alike, Aemilia, we need each other." His voice was low and compelling and my body was feeling a need for him as much as his for me as my blood responded to his touch. I led the way unhesitatingly upstairs to the bedchamber, knowing that was what he expected of me. Once behind the closed door he undressed me slowly because I intuited that was what he wanted, each phase interspersed with caresses and intimate fondlings. I had not known a man for several months, longer than at any time since I was eighteen, my body was aching for physical satisfaction and Simon Forman's saturnine appearance had a strange attraction, strong and compelling. I lay in my shift while he kissed every part of my body, pausing as he reached the mole on my neck.

"Ann Boleyn's mark," he murmured, "a beautiful woman, dark and mysterious like you. They said she was a witch. And they say I am a wizard. We are a pair, Aemilia."

I responded to him, enjoying his strength with its hint of menace. Then suddenly without any warning an image flashed into my mind and I was filled with a sense of revulsion. An image of another man. Not my husband Alfonso Lanier somewhere on the high seas and probably in danger while I was betraying him in his own bed. It was an image of the only man I had ever loved, Will Shakespeare in his attic room in Gracechurch Street. As I remembered our love which had united body, mind, and soul, it seemed a betrayal of the grossest kind to sully true love with mere animal instinct, a betrayal of a memory that would remain with me for ever. I pushed him from me with all the strength I had and leapt from the bed to his great amazement. "No, no, I cannot. I have changed my mind. Please go," I cried frantically, reaching for a robe that hung behind the door and covering myself with it.

Simon Forman looked as if he had been dealt a great blow and did not know from whence it had come. The expression on his face was one of puzzlement turning slowly to anger as I stood defiantly by the door. "How now, what mischief is this?" he cried. "Is this some of your whore's tricks, to lead a man on then torment him with refusal at the last leap. Are you angling for more payment than a waiving of my fee?"

"No, nothing was further from my mind, I assure you. I cannot do it, that is all."

"You cannot do it after all your encouragement, what talk is this?"

"I have a husband, I cannot betray him."

"You didn't think of that before and you have betrayed him often enough. We shall see whether you can stop me now," he roared, lunging for me.

I screamed and opening the door began to run down the stairs. He did not follow me but stood in the doorway hollering, "You are a whore of the worst kind, showing your wares then refusing to sell. Why make me privy to your intimacies in the first place?"

I was crying now as his words were carrying all over the house. He dressed himself then came down the stairs, his face a mask of fury. "I lied about your prognosis. Your husband will come to nothing and you will get nothing by him. You will never be a fine lady again because that came only through whoring and what man wants a whore past thirty years of age."

He stormed out of the house slamming the door and as I sat weeping on the stairs I was aware of young Nan with a tousled yawning Henry together with Mistress Wayman, all staring in amazement from the top of the staircase. I motioned the maid to return to bed with Henry but as she turned to go I caught a glimpse of a smirk on her face. Mistress Wayman however came down the stairs muffled in her voluminous linen shift and said apologetically but firmly, "I shall leave tomorrow, Aemilia. I really cannot stay any longer in such a disorderly house."

Mistress Wayman was as good as her word and after the time necessary for her to pack her belongings and find alternative accommodation I was bereft of my lodger and her necessary rent. I was dismayed and ashamed. I sensed that Nan was regarding me with different eyes and imagined a new air of insolence about her. For a few days I was racked with despair and self-pity. I seemed to have lost everything except bitter memories and the future looked bleak, especially if what Simon Forman said was true. Then after a few days my spirit reasserted itself. I would not be defeated by a temporary reversal of fortune. I would fight back. I would put Simon Forman from my mind and ignore his negative predictions which were probably only the result of his anger and frustration, for which I had to admit that I was greatly to blame. As an educated woman I must not let myself be a victim of superstition but believe that we are the makers of our own destiny and not at the mercy of the stars. I would recommence my regular visits to the playhouses, not allowing Will to have such power over me as to keep me from what I loved even at the cost of heartache. I would borrow some money from Lucrezia to tide me over until Alfonso returned. I would re-establish my authority over the impertinent Nan. And I would start to write poetry again. What had Will said, "It is worth the effort if only to empty the heart of the pain that might otherwise kill you."

Chapter 13

CONCERTO

Unexpectedly it was to be one of the happiest years of my life. Alfonso returned sooner than anticipated for the privateers were back in London by February, disappointed of their aims. Unfortunately the expedition had been a disaster, fraught by bad weather, ill luck and Spanish dominance on the High Seas. There was no treasure to be brought home and the Queen was noted to be angry at the failure. When I heard the news I too was disappointed at the knowledge there was to be no quick solution to our financial problems yet for the moment that was overlaid by an unanticipated eagerness to see Alfonso again. I didn't know when to expect him and I was in the larder checking on the remainder of the preserves I had made in the autumn when I heard the front door open and the tread of his boots on the stone flags. I felt a moment's uncertainty then I walked into the hall where he was still standing, his sack at his feet, and we stood looking at each other for a time. His skin was bronzed, his curly hair was longer, reaching his shoulders, and he had grown a moustache and small pointed beard. There were faint lines round his eyes through squinting at the sun and he sported a gold earring. He smiled and his teeth shone white against his brown skin, making my heart leap a little as I said, "You look like a pirate."

"I am," he laughed. I was conscious of my working dress of mustard yellow wool and my hair drawn plainly from my face but he said, "You look very beautiful, Aemilia." He came towards me and took me in his arms saying, "I've missed you."

It was the first time I had ever heard him utter such a sentiment and I replied, "I've missed you too," realising that I meant it.

The sweetness of his homecoming was a surprise to both of us and we made love with all the refreshment of a year's absence. "I've thought about you often, dreamt of you when we were isolated in the vastness of the ocean and I feared I might never see you again," he said as we lay entwined and I could feel the taut muscles of his body, hardened by toil and fighting.

"I have been faithful to you," I said, realising it was only half true but nonetheless wanting him to believe it as I nuzzled against him enjoying the comfort of his nearness.

Afterwards came all the stories - the gales and mountainous waves when they struggled to control the ships as they were tossed hither and thither like spillikins, the hard fighting when companions were mown down by ball and shot in the fierce melee of an assault. Later still came the apologies, for not having returned with any spoil, for not having gained any preferment.

"It matters not," I assured him and in the aftermath of our reunion I meant it at the time. Henry was ecstatic at his return, not wanting to be out of his sight and eager to show his father the progress he had made in a year. "I have practised music with him and begun to teach him his letters. He's very quick," I preened.

He never tired of hearing Alfonso tell him his adventures over and over again. "Tell me about how you climbed over the side of the Spanish ship and killed one of the soldiers before being knocked into the water. Tell me about how the Earl of Essex went in the landing boat under fire without his armour because he wanted to be the first to take the island."

Alfonso was full of praise for Robert Devereux. "He is a wonderful leader, he inspires men to follow him and he's always in the van. He took much notice of me. He said I had the makings of a good soldier, though he complimented me on my music too. He once spoke about you, Aemilia, recalling the time you first met at Lord Burghley's. I prefer him to Raleigh who can be arrogant and though the two concealed their animosity on the voyage there is no love lost between them."

"What about the Earl of Southampton? How did he fare?"

"Surprisingly well. He isn't as effeminate as he looks and he and Essex work hand in glove."

From the gusto with which he regaled his adventures I realised that far from being deterred by his first military experience he had got a taste for fighting and I wondered where this would end. He showed no great enthusiasm about returning to his post with the Queen's Musick except for the opportunities it afforded for keeping in touch with the Earl of Essex who once again was the constant companion of the Queen, and I knew that if Essex planned any more military expeditions then he would want to be a part of them. But for the moment we were more content together than we had ever been. He had a new appreciation for the comforts of home and I liked having him around. I loved to hear him rehearsing again with his friends and kin in the parlour that Mistress Wayman had vacated and I enjoyed his company as we did share many things in common. Our new-found satisfaction in each other resulted in new bed pleasure and I soon realised I was pregnant again. Since his return I had been taking the potion Simon Forman had given me and I experienced none of the problems I had hitherto known. I felt well and strong with a certainty that this time the child would come to full term and I remembered Doctor Forman saying the best cordial for a successful pregnancy and healthy child was a calm and contented spirit, which I had for the first time for many years. Alfonso was exhilarated and stopped going to the taverns and spending time with his gambling associates, promising to be thrifty in anticipation of his new responsibilities. He was maturing at last as a result of his soldiering experiences and prospective fatherhood. It was the happiest year of our marriage.

"Southampton's been imprisoned," Alfonso informed me one day on his return from the Court.

"In the Tower? What has he done?" I was aghast.

"Not in the Tower, in the Fleet."

"In the Fleet? For what?" I was astonished. The Fleet was one of the worst jails in London situated near the stinking Fleet ditch and usually reserved for debtors. Most noblemen were put into the Tower, surely Henry Wriothesley couldn't be in debt.

"For marrying Elizabeth Vernon secretly. She's in the Fleet too. Apparently while in Paris with Cecil he received word from her that she was pregnant so rushed home and married her in secret."

Robert Cecil had been sent on an embassy to Paris to sound out the French about a possible peace treaty with Spain and the Queen had ordered the Earl of Southampton to accompany him, knowing full well he was against the proposal. Cecil led the anti-war faction at Court and they had been exerting more pressure on the Queen to make peace with Spain after the fiasco of the Azores expedition, much to the displeasure of the Earl of Essex and his supporters.

"The Queen really has taken against Southampton hasn't she," I mused. "I know she always punishes those men who get her maids with child, like Raleigh, but at least Raleigh was put into the Tower and he was one of her favourites and considered her property. Southampton never has been. What has she got against him?"

"I think she's using him to get at Essex," Alfonso replied shrewdly. "He's his closest friend and like him is against peace with Spain. To make him part of Cecil's embassy was a deliberate provocation and a humiliation for both of them. And Elizabeth Vernon is Essex's cousin."

"I don't understand it," I confessed. "I thought Essex was back in her favour."

"Oh he is, on the surface. He's always by her side, but she doesn't know what to do with him. I've seen them together and half the time she treats him like a cosseted favourite nephew and the other half she bills and coos with him like a suitor for her affections."

"She's getting old. She likes to see him as another Leicester and plays the coquette with him." I understood all too well the frustration that old age could impose on a woman always accustomed to the adulation of men and now losing her attractions.

"If that were all it were no great problem, but she fears his ambitions. She fears that if she gives him too much power over her he will use his control to rule England himself. So from time to time she acts to put him firmly in his place and encourages Cecil to oppose him."

"You're becoming quite a politician yourself, Alfonso," I remarked with some admiration.

"No, it's just talk that I hear at Court," he shrugged. But I enjoyed discussing the news with him as we shared more time together. When it was possible he would let me accompany him to concerts and entertainments and for the first time seemed to take pride in my appearance once my condition became visible. All my kinsfolk were full of compliments, while for once my father-in-law was pleased with me. Even the Queen deigned to speak to me on one occasion and I noticed how old and fragile she was looking, her cheeks hollowed, her eyes sunken though still shrewd, her gowns still as magnificent though their splendour served to emphasize more her decaying beauty. There was a marked melancholy about her as she realised Lord Burghley was dying, her "alpha and omega" and the last of the companions and advisers of her youth. During his final days she personally spoon-fed him broth and when he died in August, aged seventy seven, she wept for a month. I mourned him because he had always been kind to me but I wept his passing for another reason. Henry was now nearly six years of age and I had hopes of him being admitted as a scholar to Westminster school, situated near us and known for its excellence. He was after all the son of a nobleman and I intended him to have a good education, hopefully at the university or the Inns of Court later. Although the school master was William Camden, Lord Burghley had been the unofficial power behind the school for years for he had always had a great interest in learning and in children, and I had thought to have made use of his acquaintance to gain a place there for my son. All hope was not completely lost however because out of a total of more than a hundred boys nearly half of them were poor scholars on a free scholarship, and living in the area as we did Henry would have no need to be a boarder. At the moment I was teaching him myself and I knew that in another year or two he would have more than sufficient knowledge for entry.

I took him with me to watch the funeral procession as it passed through Westminster to the abbey, Alfonso being part of the music. Leading the five hundred official mourners was not his son, Robert Cecil, but Robert Devereux who had been his ward and to whom he had been the nearest figure to a father.

The Earl had only recently survived another altercation with the Queen. During an argument over the situation in Ireland, where the rebels were being increasingly successful over the English forces and had inflicted another great military disaster upon them this summer, Essex had turned his back on the Queen and she had struck him a violent blow on the head. To the consternation of all present he had drawn his sword, a treasonable action in the presence of a sovereign. A reconciliation of sorts had been effected, chiefly by Lord Burghley, but Essex had subsequently withdrawn from the Court and only returned for the funeral of his mentor. People wondered what he would do now.

The country was in a great state of unrest with worries about the ageing Queen and no declared heir to succeed her, the crisis in Ireland and the renewed threat of an invasion by Spain who were supporting the Irish rebels with money and men. However I felt the same aura of serenity that I had known when carrying Henry, as if I were cocooned in a soft cloak of impermeability. My aggressive independence loosened into a reliance on Alfonso that was involuntary and unexpected, and I realised that it was nature's way of ensuring protection for a woman carrying a man's child. The summer was warm and sunny in contrast to the bad weather of the past three years and occasionally Alfonso was willing to accompany me to the playhouses. We went to The Rose to watch 'Every man in his Humour' by Ben Jonson, not noticeably chastened by his spell in prison, performed by the Lord Chamberlain's men with Will Shakespeare a member of the cast. I noticed that Will hadn't written much of late although some of his plays had been published and I had bought 'An excellent conceited tragedie of Romeo and Juliet,' though I feared it was a pirate copy. It had been a poor season for new plays and I couldn't help thinking that Will had written most when we were lovers and that perhaps I had inspired him. Perhaps his creativity was spent and young Jonson was about to take his place. Then the following month Ben Jonson almost left the stage for ever. After challenging to a duel an actor in the Lord Admiral's company by name of Gabriel Spencer, he killed him and was set for hanging at Tyburn had he not pleaded benefit of clergy by reciting the 'neck verse' and had his sentence reduced to branding on the thumb. It would seem the young playwright courted trouble as much as Christopher Marlowe had, and William Shakespeare almost lost his second rival. As it was the affair once again added fuel to the Puritan animosity about anything to do with theatres, especially as a few months earlier the playwright John Day had been killed by a fellow writer in Southwark.

At the end of November I was safely delivered of a girl after another relatively easy birth and I thanked Simon Forman silently but fervently for his assistance in bringing this to pass.

"I'm sorry it's not a son for you," I said to Alfonso but his excitement was joyful and spontaneous.

"We already have a son, it's wonderful to have a daughter as well," he said, holding her in his arms. I was happy too. She resembled both of us with olive skin and thick black hair already curling though her eyes were still blue, and the fact that Alfonso and I now shared a child together welded us closer. I looked forward to rearing her according to my own beliefs and had many ambitions for her education. We named her Odilya and in early December she was baptised at our Parish church of Saint Margaret's in Westminster with Alfonso's sister Ellen Ferrabosco and her husband as godparents. Afterwards we celebrated at our home in Longditch with our kin, none of them remarking on the emptiness of the house nor the disappearance of so many of our fine things.

All through the autumn there had been much talk about sending another army to Ireland to challenge the supremacy of the rebel leader, the Earl of Tyrone. By December it was an acknowledged fact and the anti-war party had lost the vote. Robert Devereux was being suggested as commander of the army though it was known that he did not want the honour. Ireland was a thankless task, his own father had died there, and besides he feared that while he was out of the way his enemies, like Cecil and Raleigh who had refused the Irish appointment, would work against him. In December a notable visitor came from Ireland with an appeal to the Privy Council for them to send help to the now beleaguered settlers. It was the poet Edmund Spenser who had lived in Ireland for twenty years on an estate confiscated from the Irish, as did many Englishmen. He was lodging near us in Kings Street and because I remembered hearing him read 'The Faerie Queen' at Court when I was with Lord Hunsdon and how it had inspired me to start writing poetry myself, I wondered if I might be able to find an excuse to call on him although his society was greatly sought after by poets and writers.

On Saint Stephen's Day I was fortunate to receive a pass to accompany John Lanier's wife, Frances, to Whitehall for a performance by the Lord Chamberlain's Men. It was a sequel Will had written to his 'King Henry IV' at the request of the Queen, for the fat rogue Falstaff was a favourite character of hers. We were as usual seated near the back of the Great Hall but during the crush at the end of the performance I was pleasantly surprised to be greeted by the Earl of Essex, returned to the Queen's favour and her dancing partner for the Yuletide festivities. Robert Devereux was now thirty two years old and more handsome than when I had first seen him, the lines around his eyes and running from nose to chin giving him more distinction now but his hair as deeply auburn, his eyes as strikingly blue. His tall figure with broad shoulders and well-shaped legs in silver and white hose, together with his distinctive square-cut beard, ensured attention.

"Mistress Lanier, Aemilia, what a pleasant surprise. Your beauty is as fresh as ever," he said with the ease of the practiced courtier. "And I can see you blooming with health after presenting your husband with another child," he added tactfully. Then he began to talk about Alfonso's part in the Azores voyage. "What do you think of my offering him a commission as a captain in the army I am taking to Ireland?" he asked. It had recently been confirmed that he was to head the army, the talk being that although he was not eager for the assignment he was too proud to refuse.

The news came as a terrible shock to me but I did not like to admit that my husband had kept me in ignorance of his intentions so I replied as calmly as I could, "If Alfonso prefers being a soldier to a musician then that is a decision he must make for himself."

"I know it will be hard for you," he said sympathetically, "but I like to have people around me that I can trust. I also must leave my wife and children, as must the Earl of Southampton with a child new born."

"I am sure my husband must be honoured by your attention, Sir," I said, thinking that it was I myself who had told Alfonso to put himself in the way of the Earl of Essex so I could hardly complain. There was after all no knowing what his favour might bring. We talked generally about the play for a little while longer and I asked about his sister.

"Penelope is well but I am afraid not welcome at Court. She has seven children now," he said ambiguously for he would know I was aware of the rumours and I detected a twinkle in his eyes, his love for his sister not impaired by her peccadillos.

As we prepared to make our farewells I said impetuously, "Would you be so kind as to grant me a favour? Could you introduce me to Master Edmund Spenser."

"Most willingly," he accepted readily and led me to where the poet was surrounded by a group of admiring well-wishers, amongst them several of the actors, one of whom was Will. With such a celebrated promoter as the Earl of Essex, Edmund Spenser could not help but acknowledge me and I complimented him on his poetry, saying how much I enjoyed reading it. If only I were a man I could tell him that I myself wrote verse and that he had inspired me, I thought longingly. I could have been part of his coterie and talked freely with him. Then on sudden impulse I decided to make use of the information Essex had given me and ventured, "My house is not far from where you are staying in Kings Street. My husband Alfonso Lanier will be a captain in the Earl of Essex's company going to Ireland. Perhaps if you have time you would take a cup of wine with us. My husband is also a member of the Queen's Musick and would be delighted to play for you."

"If time affords that would be a great pleasure, Mistress Lanier," he replied courteously. "I have much to do with business while I am here but if I have occasion I shall certainly do so."

But I thought how ill he looked since the last time I had seen him.

Alfonso had spent the evening playing in a private concert at Sir William Petre's house and when he returned home I challenged him about what Essex had told me. "Why didn't you discuss it with me?" I asked angrily, feeling ill done by.

"Because I thought you would be against it," he replied uncomfortably. "I know you prefer me to be a musician but you also told me to seek Essex's favour and it would seem I have done so. Who knows what will become of this. If I can distinguish myself I might receive a knighthood, military service is the best way to such an honour. Then I might receive some kind of employment in the Earl's service."

I acknowledged the truth of it but the acceptance was tinged with bitterness that he had not discussed it with me, especially since we had reached a period of some contentment in our relationship.

"And how am to cope alone with two children to maintain, have you thought about us?" I asked resentfully. I didn't like to add what was really in my mind, the possibility that he might be wounded or die but my anxiety made me say, "Half the men who go to Ireland never come back. It's a graveyard, everyone knows this."

"This time will be different, have no fear. Essex is a great commander and it's going to be the largest army assembled since the Armada. We will be victorious in

Ireland and crush the rebels once and for all. Everything will go well and I should be able to restore our fortunes."

He was full of optimism and I tried to share his confidence. His faith in the Earl of Essex was shared by a lot of people and it was true that the venture held opportunities. I could hardly complain when I had chafed at his lack of ambition but I had difficulty in reshaping my image of the musician I had always known into that of an army captain.

Two days later on the 28th of December an event occurred which filled people with amazement. The Theatre, that unholy edifice which had given so much pleasure and roused so much anger in diverse sections of the London populace, was no longer standing in Shoreditch. It was not demolished by act of God as the Puritans had long prophesied, nor dismantled by the City authorities as they had often threatened, but by the members of the Lord Chamberlain's Company themselves. Bitter and frustrated by the legal wrangles concerning the lease they had taken matters into their own hands. Armed and determined they had marched to Shoreditch at break of day and in a snowstorm and while householders stood alarmed and bewildered and some offered violent opposition, they took down the timbers, frame and posts of the playhouse and loaded them onto carts. By nightfall it was largely done and the loads were borne away in the darkness. But to where? Some said to secret warehouses, some said they had seen them cross the frozen Thames to the South Bank. It was soon the talk of London. No-one knew what the actors had in mind but what was certain was that Shoreditch had lost the edifice that for nearly twenty five years had been its most distinctive feature. What else was to go people thought as the year drew to its close. There was definitely a feeling of change in the air.

CHAPTER 14

MOTET

Last year had been a year of births and deaths. The new year began with attendance at another funeral as I went to Westminster Abbey church to see Edmund Spenser buried beside Chaucer. He was forty six years old. He had never made the visit I had ardently hoped for, but when he had said he had little time available neither of us realised just how little that time was. Other poets carried his hearse but it was the Earl of Essex who paid for the funeral, for despite his estimation as a poet Spenser was not a rich man.

As I watched Robert Devereux lead the funeral procession I hoped the burial was not a prophetic omen for the Irish campaign on behalf of which the poet had been sent.

Many eulogies were written on his death and when the coffin was finally lowered into the vault fellow poets ostentatiously threw their quills into the tomb. Although Will was present with the actors of the Lord Chamberlain's Men and others, he did not follow suit nor did he compose any epitaph on this poet he greatly admired and who had paid tribute to him as a "*gentle spirit from whom large streams of honey and sweet nectar flow.*" I was sure he must have grieved as sincerely as anyone for the loss of the man who had often inspired him but I knew he shunned display and I had discovered from my own experience how much of a private person he was, often finding him hard to deal with when we had been lovers because of his reticence in revealing his personal feelings. I too, though I wrote poetry and owed much to Spenser's example, was an outsider in this circle of grieving poets, although these days I had lost much of my incentive to write and I had no spare money to waste on expensive paper and ink. Perhaps my poetic ambitions were also being laid to rest.

Amongst the mourners I caught sight of the poet's cousin Alice, Ferdinando Stanley's widow lately remarried to the Lord Chancellor Sir Thomas Egerton, and this called to mind the loss of the generous attractive nobleman who had once been the patron of Will and other members of the original company. I made an effort not to let thoughts of death and mortality consume me as the Irish campaign was imminent and Alfonso preparing to depart.

Alfonso was completely absorbed in the project though he did go, albeit impatiently, to Richmond with the Queen's Musick when the Queen removed herself there for a time. She had never really cared for the palace of Richmond when she was young but now in old age she appreciated all the latest comforts her "warm box" offered. I used his short absence to prepare myself for being long alone, not relishing the prospect, though I already felt that Alfonso was far away as he thought of little but the coming adventure and the rapport we had known for the past year had gradually been eroded by his impatience and my resentment.

All talk now in the city was on the Irish campaign and men were being pressed into the army. At Whitehall over Christmas we had laughed at such a scene in Will Shakespeare's history of King Henry IV but what had been found amusing on the stage was now a terrifying experience on the streets. The pressing of men into service was especially rampant in the Liberties where so many of the vagrants and masterless men hung out, though players and musicians were exempt being in the Queen's employ. I felt the irony keenly that Alfonso Lanier, Queen's musician, was actually volunteering for service in this unpopular war.

Meanwhile in the Liberty of the Clink it now became obvious what was happening to the dismantled Theatre. To everyone's amazement it was being rebuilt on Bankside, supervised by the carpenter responsible for the original construction in Shoreditch. In company with many other curious spectators I went to look. Although a little further from the river than The Rose, people were saying that Philip Henslowe and Edward Alleyn were not at all pleased by the prospect of such close competition from their nearest rivals. Edward Alleyn had recently married Henslowe's daughter Joan and severed his contacts with other theatre companies as he entered into partnership with his new father-in-law in managing The Rose. However the innkeeper at The Angel informed me that the sharers of the Lord Chamberlain's company had leased the land for thirty years so were definitely planning a permanent structure. "Everyone in Southwark will be watching the project with interest," he said. "For a start the land isn't good, it's marshy and full of ditches and construction certainly won't be without its problems. And whoever heard of dismantling a building then re-erecting it." He shook his head in bemusement and most people shared his opinion.

On the twenty seventh of March the Earl of Essex and the army for Ireland made their official departure from Tower Hill, the open space to the north of the Tower.

Alfonso and I had already made our farewells and he had wept when parting from the children, but I took them to watch the triumphal procession through the streets of the city, a total of 16,000 infantry and 200 cavalry in all it was said. The Earl of Essex rode at the head on a white horse, tall and magnificent in shining armour with the Earl of Southampton close behind him but we were unable to catch a glimpse of Alfonso in the press. As I was standing in Cheapside I saw amongst the crowd John Florio, one time Southampton's tutor. The gregarious Italian returned my greeting and told me proudly that he was ready to publish his lexicon of English and Italian words which I assured him would be greatly appreciated by poets and playwrights. We talked companionably for some time and I had just bade him farewell when I heard from behind me a deep voice that I recognised saying, "Give you good day, Mistress Lanier. I see you have been successful in bearing a child," and turning I came face to face with Simon Forman. For a moment I felt abashed and avoided my eyes from his face but when I looked up into his striking features I found no trace of former resentment, in fact I thought I caught a glimmer of a smile hovering at the corners of his wide sensuous mouth.

"I have you to thank, Doctor Forman, I am most grateful," I said sincerely and he nodded in acknowledgement.

"This is quite a show isn't it," he said, "It puts the playhouses to shame and I considered it a spectacle not to be missed. Let's hope their homecoming is with such honour."

I looked at him questioningly because of his reputation for divination but before I could ask his opinion everyone was suddenly startled by a great clap of thunder that seemed to shake the very foundations of the street, followed by a sudden downpour of rain even though the sky had been a cloudless uniform blue almost translucent in the weak beams of early spring sunshine. The astrologer seized my arm, saying, "Come let us take shelter," and dragged us all into the nearby Falcon inn out of the rain, suggesting he buy us a beaker of wine. As we sat together at one of the tables he said, "Shall we forget our differences and be good fellows again?" I wasn't sure what he meant and wondered if he knew that Alfonso was with the army but he continued, "I repent my share of what happened at our last meeting but I was myself somewhat distracted. I had recently lost a woman I loved, whom indeed I had hoped to marry. Her name was Avisa Allen and I had loved her for a long time but she was married to another man. Then he died and the opportunity came for us to wed but before we could do so she died herself. I hope you will forgive me." I murmured my sympathies, not knowing how to reply, but he went on, "I hope you will not hesitate to visit me again should you have need," and I found myself promising him that I would do so if I ever needed his help.

"What signifies this sudden strange storm? Is it an omen?" I asked anxiously after I had told him that Alfonso had gone with the army.

He paused deep in thought before replying, "I am afraid the Irish expedition is doomed."

I felt a surge of fear but noticing that Henry was listening carefully with his eyes fixed on Simon's face, I laughed and squeezing the child's hand said, "I'm sure the Earl of Essex knows what he's about," not wanting him to hear any more.

But when the rain had stopped as suddenly as it had begun and we were preparing to go our separate ways Simon Forman took my arm as he said, "Be careful,

Aemilia, the portents are not good. You were born under the sign of Aquarius were you not? The water-carrier, a fixed sign in the element of air, ruled by the planet Saturn. I can see dangers and loss but ultimately you will survive by your own strength of will."

As I made my way home with the children I pondered anxiously on his words. He had been right about the Azores expedition which had come to nought for us. God knows what would happen if Alfonso were not to return. He was not the ideal husband but we had reached some equanimity and my situation as a widow with two children would be very difficult. As it was I would need some will to survive in the near future. Alfonso had left me with some money, borrowed he said but would not reveal the source, but I did not think it would be enough to tide us over until he returned, if he ever did. Odilya began to cry hungrily and I roused myself impatiently. Once before I had told myself that I would not be a slave to superstition and I must hold to the belief that Alfonso would return with some remuneration and prospects.

One fine day in May, bathed in sunshine but chilly for it had been a dry though very cold spring, I decided I needed some diversion so hearing that a new play by William Shakespeare was being presented at The Curtain I left Nan in charge of the children and made my way there. It was strange to see The Curtain standing solitary without the neighbouring Theatre and I remembered my first visits to the Shoreditch playhouses when they competed with each other for the largest audiences. I paid for a seat in the cheaper gallery at the top, none of the gatherers would think of offering me a free seat now I thought ruefully though I always made a point of dressing as well as I could. I was impressed with 'Much Ado about Nothing', liking the forceful heroine Beatrice, enjoying her attempts to get the better of Benedick much as I did with Alfonso, and laughing aloud at the incompetent Dogberry who reminded me of a constable we had in Bishopsgate ward when I was a child. I had made up my mind not to be deterred by our past history from speaking to Will if we ever encountered each other, and today I decided that congratulations were well deserved. At the end of the performance I made to approach him then I was suddenly overcome with a feeling of embarrassment and would have retraced my steps had he not seen me. "Give you good day," he said carefully.

"Good day to you," I replied. We stood looking at each other awkwardly for it was two years since we had last spoken together.

"You look well, Aemilia," he said, admiration in his tone.

Everyone told me so I must believe it, my figure and my features had rounded somewhat and I was wearing a plain gown of russet wool with a neat pleated ruff and a small cap of yellow velvet. He looked older, not so much that his features had aged but that they had acquired a sober cast more suited to a man of more years than someone not yet forty. His body had thickened and his hair receded more, emphasizing his high forehead. His intelligent thoughtful eyes were the same.

"The play was excellent," I said. "I loved every part of it, the wit, the romance, the humour."

He smiled then as he always used to when I complimented his work and his face took on the vitality it used to have. "At last I have written a play to please you," he said with some mischief, though I recognised the underlying note of sadness in his tone.

I shook my head. "No, you have written many excellent plays that have pleased me much."

For a few moments our gaze held in remembrance.

"To be frank I haven't written a lot this past year. My inspiration seems to have deserted me," he said sadly and once again our thoughts merged in the ensuing silence. Then he said more buoyantly, "But I'm working on a play for the opening of our new theatre. Though heaven alone knows when that will be. We are hoping for June but the ground is marshy with a great ditch and though Peter Street our carpenter is working all hours it's no easy task assembling a new theatre from the old parts. Everyone thought we were mad at first but it is costing us less than building a completely new construction and we were certainly not going to let our rascally landlord have it."

"It must still be expensive. Is George Carey helping you with the cost?" I still had difficulty in giving him his title of Lord Hunsdon.

Will laughed dismissively. "We are bearing the cost ourselves. The Burbages are paying half but the other half is being shared by five of us actors so I now have a tenth share in a playhouse."

The investment must still have been high, I mused. He was putting Southampton's money to good use - a large house in Stratford and now part-owner of a new playhouse. William Shakespeare was becoming richer as I was growing poorer. Where had I gone wrong? But I wished him well and when I departed I sensed his reluctance to see me go.

On the way home to Westminster I decided to call at the bookstalls in Paul's churchyard to see what was newly on offer. I couldn't afford to buy any books but I could do what Will often did, contrive to read some things while I was browsing. At William Leake's bookshop I saw to my amazement a book entitled 'The Passionate Pilgrim by William Shakespeare'. It was a slim volume of a few poems and I began to read.

> *When my love swears that she is made of truth*
> *I do believe her though I know she lies*
> *That she may think me some untutored youth*
> *Unlearned in the world's false subtleties.*

I realised he was speaking of me and continued to read until the last two lines;

> *Therefore I'll lie with her and she with me*
> *That in our lies our faults may flattered be.*

The second one was even more explicit, referring to Southampton and myself.

> *Two loves I have of comfort and despair*
> *Which like two spirits do suggest me still:*
> *The better angel is a man right fair*
> *The worser spirit a woman colour'd ill.*
> *To win me soon to hell, my female evil*
> *Tempteth my better angel from my side,*
> *And would corrupt my saint to be a devil,*
> *Wooing his purity with her foul pride.*
> *And whether that my angel be turned fiend,*
> *Suspect I may, yet not directly tell;*
> *But being both from me, both to each friend*
> *I guess one angel in another's hell.*
> *Yet this shall I ne'er know but live in doubt*
> *Till my bad angel fire my good one out.*

I turned the page but there were no more. The next four sonnets were from 'Love's Labours Lost' and the rest a small selection of some other verse, markedly inferior it seemed to me. But I was horrified, bitterly hurt and furiously angry. The bastard! How could he publish to the world such an indictment of our relationship, a relationship I believed was born of true love even when we parted. I was choking with a mixture of anger and grief.

"Do you want to buy a copy? They're selling very swiftly, anything by Master Shakespeare is greatly sought after," said the bookseller eagerly, but I threw the little volume back onto the pile and impervious to his recriminations dashed out of the shop. I had to see him, challenge him. I had to do it immediately, I couldn't go home in this state. I retraced my steps into Westcheap then turned up past the Exchange and cut through to Bishopsgate and onto Gracechurch Street but the door of the tenement was locked and there was no answer when I knocked. The musician Thomas Morley, a corpulent cheerful man in his early forties, was just entering his own lodging two doors further down the street and he saw me and greeted me courteously. "Are you seeking Master Shakespeare?" he asked. "He no longer lives here. He's recently moved to Southwark to be near the new theatre they're building." My distress must have shown on my face because he said kindly, "Would you like to come and share a cup of wine with me." I thanked him gratefully but refused and he said, "I shall miss Will's company, I enjoyed working with him. His lyrics flow so smoothly that it's easy to compose music for them." I nodded and made to go but he added, "I was sorry to hear of the death of your uncle Giovanni. That's the last of the Bassano brothers now isn't it. They'll be greatly missed in the musical world."

I bade him farewell and made my way to the river steps to find a boatman, the quickest way back to Westminster rather than going through the city. I didn't usually expend the money but there might be someone to share the fare with me. I was still distressed by the poems but I couldn't go looking for Will in Southwark at this hour and mention of my uncles made me realise again that my old world had ended, the world of my father, Lord Hunsdon and also of Will Shakespeare. But there was a great pain in my heart at the thought of how he had tarnished our love. He can't have loved me, I sobbed inwardly though the chill wind now whipping from the river excused my tears, not as deeply as I had loved him.

When I reached home I took from my jewel box the sonnet he had written for me when I had played the virginals at Lord Burghley's house. Lying on top was Lord Hunsdon's cross but apart from that the box was almost empty. As empty as my heart. The two men who had sworn their love for me had both failed me. I acknowledged that I wasn't blameless. I had accepted Lord Hunsdon for gain, knowing the risks involved, and I had succumbed to Henry Wriothesley's attractions. But I had loved Will Shakespeare on every level of my being and I had believed our mutual love strong enough to overcome a dalliance which in part had been fuelled by jealousy of my rival. Because our love affair was over, the publication of two poems could not affect its outcome but the fact had sullied the treasured memories I held in my heart and changed my perception of Will. With some bitterness I recalled how I had always longed for people to read poems written about me by a great poet and now my wish had come true.

My low spirits continued to oppress me as spring progressed into summer, exacerbated by the growing realisation that I couldn't keep the house in Westminster and would have to think seriously about moving. The house was half empty anyway and my debts were mounting. Regretfully I began to consider taking up our old house in Bishopsgate, reflecting bitterly that at least I now wouldn't have to run the risk of frequently running into Will. My ambitions of rising in the world again seemed doomed to disaster, unless Alfonso returned from Ireland with a promise of preferment in service to one of the great lords. However the news coming from Ireland was generally bad and the sultry days buzzed with rumours like swarms of summer flies. As I shopped in the markets I would stop and listen to people talking and even allowing for uninformed gossip the overwhelming opinion was that the campaign in Ireland was not going well. Men who had returned had brought news that, contrary to expectation, the rebels outnumbered the English force by two to one and the fighting generally took place in bogs and woods where the army were unable to use their horse and artillery. There was also renewed fear of an invasion by Spain, eager to take advantage of the absence of Essex and a large English army. London was placed in a state of alert and the whole city was once again filled with an atmosphere of foreboding reminiscent of the great Armada eleven years ago. Ships were guarding the coast, the army was recalled from the Low Countries and all householders in London had to keep a lantern burning before their houses during the hours of darkness in case of a night attack. The events kindled in me a nostalgia for those heady days of 1588 when my circumstances were so different. Now I had the responsibility of two young children to worry about as well as knowing nothing of Alfonso's fate.

"Do you want to come and stay with us for a time?" Lucrezia asked but I refused, determined at all cost to keep what little independence I had. All Alfonso's family were worried about him but his father was still angry at his defection and I felt that for some obscure reason he put the blame on me.

"Robert Cecil says that peace with Spain would remove at one stroke both the fear of an invasion and Spanish support for the Irish rebels, solving the Irish situation better than the Earl of Essex's futile military campaign," he said with derision.

"But Cecil is of the anti-war party and it is in his interests to discredit Essex," Innocent, always willing to support Alfonso, reminded his father.

"Musicians should stay clear of politics," Nicholas Lanier snapped. I agreed wholeheartedly with the opinion but nonetheless I felt my father-in-law was being somewhat hypocritical as, like all foreign artists, he passed relevant information to the Government on his occasional visits home to France.

In June the opening of the new playhouse on the South Bank was a pleasant diversion to lighten the mood of Londoners at least temporarily. To everyone's surprise it was no longer called The Theatre but had been renamed The Globe. The opening performance was a new play by William Shakespeare entitled 'Julius Caesar' and although I would love to have attended I was deterred by the fact that the admission price was to be doubled for the occasion. However as the performance was to be repeated the next day I decided to wait until then to take the ferry to Bankside. The outside of the building was no surprise and looked like the old Theatre, which indeed it was, polygonal in shape, constructed of timber and wattle and daub, the plaster painted white. But inside it was the most splendid playhouse I had ever seen, larger than the others being more than a hundred feet across. The stage must have been fifty feet wide, cornered by classical pillars of wood painted to resemble marble and jasper, with gilt and gold decorations and vivid hangings. I caught my breath at the dazzling splendour. Above the stage was a representation of Hercules holding the globe of the world on his shoulders and underneath the Latin motto 'Totus mundus agit histrionem.'

"All the world plays the actor, but I suppose you know that," a voice behind me spoke and I turned to face Simon Forman. "Splendid isn't it. But perhaps we had better take our seats, Aemilia, or we shall have to stand here in the pit." He led me to one of the best seats in the second gallery, paying our admission, as the playhouse was rapidly filling with eager playgoers. "It holds more than three thousand spectators," he informed me, "and it is so cleverly constructed that the actors are always out of direct sunlight for the entire performance, a boon for them and of great advantage for night-time scenes."

"I thought you would have been present yesterday for the opening performance," I surmised, "or did the play please you so much you have made a return visit?"

"Unfortunately I was much occupied yesterday although it was on my recommendation that the day was chosen. Master Burbage consulted me as to an auspicious date and I divined the twelfth day of June, the summer solstice being particularly important as the playhouse is in direct alignment with the midsummer sunrise, while a new moon is the most opportune time to open a new house."

The play was a great success and most people recognised their own city of London in the depiction of ancient Rome, the opening triumphal procession with its noisy spectators reminding them of the Earl of Essex's recent parade through the city streets.

"Am I alone in seeing the discrepancy between the official presentation of Caesar as a God and the mundane reality of a deaf old man with the sleeping sickness, to be a veiled reference to our own dear Queen - immortal Gloriana we are led to believe but actually a fading old woman losing her grasp," Simon whispered.

"Treason, Doctor Forman. Look to your head," I whispered back. But most people were aware of the recent spate of assassination attempts on the Queen, more than at any time since the execution of Mary Stuart, as it was feared she was becoming too capricious to rule and resolutely refused to name an heir.

When the play was finished and we made our way out of the playhouse Simon said, "As my house is so close would you do me the honour of taking a cup of wine with me?"

I would have liked the opportunity to ask his opinion on the importance of omens and predictions in the play and what he thought of Cassius's statement, '*The fault lies not in the stars but in ourselves that we are underlings*'. However I had more pressing matters to attend to so I answered, "I thank you but no, I seek a word with Master Shakespeare." A lapse of time had not weakened my intention of challenging him about 'The Passionate Pilgrim'.

"He has lodgings here in Southwark now. Not in the best area, across one of the bridges over the ditch in a rather dark alley but it brings him close to The Globe. Yet not quite so salubrious as Bishopsgate, despite its rotting heads."

"I am returning to live in Bishopsgate. I am in process of leaving my house in Westminster. Was this the loss you referred to at our last meeting?"

He looked closely at me. "One of them perhaps, I never know the precise details of my predictions. Why don't you come to visit me again and I will recast your horoscope."

"Some time perhaps I will." We made our farewells and I was unsure whether my reluctance was because of him and our chequered relationship or because of what he might foretell for me.

Will saw me first and approached me, his first words being, "How did you like the play?"

"I liked the play very well and the new playhouse is magnificent but I did not come to talk about either," I informed him coldly. "Rather about some poems written about me and published in a book called 'The Passionate Pilgrim'."

"Not with my permission," he replied adamantly. "The compositions were stolen without my knowledge, it is a pirate copy. There are always unscrupulous publishers, printers, actors and theatre managers trying to steal our work. We keep our plays in locked chests and the only people to have a copy are the writer himself and the book-holder. Even so actors are bribed to copy out half-remembered versions or playgoers scribble down as much as they can remember during a play. God's bones, do you think I would be responsible for the shit in that book? The sonnets from 'Love's Labours' were meant to be bad, they were put into the mouths of idiotic characters and taken out of context they are meaningless inferior poems. The following sonnets are not even mine, surely you could see that. I don't write such bad verse. How dare someone put my name to such ordure."

With a shock I realised he was more concerned with his reputation as a poet rather than with my feelings. "But the first two sonnets are yours," I persisted. "About me........and the Earl of Southampton," I added reluctantly.

He paused then admitted, "Yes they are mine. But they were never intended to be published. I told you once that my sonnets were private and not for publication. Someone stole them."

"But you did write them. You penned such sentiments," I persisted. He shrugged, seemingly not willing to admit to it in the face of my accusatory expression. "And your verses to Southampton were circulated around the Court so presumably you showed them to someone. Was it him?"

"I suppose he could have been careless," he said reluctantly.

I breathed deeply. "You still don't understand do you, Will? What has hurt me so bitterly is not in the main that they were published, after all my name does not appear, but that you thought so little of me. I loved you, more than anyone in my life, and I thought you loved me." I choked and couldn't continue.

"I did love you, Aemilia, believe me. But you do not know how much your betrayal hurt me. You destroyed me and you destroyed my faith in him."

"And that is what you couldn't take. Not my betrayal but his. And for this you have wiped out all recollection of the love we shared, the passion we knew, the union of our minds. You have turned the gold of our beautiful love into the dross of lust and ugliness and left a permanent record for all men to read." I turned on my heel and began to walk away, then I turned and added, "And I was not diseased, you know that. I am not a whore, I have had but four lovers and you know who they are. But it seems you always thought I was. I don't understand why I ever loved you because you are not worth it."

His face was white but I ignored the appeal in his eyes and walked away. I was trembling but I felt strong. I had never before denied that I was a whore because it was true that I had given myself to Lord Hunsdon for gain. And if circumstances had worked out differently I might well have taken other lovers because many men desired me and I enjoyed being loved by handsome men. On every level I preferred the company of men because they had experience of a world I would love to have shared. But only with the Earl of Southampton and perhaps Simon Forman had I indulged the sensuous weakness in my nature. I had really loved Will and the one time I had known true love I had been cruelly disappointed.

As I thought about my dealings with men I called to mind Alfonso and pondered my erratic relationship with the man who was legally my husband. He was rash and thoughtless. He had wasted my money and was not faithful. He enjoyed me in his bed but showed little signs of devotion. Yet I had grown accustomed to having him in my life. He could be amusing and entertaining and we shared much in common, not least our background and families. Robert Devereux seemed to think well of him and as I made my home I wondered how he was faring. The news reported in the streets by those who returned from Ireland both on business and as deserters from the army was not good, and English casualties were said to be very high. The news coming from the Court which I heard from the musicians was no better. The Queen was blaming Essex for all the failures and even when he showed some success in capturing a town or castle she dismissed it as, "an Irish hold taken from a rabble of rogues," and similar language. She was furious at the number of men he was knighting on the campaign, believing that he was building up a body of followers with sworn allegiance to him rather than to her and which he intended using against her. She had reacted to the information that he had granted the commission of General of Horse to his friend and close companion,

Henry Wriothesley, by giving to Robert Cecil the post of Mastership of Wards, a lucrative office coveted by Essex with his financial difficulties and which she had previously promised to him. Her total animosity to him was hard to understand except that rumour was that his enemies, especially Cecil and Raleigh, were blackening his name and hinting to the Queen that the army he had ostensibly raised for Ireland was really to use against her for his own royal ambitions. I had always liked Robert Devereux and I feared for him, as well as for Alfonso in his train.

By August I was back at my old house in Bishopsgate in company with my children and our maid Nan. I had at last been forced to surrender our house in Long Ditch and many of my dreams with it. Nothing had come to pass as I had hoped. In my first delight at moving into the house I had fantasised about entertaining poets and patrons, composers and men of letters in the style of the Venetian courtesans, feeding off the position Lord Hunsdon had given me. I had fondly imagined that being so close to Whitehall and in the vicinity of Saint James' palace and the Strand some of the prestige might have caught us in its glow like a candle flame which burning brightest in the centre still casts its flame dimly into the furthest shadows. However once I had left the privileged protection of the Court my identity had gone and we had neither the money nor the distinction to make our mark in society. I was back where I had begun, at the house I had left twelve years previously and had sworn never to return to, believing my life had changed forever. I hated the house, shadowed by too many memories. I couldn't walk into the kitchen without seeing my mother working or go up into the parlour where her last agonizing months were spent lying on the settle surrounded by cushions. I lay in the canopied bed where my parents had slept uneasily together, while Henry slept in the bed Angela and I had shared and where all my dreams of a better life had taken seed and blossomed. But at least I was fortunate to still possess this survival from our family properties for it could have been much worse. It was also fortunate that it was still furnished for I had little of my own to fill it apart from my father's Italian picture, the Flight into Egypt, which went back over the paler patch on the wall - a link with him.

"I like it here," Henry said. He liked the hustle and bustle of Bishopsgate, the business of the streets and the markets, the constant tolling of the bells from the many churches. I would let him walk as far as the gate for he showed a boy's gruesome fascination with the heads hung there and would make up stories about the malefactors, and he liked to watch the many travellers passing on horseback or in carts for it was the main thoroughfare north from the city. The fact that he was happy here gradually helped me to change my perception of the house and the ghosts began to fade, for Odilya was thriving and growing more beautiful with her dark eyes and black curls and at eight months could sit straight. I was proud of her and neighbours always stopped to talk and dote on her. It never crossed my mind that in a few weeks I would be laying her in a tiny coffin in a grave close by my father, mother and Angela in St. Botolph's churchyard.

Her death was so sudden and unexpected that I did not even have time to take her to Doctor Forman who might perhaps have been able to help with the crucifying pains that tore her little body. I held her weeping in my arms as the last breaths escaped in ragged gasps and gazed in disbelief as after one long shuddering convulsion she lay lifeless at my breast. I held her for an hour, all alone. She did not look as if she were dead but sleeping calmly after the passing of a childish ailment, her colour not yet gone, her black curls wet with the perspiration of sleep. I thought back to the moment of her first newborn cry as I had reached hungrily for her and in utter desolation felt an agony of loss that I had never before experienced, the loss that Simon Forman had perhaps foreseen. All other losses seemed small in comparison to this, my beautiful daughter for whom I had waited so long and for whom I had such plans for her upbringing. In my distress I cursed God for deceiving me by first giving me a priceless gift then dashing it from my hands, and another ghost joined the company that flitted periodically through the house. All our neighbours and the kinsfolk who lived close by in Mark Lane came to watch her buried and comfort me, and Lucrezia held the weeping Henry in her arms. "I cannot let Alfonso know. How can I meet him with this news when he returns," I sobbed to his mother. If he ever did return. London was now full of deserters from the campaign, relating horrendous stories about atrocities, disease, and English losses. Odilya was another loss for me, as Simon Forman had predicted, but was there still more to come? Would it be Alfonso? I tried not to let my sadness overwhelm me for the sake of Henry who took the death of his little sister to heart. I tried to console myself by the thoughts of others close to me who had suffered such a bitter loss, my mother with her two little sons, Angela with her firstborn, Will with Hamnet. I had suffered with him then but now I understood more fully his agony at losing a child. Odilya's existence began to seem almost a dream and I wondered why she had been sent to me for such a short time.

"To show that you can have children," Lucrezia replied firmly to my question. "You will have others when Alfonso returns." But in my melancholy state of mind I began to fear he would never return alive and Simon Forman's predictions began to assume terrifying proportions. I could keep my panic in check during the day but it surfaced uncontrollably in my dreams at night making me wake trembling and drenched in sweat.

A week after Odilya was buried the Earl of Essex returned to England in company with his friends and high-ranking officers. The Queen had accused him, amongst other charges, of making peace with the rebel Irish leader, the Earl of Tyrone, independent of her consent and for his own devious means. He had returned in haste to defend himself from these treasonous accusations, and the subsequent events were soon common knowledge around the Court as people couldn't wait to pass on the scandalous news. Knowing that the Queen was in residence at this time at the fabulous palace of Nonsuch in the shire of Surrey, Essex had ridden there immediately. Instead of asking for an audience he had leapt from his horse, gone running through the palace to the Presence chamber and to everyone's amazement pushed through to the Privy chamber, then not finding the Queen there, she being still abed, had burst into her bedchamber. The chamber was sacrosanct, out of bounds to all but her lady attendants who now stared in horrified disbelief as the Earl burst in upon an Elizabeth no-one but they had ever seen, without her face made, without her wig, her thin grey hair in disarray. The Queen, regal as ever, controlled her discomposure and told him to return later when she was ready to receive him. When he did so he found her in the full panoply of Sovereign Majesty, surrounded by her bodyguard, and she had him committed to house arrest. Queen Elizabeth and Robert Devereux were never to meet again.

By October the rest of the army were trickling into London, many of them wounded, most of them disillusioned, some of them angry, but there was no news of Alfonso and my fears grew. What could have happened to him. He certainly could not have received the preferment he had hoped for or he would have been with the Earl of Essex though that might not have been good in the circumstances. I tried to keep my worries from Henry who was constantly asking about him and worrying that he wouldn't know where we had gone. Then late one afternoon I heard someone opening the door and went downstairs to find him in the reception room.

"I went to Long Ditch and when there was no sign of you I went on to my mother in Chelsea. She told me where to find you. She also told me about Odilya."

He looked desperately tired, lines of weariness etched on his face, his clothes dusty and travel-stained with a tear in the sleeve of his jacket. I pulled him wordlessly towards me and put my arms around him. "I'm so sorry about the baby," I said finally and began to cry in a mixture of sorrow and relief.

There were tears in his eyes also as he said, "I'm sorry for you too, Aemilia. For having to bear the loss of the child without me, for having to give up the house, for not bringing you back any recompense. I know you didn't want to come back here and the loss of the child must have been unsupportable." For a few moments we found solace in each other's nearness as we wept together for the loss we shared.

But later when he had washed in the large stone sink in the kitchen and I had found him fresh clothes and prepared food he recovered his spirits, aided by Henry's joyous excitement at his return.

"It wasn't all bad, we had some successes and there were good times with entertainment and spectacle," he said, leaning back in his chair revived by a hearty meal and a flagon of wine. "On St. George's day we were in Dublin and Essex arranged a garter feast with jousting, tilts, music and ceremonies of knighthood which was more splendid than any I have ever seen at Court. I was part of the music on that day and was personally complimented by the Archbishop of Dublin, Thomas Jones, a man of culture and discernment."

"Did you ever get close to Essex?" I asked.

"Often. I was one of his captains. But if you mean did he never consider a knighthood for me let me explain something to you. The Earl of Essex is courteous, generous, amiable to all and gives the impression that he is a man amongst men. But make no mistake he considers himself one of the greatest lords in the kingdom, descended from kings. He knighted many men in Ireland because he believes the Queen has deliberately decimated the nobility to strengthen her own power. But it is the nobility he wishes to revive and I am afraid that I, a French-Italian minstrel, do not come into this class. However," he continued after seeing the disappointment evident in my face, "he thinks highly of my conduct and I am sure he will find some post for me in his service once the Queen's anger has dissipated."

"She has put him under house arrest in the care of Lord Chancellor Egerton. She won't even let him see his wife who has just been delivered of a child."

"Did you know that he also lost his little daughter Penelope whilst we were in Ireland? Infant mortality is no respecter of persons." I hadn't known and the knowledge of our shared experience brought me close again to Robert Devereux. Alfonso was continuing to talk, "I am sure that in due course he will be restored to the Queen's favour, you know she has always blown hot and cold about him. She likes to demonstrate her power over him but she loves him too much to be at odds with him for long. You'll see that come Yuletide he'll be dancing with her again at the Court festivities and then he will be in a position to grant me some service. Our fortunes will be on the rise again soon."

He spoke confidently and despite my own reservations he was so sure of how events would turn that he did not return to his position with the Queen's Musick. At the Christmas celebrations he was not amongst the musicians. But neither was Robert Devereux amongst the revellers. He was still under house arrest and though the Queen allowed his wife Frances a brief visit, his sister Penelope was refused together with any of his friends. It was given out that he was sick and prayers were said in city churches for his return to health and to the Queen's favour. But she only responded by returning the New Year gift he had sent to her.

Chapter 15

SONATA

"I think I must tell Henry who his real father was," I said to Alfonso soon after his return.

It was something I had been thinking about and in the new year I considered it was time to do so. Alfonso had more than fulfilled his obligations as a father to my child but I wasn't prepared for the look of anguish that crossed his face as he cried, "No Aemilia, you can't do that. You can't take Henry away from me too."

His choice of words startled me though I was aware that he was feeling depressed about the way events were shaping with Essex's disgrace. However I continued with my reasons. "He's going to school soon, you did agree that. I can continue to teach him but it's best he meets with other boys now he is seven."

"I agreed that he should go for a time, until he is twelve or so, old enough to be apprenticed as a musician. He loves music and shows a real gift. Why is there need for him to know he is not my son?"

"Because someone will tell him, either at school or at Court if he is going to be a Court musician. It isn't exactly a secret and I think it best if I tell him myself, it will be less of a shock than hearing someone make a jest of it to him."

"Yes a jest! You will humiliate me further when he has always known me as his father," Alfonso said bitterly. "You have always humiliated me and now you are going to do so again with our own son."

I knew that despite his nonchalant attitude he had always been sensitive to the gossip surrounding us but although I respected his feelings I was sure it was essential for my child to understand his real paternity which was aristocratic and probably royal. He had been deprived of much but I did not think he should be deprived of his birthright. Some day it might matter to him.

One day when Henry and I were alone together I considered it an opportune time. He listened carefully as I told him as honestly but as simply as I could how I had lived at the Court when I was young with a nobleman who was now dead and that he was his real father. To my surprise he remained silent, asking no questions nor showing any reaction. "Do you understand?" I asked gently.

"Yes Mama," he replied. "Can I go and play with my hobby-horse now?"

I was anxious, wondering what emotions he was hiding and fearful of what Alfonso might say when I told him. But as soon as the door opened and Alfonso walked into the reception room where I was clearing away the remnants of our meal Henry went running to meet him. "You are my father aren't you?" he asked immediately, seizing his hand. "You are my real father? It doesn't matter what Mama has told me because this nobleman didn't want me and you wanted me and looked after me and cared for me so this makes you my real father doesn't it? I don't want any other father except you."

An expression of surprised joy flashed across Alfonso's face as he looked down at him tenderly. "Yes, son, I am your father, your real father. I've brought you up and I love you very much so that makes me your real father doesn't it."

"You won't ever leave me, will you?" Henry asked anxiously, still needing reassurance.

"I won't leave you ever," Alfonso knelt down beside him and pulled him close.

There was a compact between them and for a moment I felt excluded. As I watched them together a multitude of emotions suffused me, not least gratitude to Alfonso for not only fulfilling his share of the bargain but for the genuine attachment he had forged with the boy in giving him the father he might otherwise have lacked. He often exasperated me and our volatile relationship had never settled into a comfortable marriage but I could make no complaint of his care of Henry.

"That's settled then isn't it," said the child, relief crossing his features. "If I get my sword can we go into the garden and you can teach me to fight some more." They didn't even look at me but went out together, Henry chattering away ten to the dozen.

Later when Henry was in bed I said to Alfonso, "There was no need to fear after all. It's done now and no-one can take him by surprise." I wasn't certain that when Henry was older he might not wish to pursue his heredity with more interest but at least the knowledge would never come as a shock to him. I paused then said, "Thankyou for accepting him as your son. When we first married I said I had no intention of being grateful to you but I am, for his sake."

Alfonso looked surprised. "But he is my son, Aemilia. I didn't sire him but I have been with him since he was born and we have reared him together, he is ours."

"And you intend him to be a musician, even though you are no longer playing?"

"I thought he could be apprenticed to my brother John if he would take him, or my brother-in-law Ferrabosco. I know you would have liked him to have gone to

Westminster school and then to the university but what then? He could never be a nobleman despite your hopes. Perhaps a lawyer, a clergyman, a schoolmaster. A life of tedium. No, music is in his blood and he has a real gift, and a musician's life can be full of interest," he grinned.

"Then why are you not back at your post?"

"I'm waiting for Essex. He said he would do something for me. You don't like being poor and if I can rise in his favour it will change our fortunes, you have often said that." He was supremely confident and I had to admit that I had been the instigator of his quest for advancement, a quest all the more urgent after our recent reversals.

However as the new year progressed the Queen showed no change of attitude to the Earl. But while he was still being held under arrest at the house of Sir Thomas Egerton his friends and supporters, led by the Earl of Southampton, were meeting regularly at Essex's own house in the Strand, one of the string of great noblemen's houses with gardens leading down to the river, and Alfonso was often amongst them.

"What are you plotting?" I would demand on his constant absences from the house. I feared that they were going to try to rescue Robert Devereux, but he was secretive and would tell me nothing beyond saying that Essex had a lot of support. I had been worried about losing his wage as a musician but he would regularly bring home enough money while being vague about its source.

"It's Raleigh encouraging the Queen's hostility," he would say ferociously, "and perhaps Cecil, though he's more cunning in hiding it and swears he holds a neutral position."

"Robert Cecil has always been jealous of Essex, since they were boys and living in the same household,"

I remembered. Essex was always the favourite, strong and athletic, excellent at dancing and fencing while the pygmy, as the Queen called Cecil, was hindered by a deformed body although compensated by exceptional intelligence. In a battle of wits I wasn't sure who would be the victor and longed for Lord Burghley, who could handle both of them, to be back at the helm. Essex was the more popular figure and had the good will of the people with hundreds of pamphlets now flooding the streets in his support but his critics said he was emotional, impulsive, and rash, qualities I had seen evidence of myself.

In March he was allowed to return to his own house but Alfonso was angry when he told me that none of his friends and supporters was permitted to visit there and even his wife and new baby were refused permission to live with him. My heart went out to Robert Devereux but I was also worried about Alfonso, idle, angry and keeping dubious company and we had many arguments, our essentially fragile rapport being continually fractured. Finally in June the Earl was brought to trial in a specially convened court at Chancellor Egerton's house. The charges against him included accusations that he had conspired with the Earl of Tyrone to reinstate the lands of Irish rebels and return Ireland to the Papist religion, and that he had planned to use the army to make himself King of England and Tyrone Viceroy of Ireland. However much of the evidence was judged to be forged and he was finally cleared of the charge of treason, though found guilty of contempt and disobedience to the Queen. He was not allowed to go back to his own house but until his sentence was pronounced he was sent to the Oxfordshire estate of his uncle Sir William Knollys, brother to his mother Lettice. Alfonso was almost rabid with frustration and anger. "How long is it going to be before she makes up her mind about him," he stormed. "She thinks she is teaching him a lesson but instead she is merely turning his supporters against her."

"Alfonso you are talking about the Queen," I shouted in return. "You used to be in her service as a musician, as my father was, as our families are. I don't understand this new Captain Lanier."

He stormed out of the house and when in August Essex was finally set free he was more angry than relieved, crying, "He has not been released by a statement of his innocence, oh no, only 'by clemency of the Queen.' Is that provocation or not?"

"This whole year has been a waste," I stormed at him, thinking how we had lived in a continual state of uncertainty. But I was mistaken in thinking that matters might now improve. Because he was no longer playing with the Queen's Musick I lacked the opportunity to go to Court even in a mean position and my only diversion had been my visits to the playhouses, though during the drama of the Earl of Essex's trial theatre performances had been limited to two a week for fear of public support, a move not popular with actors, playgoers or managers. Philip Henslowe, with the co-operation of his son-in-law Edward Alleyn, had recently built a new playhouse, The Fortune, on the opposite side of Finsbury fields to where the old Theatre had stood. Vexed by the close competition of The Globe he had leased out The Rose and moved the Lord Admiral's Men back to their original area north of the city. There was a new spate of playwrights now competing with each other but Will Shakespeare continued to be one of the most popular and I watched his 'Hamlet, Prince of Denmark', a vastly improved version of a very old play, while some of his previous works went into print.

Alfonso continued to be often away with his new crowd of companions - soldiers from the Irish war and Essex supporters. When he was at home he was restless and irritable and his bad humour communicated itself to me. Because he had no occupation he returned to his old habits and filled idle hours with drinking too much and playing cards and dice. The close rapport we had known two years ago when Odilya was born had been completely lost.

"The Earl of Essex is finished now," I said. "Much as I like him, and God knows I have always done so, his public and political career is over. Since the Queen still won't forgive him, even though she's pardoned him, and won't receive him at Court, everyone is saying he will live retired on his country estate. So why don't you accept that it has all come to nothing and return to the Queen's Musick while you know you still have a place open there."

"So you think this is the end, do you?" retorted Alfonso aggressively. "You don't understand anything at all. Do you think Essex and his supporters will tolerate this injustice and humiliation. The Queen is old and no longer fit to rule, completely at the mercy of unprincipled counsellors who work only for their own ends. They have to go."

"What are you saying," I was aghast. "Alfonso, this is treason of the highest order."

"Not if we can get King James of Scotland to support us and although I shouldn't be telling you this I can let you know that favourable overtures have been made to him, which counts for a lot seeing he's most likely to be our next monarch."

"The Queen has not named him as her heir. Nothing is settled. And there is Arbella Stuart." I thought of the little girl I had met at Grimshorpe castle when she visited the Duchess of Suffolk in company with her grandmother Lady Shrewsbury. Arbella was now twenty five years old and reputed to be the most learned lady in the kingdom. One day at Court the Queen had been heard to say, "One day she will be as I am," and there was considerable foreign interest in her as future sovereign with many overtures of marriage from royal princes of Europe.

Alfonso laughed dismissively. "You can forget about her, do you think Englishmen will tolerate another woman to rule over them. The Scots are not popular but anything is preferable to petticoat rule. God knows I have some experience of it myself."

I was furious and screamed at him, "Don't bring treason into this house, Alfonso Lanier."

But he merely smiled mirthlessly saying, "I'm going to Southampton House now, we have some important matters to discuss and it's safer to use Southampton's place rather than Essex's. There will be poetry and music as cover."

I thought of the time I had gone to the house asking Henry Wriothesley to do a favour for Alfonso. I was responsible for getting him into this company through my own association with Southampton. I had to try and extricate him but I was at a loss how to do so. All over Christmas he was in a ferment of excitement and took no part in the Court festivities held this year at Whitehall with Essex and Southampton noticeably missing. He wasn't sleeping and I would often hear him rise and walk about. Next morning he would look weary yet his movements would be quick and restless, his eyes unnaturally bright. One night as I lay beside him in bed he could contain himself no longer and burst out, "I will tell you a secret but you must swear to keep silent or you will endanger my life." My heart lurched sickeningly. "I'm telling you so that you will know the circumstances should anything go amiss. When the Yuletide season is over we are going to seize Whitehall, take possession of the Queen, force her to accept Essex, dismiss all her councillors and call a Parliament, though we intend no harm to her. We merely want a change of the government that is ruining England. We have support from the King of Scotland on the understanding that the crown will definitely be offered to him when the Queen dies."

All thoughts of sleep were banished from my mind at the enormity of such a proposal. "This is a mad scheme, in fact it's treason, you'll never do it and you all risk losing your heads. Whose idea is this, Essex's?"

"Southampton's."

I was too shocked to say anything. Why in God's name hadn't Henry Wriothesley kept himself to patronising poets and writers, diverting himself with the playhouses not treasonous plots. I remembered how I had once told Will that he thought himself a player on the stage and thinking of Will put an idea into my mind, inadequate but the best I could propose. I had heard that the Lord Chamberlain's Men were to entertain the Queen on Twelfth Night with a new comedy of that title written by William Shakespeare and I coaxed Alfonso's brother Innocent to get me permission to accompany him as I knew he was playing that night.

"Santo Cielo, why isn't Alfonso playing," he cried in exasperation as he left me at the door of the Great Hall after I had shown my permit for admission and found my place on the rear bench beside other musicians' families. I was greeted by many acquaintances including some old courtiers and was glad I had made a great effort with my dress, combining two old gowns to create a very favourable impression in tawny velvet and blue taffeta with the new-fashioned long pointed stomacher. I had spent hours in an occupation I hated, covering the joins with amber beads and gold lace taken from two other gowns, but reckoned the sacrifice worthwhile for an appearance that did not shame me in the elevated company and gave no indication of my straitened circumstances. At the close of the performance I intended, albeit unwillingly, to talk with Will Shakespeare but knew I would have to wait some time as he was being complimented by many nobles and lesser admirers after having first been summoned by the Queen herself.

Innocent appeared in company with a man of about my own age. "This is John Daniel, composer of lute songs. I don't know if you have ever met," he introduced us.

"I've heard your music with pleasure," I replied, "and I know the poems of your brother, I have bought several copies of his verses."

"Samuel always outshines me," the young man laughed. "At the moment he is chafing at having to spend his time tutoring the Lady Anne Clifford instead of being able to devote time to his writing. There she is," pointing to where a young girl of about ten years old, splendidly dressed in a gold farthingale with an elaborate ruff, stood beside an older woman equally distinguished. "Her mother, Countess of Cumberland," he added. I studied the dignified noblewoman with the pale face and serene features and realised it was Susan Bertie's good friend who had been Lady Margaret Russell, the Puritan Earl of Bedford's daughter whom I had often met many years ago. "Young Anne is a great favourite with the Queen," John Daniel added.

Samuel Daniel moves in elevated company for a poet I mused, knowing one of his patrons was the scholarly Countess of Pembroke, Philip Sidney's sister, whose son he had also tutored, and other patrons included Sir Thomas Egerton and Sir Christopher Blount who had recently married Essex's widowed mother Lettice. The name of Essex reminded me of my intentions and as soon as I caught sight of Will Shakespeare I excused myself from the musicians whom I left talking together. I felt ill at ease about meeting him after our last bitter encounter but I knew it had to be done so I squared my shoulders determinedly and accosted him with a direct, "I see you used the Italian story I once told you," looking him boldly in the eye. He seemed surprised to have me speak to him and not a little embarrassed, but in a moment of silence our thoughts merged inescapably backwards in time and I saw a flicker of emotion in his eyes as he looked at me. "It was excellently done and the music was perfectly attuned to the mood," I continued as impersonally as I could.

"Thanks to Tom Morley," he acknowledged with a brief smile. "But you must have realised we have a new clown, Robert Armin," he continued, seeming eager to carry on the conversation. "Will Kemp has left us and Armin is of a more melancholy nature with a beautiful singing voice which demands a different sort of character for him."

Much as I would have loved to have lingered and talked longer about the play and the music I was afraid of being interrupted so I asked bluntly, "Do you see much of Henry Wriothesley these days?"

He looked surprised and hurt by the change of subject then said belligerently, "Is this because of what you see as ambiguous nature in my play?"

I ignored the provocation and the temptation to have discussed the play with him, insisting merely, "This is very important, I need to contact him."

He studied me with a return of his old coldness then said bitterly, "I would have thought that would have been easier for you than me."

"Listen, he is in great danger and I thought that might count with you. I need a message to be sent to him anonymously warning that the plot has been discovered and it is not safe to go ahead."

"What plot? What is happening and what is it to do with you?"

"It has nothing to do with me but I know from unofficial sources that Southampton and his friends are being led into a trap by their enemies and I would like him to be warned. Trust me."

"Do you still love him?" he ventured, not looking at me now.

"I don't want to see his head on London Bridge."

"Will, your presence is required."

"Aemilia are you ready to leave?"

The calls came simultaneously from Henry Condell and Innocent Lanier.

"Please, Will, get a message to him, but secretly, anonymously, you must not get involved yourself," I insisted, passionately now. "But if you have any thought for Henry Wriothesly you must do this." I couldn't say more because we were no longer alone and I had to leave him hoping that enough, but not too much, had been said and that my manner had convinced him of the seriousness of my request.

"A very pleasant evening, Aemilia," Innocent was saying contentedly, "What a pity Alfonso has missed it." I agreed wholeheartedly, wondering where he was.

For a few days I was in a ferment of anxiety for all concerned, not least for myself should Will have been indiscreet, but time went on and nothing further was heard of the plot to seize Whitehall so eventually I mentioned it tentatively to Alfonso.

"It had to be called off. The plan was somehow discovered. We were told that the Privy Council had wind of it so we had to abandon it," he replied shortly with subdued anger. I breathed a sigh of relief but only temporarily as he continued with a cryptic, "Essex has another plan."

His visits to Essex House and Southampton House increased in the new year and although he confided nothing further he did tell me that Puritan divines sometimes preached at these meetings assuring them that all London was in support of the Earl and would follow where he led. Essex had always been favoured by the Puritans because of his hostility towards a peace with Catholic Spain and many Puritan writers had basked in his patronage. Then the meetings were moved to Drury House, the new home of Sir Thomas Drury in a quiet place at the end of Drury Lane, midway between the residences of Essex and Southampton and less conspicuous with a convenient large coachyard in front and a private garden at the rear. January was not a restful month for me and I dreaded a repeat of last year's uncertainties having little to distract from my worries, deprived even of Henry's company now that he was attending school and I no longer had to teach him.

Very early on the first Sunday in February I was aware that Alfonso was not abed and going downstairs I found him ready to leave the house, wearing his armour from the Irish campaign and carrying his sword. "Where are you going?" I asked brusquely.

He hesitated then answered, "To the greatest enterprise of my life. Today there will be a new England and with the Earl of Essex in charge our fortunes will rise."

I was horrified by his words but before I could say anything further he had gone, closing the door firmly behind him. I dressed as quickly as possible then giving Nan strict instructions to look after Henry I went through the gate and into Bishopsgate Street within. The city had the air of a normal Sunday morning, empty of its markets with shops and businesses shuttered and church bells tolling as I made my way towards Paul's and the centre. However all along the Poultry and Cheapside people were leaving their houses and the crowd steadily grew in number as news passed around of an uprising. By the time we reached Paul's cross where a Puritan preacher was exhorting people to support the Earl of Essex the crowds were vast. Then those at the front began to shout and point up Ludgate Hill as through the gate came hundreds of armed men, half of them on horseback, led by the Earl of Essex. As he rode brandishing his sword he called for all Londoners to join them and put an end to the ruination of England by the incompetent and self-seeking government, playing on high taxes, food shortages and the unpopular foreign policy of appeasement with Spain. But although many sympathised and though Robert Devereux was a popular hero, hardly anyone had discontent strong enough to join him and merely watched as they passed. They had been loyal to Elizabeth for more than forty years and though Essex insisted his intention was not to depose the Queen but surround her with more sincere and patriotic counsellors, no-one was willing to see her sovereign powers entrenched. So as the small army of rebels rode through London their number was not increased as had been their fervent expectation. They made their way to Ludgate Hill, but without the anticipated reinforcements they were planning to retire in disappointment to the Strand with further intentions unclear. However by this time the Bishop of London had managed to get together a troop of soldiers who immediately opened fire and in the resultant confusion they were separated and dispersed in different directions. All this I saw but no more. London was agog, many people were filled with panic at the musket shots and ran to their houses, others crowded the streets trying to find out more news, some walked to Essex house in the Strand to discover more though this was dangerous in case they should be thought sympathisers. In some trepidation I made my way there trying to find Alfonso. A small group of important officials were leaving the house by barge and the news was that they had been kept as hostages but were now being released and amongst them I recognised Sir Thomas Egerton and Essex's uncle, Sir William Knollys. But the mood was ugly with a great number of soldiers now surrounding the house so I decided it would be safer to go home and wait for news.

The day wore on but Alfonso did not return and I grew increasingly anxious. Towards evening there was a knock on the door and opening it I was surprised to see Innocent Lanier with his sister Ellen, in the early stages of another pregnancy, and her husband Alfonso Ferrabosco. The whole city was a hotbed of combined rumour and news and they had heard that Alfonso was implicated in the aborted rebellion. "Has he returned home?" they wanted to know and when I replied in the negative Innocent said, "Then he must have been arrested. As many as could be caught were placed under arrest. Essex and Southampton have been taken to the Tower and the others dispersed amongst all the London gaols."

"We must try to find him but it is too late tonight," said Ferrabosco. "Tomorrow we will divide and try all the prisons." They had some further news, relayed to them by the young musician Robert Johnson, son of my mother's cousin, who had gone to play for the performance at The Globe.

"The Lord Chamberlain's Men are all in The Clink," said Ferrabosco. "Apparently they were approached by the Earl of Southampton and paid forty shillings to play 'Richard II' on Saturday afternoon, including the deposition scene which has never been allowed on the stage. The authorities are looking upon it as done with deliberate intent to influence the populace in preparation for the next day's rebellion and they could be charged with treason." We parted in serious mood promising to meet early the following day.

I didn't sleep at all, riven with torment about what was going to happen to all these men, my husband, my friends and lovers, all of them imprisoned. Memories of them all surfaced and sank in the whirling eddies of my consciousness like men already dead. Memories came randomly - Will smiling when I praised his work, lying on velvet cushions with Southampton in his barge, the young Robert Devereux at Lord Burghley's house, Alfonso playing his recorder with Henry. In a confusing nightmare I longed for them all, the sight of their faces, the touch of their hands.

Early next morning Ellen and Alfonso Ferrabosco in company with Innocent Lanier and his younger brother Jerome arrived at the house. "Ellen will keep you company while we split up and try all the prisons in turn," said Innocent.

"No," I was adamant, "I'm coming too. I can't bear to sit at home waiting and doing nothing."

"Very well then, Innocent and I will cross over to Southwark to try The Marshalsea, The Clink and The Borough Compter," said Ferrabosco, "Jerome can accompany you and Ellen to the city jails."

We went our separate ways, our group trying Newgate, The Fleet, and The Counter, but in every case the prison sergeant was deliberately obstructive. "Is he an important prisoner?" asked the sergeant at The Fleet.

"Important to us," I replied but had to admit he was not a nobleman.

"Then we have no record, there have been too many arrested and we haven't been able to take the names of all the meaner sort," he retorted harshly, slamming the door against us. The same procedure was repeated at The Counter, while at Newgate the prison-sergeant informed us that if we had come with garnish they might take the trouble of looking for him.

Ellen looked blank but I explained, "Money to pay for bribes to get food and a single cell. It's all they're interested in but if we came with money it's highly unlikely it would go any further," I added wearily and we returned home disheartened.

When Innocent and Ferrabosco returned they had ascertained that he was not in any of the South Bank gaols and did have some other news. "The actors are released from The Clink," said Innocent. "They were brought before a committee of judges who accepted the fact that Southampton's bribe was sufficient inducement for the actors to have put on the play so they have been released with a reprimand and a heavy fine."

I breathed a sigh of relief for Will, he was no Ben Jonson who was familiar with the inside of prisons, but I was now increasingly worried about Alfonso.

"Innocent and I will try the city gaols again tomorrow, we shall have more force than you and we'll make sure we have some money," Ferrabosco promised. "If we have no luck we will try the Tower."

They were as good as their word and on the morrow I provided them with some clean clothes and food should they be successful in their search. Ellen stayed with me but we were both too fraught to do anything but move restlessly about the house, constantly looking from the window and occasionally wandering into the street. "He was always my favourite brother, why did he not stay content with being a musician," Ellen bewailed, reminding me of Alfonso with her dark curls and brown eyes. "I can't return to my mother without some news of him."

"Try not to upset yourself too much, it isn't good for you in your condition," I soothed her while trying to keep my own anxieties under control, glad that Henry was at school and I had been able to spare him from knowing the worst.

At last the men returned with the information that they had tracked him to The Counter. "We left the things for him and gave the prison sergeant money to see they were delivered to him but I have severe doubts as to whether he will do so," said Innocent gloomily. There was relief in knowing where he was but no lightening of our anxiety for The Counter, in Wood Street leading up to the city wall and Cripplegate, was one of the worst prisons in London. We were also very worried about his prospective fate but resigned to the fact that we could do nothing in the interim. But the strain of waiting for news was intolerable although I tried to hide my fears from Henry who was constantly asking about him. I also made a couple of visits to The Counter but the gatehouse was crowded with other petitioners and they would tell us nothing.

The Queen had immediately issued a proclamation thanking Londoners for their loyalty and a week later a trial of the leaders of the rebellion was held in Westminster Hall. People waited for the verdict but they all knew what the outcome would be and there was no surprise when it was announced that the Earls of Essex and Southampton were to be executed. I wept for both of them when I heard the news. Late the following afternoon Alfonso returned home.

The door opened laboriously and he staggered into the house collapsing onto the nearest chair. He was filthy and stinking, his clothes covered in indescribable foulness. His curly hair was matted and his face grey with weariness under the beard that had grown, a large ugly bruise under one eye. I didn't know what to say so I poured a tankard of ale and put into his hand. His hand shook uncontrollably as he took it and he gulped it down greedily, afterwards seized with a paroxysm of coughing.

"They let us go. We weren't important enough," he said when he had stopped gasping for breath, his voice hoarse and grating.

"I tried to find you. I sent you clothes and food but obviously you never got them," I said sadly, moving towards him.

"Don't touch me, Aemilia, I'm too disgusting," he cried, "I'll wash as soon as I feel better." He slumped in the chair, breathing heavily, then he looked up at me, his red-rimmed eyes glistening with tears. "I have to ask your pardon, it was all a mistake, you were right."

"You did what you thought best and you have paid for it." There were tears in my eyes too.

"Not as much as I expected to," he confessed. "We thought we would all die in that dreadful place. So many of us crammed together in a windowless cell, no air, no sanitation, no room to lie down so that we had to get what sleep we could sitting up with rats running over our feet. They gave us nothing to eat but a dry crust and watery gruel, just enough to keep us alive." He was seized by another fit of coughing.

"It's over now," I said comfortingly. "Let's get you cleaned up then I will make you a meal and afterwards you must rest. We can talk later." I was glad Henry was at school so as not to see him in this state. I began to boil water to fill the wooden tub and took his clothes into the garden where they could be burnt later. When Henry arrived home he was clean and fed and fast asleep on the bed. "I have a surprise for you," I said when he walked through the door and took him immediately upstairs. "But don't waken him," I warned as he made to leap joyfully onto his father, his childish face alight with happiness. Later I supposed there would inevitably be recriminations as I felt the full extent of his folly and its repercussions. But for the moment all I could feel was relief to have him safe. All night he lay beside me unstirring while in my waking moments I touched him, feeling reassured by his presence. I was angry with him, but some warmth flickered within me at the realisation that he was back home and I pondered again the chequered relationship I had with Alfonso Lanier, my husband. When he finally awoke at midmorning the following day his first words to me were, "Do you know what I was thinking while I was in prison, that I would be better off being a musician." I agreed wholeheartedly with him, neither of us realising the irony in our convictions.

On Ash Wednesday Alfonso and I went to Tower Hill to join the crowds there for the execution of Robert Devereux, Earl of Essex. For the past two weeks since Alfonso's safe delivery I had suffered for him and for Henry Wriothesley and the end to be meted out to them. My mind wandered constantly to the past and I thought of the young laughing Robert Devereux, at Lord Burghley's house, at the playhouse, introducing me to his sister, stalking out of the Queen's presence with her. I knew Penelope's grief would be unsupportable and I thought how I had once envied her. I kept thinking also of Henry Wriothesley and the intimate times I had spent with him, reliving the sensation of his powerful body but also remembering his sardonic wit. I knew that Will would be suffering and the certainty of his distress was another knife plunged into my heart. My imagination leapt constantly between what they must be feeling now in anticipation of their fate, and the final moments when the axe would descend and deprive them of life. Then came the news that the Earl of Southampton's sentence had been commuted to life imprisonment in the Tower. His beautiful body would not be mutilated but I wondered what incarceration for ever would do to his soul, and if death might not have been more merciful. Everyone expected the Queen to pardon the Earl of Essex and after his humble repentance he expected it too, holding onto hope until the last minute. It was common knowledge how much she had loved him. But no word came and the date of his execution was set for Ash Wednesday, the day of repentance, dramatically symbolic for his last appearance on the stage of national events.

It was early morning and cold as Alfonso and I joined the crowds on Tower Hill so I was well wrapped up in wool cloak and hood, but I was shivering from more than the sharp frost. My body was trembling from head to toe, my heart thumping uncomfortably in anticipation of what was to happen. I didn't want to be here but felt that I must. The waiting was excruciating and seemed endless though in actual fact it was but a short time. The grass was covered in rime and the iciness seeped through my bones as the crowds, strangely silent, passed unseeingly before my eyes. It was as if I were watching a scene in the playhouse, detached and unreal. Then the drums began to roll and everyone's attention stiffened. As the procession approached a watery sun parted the leaden skies and shed its weak beams directly onto the scaffold so that it stood illuminated and an audible gasp rose from the crowd. The Earl of Essex walked slowly but with a firm tread, escorted by the lieutenant of the Tower and an armed guard. He was dressed entirely in black, a silk suit covered by a black embossed velvet mantle and black wide brimmed hat. His expression was grave but resolute as he ascended the steps of the scaffold. He put off his hat in deference to the lords assembled then began to speak, clearly and firmly, acknowledging that his sentence was just, that he was a grievous sinner with the number of his sins greater than the hairs on his head yet insisting that he never intended any harm to the Queen's person or dignity. Then he divested himself of his mantle and black silk doublet, ready for the executioner, and there came a loud unanimous intake of breath from the crowd. For underneath his black outer garments Robert Devereux wore a bright red satin waistcoat. As people whispered together I remembered hearing how Mary Stuart at her execution had been wearing a crimson petticoat when she divested herself of her black gown, red the colour of martyrs, an act of defiance to the Queen. The Earl of Essex had confessed his sins and acknowledged his pride but the message was clear. He considered he had been thrown to his enemies. He paused dramatically for a few moments and once again I had the impression I was watching a play, that what was to take place couldn't really be happening. He knelt and laid his head on the block, requesting that when he stretched out his arms to signify to the executioner that he was ready and prepared all present should join with him in prayer.

There was a hush broken only by the cawing of the ravens and my heart was thudding like a hammer in my breast. I didn't want to watch but felt compelled to do so, as if by my attention I could in some way communicate my fellowship with him, help him bear the ordeal. Then he spread his arms and the executioner brought down the axe. There was a gasp of horror as the head was not severed and it took three strikes of the axe to do so, though there was no movement on the scaffold after the first blow. This was no mock death in the playhouse. This was real. I was shuddering, my stomach heaving, and reaching out for Alfonso's support I saw that he was crying. "I liked him," he choked, as he took my hand.

I was too shocked to cry and it seemed as if my heart was full of splinters of ice. I pressed his hand and when I could trust myself to speak I said, "Many people did."

As we made our way home, sad and subdued, we mused on the fact that Walter Raleigh had been noticeably absent though he should have attended in his office as Captain of the Guard.

"Perhaps he rued his enmity when he realised where it had finally led," I surmised.

"More like he didn't dare to face Essex," retorted Alfonso. "But Raleigh had better watch his own head. He collaborated with Cecil for his own ends but Cecil has no love for him. Cecil cares for no-one with ambition, his own is too great to suffer competition."

After Essex's death poets and musicians busied themselves with epitaphs and many anonymous ballads were sung by the common folk. One day at home in Bishopsgate I leant out of the parlour casement and heard someone singing -

"England's sweet pride is gone
Welladay oh welladay,
That makes us sigh and groan
Evermore still,
He did her fame advance
In Ireland, France and Spain,
And now by sad mischance
He from us is ta'en."

I colluded with the sentiments, realising the full impact of the blow that Robert Devereux's death had dealt to our own hopes of advancement.

CHAPTER 16

PLAINSONG

The Queen was dying. She never fully recovered from the death of the Earl of Essex and although she made an effort to be as gay as possible, dancing at Court festivities and going a-Maying, the blow that had struck off his head had been a blow to her heart. It had also been a disaster for us. Although Alfonso was still officially a member of the Queen's Musick and received his wages it was considered not appropriate that he should play before the Queen. How much she knew about the rank and file supporters of the Essex rebellion was debatable but Alfonso had been one of Essex's captains and it was common knowledge that she had her finger on the pulse of everything within her orbit. Nicholas Lanier was particularly angry with him, blaming him for bringing the family of musicians into disgrace, though his brothers and cousins all rallied around him and it was his older half-brother John, a favoured musician at the Court, who got Richard Bancroft, Bishop of London, to include him in the music for church services. Alfonso had another problem however. The campaign in the damp bogs of Ireland together with the hardships of military life, followed by his spell in the Counter jail, had left him with a racking cough which was often accompanied by a shortage of breath. "Sometimes I don't have enough breath to play long complicated sequences," he confessed miserably to me.

"It's only temporary, you will improve now, especially with the coming of the warmer weather," I consoled him. "Play the lute in the meantime."

"But I'm a recorder player. That's my forte and my position in the company." I could tell he was worried.

We were not the only ones with difficulties after the rebellion. Penelope Devereux had been turned out of her home by her husband, Lord Rich, who proceeded to sue for divorce on the grounds of her adultery with her lover Charles Blount. I had often wondered how she had contrived to survive her irregular lifestyle, ascribing it to her beauty, her birth, her accomplishments, her popularity, but I now realised I had been mistaken. It had been solely on account of her brother's position and power. The splendid aristocratic Penelope was as much at the mercy of men's control as I was myself, as all women were. She had sheltered in the shadow of Robert Devereux and once he was no longer there to protect her she was persona non grata. When I heard that during the divorce hearing she was staying in the Strand house of her uncle Sir William Knollys I decided to visit her, realising it was presumptuous of me and half expecting to be turned away. However remembering how I had broached the Earl of Southampton in his palatial residence I knocked purposefully at the door and gave my name to the footman. In a short time I was surprised to find myself escorted by a neat young maidservant up the wide imposing staircase to a large and lavishly furnished parlour. As my name was announced I just had time to register the wide mullioned window pouring light onto the silver sparkling on the polished oak furniture, the portraits on the exquisite panelling, the jewel-bright rugs on the floor before Penelope came towards me, holding out her hand in welcome. "Aemilia Lanier, what a pleasant surprise after such a long time." She was dressed in a simple black gown devoid of all ornamentation save for a small gauze ruff and there was an unmistakeable air of fragility about her. Her face was pale and drawn, her eyes red-rimmed, but her vivid red-gold hair shone like a luminous aureole around her, giving her an ethereal beauty. Now that I was in her presence I felt embarrassed, not knowing what to say and realising that any mention of her present circumstances would be unacceptable presumption on my part. But Penelope pre-empted me by saying, "I know your husband supported my brother and for his sake I am most grateful. I am also well aware of your own warm regard for Rob, and his for you." The ice was broken between us and we found it easy to take up the threads of our previous acquaintance. Penelope wanted to talk about her brother and I was content to listen as she reminisced over the years, sometimes with tears in her eyes. Then she said, "Enough of talk, will you play some music for me," and she handed me a beautiful lute which had been lying on a tapestried daybed as if only recently laid down. I found relief for my own turbulent emotions as always in music, playing some gentle reflective airs including a beautiful new song by John Dowland, 'Come again sweet love doth now invite', and afterwards she accompanied me on the virginals in some of William Byrd's compositions. Then as I made my farewells, not wishing to outstay the warm welcome I had received, she surprised me by saying, "One of the conditions of the divorce is that I must not remarry but I shall not obey. Charles and I intend to marry, albeit in secret, as soon as we can. I love him so much and we want to be together, no matter what it costs us. An

arranged marriage can be a cruel fetter. I wept all the
way to the altar when I married Lord Warwick."

My envy of Penelope Devereux had been ill founded
as I realised her difficulties were only beginning. The
divorce would be a public and shaming procedure and if
she and Charles Blount then flouted all conventions by a
subsequent marriage they would be ostracised by society.
Yet I envied her the deep love they shared and I said, "You
are fortunate to have found true love to compensate for
all your sadness," and her ravishing smile transformed
her dejected features.

On the walk home I contemplated the strength of her
devotion. A poet's inspiration and a great lord's wife, she
had found true love with a man of lower position and
lesser talent and had the courage to follow her heart. It
was true she had been protected by her brother but with
his loss she was continuing to follow her own path and
break with all the conventions imposed upon women,
and I admired her for that. I thought momentarily of Will,
of what could have been, and a pain pierced my heart.
Afterwards I was surprised by the sensation for I thought
of him rarely these days and could visit the playhouses
and watch him act with only occasional memories to
disturb my enjoyment. His latest play had been a
reworking of the classical story of Troilus and Cressida
in which he had cynically portrayed love as futile and
faithless, and I wondered if in his interpretation of
Cressida's betrayal he still harboured bitter feelings
about me. He had also portrayed armed conflict as a
futile ignoble exercise and I surmised that when he wrote
it he was also feeling bitter about Southampton. I had
found it a dark cynical play lashed with anger.

I was now forced to accept that I had to make the best
of my life with Alfonso, though since the rebellion and
its aftermath the element of trust and mutual acceptance

that we had forged together had splintered and I didn't think it could ever be repaired. However there was nothing else, and little I could do to make myself independent. Matters were not helped by Alfonso's frustration about his poor health, a completely new experience for him and which often made him bitter and angry so that he was not easy to live with. There was also a matter of how we could live if he could no longer play. But one day he told me, "Bishop Bancroft thinks he might be able to find some work for me with Sir Thomas Egerton whose chaplain he once was, to tide me over until I feel better."

"The Lord Chancellor!" I exclaimed in surprise. "What on earth could you do for him?"

"As you would expect, he has a lot of secretaries but not all of them are linguists, not even the Latinists have always got sufficient French or Italian, and Bishop Bancroft thinks he might be able to arrange for me to give some assistance with translations from time to time, nothing permanent of course but it would help in the meantime. As a matter of fact Egerton's just lost one of his most able secretaries, someone I got to know quite well on the Azores expedition. Do you remember John Donne who used to pass around the poems he wrote?"

I nodded, remembering how Will and I used to read some of them together. "Yes, I often saw him at the playhouses, a really handsome young man who always dressed to attract attention."

"Well he's now attracted more attention than is good for him. He fell in love with Egerton's niece, Anne More, married her secretly while she was under age and for his presumption has been put in the Tower. Apparently the Lord Chancellor's liking for his capabilities and his witty conversation did not extend to welcoming him into the family, both his humble background and his Catholic religion being great impediments."

"Well an introduction to such a great personage certainly can't do you any harm," I said with some satisfaction. "Egerton tried hard to smooth the Earl of Essex's path and he has been good to poets and musicians, I know Samuel Daniel has dedicated several works to him and he was known to my father." He had also taken Lord Strange's widow Alice as his second wife though gossip intimated that it was not a happy union and they spent much of their time separately between his many great properties. Easy to do when you have several estates I thought wryly, mine and Alfonso's disagreements echoed around our small house.

It was a strange unsettling year when not only us but the country at large seemed to be waiting for something to happen, the sensation was of living in an interim with anticipation as the general mood. For most people it was the expected death of the Queen and the apprehension of the end of an age. No-one knew what the new age would bring and even the succession was uncertain. Wherever people met together, in the taverns, playhouses, markets, their own homes, debate would open on the relative chances of King James of Scotland, Arbella Stuart, the Spanish Infanta, even Lord Derby with his Tudor antecedents through the princess Mary Rose. Bets were placed and people also argued about who would make the final decision.

"The Queen of course," I said.

"Robert Cecil," declared Alfonso emphatically, and once again we were at odds.

Christmas dragged wearily to its close as everyone but the Queen herself knew she was dying. Refusing to accept the inevitable, declining even to lie down, she struggled on until March. Then in the early hours of the

24th of the month, symbolically the feast of the assumption of the Blessed Virgin, she surrendered to mortality at the palace of Richmond. By order of Robert Cecil news of the Queen's death was carried post-haste to Scotland by Sir Robert Carey, Lord Hunsdon's youngest son as he was mistakenly designated, but Londoners had to wait to hear who would succeed her. Crowds gathered at Whitehall and the public places where news was always announced and I made my way to Cheapside to hear a herald proclaim King James of Scotland, son of Mary Stuart, the new sovereign of England. The news was accepted with equilibrium but no great excitement by Londoners who were more saddened by the Queen's death than eager for a new monarch. All that mattered to the majority of people was that the succession had been achieved smoothly and without bloodshed and at least the new King had a young wife and three children including two sons. I myself was disappointed as I listened to the announcement. I would have welcomed another female sovereign and had hoped the crown would have passed to Arbella Stuart when I might have stood some chance of employment at the Court. Alfonso however was hopeful saying, "You know he connived at the Essex rebellion which means that he will be ready to pardon and re-instate those whom the Queen punished."

We took Henry to see the Queen's body lying in state at Whitehall, where it had been ceremoniously conveyed on a torchlit barge, and I found myself weeping as I took my last look at the great Queen I had known personally and who had ruled England for so long. I said nothing but I wondered if my son, now ten years old, recognised that he was also saying farewell to a kinswoman. A month later we watched the magnificent funeral cortege process to Westminster Abbey. The coffin, surmounted by a lifesize wax image of the Queen in her crown and robes of state, was borne on a bier drawn by four horses draped in black velvet while behind walked hundreds of black-clothed lords, ladies, councillors, retainers, and finally Sir Walter Raleigh bringing up the rear with the Gentlemen Pensioners, their halberds pointing downwards. The press was so great that we were afraid of being suffocated in the crush as all London turned out to watch and pay their last respects, the oldest to the youngest, the richest to the poorest.

Some weeks later many of the same crowd, though by no means all, came to watch the new King ride into his city, in his eagerness undeterred by the plague raging again in this very hot summer. Speeches were made by the actors, including Richard Burbage and Edward Alleyn, and poets wrote eulogies and mottos to be displayed on triumphal arches. Most prominent was Ben Jonson but as usual William Shakespeare was notable by his absence from the arena of official panegyric.

"The King wasn't exactly a prepossessing figure was he?" I said afterwards in disappointment to Alfonso. I had not been impressed by this little man in huge bombast that made his weak spindly legs look as if they could not support his body, his pale rolling eyes, tongue that lolled from his mouth and his reddish-brown hair already thinning.

"You're biased because you would have liked another Queen," retorted Alfonso. "He's reputed to be very clever. If anyone can understand him that is, they say his Scots accent is incomprehensible."

"Well let's hope the Queen is more attractive," I groaned but when Queen Anne and the royal children finally made their entrance into London a few weeks later I had to admit they made an enchanting group. The young Queen was tall with a ruddy complexion and yellow frizzed hair but she smiled continually and waved graciously, while the ten year old Prince Henry was handsome and well built with an open countenance and confident demeanour, and his younger sister Elizabeth was sweetly featured yet suitably demure.

Then in July we were favoured by another great spectacle, the Coronation. "God's bones, I'm weary of processions and ceremonials," I complained to Alfonso in the aftermath of another hot summer day.

"I thought you liked spectacle. Don't tell me your love for theatre is waning," he mocked. But secretly I had to confess that much of it was sour grapes. Alfonso had been included in some of the music while I had to watch many of the people I had known at the Court, splendidly dressed and flaunting positions of high authority, looking forward to the new reign which promised so much, while I stood as one of the crowd, my gowns rather shabby now and lacking the impact of the new fashions. Even Will Shakespeare had walked in the coronation procession. To everyone's surprise King James had volunteered himself as the new patron of the Lord Chamberlain's company who were in future to be known as the King's Men. The actors had all been made grooms of the bedchamber and provided with liveries of red velvet in which they paraded.

Back home, hot, tired, and disgruntled, I pondered the fate that had separated Will and me. My time of glory had been so brief though it still remained bright in my memory, perhaps my problem was that I couldn't let it go. But I was back where I started in my father's house in Bishopsgate while Will and the other actors were royal servants. Who could have foreseen such an event ten years ago. The Earl of Southampton had been released from prison and Penelope Devereux and her illegal husband basked in favour again at the new Court.

The only way I could have held my position would have been through a rich lover and now it was too late, I was thirty four years old and though I was still admired I had not the money to compete with young beauties in this new age. As usual I drowned my melancholy in music and poetry.

My diversion continued to be the playhouses, easier of access now that I lived in Bishopsgate again, and one afternoon I made my way across the bridge to Bankside only to find all the theatres shut. I should have expected it because the plague had become increasingly virulent and it was a measure of my lassitude that I had not paid sufficient heed to news, though I had heard somewhere that Will Shakespeare had moved back into the city from Southwark. I returned home dispiritedly and as I climbed the stairs to the parlour I heard sounds coming from the bedchamber above. As I climbed the further staircase I became uncomfortably aware of what those sounds were. Breathing deeply I opened the door and saw Alfonso on the bed with our maid Nan. My first involuntary reaction was fury but contemporaneous with it was a pain that convulsed my whole being as if my heart was being sliced in two. In the noisy climax of their coupling they had not heard me enter but as Alfonso rolled away from her they both saw me standing transfixed. Nan made a clumsy attempt to cover her nakedness while Alfonso scrambled up, reaching hastily for his netherhose. "Get out!" I screeched to my maid, and as she made a frantic attempt to gather her clothes together and make for the door I screamed, "And I mean out, out of this house for good."

"Aemilia, you can't turn her out, where can she go?" Alfonso uttered feebly.

"I can and I will and I don't care where she goes," I shouted, "And you can get out too."

Alfonso was now tucking his shirt into his hose and though looking pale and shocked began to cajole with his usual mixture of charm and helplessness, "It was just a moment of weakness, nothing more, it meant nothing. God's teeth, I am a man and she tempted me." I fixed him with a contemptuous stare as icy as the tremor spreading through my body and he continued less confidently, "It was the first time, I swear it."

With a sickening suspicion that it was not true I cried, "How could you! A servant in our house. I know you have never been faithful but to find you making love in our bed is unforgivable and with our own servant too, that is beyond anything that I could believe of you."

"And what about you? She told me you had Simon Forman here in our bed. Do you deny that?" he retorted, angry now.

"Yes I do deny it. The girl's a liar as well as a whore." I heard the door slam. "Now you can go too. I mean that, Alfonso Lanier. I do not want you in this house a moment longer and I never want to see you again."

"Calm down, Aemilia, and let me explain. It was just something that happened on the spur of the moment and meant nothing to me, believe me."

"But it means everything to me to find my husband seducing our maid in my absence, most probably not for the first time. Believe me when I say I want you out of this house NOW."

I could see the conflicting emotions on his face as he looked at me with the dawning realisation that I might mean what I said. "Don't be hasty, Aemilia. Let's talk about this. You can't turn me out for something so trivial."

"That is precisely the sort of reasoning that confirms my intention," I retorted furiously.

"But where can I go? And how can you manage without me? What about Henry?"

The words struck with sickening force into my thinking but I was determined to ignore them as I replied, "You can go where you like, that is up to you, no doubt you have many places open to you. As for Henry and me, we are better off without you."

His face was agonised now as he began to realise how implacable I was. "Just rethink Aemilia. I'm sorry, it won't happen again, I promise. Give me another chance. You can't turn me out of my own house." A fit of coughing overcame him but I ignored it.

"This is **my** house, Alfonso. Only mine." Even as I said it I knew that it was not true because in law all a married woman's property belonged to her husband, but it was my family inheritance and I repeated it defiantly, "**My** house, and I don't want you in it a moment longer. Take all your belongings and go."

He bowed his head in submission then said, "I can't go so quickly. It will take me some time. You must give me at least an hour."

"Very well then, an hour. I shall take a walk and when I return I expect to see no sign of you. And no sign of you ever again in this house." I didn't look at him as I left the room and made my way down the stairs to the front door and the street. My emotions were in turmoil, tearing me apart in ferocious confusion so that I walked heedlessly with no recollection of where I went. I had been so angry at the sight of him making love to the silly, smirking Nan, our maid whom I employed and paid, the girl who despised me because of what she knew about me and who would now triumph over me more. A girl more than ten years younger than I was, fresh and plump and pretty. Tears ran down my cheeks as I began to realise the full import of my distress. It was irrefutable that he should never have compromised a servant of ours, but it was true that I myself had been willing to let Simon Forman into our bed. The reason I had dealt so harshly with him came to me as a great shock, illuminating my consciousness with terrifying clarity. I had not been able to accept him making love to someone else because I was in love with him myself, it was as simple as that. After so long, and unbeknown to me until now, I had fallen in love with my wayward husband. I found it difficult to accept the bitter irony of the truth. I had disregarded him for years, given myself to other men, used him when it suited me, and only now at this moment of loss did I realise I wanted him. The anguish of seeing him making love to someone else had revealed like the alchemy of invisible ink the hidden imprint on my heart - I loved him.

I returned home sooner than the hour I had given him, hoping he had ignored my command and was still there. But he was gone and there was no sign of him in the house. He had taken his clothes, his music sheets, his books, his musical instruments. Alfonso Lanier had gone from my life as I had told him to.

I was vague about his absence to Henry but later that night as I lay in bed I was wracked with sobs. Why had it taken me so long to realise that over the years we had been together I had grown to love him. He had been foisted upon me, I had been unfaithful to him, taken him for granted, fought for mastery with him. But we were alike in many ways, sharing a common heritage that had bequeathed us passionate and reckless personalities. We had many mutual interests, especially our love of music. He had proved himself a good father to Henry, devoting much time to him and forging bonds of affection as genuine as any natural parent. He had always been a satisfying lover and our frequent disagreements had added spice to our lives. I had rejected him for what I had thought was true love with Will Shakespeare and for ambition and sensuous infatuation with Henry Wriothesley. Beginning with Lord Hunsdon all my lovers had failed me, or at least disappointed my expectations, and now I had lost the man who was legally my husband. Then the image of him with Nan recollected me to the fact that he had often been unfaithful and never once said he loved me. Even in our most passionate lovemaking he had never murmured words of endearment. He had married me for his own advantage and after the shock had worn off would care little for the fact I had turned him out except for losing a comfortable lodging. The realisation that I had fallen in love with him did not mean that he felt the same about me, experience spoke otherwise. I would not allow him to humiliate me by changing my mind and taking him back, I would be resolute. I had always believed women to be equal to men and capable of being independent of them and then betrayed myself by weakness of the flesh. Now I had to find the strength to put my beliefs into practice.

The following day I was not surprised to find Lucrezia at my door. "I suppose you are here about Alfonso," I said wearily as I let her in. "Is he with you?"

"He stayed last night but he's gone now, I don't know where. Are you going to allow him back?"

Her look was uncompromising but I knew she was shocked. However I shook my head saying firmly, "No. I meant what I said and nothing will change my mind."

My cousin made a valiant attempt to do so but I was adamant to all her powerful arguments, even to her final coup de grace of "However can you manage on your own?" I did not know and merely shrugged as she left in disappointment, looking suddenly older and no doubt having to withstand the fury of Nicholas Lanier at his son's latest offence.

The following day I opened the door to find Innocent, Jerome and Clement on the doorstep.

"No, no, no!" I said firmly and made to close the door against them but Innocent put his foot inside the threshold.

"I know Alfonso is not without blame but he is only a man," he began, then seeing my face he shrugged his shoulders with Italian eloquence. I remained silent and he asked in some embarrassment, "How will you manage on your own?" As I still said nothing he continued, "We are still kin if you have need. And as Henry is now of an age for an apprenticeship I'm sure our brother John will take him, his standing at Court is even higher under the new King. I know that is what Alfonso intended and you won't have to worry about him."

I thanked him but refused to have further dealings with the brothers except to say that I would be willing to send Henry to John Lanier and I would be grateful if they could make the necessary arrangements. Henry was happy when he heard the news, though by now concerned about his father's absence. "You will no doubt see much of him," I said sharply, upset by the fact he seemed more excited about taking up his apprenticeship than sorrow at leaving me.

Then he said anxiously, "But how will you manage, Mama, if father does not come back to the house."

This was becoming a constant refrain and the sobering fact was that I didn't know. I had never had to cope on my own before. As a young girl I had considered myself independent but in actual fact I was kept by my mother and I had made use of all my male relatives and friends to accompany me in public. I had always believed that women were equal to men and should be able to live independently of them but I had never had to put my beliefs into practice. I sensed the disparity between idealism and reality. The new century and the new reign were bringing in their wake more changes than I had expected.

CHAPTER 17

RICERCA

The Earl of Southampton was out of the Tower and Walter Raleigh was in. A plot had been discovered to assassinate the new King and Raleigh was judged to be behind it. He was accused of treason and though at first condemned to death his sentence was later commuted to life imprisonment in the Tower. No-one believed the accusations and Robert Cecil was suspected to be the instigator. He had mistrusted Raleigh as much as he had Essex but had needed his co-operation to bring down Robert Devereux. Now however he was in a position to rid himself of his other rival aided by the fact that King James, influenced by information Cecil had fed him, hated Raleigh on account of his colonialism, his purported atheism and the fact that he had not supported his accession. I remembered what Alfonso had said of Raleigh's chances of escaping the axe and wished he were here to talk about the political situation and keep me up to date with Court news. Every day I was beginning to realise how I had taken his presence for granted and how I missed him.

One day I answered a knock at the door to find the musician John Daniel on the doorstep. I was surprised but invited him into the house, offering him some home-brewed ale. I poured some of my elderflower cordial for myself and while we drank together we discussed music and commiserated on the recent early death of Thomas Morley. "He will be missed by Master Shakespeare," said John, "he composed some beautiful music to complement his lyrics." There was silence then and I wondered why he had come. Then he said hesitantly and with some embarrassment, "I beg pardon Mistress Lanier but it is common knowledge in musical circles that you are estranged from your husband." I looked at him in surprise, feeling ill at ease, and he continued uncertainly, "I do not wish to intrude but I have a proposition that I think could be of help to you. As I once told you, my brother Samuel has been tutor to Lady Anne Clifford but now with this new reign he is much in demand at Court for the writing of masques and other entertainments. Also Lady Anne at fourteen years of age no longer needs his tuition in general subjects. Her mother however would still like her to have tuition and guidance in her study of Italian and music and my brother suggested that if you were willing to undertake such a commission he could arrange for your appointment. He is familiar with your expertise in these spheres and as you probably know is brother-in-law to John Florio who speaks highly of you. It would seem the Countess of Cumberland also has some knowledge of you from earlier days. Of course, if we have been presumptuous with these overtures please feel free to refuse," he added hastily, "I merely hope that you will not be offended."

"No I am not at all offended, indeed I am most grateful for your consideration," I replied warmly. "If such an opportunity could be arranged I would gladly accept it."

"Samuel will certainly confirm the matter with Lady Clifford now that he knows your mind," John said. "Wait to hear further, either from him or me, before very long."

When he had gone my mind was more at ease than at any time since Alfonso had left. The house had been unbearably quiet without either him, Henry, or even our maid, and in the laggardly hours of silence I had had much time to worry about my situation. I had half expected my husband to come creeping back asking for another chance but I knew he was proud in his own way and his military experiences had hardened him from the mild natured young man I had married. I had also considered burying my own pride and going to seek him but I couldn't bring myself to show such weakness when he had wronged me. I had always believed that women were the equal of men and the real proof of that was to be independent of them though this was exceedingly difficult to do. I would have to find some employment and neither my education nor my inclinations fitted me for manual labour. Now I had been given the chance to use my skills in a meaningful and advantageous way.

While I waited for further news from the Daniels I pondered on this turn of events. The Cliffords had several properties in London and in the country while George Clifford as Earl of Cumberland had his ancestral lands in the far North so I had no idea where I was to go. I had once or twice seen George Clifford during my time at Court, a larger than life figure, tall and imposing, a loud laugh, a roving eye. He was something of a pirate having been party to most of the buccaneering voyages, even making independent expeditions with his own ships, and as an expert in the tiltyard he had been for a time the Queen's champion. He was just the sort of man the Queen had liked, handsome, red-blooded, adventurous and spirited even to the extent of recklessness. It was well known that he kept a mistress but I didn't know who she was. In contrast his wife Lady Margaret was a devout Puritan as I knew from my time with Susan Bertie. It was therefore not difficult to believe the rumours that the marriage was not a success. Lady Margaret lived apart from her husband with their only child so her present position was not unlike my own. I tried to recall my impression of her from the time John Daniel had pointed her out to me at Court, a figure of dignity, richly attired, an older version of the pale, serious young companion of the Countess of Kent.

When the news came to me it was brought by a liveried servant. The Countess of Cumberland and her daughter Anne were residing at the estate of Cookham in Berkshire and I was to attend them there. I would be taken by coach and I was to be ready the following week, the week after Michaelmas. Making enquiries I discovered that Cookham was a royal manor leased to Lady Margaret's brother, Lord William Russell, and that it was not far from Windsor. It was however some twenty five miles from London and London was where I belonged. My only other forays into the country had been the journey I made to Warwick with my father and my journey to Lincolnshire with the Countess of Kent. I remembered how I had hated the solitude of Grimsthorpe castle and the tedium of the flat monotonous landscape and I feared something similar awaited me.

When the time came to depart I felt a great sadness as the coach left the city through Ludgate and the hustle and bustle receded behind me, and my sense of estrangement increased as the familiar landmarks passed out of my sight. I had much time to think melancholy thoughts on the journey for no-one accompanied me inside the carriage, some of the space occupied by possessions which the Countess wished to have transported, but I tried to while away the time with reading and playing my lute to minimise the discomfort of the rolling and bumping of the vehicle as it rumbled along the rutted country roads. How much pleasanter it had been to ride on my father's horse with his arms comfortingly around me as he pointed out to me the things of interest. For a time I relived the whole of that glorious ten days in my imagination. But then I thought how he too had made this journey to Windsor occasionally to be part of the music there for special occasions, as had many of my relatives including Alfonso whose remembrance I tried to smother. And I was forced to admit that the countryside here was gentler than Grimsthorpe, the landscape of romance with rolling hills, woods and rippling streams reminiscent of 'The Faerie Queen'.

When we arrived at Cookham in the dwindling brightness of a late September afternoon my first impression was that the estate was one of the most beautiful I had ever seen. As the light faded in a soft luminence over the hills folded in chequered shade, a view across thirteen shires I was told later, the landscape was suffused in the golden glow of autumn with the beech trees red against the setting sun. I was aware of driving along a seemingly endless approach with shadowy vistas of groves and formal gardens, hearing the unmistakeable tinkling of running water at every turn. When the house eventually came into sight its heart was a modest medieval timber-framed building but at every point were extensions, tastefully wrought to blend harmoniously into the original structure so that they seemed not to have been added but to have grown organically as the old dwelling matured into its resting place like a spreading oak tree. I sensed immediately an aura of calm, as if people had been happy here over a long period of time and I felt reassured, and for the first time optimistic.

I was welcomed by Mistress Taylor, who had previously been Lady Anne's governess but who was still retained in a sinecure of general helpmeet, and led to a spacious chamber which was to be my own. It was comfortably furnished with everything I needed, warm and bright with soft green curtains of linsey-wolsey at the casement window and a matching counterpane on the uncanopied bed. Through the casement I could see below me the extensive gardens ending in a grove of cherry trees, beyond which could be glimpsed the silver meanderings of the Thames. The fact that I could see the river cheered me as it still provided a link with London and I didn't feel so far away after all. A maidservant brought me a cold repast which she laid out on the small table beneath the window, informing me that I would be called upon to meet the Countess of Cumberland when I was rested and refreshed. So after I had eaten and washed, a jug of hot water already placed beside the bowl on the marble washstand, I changed from my dusty travelling clothes into a neat plain gown of a dark green cut velvet with a small ruff which I considered suitable, not wishing to look too forward but neither too subservient for I was giving them something in return for their hospitality. Then I composed myself ready for the interview, curious to know how Lady Margaret Clifford would receive me.

My remembrance of her was vague after such a long time but I recalled the soft voice, the serenity, the dignified confident demeanour she shared with Susan Bertie, not surprising since they were of the same class and background, Lady Margaret's father, the Earl of Bedford, having reared his family in the tenets of the reformed religion. I remembered how I had not considered her beautiful when young with her pale complexion and her grey eyes set unevenly, and now her face was fuller and her brown hair streaked with grey beneath her jewelled cap, but there was both intelligence and deep warmth emanating from her, especially when she smiled. She was now about forty years of age, richly dressed in dark red brocade, heavily jewelled and with an enormous fan ruff, but she greeted me without any semblance of haughtiness or superiority, rising to her feet and saying, "Mistress Lanier, how glad I am that you see fit to join our household for a time. Master Daniel has spoken highly of your talents and your willingness to share them with my daughter Anne. But though you will indeed spend much time with her I hope also that you will accompany me with your music and reading. I remember how you sometimes used to do so when you were a young girl under Lady Wingfield's tutelage." I murmured my pleasure and though I returned her smile I also made a formal curtsey to her.

In the company of the Countess of Cumberland I had the strange sensation of being transported back twenty five years into the household of the Countess of Kent. Lady Margaret Clifford was deeply religious but like Susan Bertie she wore her faith lightly as a summer gown, never enforcing her beliefs but touching all who knew her by her calm strength and the equality of her words with her deeds. Also like the Countess she had the inborn consciousness of her high position which, though she looked upon it as a responsibility rather than a distinction, was never allowed to let fall. I found that much of what I had absorbed unconsciously in the Suffolk household began to trickle through into my memory again after nearly a quarter of a century and the sensation was not always pleasant as I recollected my rebellious nature and all the dreams I had nurtured, most of them come to nought. However my circumstances were different in that I was now the teacher and I was handsomely reimbursed for my services, whilst also being provided with food and accommodation together with seasonal gifts, so that I was able to save up a sum of money. As Lady Anne Clifford's tutor I was responsible for improving her music skills and her imperfect knowledge of Italian though I often acted as partner in games of shuttlecock, bowls and barley-break, or indoor pastimes like dancing and cards. Anne Clifford was a younger version of her mother, pleasantly featured rather than beautiful, soft voiced and dignified and with a personality not yet fully developed. However her seeming pliancy was deceptive because she too was imbued with a strong sense of her high position together with a resolution that owed more to her father's self will than her mother's faith. When I was not busy with Anne I often shared the company of Lady Margaret. Although never proud and domineering there was nonetheless a distance of class and position between us for the fact remained that I was a paid servant. Though allowed to be a companion I could never have been allowed the intimacy of being termed a friend. However as time passed we unexpectedly discovered a mutual liking that developed through the time we spent together. It was my first experience of close companionship with a woman, most of my life having been spent in the company of men, and I was surprised to discover how much pleasure I found in the times we spent together. Lady Margaret liked to have me play music for her or read to her while she worked at her needlework, an occupation that excused me from a pastime I had always loathed. Like Susan Bertie her preferred reading was the Bible or other religious works but through her encouragement I began to appreciate for the first time the poetry of the psalms, her favourite book. Sometimes we would read the Countess of Pembroke's translation and sometimes we would sing metrical versions together. The house had many rooms all sumptuously furnished but in fine weather we would often sit out in the grounds, her favourite place being an enormous spreading oak with a seat beneath, shelter from both sun and chill winds. Sometimes we would walk on the estate, its vast acreage providing constant novelty with gardens, groves and orchards interspersed with rippling streams. Another form of exercise that she enjoyed was archery and she taught me to use a bow.

I began to settle into the routine of the house - its size, the novelty of my new life and the opportunities for music and poetry rescuing me from the boredom I had expected to experience in the depth of the country, as well as my growing appreciation of Lady Margaret's company. At first our discourses were impersonal, limited to commenting on what we read together, but she occasionally would refer to my time in the Suffolk household. She never made mention of my subsequent history even though she must have known about my time with Lord Hunsdon but one day she surprised me by suddenly saying, "You are too sensual, Aemilia. To be free of the power of men you must first rid yourself of your sensual nature."

Taken aback and wondering what she had heard about me in more recent years I nonetheless permitted myself a half-smile as I asked, "Is it so obvious?"

She did not reply directly but said, "It is possible when disappointed by men to channel the need for love, the need to give and receive, into love for Christ. There is no disillusion in heavenly love, no limit as to what we can give and what we can receive. I have found my salvation in God's infinite love and in serving him more than the whims of men." It was a simple statement of fact for it was not her habit to preach.

Another day she ventured to say, "Ours was an arranged marriage. George Clifford had lived in our household since we were both children because when his father died young he was made a ward to my father, the Earl of Bedford. It was always recognised that we were to marry. However though we had a genuine affection for each other we were both too different in temperament and character. I have no liking for his way of life and indeed little liking for the Court as a whole."

At one time of my life I would have considered Lady Margaret weak and foolish, sitting at home reading the psalms instead of beating George Clifford at his own game. That would have been my rebellious reaction to a man's philandering. But recently I had begun to think differently. That was not rebellion but rather the acknowledgement that women need men to survive and by allowing men to dictate their behaviour they allow themselves to be controlled. On the contrary Margaret Clifford was really independent, building her life in the way she wished, living separately from her husband, running her own household, bringing up her daughter single handedly, in charge of her own money, accountable to no-one. She travelled amongst her properties, attended Court when it suited her, entertained poets, musicians and divines at Cookham and other places, patronised writers and distributed alms to those in need, personally supervising the distribution. Like Queen Elizabeth she danced to her own tune without needing any men to play the music. My admiration for her grew.

One day I came across Lord Hundson's cross which was still in the ivory box where I used to keep all my jewels, practically the sole survivor of my once substantial collection. On an impulse I took it down to where Lady Margaret was seated at her tapestry frame in one of the parlours. "I would like to give this towards your charitable donations," I said, holding it out to her.

She laid down her needle and took it gently, turning it over carefully in her hands and studying the beautiful craftsmanship, then she looked at me consideringly. "It is of excellent workmanship and very costly. Was it a gift?" she asked. I'm sure she must have guessed from whence it came but as I didn't reply she continued, "Are you sure you want to surrender it?"

"Yes I am certain. It belongs to a part of my life that now has no interest for me. But I would like it to be used for some charitable purpose, to help those in need, especially poor women."

"It cannot be used as it is. I would have to sell it and then distribute the money." I nodded my agreement and she went on, "I know a reputable goldsmith in London whom I am sure will give us a fair price and then I promise I will put it to good use in the way you have stipulated. Thankyou, Aemilia, your feelings do you credit and I do not think you will have any regrets."

Back in my room I saw Will's poem still in the bottom of the box. I picked it up, mindful of destroying that too for it was also a part of my life that was past. But before I could tear the paper my hand was stayed. I couldn't destroy a poem no matter what painful feelings it caused me. A jewel was something that had been bought with money, casual money because there was so much of it. A poem was the product of the soul, of a creative impulse that was unique and to destroy it was like killing a child. I folded it carefully and put it back into the box.

I remained at Cookham for more than a year and a half. Amazingly for one who considered it impossible to be happy from all the activity that was London it was one of the most contented periods of my life. The estate was a world in miniature and though there was often solitude there was also much company and diversions with the members of the large household and visits from all sorts of people. I would walk in the grounds, often as far as the River Thames which lay at their feet, and sometimes to the village talking with the blacksmith, the maltsters, the cottagers, and watching the children playing on the green. There was always news arriving and letters to be delivered and I learnt of a plot which had been discovered to depose King James and put Arbella Stuart in his place, of the King's project to supervise a new translation of the Bible, and of a peace treaty with Spain engineered by Cecil, which must have had Philip Sidney and the Earl of Essex turning in their graves. When the Countess and Lady Anne made brief absences from time to time I was given the opportunity to leave myself but I did not welcome the long journey back to London. There was little to take me back there except for the longing to see my son but he wrote to me occasionally and was obviously happy in his apprenticeship with John Lanier so I had no fears for him. I sometimes thought of Alfonso but I knew nothing of his present whereabouts and with time my distress had buried itself in the well of pain dug by all my dealings with men. I was learning to live without dependence on men and I was living contentedly, supporting myself.

Much of my time at Cookham was spent in writing, Lady Margaret providing me with an endless supply of paper and ink. I had never before appreciated the beauties of nature but here they forced themselves onto the senses with their constantly changing colours and sounds as the seasons turned, transforming the perspectives in unexpected ways. Instead of merely expressing my own thoughts and experiences as I had previously done, I began to put down in verse my response to this place in the style of classical eclogues. I was also toying with a composition about women whose beauty and sensuality had been their ruin - Helen of Troy, Cleopatra, fair Rosamund, an ancestor of the Cliffords. One day I had shown to Lady Margaret something I had penned on Cookham and she had been surprisingly complimentary which led to my confiding in her some other compositions. Later she said, "Why don't you write a poem about the Passion of Christ, a long poem in the romance tradition of 'The Faerie Queen' perhaps."

"I think that would be beyond me," I demurred.

"Why not look at it from the viewpoint of the women involved - the Virgin Mary, Mary Magdalene, Pilate's wife, go back to Eve and her share in the felix culpa. I think that could be something to employ your talents, Aemilia, talents which you undoubtedly possess and which I think could be a project dear to your heart." The idea interested me and I promised to think about it. Poems with women as their subject were usually devoted to themes of love. No-one had ever considered a poem about women's involvement in Christ's Passion, it was decidedly male centred. In fact traditional theology from the time of the early Church fathers had put the blame for Christ's sacrifice on the first woman, the original sin committed by Eve which resulted in the dismissal from Paradise and thus rendered salvation necessary.

Then unexpectedly came my own dismissal from Paradise. One day Lady Clifford said, "I'm afraid it is time for Anne's education to end. Her father is in the process of arranging a marriage for her now that she is fifteen and he has called for her to spend some time at his house at Grafton so that he can sound her out about prospective suitors, although he has given his word to do nothing without my final agreement. I am myself to leave Cookham for good, in fact when Anne is safely married I intend to go and live on my estates in Westmorland, lands given to me as part of my own marriage settlement."

The news rocked my tranquil progress like the jolt of a broken axel, even though I knew my employment could not last for ever. But I had cherished the hope that once Anne's tuition had finished the Countess might still keep me in her service, as I had once hoped with the Countess of Kent, and I felt a deep disappointment at being cast off. Once again I had been made aware of the great differences between the nobility and others. My own circumstances somewhat resembled the Countess of Cumberland's - we were both separated from our husbands, my education and accomplishments were equal to hers, and without undue vanity I knew I had been given a beguiling attraction - but birth and breeding were the ties that bound and divided. The hopes I had nourished of being accepted as a friend of Margaret Clifford had not been allowed to flower though this did not change my estimation of her as an independent woman, while her serene contentment had helped me come to terms with the circumstances of my own life. I had discovered a new strength within myself that had nothing to do with dependence on others and had come to realise that I had a vocation for writing even though it seemed unlikely that I would be able to develop it profitably.

The day before the carriage was to return me to London I walked around all my favourite spots, touching the trees and benches where I had spent many happy hours in conversation and meditation, dappling my fingers in the streams, even kissing the harsh bark of the spreading oak. Then at our farewell Lady Margaret had surprised me by saying, "I sometimes ponder on what has been my purpose in life. I have not been able to satisfy my husband and have been unable to give him the sons he so desired." (Her words struck a chord in my own heart.) "But I trust and pray I have been able to reflect something of God's love in the world and it will be of eternal satisfaction to me Aemilia if you can write what I have suggested to you."

We parted with affection and the first few miles away from Cookham were full of regret. When I had first arrived I had seen the river as a necessary link with London and I would walk to the banks and feel solace in the fact that as it rolled by my feet it led directly to the city, but over time my nostalgia had weakened. However during the journey back my spirits rose again and I began to feel excited about returning to London. Cookham had been for me an interlude that had gifted me the time and inspiration to write, and to acquire through my own abilities a tidy sum of money which meant I had no need to worry about financial problems for the immediate future. It had also given me the chance to reassess my life away from Alfonso and to realise that it was possible for a woman to be independent. In the past I had looked to Lord Hunsdon, Will Shakespeare, and the Earl of Southampton to transform my life but two women, Susan Bertie and Margaret Clifford, had given me the opportunity to have my own freedom, through the education provided by one and the creative encouragement by the other.

As the carriage neared London anticipation warmed my spirits and my sojourn with the Cliffords already seemed as much like past history as my time in the Suffolk household. I leant from the window to survey the familiar outline of the walls then the tall spires of the many churches and the looming bulk of palaces came into view. As we clattered through Ludgate and into Fleet Street, into the teeming mass of humanity with its noise, smell and ceaseless activity, my heart soared at the thought that I was home again.

Once established back in my house in Bishopsgate I contacted John Daniel asking him to thank his brother for his help and to discreetly make known among the musical fraternity that I had returned home. I did not want to make contact with any of the Laniers at present but I wished to see Henry. True to my hopes he soon appeared at the house and we hugged each other joyfully. He was twelve now and going through the awkward stage of growing up, his body gangly and unco-ordinated, the pitch of his voice uncertain. But he was full of enthusiasm for his life as an apprentice. "Uncle John is an excellent teacher and he is going to arrange for me to play in public soon. He has already got my cousin Nicholas a position as a flautist in the household of Prince Henry."

John Lanier had long been a popular Court musician and there were obviously more opportunities for employment now that there were no fewer than four royal households in this new reign - the King's, the Queen's, Prince Henry's and the Princess Elizabeth's. I told him how pleased I was, then because he had made no mention of his father I dared to ask about him. "Do you see your father?"

Instead of answering he asked his own question, "Are you going to see him?"

"Has he asked about me?"

"No," he replied unwillingly. Then he added, "He doesn't play music any more, he says he doesn't have enough breath. Sometimes he is ill with his breathing." He looked at me appealingly but when I didn't respond he said, "He isn't always in the city, he moves about."

"If he doesn't play music what does he do?"

"I don't know. He still gets his fee as a royal musician because he is sick but he told me he also does some work for some important people."

I supposed that must still mean Sir Thomas Egerton but my son's words had unexpectedly disturbed me. However I was determined not to be troubled by the emotions his information had spontaneously roused in me and changed the subject, although some obstacle had now come between us. But I was glad that Henry was on the whole happy and knew he was in safe hands. Although I would love to have had him stay with me I knew it was better he should be in the company of men. It was all very well for Margaret Clifford to bring up her daughter single-handedly but a son was different, I had to sacrifice him for his own good. However I now had to decide what to do with my own life. For the moment I had enough money to live on but it wouldn't last for ever.

The autumn after my return was noticeable for another plot against the King's life, called the Powder treason because the intention had been to blow up the Parliament House when King James was opening the new session. Fortunately the barrels of gunpowder had been discovered at the last minute and the news relayed to Robert Cecil. The perpetrators, all said to be Catholics, were gruesomely executed and the Papist religion, which had of late been gaining some favour from the King who hated the Puritans, was now discredited. For weeks it was the talk of London and crowds gathered to watch the prisoners hanged, drawn and quartered but I stayed well away, I'd had enough of executions and these were particularly violent. I knew that some of my Bassano relatives, as Catholics themselves, were distressed by the turn of events and it was whilst discussing the subject with my cousin Augustine Bassano, son of my uncle

Alvise, long since dead, that I was also given some interesting news. Angustine's son Lewes was planning a visit to the family properties in Bassano del Grappa. The Bassanos had returned to Italy from time to time and my father had made two such journeys but Augustine now felt himself too old for the long hazardous expedition and Lewes, at thirty years of age, had volunteered. An idea began to take shape in my mind. I was alone and independent, I had some money and I had always wanted to go to Italy. My father had promised to take me and it would be an act of faith to him if I could accomplish his wish. It would also solve the problem of immediate dealings with the Laniers and the risk of meeting Alfonso, though I knew I would have to do so eventually with Henry beginning his musical career, but I hoped that time would smooth the path.

I put my proposition as forcefully as I could to Augustine and Lewes, knowing full well that I would face fierce opposition. At first they were adamant that it was no enterprise for a woman, then faced with my annoyance they listed all the disadvantages, the dangers and hardships to be met. But I was not unfamiliar with their tales having heard them all from my father and when I insisted that he had always promised to take me they finally, reluctantly, capitulated.

There was much to occupy my mind before we departed, intending to do so as soon as the first signs of spring showed themselves. We had to apply for permission from the Privy Council, giving reasons for our visit and our expected length of stay. They were never keen on giving passports to Catholic countries but because we were visiting family and because Lewes promised to furnish them with any relevant information gathered on our journey they were issued promptly. As expected, most of my own energies were directed to confronting the disapproval of others though I did suffer some qualms about what I was undertaking and in the loneliness of the nights all kinds of fears beset me with no-one to share them. But in my heart I was sure it was something I had to do and I was proud of my independence.

In the meantime I found pleasure in returning to the playhouses after my long absence. I visited them all, in Shoreditch and on Bankside, to watch plays by new writers - George Chapman, Thomas Dekker, Thomas Middleton, John Marston - and at Henslowe's new Fortune a Roman tragedy called 'Sejanus' by Ben Jonson who was becoming a prolific author. Finally I made my way to The Globe to see William Shakespeare's new play which I was told had first been performed for the King at Whitehall, the renamed company now receiving many royal commissions. It was called 'Othello the Moor of Venice' and aroused many emotions in me. It was a tale of violent unjustifiable jealousy and my mind flashed back to his little attic room in Gracechurch Street and my taunting him that he should write a play about jealousy since he had so much experience. Did he still remember those feelings? Surprisingly he was not a member of the cast himself and when I commented on this casually to the playgoer seated beside me I was told that though he was still a sharer he no longer acted with the company. I reflected how at one time his interests were shared equally between acting and writing and that strutting upon a stage must now have lost its appeal for him, though he was still younger than some of the actors. The play began in Venice, coincidence for me at this time, and had as its source an Italian story I had once pointed out to him. But I couldn't deny the effect of the powerful writing as a black-faced Richard Burbage thrilled the audience with his terrifying portrayal of the Moor and a new boy apprentice brought unprecedented emotion to the role of the tragic heroine Desdemona.

"A boy of rare talent and a great find for the King's Men. Will Shakespeare is now able to write more demanding roles for his boy heroines," a voice behind me said as I was making my way out of the theatre, still stunned by the impact of the final scene. Turning I came face to face with the enigmatic figure of Simon Forman who continued, "I have not seen you here for a long time, Aemilia, and I heard that you had left London."

"Did you not divine that, Sir?" I asked him with mock surprise and as he laughed I proceeded to tell him my recent history. "So you see you were right about my losses. I lost my house, my child and my husband."

"But you also found. Perhaps something in yourself that you did not know was there. I have also found - a wife to console me, Mistress Jane Baker as she was, the daughter of a Kentish knight whom I met on one of my business ventures in the shire."

I complimented him then told him about my proposed journey to Italy. "Will all go well?" I asked in some trepidation.

"That I cannot tell without proper consultation," he replied cautiously. "But I think now you are more likely to find than to lose." He wished me well for the adventure adding, "Take great care. And do not be seduced by every seemingly fair proposition. Come and see me when you return." With those cheering words he left me and I felt a thrill of anticipation. For a short time I had been in Venice in my imagination in a London playhouse. But before too long I would be there in reality, in my father's home town. It was a hope I had cherished for a long time. Would it fulfil my expectations or would it be a disappointment after so long waiting and, indeed, would I ever reach there, I wondered.

CHAPTER 18

LA VOLTA

"There's Venice, just across the water," said Lewes as we stood by the white tower of the little port of Marghera, ready to take a boat across the lagoon on the last stage of our journey.

"I never thought we would make it," I confessed, somewhere between laughter and tears.

"Sometimes neither did I," Lewes admitted. "I think I might have turned back except for being shamed in your eyes. For that reason I'm glad you persuaded me to bring you. Though I'm glad for other reasons too," he added and the look in his eyes was enigmatic.

We had set off from Dover at the beginning of April in the company of a group of merchants, for no-one made the journey to Italy without the security of numbers as lone travellers were ideal prey for the robbers and bandits who lurked in the less populous regions. At Boulogne we were joined by more merchants and we then had to take to horses.

"I can't ride," I had told Lewes when we planned our journey.

"Well you are going to have to learn," he had retorted brusquely, still unsure about my participation.

I had thought the fear and discomfort of riding would be the worst part of the trek for me, but I was soon proved wrong.

As we rode through the Low Countries we increased our party all the time and made steady progress, staying usually in decent inns and every week taking a day's rest. I did find riding uncomfortable but it was never tedious with the unfamiliar ever-changing landscape and strange sights to divert me, and there were always people to talk with as we rode. In the evenings seasoned travellers entertained us with tales of their previous adventures. But when we turned to follow the course of the River Rhine we entered into perilous country full of bandits who were not content with robbery but would finish off their work by cutting the throats of travellers. All along the route were gallows festooned with malefactors who had been caught by the authorities, but it was also not uncommon to find decaying bodies of unfortunate victims, sometimes rotting and sometimes their bones picked clean by carrion crows. So we stayed close together, always on the watch with a guard front and rear, and at night a number took turns at keeping awake through the hours of darkness. I was the only woman in the party which presented particular problems for me. Most of the men disapproved of my presence for they were nearly all merchants on business with little time to lose and were fearful that I might delay them so that I dare not request any special concessions or betray my ineptitude with the horse. Some of the others, and not only the younger men, were too familiar and lost no opportunity to take liberties to enliven the monotony. It was not unusual in the mornings when I took off my bodice to wash in a bucket of cold water to find myself surprised by one of them putting his hands on my breasts and pushing himself against me or lifting up my skirt from behind. When I had first prevailed on Lewes to let me accompany him I had been determined not to lean on him, but in reality I was glad of his protection for he was young, strong and well-built. However I never made any complaint, not wishing to be a burden when he had not been enthusiastic about my company in the first place, and we soon slipped into an easy comradeship when he realised I was not going to be a problem even though my clothes and my feminine needs sometimes made life difficult. Then when we came to Basle and began to cross the Swiss federation of states the problems were of a different nature as we had to negotiate the mountains. We had been on the road for six weeks and were making good time but now our progress was slowed as the gradients became ever steeper. I at last abandoned the uncomfortable practice of riding side saddle and defiantly tied my skirts between my legs to ride astride. The horse was easier to control even though my appearance was indecorous and when Lewes offered to lend me his spare pair of cloakbag breeches I accepted eagerly. "I used to want to be a boy then I could be a player in the theatre," I laughed.

"I must say you make a very fetching boy," he grinned.

But the horses were forever stumbling and we had to rest them more, and the nights were cold even though it was now June. At a certain point we were forced to leave the horses and take to mules. As we reached the snowline we had to wear our cloaks even during the day, while the nights were bitter and it was difficult to sleep. I slept always beside Lewes and I found myself creeping closer to him but he didn't object and we shared the warmth of our bodies. The crags of the mountains towered above us, black and menacing where the snow didn't cover them, ghostly in their white shrouds when it did. Below us were huge chasms, sometimes unseen in the icy carpet so that every step became a hazard, every stumble could mean a plunge to extinction. The men took it in turns to lead the way, though we also had a guide, but we had to go on foot now, roped together for safety, while the mules carried our belongings. One night when we were close to the top of the pass, the Col San Bernadino, we lay shivering in our blankets in the hut where we were sheltering when we were attacked by a large band of brigands demanding that we surrender all our goods to them and brandishing long knives whose steel shone in the moon's cold beams reflected on the snow. Knowing we could not defend ourselves the men made as much noise as they could, hollering and shouting, and the bandits, surprised by our number and thinking us more than we were, turned and fled. I was trembling with cold and fear, never having been so afraid in my life, and I clung to Lewes with my arms around his neck and my body pressed against his for comfort. When we lay down he wrapped us together in the blankets and I didn't resist, glad of his nearness. But the closeness of his body made my blood rise and I longed for contact with a man after being so long alone. I found his lips and he returned my kisses, at first gently then more insistently. His hands moved along my body and I could feel his hardness as he pressed against me. I wanted desperately to succumb to him for he was young and strong and I yearned for physical satisfaction and the temporary oblivion that consummation would bring, well aware that he wanted it too. All our pent up fears and the aching of long abstinence craved release. For a short time we had been close to death and now our needs were life-affirming. We teetered on the brink but finally something stayed us and we pulled back. As much as my body craved physical contact I knew that if I surrendered to him it would change the delicate balance in our partnership and I would no longer be undertaking the journey as a test of will and independence. I wasn't sure how Lewes decided, I knew it was a great effort for him, but I wondered if he was thinking of Alfonso, his cousin. Whatever the reason, we both realised it was a line we must not cross. So we went no further than our kisses and caresses and finally we slept wrapped in each other's arms. Next morning neither of us spoke of it.

The following day we reached the pass where there was a refuge and refreshment for travellers though the monks were surprised when we told them we had been attacked so close to the summit. "The robbers are getting ever more ruthless and unpredictable", they said.

The slopes on the other side were easier, the sky above a cloudless lapis lazuli blue, the verdant fields below us spangled with wild flowers, the sun increasingly hotter as we descended.

"Are we in Italy now?" I asked Lewes, amazed, warmed and excited by the change, not only in the landscape but in the atmosphere, in the air itself.

"I don't know," he admitted. "I think we are in Lombardy but I won't know definitely until we get to the Republic of Venice, it's the only part I've been told about."

I studied him as he gazed speculatively into the distance, broad shouldered and bronzed, his chestnut hair ruffling slightly in the breeze, his brown eyes narrowed against the sun. There was a look of Alfonso about him which was another reason I had drawn back on that night of near-love. He was more thick-set and not so tall, his eyes and hair a lighter brown, his hair shorter and less curly except where it was damp with sweat in the nape of his neck, his beard fuller, yet there was an unmistakeable family resemblance and he stood in the same relationship to me as did Alfonso - my cousin's son.

Now we were indeed in the Republic and only the lagoon separated us from Venice itself as we stood at the little port of Marghera and breathed in the salt tang of the Adriatic.

We had gone first to Bassano del Grappa and during our stay there had met many of our distant relatives and been entertained and feted in different households with a mixture of plentiful food and wine and abundant curiosity, even if imperfectly understood for they spoke a Venetian dialect. Their life was surprisingly simple, and arduous. Lewes had put his hand to helping the men on their land where they cultivated fruit, vines, the characteristic bisi (small peas) and white asparagus, as well as mulberry trees for the thriving silk production. In return for their hospitality I had joined the women in their household tasks and in the complicated process of producing silk thread from the larvae of the silk worms. It was unlikely that I would again own a silk gown but I thought ruefully that if I ever did so I would appreciate it the more. But though the hours were long the pace was leisurely and I was surprised by the calm exuded by this simple life. Bassano itself was a prosperous town with large piazzas and impressive houses of stone, plastered and painted with frescoes of religious or allegorical scenes and all with upper storeys and balconies. There was a castle and watchtower, a stone arched bridge designed by the famed architect Palladio to cross the rushing torrent of the Brenta, and many splendid churches including the ancient church of San Francesco so familiar to me from my father's description. His presence had felt very close to me in this town of his birth. Because he had told me so much of the town, its buildings, its history, it was almost like having him beside me as the Italian part of my heritage began to seep into my bones and the unfamiliar blazing orb of the sun shed its beams like liquid gold into my veins. I felt freer than I had ever done in my life, free from anxiety, free from convention, and marvelled at it.

But once the oppressive heat of summer had passed we bade farewell and took our horses again for the two day journey to Venice, leaving behind the hills until they were merely misty outlines in the distance and riding through countless fields of maize, interspersed sometimes with woodland, until finally the smell of the sea tickled our nostrils and we could see the Adriatic in front of us with the white tower of the little port of Marghera in the distance. Now we were almost at our final destination of Venice.

After surrendering our horses we stood for a time gazing in wonder across the tranquil blue waters of the lagoon before going to find a boat that would take us into the fabled city. The lagoon was a much bigger expanse than I had imagined but with many fishing boats and nets strung out over the water as our little craft threaded its way through. Then suddenly the watery expanse transformed itself into a city, an astonishing city of a thousand islands joined together on piles to make one entity linked by waterways instead of roads, and I felt the same sense of unreality I had known as a child when I first saw the faerie castle of Kenilworth rising from its enchanted lake. We could see only in the distance the shapes of great buildings, towers, and spires, because our boat entered the city from the back along the Cannaregio canal for this was the district where our cousin Antonio lived. Antonio was the son of my uncle Giacomo, the eldest of the six Bassano musicians, who had died many years ago. Giacomo was the only one of the brothers not to have stayed in England, returning after a time to Venice to work in his father's workshop where they had made musical instruments for the Doge, a craft now continued by his own son Antonio.

Following our directions we found his house easily enough once we had disembarked, entering from the canal through a sotoportego into a narrow alleyway lined on each side by very old buildings, almost touching each other so small was the cobbled walkway between. The door was open and on crossing the threshold we found ourselves immediately inside the workshop, astounded by its size as it comprised all the ground floor of the building. The first room was the show room in which were laid out lutes, recorders, shawms, flutes, theorbos, some on shelves and some hanging on pegs on the walls with the most beautiful and valuable instruments resting on silk covers on tables. This room led into other rooms in which many people could be seen working - sawing, scraping, planing - and there was an overpowering smell of new wood, shellac, glue and linseed oil. Two men were deep in conversation and studying a lute, the one in the leather apron was short and squat with a ruddy face and grey curly hair, the other tall and elegantly dressed in a long red velvet robe over tunic and hose, obviously proprietor and customer.

The first man looked up enquiringly then nodding us a greeting said, "I will be with you shortly, please feel free to look at the instruments."

The other man was touching the lute with something approaching affection and said, "You may leave me for a time, Signor Bassano, while I try out the instrument if I may." The grey haired man was all encouragement, then he turned towards us.

"Antonio Bassano?" asked Lewes.

"I am he," he replied gravely. "You are strangers here?"

Lewes and I let out peals of laughter though not sure why - relief perhaps at having come to the end of our quest but touched with amusement - and our cousin looked at us with some alarm whilst the customer took his eyes from the lute in curiosity. Lewes introduced us, smiling mischievously, "We did not think we were complete strangers. I am Lewes Bassano, grandson of Alvise and this is Aemilia Lanier, born Bassano and daughter of Battista."

For a moment Antonio looked as if he couldn't believe his ears then he studied us carefully, then his solemn face broke into a smile, then he was embracing us both together and a torrent of words poured from his mouth which we managed to understand enough to realise it was welcome, amazement, excitement and joy wrapped up together. He turned to his customer with profuse apologies, explaining all his family history from when his father Giacomo accompanied his five brothers to the Court of England's King Henry more than sixty years ago. The stranger listened with courteous attention, but a flicker of amusement in his eyes, then said, "I shall take the lute, Signor Bassano, and I have a proposition to make. Tomorrow I am holding a musical evening at my house. Perhaps you and your wife would favour me with your presence and bring along these visitors of yours to enjoy some of our Venetian culture." His eyes rested upon me and as Antonio made a gracious acceptance Lewes and I had no choice but to follow suit. There was too much newness assaulting me from all directions so that I was aware of little except a tall, imposing, well-dressed man of middle age as he bent over my hand in farewell.

Antonio could not wait to take us to his wife in the house so leaving the business in the hands of one of his apprentices he led us up a flight of rickety wooden stairs to their simple but comfortable living quarters above. There in a volley of excited explanations we were introduced to Adriana, a tall thin woman in a brightly striped linen skirt, nearing fifty years old with narrow features, eyes that were almost black, and black hair streaked with grey. They made a curious couple, he short and squat, she tall and thin, but their childless marriage had engendered an obvious affection and her welcome for her relatives by marriage lacked nothing in warmth and generosity. The chamber we were given was narrow and dark with a small shuttered window but comfortably furnished with two iron bedsteads covered by colourful linen counterpanes, painted wooden chests for our clothes and a decorated ceramic wash bowl and jug. Although we had enjoyed separate chambers in Bassano del Grappa Lewes and I had become accustomed to sharing a sleeping place in inns or in the open air and had never been tempted to repeat our amorous encounter in the pass.

During cena, the first of many plenteous meals well-prepared in typical Venetian fashion with lots of fish and rice, Antonio informed his wife of the invitation we had received for the morrow. "Vincenzo Albinoni is one of the cittadini originari, the highest caste in Venetian society from whom all the government officials, including the Doge, are selected," he explained further to us. "He has a palazzo on one of the canals leading from the Canale Grande and often entertains there but he is very fond of music and is to be found at all the concerts in Venice. He was married young but his wife died of the plague and he has never remarried, preferring the company of the cortegiane oneste, the high-class courtesans for which Venice is noted." This was said casually without embarrassment or censure and Adriana continued the information by describing how the best courtesans were highly educated and cultured with skills which included music and literary compositions. I remembered how the Earl of Oxford had once told me the same, mentioning a courtesan called Veronica Franco who wrote poetry and was considered equal with male poets in the literary salons.

The following day, leaving Lewes absorbed in Antonio's workshop, I walked with Adriana to the shops determined to buy a new gown for the evening. As we crossed and re-crossed the wooden bridges over the canals in bewildering changes of direction I was stunned by the magnificence of the many churches and the palazzos we passed along the way, especially once we reached the broad sweep of the Grand Canal and saw soaring in front of us the arched stone bridge of the Rialto.

"The Rialto is the old trading centre of Venice and this new bridge has replaced an old wooden one," said Adriana as we climbed the white stone steps and saw all the shops arcaded along its length. "Here you will find what you want."

I returned to Antonio's house with a creation of red cut velvet and gold brocade with enormous padded sleeves, altered to fit me by a deft seamstress. Lewes's eyebrows rose as I swept downstairs, somewhat disapproving of the blatant colours and the low neckline revealing much of my breasts, but I had already surmised that sobriety was not a Venetian characteristic. When we arrived at the Albinoni palazzo, in one of the swan-necked barges called gondolas which served the same purpose as the less elegant ferry boats on the Thames, I was proved right. I did not call undue attention to myself in the glittering throng and indeed merged comfortably with the Venetian ladies with my head uncovered and my hair bound in coils with gold braid. The Albinoni palazzo was certainly impressive, the sala larger than many of the rooms at Whitehall and more lavishly decorated with gilded paintwork, a high painted ceiling embellished with arches and gold bosses, and colourful frescoed walls. The concert was of an exceptionally high standard and the banquet generous with many imaginative dishes, colourful rice, strange fish, ornately dressed meats, sugared confections in fantastic shapes. I had the uncanny sensation that I was back at Whitehall under Lord Hunsdon's patronage.

Our host had naturally greeted us when we arrived but he was greatly in demand and it was not until I was helping myself to wine and one of the little sugared almond cakes that I found him at my elbow. "Is everything to your satisfaction? Are you enjoying the evening?" he asked. While I praised everything with enthusiasm I had the first chance to study him in detail. He was nearing fifty years of age with more grey than black in his hair, cut short around the ears but full and wavy on the crown. His features were patrician with high cheekbones and an aquiline nose and though his lips were thin his gentle smile softened their severity. His eyebrows were arched above grey eyes that were intelligent and scrutinising but in which flickered a hint of amusement. His rich fashionable clothes showed to advantage on his tall slim figure but he wore no jewellery nor obvious adornment, not even a single obligatory ring on his long tapering fingers.

"Come and talk with me," he said, leading me to one of the red velvet benches, "tell me about yourself and why you are here alone with your cousin." The information I gave him was strictly impersonal, about my family and my father's wish that I should see his native Italy, about the Bassano musicians, about my own love of music and poetry. "Then you must come to more concerts here and if you are willing I would like to take you to others in Venice, some of them public and some in private houses."

Back at Antonio's house I reflected on how many journeys into the past I seemed to have made of late.

My residence with the Countess of Cumberland had mirrored that with the Countess of Kent, the childlike freedom of Bassano del Grappa and the constant memories of my father had brought to mind the carefree days of my youth, and now the luxury of a palace as an admired guest of a wealthy lord could not help but remind me of my time with Lord Hunsdon. I had the strange sensation my life was beginning again.

When I told Lewes of Signor Albinoni's invitation he pursed his lips, not exactly disapproving but lacking in enthusiasm. Antonio however was confident in its propriety, saying, "He is a well respected citizen of Venice, wealthy and with many important contacts. It will be an excellent way for you to enjoy the entertainments of our city," and Adriana confirmed this. "No doubt also Giovanni will be able to provide you with an entree to his own performances," he continued. "Tomorrow I shall take you to meet your other cousin." His brother Giovanni Bassano was a professional musician in the city. Younger than Antonio, Giovanni could not have been more different - loud, exuberant, uninhibited and unmarried, preferring the company of young men. But he found great delight in introducing us to the inner circle of the Venetian musical world.

For the next few months my life in Venice took on the whirl of social engagements that I had not known since I was with Lord Hunsdon. Besides providing me with invitations to grand palazzi, Vincenzo Albinoni would often escort me around the city, sometimes by gondola, sometimes walking, showing me the beauties of the art and architecture for he was a mine of information. But I would often wander alone, exploring the wealth of art that was in the public buildings and the churches. I never tired of these meanderings because I had never before seen such paintings, large and luminous, depicting with vivid realism stories from the classical authors and from the Bible, stories I had always known but never so intensely visualised. The churches were a source of constant amazement to me, not only in their size and magnificent decoration, their sheer golden opulence, but in the mosaics, frescoes and the wealth of paintings by artists of genius, many of whom I had never heard like Tintoretto, Carpaccio, Veronese as well as Titian and Bellini. I spent many hours studying the paintings, sometimes on my own, sometimes in company with Lewes, Giovanni or Signor Albinoni. Such religious representations were almost unknown in England and I was fascinated by the portrayal of women, chiefly the Virgin herself but also the Magdalene, the popular female saints and the doughty heroines of the Old Testament. I had studied the stories as a child with Susan Bertie and more recently with Margaret Clifford but here the words were translated into glowing vivid scenes with a drama that was blatantly theatrical. My imagination had always been sparked by sounds - words and music - but now as the pictures coloured my senses with their visual impact I thought again of Lady Clifford's suggestion that I should write a verse treatment of the passion of Christ.

I was often in the company of Vincenzo Albinoni and with his knowledgeable interest in music, art and literature I soon began to unfold my own passions. He was a skilled lutenist himself and he encouraged me to play the instruments in his house, sometimes for his own pleasure and sometimes to entertain his friends. We talked often of poetry - Petrarch, Ariosto, Tasso - but he also introduced me to contemporary poets new to me. He would sometimes buy me gifts and one day he brought to me a book saying, "I thought you might find this of interest." Called 'Terza Rime', it was a book of twenty five poems of which seventeen had been written by Veronica Franco, a woman who had always interested me since the Earl of Oxford had told me about meeting the beautiful courtesan at the Venetian literary salon of her protector Domenico Venier and saying her artistic accomplishments were regarded equally with men's. I studied the book avidly and was amazed by the content. I knew that a few aristocratic English women wrote poetry as an approved accomplishment for their leisure hours but they were almost entirely religious works and never printed for the general public to read. In contrast the poems of Veronica Franco were frankly erotic, celebrating her life as a courtesan, advertising her skills and promising to satisfy her customers, and these had been published openly and obviously to general acclaim. Yet they were more than erotica for Franco used a forceful and argumentative style to challenge the superiority of men. Her writing disproved the traditional view of women as submissive, though she was honest enough to admit that strong sexual desire could be a destructive force. I had never read anything like them before, at least from the pen of a woman, perhaps John Donne could write so. But they were skilfully written with a sure knowledge of the arts of composition and a familiarity with classical authors.

"A woman could never publish such a work in England," I remarked to Vincenzo when he asked my opinion, not admitting that I shared many of her beliefs.

"I knew her when I was a young man," he said. I refrained from asking him how familiarly he knew her. "She was very beautiful and a skilled musician as you are. I think perhaps you are thinking you could have had such a life here in Venice." I looked at him sharply wondering if he could have heard about my time as the mistress of a great English lord. "But she was only forty five when she died, fifteen years ago now, and she died in poverty as a result of an unfortunate tangle with the Inquisition and the succeeding years of plague here in the city. In the end none of her patrons had the ability, or perhaps the inclination, to save her. Despite her early years of wealth and fame she always tried to warn others of the dangers and uncertainties of the life of a courtesan."

His attitude confused me a little because I knew he was a regular visitor to the salons of the high-class courtesans which was certainly not a secret activity in Venice. Also I recognised from his warmth and his manner that he was attracted to me but he never showed me any familiarity beyond a gentle touch, an absorbed gaze and an intent concentration when I spoke, "near-perfect Italian but not yet a command of the Venetian dialect," he gently mocked me. I enjoyed his intelligent company and couldn't deny that I found it pleasant to be admired again.

As autumn slipped into winter Venice suddenly changed alarmingly, almost overnight becoming cold and damp, the waters of the Lagoon often flooding into the streets and a thick yellow blanket of fog enveloping sights and deadening sounds. Outdoors the city took on a sinister aspect in its misty shroud with the mysterious anonymity of strange watery sound, yet the night life behind the windows of the palazzi blazed with light and colour, as did the concerts in the confraternities, the convents and the churches as Venetians continued to indulge themselves. On Christmas Eve we attended midnight mass in the basilica of San Marco and as the music floated around the golden mosaic ceiling and walls, and the scent of incense curled around the magnificently jewelled pala d'oro above the altar,

I realised my mother was right and I could easily be seduced into my father's faith by its sheer beauty. Their heritage made my father and his family such fine musicians, in fact many of Queen Elizabeth's musicians had been Italians. The Puritan religion had stripped the church of many of its abuses, rid England of the tyranny of the Pope and encouraged a more personal faith, but how could anyone doubt that God could be revealed most perfectly through music and beauty.

The Christmas celebrations were soon followed by the Carne Vale and on Shrove Tuesday, hidden behind a gilded leather mask given to me by Vincenzo, we joined the crowds of other masked spectators for a performance by a company of actors, including women, in the huge arcaded piazza of San Marco with its giant watchtower crowned by the archangel Gabriel. When I returned to Antonio's house I found everyone enjoying the traditional fritelle, fried shards of egg batter, made by Adriana.

The year was galloping on. The rains and fog of winter disappeared as suddenly as they had descended, giving place to cloudless skies and fresh breezes from the sea. Lewes and I had planned to return to England before the summer. But we were caught unawares as suddenly without warning the unbearable heat dropped on the city like a suffocating blanket and Venice turned into a baker's oven, the paving stones like hot coals underfoot, the canals a stinking cesspool. One day Vincenzo said, "I shall be going to spend the summer at my villa on the mainland, near Resana a day's ride away, it is what all Venetians do. Would you care to accompany me, it is far too hot and unpleasant to stay in the city at this time."

"We must to be thinking of going. It is what we planned," Lewes said when I told him. "If we leave it too late we won't be able to get over the mountain passes."

I recognised a note of censure in his voice and knew that he had not been happy about the time I spent in Vincenzo Albinoni's company, whether from jealousy or anxiety I was not sure.

However I had kept our relationship on a companionable level in order to avoid any surrender of my independence so I insisted somewhat sharply, "It is far too hot to travel just yet. We shall have to wait at least a few weeks." Lewes grudgingly agreed and I continued, "I'm sure Signor Albinoni would be only too happy for you to accompany us, there will be a large party of friends and dependants."

But he said, "I shall go back to Bassano del Grappa for a time, stay with Caterina and Giuseppe, help them on their lands and with the silk production, it is a busy time for them." I felt a stab of guilt and he played on the uncertainty in my face by continuing with some spite, "You go to the villa. It will be more pleasant for you to be out of the heat and no doubt Signor Albinoni will provide entertainment that will be more to your taste."

I did feel guilty but once we arrived at the villa my reservations vanished in the luxury that awaited me. Vincenzo Albinoni had told me that many nobles and cittadini originari had acquired lands in the Veneto originally as a means of securing the Republic against foreign invasion and also to provide necessary foodstuffs for the city, but now for most rich Venetians a villa had become not so much an agricultural holding as a place of recreation during the unbearable summer months. Built according to Palladio's designs the two storey house had an imposing facade of Doric columns surmounted by a classical pediment and reached by a flight of curving stairs. On either side of the main building were symmetrical loggias with stucco figures of the four seasons set in marble alcoves and surmounted by two more pediments bearing huge sundials. The stairs, below which lay the lower service quarters, led immediately into a cube shaped hall with equal rooms leading off from either side. The rooms were cool and lofty with black and white patterned marble floors, arched windows and cross-vaulted ceilings. The walls were of white plaster, cool and unadorned, and the elegant furniture was minimal. A winding staircase traced an oval pattern to the first floor and at the back of the house another flight of stairs led down to a walled garden with fountains, from which an avenue of classical figures opened out into extensive grounds. A small company of ladies and gentlemen had accompanied us to ensure there was enough diversion for the long summer days - music, reading aloud, strolls or horse-riding, cards and dancing in the evenings, long siestas at noon and exquisite meals prepared by a well-ordered unobtrusive staff of servants. But I did sometimes feel guilty when I thought of Lewes working in the fields in the heat in Bassano del Grappa.

On the first evening at the villa Vincenzo had personally shown me to a large cool bedchamber equipped with all comforts, and I had half-expected him to wish to share it with me. Indeed I had prepared in my mind what to say to him without insulting him or damaging a friendship I valued. Although I esteemed him I did not want to enter into a casual liaison and having found the strength to subdue my sensual impulses with Lewes I knew I could refuse him. I did however fantasise about what it would be like to be his mistress, to have again the life I had enjoyed with Lord Hunsdon and for which I had long craved, to be in a centre of culture and refinement, to be provided with the best that money could buy. These months in Venice had been almost a recreation of the life I had known with

Henry Carey, like watching a re-run of a play in the theatre but with different actors and an audience with changed perceptions for I was no longer eighteen but thirty eight. I knew my physical attractions would not last indefinitely and when he tired of me I had the example of Veronica Franco as a warning. And after all my struggles to be independent I was not sure that I wished to put myself in the power of a man again. However despite my expectations the subject of a closer relationship was not raised and as he left me to sleep in peace I believed I had been mistaken in his feelings towards me.

It was during our last days at the villa and we were walking in the gardens with my hand resting on his arm when he said, "Will you marry me, Aemilia? I would like you to be my wife."

The shock of his words stunned me into silence but when my astonishment had subsided I murmured, "But I am already married."

"Separated from your husband. For more than three years now. He might as well be dead, perhaps he already is. And who would know here in Venice?"

Perhaps Alfonso was dead, I didn't know. In any case he was dead to me. I couldn't believe that I was being given a second chance to have the life I had always wanted, a chance to go back twenty years and start again but not as a mistress, as a wife - a wife to a rich noble such as I had always craved.

"I would like you to be my wife Aemilia. Your beauty and talents would grace my house, your learning would give me pleasure and I know you would please the Venetians with your individuality and a little aura of mystery."

It was a great temptation to make a new life for myself in my father's country, a place I had grown to love. Yet something held me back, some hesitation that I couldn't identify, a tiny pebble chafing in my shoe that I must remove before I could go forward with certainty. "I am greatly honoured but you have taken me by surprise. It is too sudden, please give me time to think," I murmured. As usual he was polite and accommodating, saying he was willing to wait for my answer.

The decision consumed my thoughts until we returned to Venice. I was being offered a life such as I had wished for and thought impossible after Lord Hunsdon had cast me off - a life of wealth and ease, fine clothes and leisure to enjoy myself in the way I liked best. And not merely as a mistress who could be discarded at will but as a wife, the wife of one of the most important citizens of Venice, the owner of two grand houses. I could entertain people of wealth and talent, writers and musicians, have my own salon as I had always wished, be free to write poetry myself and publish it and not be condemned for invading the sphere of men. Venice was a society where merit counted as much as birth and where, unlike England, lineage was not enough unless united with service and achievement. I could truly enter into the world of the rich and noble. Literary salons, theatre with actors of both sexes, music and art would all be within my grasp. No more having to scrape together pennies to go to a playhouse or alter old gowns to make a semblance of new. Why was I hesitating at all? I couldn't understand my reluctance to commit myself to the life I had always dreamt of and for years had striven to achieve.

When we returned to Venice Lewes was waiting for me at Antonio's house. "We must be going, Aemilia, or it will be too late," he said firmly, refusing to ask about my sojourn at the villa but his eyes betraying his inquietude.

"I don't want to go. I want to stay here."

He looked at me fearfully, all his suspicions hardening into certainty. Then after a pause he said, "In some ways I would like to stay too, we do have Venetian blood after all and it flows to our hearts. But I am also English and to tell truth I am homesick for the gentle rain and chill winds of London, for a sight of the Thames instead of this interminable lagoon, for the sound of English in my ears again."

"Would you be willing to go home without me?"

He paused consideringly then said sadly, "If you really want to stay then I shall have to. But I don't know what I would have to say to our family. We are a family, Aemilia. A family of musicians. We always have been since the Bassanos left Italy to come to England more than sixty years ago. They kept some branches in Venice but it was in English soil that they transplanted their roots. Think carefully before you do anything rash."

"Will you give me a day or two to decide?"

"No longer than two days," he replied. "Then I shall have to go back, with or without you."

Leaving the house in Cannaregio I passed through the Jewish ghetto walking north towards the fondamente on the lagoon, intending to visit the church with my uncle's name, Saint Alvise. But I mistook one of the bridges and found myself further along the canal at the old church of Madonna del Orto, so called because of an ancient stone statue of the Virgin Mary found in the vegetable garden, the orto. I went inside, surprised that a church with so homely a name should be such a splendid lofty building with ten great marble pillars along the nave and vast paintings by Tintoretto because it was his own parish church. I walked around the church and above a side altar an exquisite painting of the Madonna and Child by Bellini caught my eye. The Madonna's expression was unbearably sad as she held her child close and I was captivated by the image. I was filled with a longing to see my own son. And deep in the core of my being, at a level I was afraid of touching, I realised unwillingly that I wanted to see Alfonso again. If I were to surrender my independence to a man then it would have to be to him, he was still my husband. This was the hesitation that was holding me back from accepting what all my life I thought I wanted. With a shock I realised that life with a rich nobleman and everything he could give me had become less important to me than the unpredictable partnership with the errant, impulsive, passionate musician who was still my husband. Life with Vincenzo would be trouble free, calm and passionless. "When we are married would you still go to the courtesans?" I had asked him.

"Certainly." He had sounded amused. "It is our life here in Venice, the salons of the courtesans."

Perhaps his passion would be reserved for them. I would be kindly treated, indulged, respected.

I thought of my life with Alfonso, our noisy quarrels, our struggle for mastery one over the other, his unpredictability, his volatile lovemaking that was never dull. I also called to mind the raucous hurly-burly of the playhouses and the friendly clamour of the London streets. For how long would a serene life of leisured ease content me? My life had always been turbulent, even my writing had been born out of turmoil. Would a life of predictability turn into a life of tedium, a golden cage but a cage none the less, owned by a man I respected but didn't love. I walked out of the church and back to Antonio's house thinking of Simon Forman's prediction that all would go well but that I should not be seduced by seemingly fair propositions.

The following day I thanked Vincenzo Albinoni for his kindness to me and for the exceptional honour he had bestowed on me in asking me to be his wife but I felt under an obligation to return home. I then informed Lewes that I was ready to begin the journey back. To my amazement his eyes filled with tears as he held me to him. "I have grown to love you like a sister, Aemilia, perhaps more if circumstances had been different. I'm so glad you're coming home with me."

Home was London with its noise, smells, unpredictable weather, its rich colourful language, its general exuberance and sense of companionship, it was where I really belonged. Italy would always have a place in my heart and I was glad I had come here. I had survived the difficulties and hardships of a hazardous journey and found a strength and freedom that would never leave me. I had learnt to understand that part of my heritage bequeathed to me by my father and whose recollections had been a part of my earliest memories. I had found new ideas and inspiration for my proposed writing and been introduced to the poetry of Veronica Franco. Most surprisingly I had discovered that the desires of my heart were no longer those that had consumed me in the past.

I thought of this now as we reached the borders of the Swiss federation of States. We had stopped at Vicenza to watch a play in the indoor theatre, the Teatro Olimpico designed by Palladio of which we had heard much while in Venice - a stage lit by candles, and scenery of perspectives with buildings and streets that looked real - effects not possible in the English playhouses open to the weather. I couldn't help thinking what Will Shakespeare would give for such effects in his plays, though for me the most interesting aspect was the inclusion of women actors and I hoped that one day this novelty might spread to England. On reaching Milan we had visited the wondrous cathedral just finished after three hundred years of building but now we must begin the perilous journey back home. I knew I would never again see this country where my father was born, that he had often told me of, that had provided me with new inspiration for my writing and that had offered me the gift of a wish come true. Yet despite an inevitable sense of melancholy I felt strong in the satisfaction that it was a decision I had made for myself. In front of us lay the dreadful barrier of the snow capped mountains and the hundreds of dangerous miles before we would reach England. "Please God let me see London again after I have given up so much to go back there," I prayed as we set our horses northwards. The other prayer remained unspoken.

CHAPTER 19

CADENZA

For a moment I didn't recognise the young man, tall and broad, standing on my threshold with the sun behind him. Then he said, "Mama!" His voice was deep and resonant.

"Henry," I cried in wonder and clasped him to me. Then I held him at arm's length to look at him. He had grown so handsome, his features regular, his nose long and straight like my father's, the growth of hair on his upper lip, his curly hair with the auburn tint of his own father. If only Lord Hunsdon could have seen him now he would have been so proud of him I thought as I studied him in his green doublet, the matching hose showing off his well-shaped legs. I was so happy that he had come to see me so quickly, as soon as he had heard I was home he told me.

I had only been back in London for three days but was surprised at how I had acclimatised myself to the wet chill of November. The house had been cold and smelled damp and fusty but I had lit fires, opened all the windows, bought fresh herbs to hang up and put warming pans in my bed. I had gone to the daily market at Cheapside to stock up on provisions, familiar London food - cheese, oysters, beef pies - and found great satisfaction in meeting old acquaintances, warmed by the pleasure they showed at my return. I had walked around the city, relishing the noise, the constant clamour of bells, the cries of street vendors, and breathing in the smells, the tang of the river, the tar and smoke in the air, the stench of the debris in the streets. I had visited all my familiar haunts just to make sure they were still there, walked around Paul's churchyard to see what was new in the bookshops and then into the church crowded with its usual mix of gossipers, people looking for employment, lawyers doing business, pedlars selling their wares, pickpockets and pimps. I had walked along the riverbank marvelling at the busy traffic on the water, pushed my way along the crowded narrow confines of the bridge and caught a glimpse of The Globe, The Rose and The Swan on the opposite bank, not the great palazzi seen from the Rialto bridge on Venice's waterway but my favourite places. Now I had my son back at home to tell me all his news and listen avidly to mine. He listened with wonder to the account of our long journey, following the hazardous route in his imagination, and was full of questions about his Bassano relatives, especially Antonio with his workshop. I gave to him the recorder that he had made with his own hands and sent for him as a present and he fingered it lovingly at first, admiring the careful workmanship, then he tried it by playing a tune I didn't recognise.

"It's from a book of songs recently published by John Daniel," I was informed, and I was amazed by the exquisite rendering. "When I have finished my apprenticeship my father thinks he may be able to find me a post in the household of Robert Cecil, Lord Salisbury," he said proudly.

This gave me the opportunity I had been waiting for and I asked, "How is your father?"

"He does some work for Cecil, he still doesn't play music, his lungs are not good," he replied. He paused as if wondering whether or not to continue then he said, "He's just been in prison again. He was arrested with some others in Hackney for disturbing the peace." I shook my head in exasperation and he changed the subject swiftly, telling me about a concert he had played in recently with his Lanier uncles and where he had been allowed to perform a short solo.

Later when he had gone back to the accommodation he shared with his cousin Nicholas, John Lanier's son, my thoughts returned unwillingly to what he had told me. If he had considered there was any chance of my meeting with Alfonso he would not have told me of his latest disreputable escapade. I pushed him resolutely from my mind and went upstairs to bed, hearing the watchman below the window crying, *"Remember your clocks, Look well to your locks, fire and your light, God give you Goodnight, For now the bell ringeth."* The reassuring London custom and overwhelming fatigue assured me of an untroubled sleep which otherwise might have been disturbed by regrets for what I had left behind in Venice.

The following morning busy about my tasks I heard a knock on the door but as I was in the bedchamber on the second floor remaking my crumpled bed the knock had been repeated before I descended all the stairs and I flung open the door in exasperation. Alfonso stood outside.

My heart missed a beat at the sight of him, the first time for nearly four years, and we both stood silently looking at each other, not daring to speak, weighing up each other. I was wearing a plain dress of dark red wool but I had not yet bound up my hair and it hung loose to my waist, tied casually with a length of braid as I used to wear it in Italy. He was well dressed as usual in a tailored doublet of dark blue wool edged in black, a short blue cloak flung across one shoulder and a small flat hat of black velvet, but there were bruises on his face and the skin under one eye was discoloured in shades of purple, blue and yellow. My feelings were in turmoil and I didn't know what to say so my words came out sharp and angry, "I heard you had been fighting. Were you drunk?"

"As a matter of fact I wasn't. If I had been drunk I would have been dead," he replied quietly.

He seemed thinner, his cheekbones more prominent, his eyes wary. His beard had been shaved off and his black curly hair cut short again, just as when I had first known him. A tumult of emotions rushed through me, confused and contradictory so that I was unable to deal with them, the easiest release being in anger as I cried, "Don't you know any better at your age. You are a fool, Alfonso Lanier!"

"Yes I am a fool," he retorted bitterly. "A fool for loving you and hoping you might take me back. I suppose I shouldn't have come now, I should have waited. But I couldn't wait any longer." There was a catch in his voice and he turned away.

"No, don't go," I grabbed the sleeve of his doublet, "Come inside." I pulled him into the house and closed the door then we stood awkwardly again, unsure of each other.

"I can't live without you," he said at last. "I love you Aemilia."

I searched his face as the words sunk in. Then I murmured, almost in disbelief, "I've never heard you say that before, in all the time we have been together," feeling tears pricking at my lids.

He grimaced as if in pain. "I'm sorry. I should have done, a long time ago. I've made a mess of my life," he said ruefully. "There's little to commend me to you and it's probably too late now but I thought it was worth a try and I wanted you to know that I do love you still."

I didn't know how to say what I wanted to, what my heart was urging me to. I was struggling with myself, a battle of wills such as I had always fought in my dealings with him, a fight with my pride and my independence. But if I didn't want to lose him again I knew I had to abase myself and finally the words heaved themselves out, quiet but firm. "I love you too."

The expression in his eyes was unfathomable as he stared at me, motionless. Then with a kind of wonder he said, "Never in my wildest dreams did I expect to hear you say that. Say it again, oh please say it again."

"I love you," I repeated, louder now. "I didn't realise until you went away." I was seeking his forgiveness but my pride felt unable to ask.

Still it was as if there was a great barrier between us, a wall of incomprehension, regret, remorse.

"Why didn't you come to find me?" he asked sorrowfully.

"Why didn't you ask to come back earlier?" I returned.

"You said you never wanted to see me again. I thought that was what you wanted. I tried to live without you but I couldn't do it. When I heard you were back in London I was going to come to you then I heard you had gone to Italy with Lewes. I really thought you would never come back." He paused and I recalled how I had considered it. "When Henry told me you were home I knew that I couldn't waste any more time. Even if you didn't want me I had to see you again."

"You never once told me you loved me, Alfonso Lanier. Not even when you went away to the Azores and to Ireland."

"And would that have made any difference? You always made it clear that our marriage was just a convenient arrangement. I never thought you wanted me. Sometimes we got on well together but even at the best times I never thought you loved me."

I knew that I had to be the one to move, that I had to bury my pride completely. I put my arms around him and pulled him close. "I'm sorry, so sorry. I didn't realise how much you meant to me, how I had grown to love you without realising it, until I lost you. I love you, Alfonso, since when I don't know, but I love you now and I want you as my husband, not only in name but as my true husband, to stay with me all my life."

His arms tightened around me and he put his bruised face against mine. "I've always loved you. From the moment I first saw you I think. I thought you were so beautiful, so gifted, so different from any other woman I have ever known. I couldn't believe my luck when I was actually being paid to marry you, I would have taken you for nothing."

"You are only saying that now," I reminded him severely. "It was different fifteen years ago when you were young and short of money. And it didn't keep you faithful to me."

"Nor you to me, though I knew you didn't love me so I suppose it was different. But I hated you being loved by other men and I took other women to show I didn't care. It would have been too humiliating to have people think I cared about you. But there wasn't another woman who could compare in any way to you. I know that doesn't excuse my conduct and I can't expect you to pardon me for that but I don't want anyone else, I give you my solemn promise. I want only you, God knows how much I want you."

"If only I'd known sooner," I whispered, tears choking me. "I haven't always loved you, I admit that, and I know I've sometimes treated you badly, but

I didn't think you cared for me beyond our being kin. You never said you loved me and if you had I might perhaps have realised sooner that I loved you and we could have stayed together."

"I was always afraid of showing you how much I loved you because I thought you would be embarrassed and I was afraid of being humiliated. How much of our lives we have wasted, God knows how much time we have wasted when we could have been happy together."

We were both weeping now. "We can make it up," I cried, covering his face with kisses as my tears mingled with his. Then he was returning my kisses with increasing passion and I responded hungrily, our searing emotion inflaming us and transmuting into instinctive desire. My blood leapt at his touch and my body folded into him as he pulled me close.

"There's a better place for us," he whispered huskily and throwing his hat and cloak on the chair began leading me up the stairs and into our bed. We weren't really aware of undressing, absorbed in mutual possession and not wanting to loosen our hold of each other as we tugged blindly at our clothes. It was so long since we had made love and the strength of his still-firm body, the touch of his musician's hands, made me realise how much I had missed him as my lips opened to him and I clutched his curly hair. "You are so very beautiful," he murmured over and over again, "I want you, I need you. We can begin again, we can be happy together. We are both still young, I'm only thirty-eight and you will never grow old, we have much of our lives still before us."

We had always found pleasure in our lovemaking but never in our long marriage had we experienced the unbridled passion that our unexpected reunion unleashed. As I gave myself to him for the first time unreservedly and he murmured, "My darling wife,"

I was so glad that I had resisted the tempting offer of Vincenzo Albinoni. I had a husband, Alfonso Lanier, not a rich Venetian but a half-Italian musician and against all odds I had grown to love him. It was a love more complex, more painful, more binding, than any I had known in the past. We had been thrown together but the ties that bound us, including the child we had lost, had interlaced tighter over the years so that we could not break them. Lying in our familiar bed in my family house, my parents' bed where I had been conceived and born, I realised my life had come full circle. From the beginning I had tried to break free, yet finally to end where I began had been my own choice. As we lay entwined, emotionally and physically exhausted, the thin autumn light trying to force its beams through the narrow casement, I did not think I had ever known such content. We were neither of so naive as to believe there would be no problems. We would still quarrel and disagree, we both had passionate natures and Alfonso had no drop of English blood. But we were alike in many ways and our differences only spiced what could never be a dull relationship even in our new-found need of each other.

"I'm not coming back to you penniless, I have some money," he said later when we had worn out our passion. "I have been doing some work for Robert Cecil."

"Robert Cecil! What sort of work? I didn't think Cecil was kindly disposed to those involved in Essex's rebellion."

"Oh that's all changed now. Sir Thomas Egerton introduced me to Cecil but the King has shown great favour to those punished by the Queen because he did give unofficial sanction to Essex. Essex's son, young Robert Devereux, is a page to Prince Henry and has had his father's title and possessions restored to him, while

Penelope Devereux with her husband Charles Blount and their children are greatly feted at the Court. The Earl of Southampton was, as you know, released from the Tower almost immediately. In fact I am greatly indebted to him. He has put into motion a proposal through Cecil, I don't know if you know Cecil is now Lord Treasurer, to have a patent for the provision of hay and straw in the city granted to me, which will prove very valuable to us once it is finalised. Henry Wriothesley doesn't forget his old friends."

No, I don't suppose he does, I thought warmly to myself. The acquisition of a patent, or monopoly, was very valuable and much hay and straw was used for all manner of things. "That sounds very hopeful," I said, relieved that poverty was not going to be one of our problems. "But what sort of work do you do for Cecil? You don't have secretarial skills."

"Not the sort for which I am paid officially I admit. To put it simply, I collect information for him."

A tremor of horror shivered down my spine as I realised the implication of what he was saying. "You mean spying? Oh Santo Dio, Alfonso, that's dangerous ground."

"No it isn't exactly spying," he was trying to reassure me. "Walsingham has gone now. But there is need for certain types of information and because I'm a foreigner I can move in circles where it isn't too difficult to pick up tittle-tattle, for example relating to Catholics who have been subject to more stringent regulations since the Powder plot was discovered."

"Isn't it disloyal?" I murmured uneasily. "Encouraging people to talk and then passing on the information."

"Disloyal to whom? I'm not a Catholic. It's rather a matter of loyalty to our country, to England."

"It's dangerous." A thought suddenly struck me and I asked, "Has this something to do with the fight you were involved in, come on tell me the truth."

"The fight was a result of mistaken motives and I was imprisoned for a time in order to confuse the matter, considerably more comfortably than the last time," he grinned, and I knew he was being deliberately vague. I realised my troubles with Alfonso were not yet over. "Honestly the work I do for Cecil isn't dangerous, I just tell him things that might be important and he pays me," he continued. "Our family has always done it, my father in France, the Bassanos in Italy, and I know Lewes was asked to gather information while you were away. Foreigners have always been made use of by the state."

"Oh Jesu, don't do this, it's too dangerous," I cried, unhappy about the attack on him and remembering the attempt once made on my father's life for identical reasons. "I don't want to lose you now. You've always been a madcap, Alfonso. After the Essex rebellion you said you would go back to being a musician, that's where your talent lies."

"To tell truth I don't like Cecil and I would gladly go back to being a musician if I could. I do hope that my health will improve in time but at the moment I just don't have enough breath to play though I'm still kept on the payroll."

"Perhaps now you're back home you will improve," I said hopefully, intending to go and visit Simon Forman again and ask his advice. Whatever Alfonso did I would love him but I wanted him back as a musician. I did not like the sound of "gathering information" and remembered the grisly end meted out to Christopher Marlowe, another artist seduced into this grey world. God forbid Alfonso should follow in his path. I didn't want an early death for him now that

I had found him again, or perhaps I had found him for the first time.

Yuletide was a happy season, enlivened by the satisfaction of our family and friends while Henry's delight was uncontained. My sister-in-law Ellen was bubbling with excitement, eager to tell me all the news about her husband and their rising fortunes. Happy in the early stages of her fourth pregnancy, her eyes sparkling and her brown curls escaping from beneath her cap, she pressed me to visit their new house in Westminster as soon as possible. "My Alfonso is now music tutor to Prince Henry," she proclaimed proudly, "and is much in demand as a composer for the Masques, the new type of Court entertainment. He has written the music for several masques including "Hymeneai" which is to be performed on Twelfth Night to celebrate the marriage of the Earl of Essex, young Robert Devereux, so I am sure he will be able to arrange an invitation for you both."

I was too fond of Ellen to be envious of her good fortune but I couldn't help remembering how this had been the preferment I had originally hoped for my own husband. "Is young Essex old enough for marriage?" I enquired of Alfonso in surprise.

"He's fourteen now. But he has little of his father in him, lacking both his handsomeness and his charm. In fact in his gravity of feature and manner he more resembles his grandfather Walsingham."

I was surprised, remembering my adulation of his father at the same age, but then reflected that his apparent sobriety might keep him out of trouble.

The passes were duly secured and I awaited the event with interest. The Great Hall where we had watched plays in Queen Elizabeth's time was no longer large enough for the staging of the new-fashioned masques, which I was told had become the all-consuming passion of Queen Anne, so King James had commissioned a new Banqueting House for the purpose on the other side of the courtyard. Built in brick, as the King was a fervent enthusiast for brick building in order to save timber which was becoming increasingly scarce, it had been designed by a rising new architect called Inigo Jones. I had already seen the new Exchange in the Strand which he had designed as a project of Robert Cecil and noted the obvious influence of Andrea Palladio whose buildings I had seen in Italy.

"Inigo has spent some time in Italy," Alfonso had informed me when I made mention of the fact. "He also designs all the stage effects and scenery for the masques."

"And what's an architect doing designing for the theatre?" I asked in amusement. The only stage effects I knew from the plays I had seen were limited to painted curtains, trap doors and explosives for battle scenes or storms.

"You will have to wait and see," Alfonso refused to elaborate. "I think you are going to be surprised."

But then I recalled how Palladio had not only designed the theatre we had seen in Vicenza but also the scenic effects and was even more intrigued as to what awaited me.

When we entered the new Banqueting Hall I was amazed by the sheer size though the Ionic columns set at intervals along the upper gallery, where we were seated, and the complementary Doric columns on the lower floor hindered the views of the spectators. "I think Inigo Jones worships Palladio more than is practical in a building like this," I murmured as we took our seats, thinking the views were better in the public playhouses.

Facing us was an enormous golden Roman altar inscribed with the words "Union", symbolising not only marriage but the recent union of the crowns of England and Scotland. This was flanked by life-size statues of Hercules and Atlas, behind which hung a large globe showing a map of the world in silver and blue, suspended from the roof by silver wire. Then when the strains of Ferrabosco's music signalled the beginning of the performance everyone gasped in amazement as the globe descended slowly and dramatically and on reaching the ground the bottom half opened up to shed eight masquers with drawn swords, representing the four humours and the four affections. But then from the top half of the globe the figure of Reason in a fantastic gown sparkling with gems and mathematical symbols descended to pacify them. Thirty two knights in full battle paraphenalia fought together until an ethereal messenger flew down from the heavens enveloped in a brilliant aura of white light, while at the same time a mist of delicate perfume floated over the audience. Then a curtain painted to represent clouds was raised to reveal the Queen in the guise of Juno goddess of marriage, seated on a golden throne and attended by peacocks with her feet resting upon a lion's skin. Around her swirled comets and meteors while female dancers, the ladies of the Court, descended from the heavens to dance around the newly married couple. I had never before seen a performance so elaborately presented and my gasps of amazement caused Alfonso considerable amusement. Yet despite my fascination with the show my eyes were still often drawn to where the young couple were seated in the place of honour. My opinion of young Essex was the same as Alfonso's as I noted the stiff self-consciousness that bore no sign of his father's vivacity, while the beautiful auburn-haired Frances Howard seemed to my eye to flaunt an inappropriate boldness, a maturity beyond her thirteen years. I tried to still the uncomfortable premonition that the young couple were ill suited. But fortunately on this day fate kept hidden from everyone the shocking scandal that was later to envelop them when Frances would stand in court accused of murder together with her lover, a scenario as dramatic as anything ever seen in the playhouses.

Ben Jonson had been the author of the masque and I was told that his collaboration with Inigo Jones and Alfonso Ferrabosco was a popular combination. "You've seen several of these masques I suppose, doesn't William Shakespeare write any of them," I ventured to ask my husband. I knew that in the past Will had never participated in composing the conventional celebratory poems and eulogies for official occasions and had reserved his writing for the theatre, but I wondered if he had now changed his mind.

"None," Alfonso replied. "Jonson has carved himself a niche and Samuel Daniel is also a popular author, but Shakespeare continues to write only for the playhouses, a steady stream of new plays, and I can't say I blame him. It must be more rewarding than scribbling this flattery for the nobility to indulge themselves."

I concurred with his opinion. It was obvious that though the performance had been ostensibly to celebrate a marriage, the true symbolism lay in the marriage of the English and Scottish crowns and the proclamation of a new golden age inaugurated by King James's accession. Although the entertainment had amazed me - the ingenious effects, the visual impact and last but not least the importance of music – fundamentally it had been a trifling concoction with less than subtle propaganda. I still preferred the playhouses with their simple stage effects, the rumbustious acting of professionals like

Dick Burbage and the thought-provoking complexity of Will's plays.

"Why is it not permitted for women actors to present themselves on the public stage, suitably dressed, in serious tragedies or satiric comedies, whilst noblewomen can frolic unashamedly in fantastic costumes of diaphanous materials revealing their bodies, in productions that cost enough to keep the poor of London for a year," I complained.

"It's good business for the musicians," Alfonso reminded me and I had to agree, for though music often played an important part in the playhouses it was not such an essential ingredient as was obvious in these masques. Alfonso Ferrabosco was certainly doing very well and the participation also of many of the Bassanos and Laniers in this type of Court entertainment proved the point. "You're just jealous," he teased me with a mischievous grin. "You wish you could have played a part yourself," and I had to acknowledge he was probably right. I would love to have participated in something like this when I was at the Court. But I was also aware of the regret he himself felt at not being able to be part of the music, and I had caught a glimpse of sadness behind his teasing smile. This rise in the fortunes of the musicians had come too late for us.

I couldn't deny that it was enjoyable to be part of the Court festivities again but after four years away I was aware of many changes, not only in the entertainment which had truly amazed me, but in the fashions, customs, and behaviour from the time of Queen Elizabeth - a general air of laxity with much drunkenness apparent. As we were making our way out at the end of the performance I happened to overhear two young ladies, resplendent in wheel farthingales with their hair piled high over rolls from which sprouted large ostrich feathers, talking together and laughing.

"She makes no effort to be sociable, no wonder she doesn't have any friends," said one.

"And her clothes are always so obviously out-dated. As a cousin of the King she cuts a poor figure," responded the other scornfully.

I was aware that my own gown did not correspond to the latest Court fashions for I was wearing the red and gold dress I had bought in Venice and its opulence had drawn many curious glances. I followed the direction of the young ladies' gaze and picked out the subject of their conversation. A woman no longer young, dressed in a gown covered in beads and braids but lacking any valuable decoration and obviously of the fashion of Queen Elizabeth's time, was standing alone looking both bored and lonely. After a moment's contemplation I realised it was Arbella Stuart and though I feared my behaviour might be considered inappropriate, nonetheless something urged me to approach her. As I got closer I could see she wore little jewellery, the yellow gown did little for her sallow complexion and her auburn hair had been frizzed unbecomingly into a semblance of the style made popular by the Queen. I curtseyed to her then said carefully, "I do not expect you to remember me, My Lady, but I once met you when we were children, when I was at Grimsthorpe castle with the Duchess of Suffolk and the Countess of Kent and you came to visit us with Lady Shrewsbury."

She looked puzzled for a moment, but not displeased, then she smiled saying, "Aemilia. Yes I remember. Aemilia Bassano. I remember because we talked together for a long time and I knew so few children. We talked about things that interested me and afterwards my grandmother said you were very well educated by the Countess and that I should emulate you."

"I have heard, My Lady, that you are the best educated lady at the Court," I dared to say.

"That means very little, I'm afraid. You must know as I do, Aemilia, how different life was with Queen Elizabeth. Oh I can tell you how tedious life is here with nothing but silly games, shallow gossip and play-acting. When they are not acting and dressing up, the Queen and her ladies are playing Hunt the Slipper and Blind Man's Buff till the early hours of the morning. I swear to you I am bored to tears with no-one to talk to about the things that interest me. I have asked my cousin the King to let me leave Court and live independently elsewhere but he will not agree. He is still afraid of me and must have me where he can see everything I am doing." She stopped, realising that she had probably said too much. "Thankyou for talking to me. I regret we cannot have a closer acquaintance. Perhaps sometime when I might have my own household it will be possible to do so." I was dismissed but I felt more pity for her than offence. As a child Arbella Stuart had had no friends and now as a woman approaching middle age and obviously short of money she was still as lonely. I wondered why we couldn't have been friends when our minds were so much in tune and once again the spectre of class divided me from a friendship with a companion of like mind. Nowhere amongst my acquaintances was there anyone to share my intellectual interests, only Will Shakespeare had done that. I sometimes considered my education a bane as well as a boon. I might have been better without it, I would definitely have been less restless.

As we were leaving I turned around to take another look at Arbella and I think she was about to call me back when I saw her accosted by a fair-haired young man. His demeanour and clothing proclaimed his rank though he lacked the ostentation of a courtier and there was a diffidence about his pleasant open features. She turned towards him and to my amazement a smile of such delight spread over her lacklustre face that made her seem almost beautiful.

"Who's that young man there?" I whispered to Alfonso.

He peered closely then answered, "William Seymour, the Earl of Hertford's grandson. I'm surprised to see him here, he's a quiet studious boy who loves books more than Court life. Mind you it's better for his health that way, the Greys are a dangerous family to belong to."

"As the executed Lady Jane Grey, Queen of England for nine days? And Lady Catherine Grey, dying in the Tower for marrying without Queen Elizabeth's permission?"

"The very same. Lady Catherine was his grandmother. But why the interest, he's too young for you, not much more than twenty."

I pinched him playfully, thinking again how much he knew of Court gossip and how I had always missed his tales when he had been away. However I wished for both of our sakes he was still playing music himself and though his connections with Robert Cecil would provide an entree for some Court entertainments I did not like his association with the cunning manipulator who had largely been responsible for the fall of the Earl of Essex.

"Please don't do any more spying for him," I pleaded again when we had taken a boat upriver then hired a linkboy to accompany us through the dark streets to Bishopsgate, noticing how he kept one hand on his dagger. "I'm sure there's no need for it now."

"You'd be surprised," he replied. "Spain and France have not lessened their efforts to disturb the realm. Not long ago there was a plot to replace the King by Arbella Stuart and during the Powder Plot Catholics attempted to kidnap the Princess Elizabeth. If Cecil and the Privy

Council had not already had wind of these then the results could have been disastrous."

"You've always sought danger haven't you? You need excitement. But please, Alfonso, for my sake, don't carry on with this. I don't want to lose you now."

"Just letter drops, nothing more, I promise you. The money's helpful."

"But we have Southampton's patent now." I still thought of the Earl with something approaching affection though he was rarely seen at Court, he and King James sharing a mutual antipathy, and preferred to live retired at Titchfield with his wife and family, investing in exploration and colonial ventures.

"I do hope I shall be able to go back to playing music, you know that. I'm sure I will one day, I really do feel better now I'm back at home."

But I knew that notwithstanding his regular optimistic assertions his condition troubled him more than he would admit. Despite my care of him his health was not improving and I was seriously worried though I tried not to show it. Sometimes his coughing would choke him and he would spit blood and I would have to run for a tankard of ale. Sometimes in the night I would hear him rise from bed and opening the casement he would lean out, gasping for air. I hoped he would be better when summer came and I only wished I could have gone to Simon Forman for help. I never had the opportunity to do so for to everyone's surprise he had recently died of a sudden seizure, though it was rumoured that a week previously he had told his wife the exact day and time of his death.

One day in February Alfonso came home with a present for me. "For your fortieth birthday," he said, handing me a little bag of red silk. I opened it eagerly and to my shock and amazement saw inside Lord

Hunsdon's locket with the intarsia cross and my initials entwined. "I saw it in a goldsmith's on the Bridge. The owner said it had once belonged to Anne Boleyn and those are her initials but because they say she had a mole on her neck like yours and because they are your initials also, I bought it for you."

"It must have cost you a lot," I whispered, still in shock.

"Not as much as you might think, the goldsmith said it would not find favour with everyone due to the changes in this new reign and the Catholic associations of the cross. But it doesn't matter anyway because nothing is too much for you my love. I have taken a lot from you in the past and now I want to give you something back, though not as much as I would like. You deserve more."

The tears were choking me as I put my arms around him and held him close. "My initials are A.L. for Aemilia Lanier," I assured him. "But it is beautiful and I love you." The ironies were too complex to unravel.

CHAPTER 20

MAGNIFICAT

"I want to ask you a great favour, Alfonso." I had waited until what I considered a suitable time and we were seated still at the table after an evening meal together. The flickering candle lit his face as his brows arched in surprise and he looked at me questioningly. "I want to publish a book of poems and I need your support." He waited for me to say more and I continued, "I have been writing poetry for a long time, since I was with Lord Hunsdon in fact, but only for my own satisfaction and often to keep myself occupied. A suitable accomplishment for a woman," I added with conisderable irony.

The irony was not lost on Alfonso as he said, "For an educated woman. Usually an aristocratic lady. You have always been capable of surprising me, Aemilia."

"These early attempts were of little worth except to myself, as a release and as a learning process. But when I stayed at Cookham with Lady Clifford I had the time and opportunity to write in earnest and it was she who encouraged me and gave me a subject. I am now not content for this to be merely a private exercise. I want it to be published."

"Women don't have books published," Alfonso said evenly. "They write only as a recreation, for private

4 2 1

perusal, you said that yourself. Writing for publication is a man's sphere."

"I know."

The desire to try and get some of my verse published had been growing for some time, strengthened since my return from Venice where I had discovered the writing of Veronica Franco and developed a confidence in myself. I had shown my compositions to few people but those I had, like Lady Clifford and Will Shakespeare, had been complimentary. However one particular event had been the final spur to my irresolution.

Alfonso came home one day with a copy of 'Shakespeare's Sonnets, Never before Imprinted' which he had bought for me from the bookseller John Wright in Churchgate, saying in amazement, "Would you believe it, he's actually had printed the sonnets he wrote to Southampton which were being circulated ten years ago."

"It must be another pirate edition," I said, trying to keep my voice from trembling.

"No this seems to be fully authenticated by the poet himself, he's obviously waited until he no longer lives in London. There are over a hundred sonnets, most of them written to a man but some to a woman."

"Is Southampton mentioned by name?" I asked, not daring to ask the question which was really uppermost in my mind.

"No, no names, but many people around the Court are aware of the association. No name of the woman either though that could be an invention in keeping with many sonnet conventions."

"Sonnet sequences usually have a real person as a subject, even if greatly idealised," I forced myself to say. "Like Sidney's Penelope Devereux for example."

"The woman in these sonnets is scarcely idealised, in fact there seems to be a lot of venom in the portrayal, maybe Shakespeare is a pederast after all. But read them yourself, see what you think. I thought you might like to have a copy knowing how much you admire his plays. For myself I don't care for them, though I must admit I've only skipped through it. Whether it's an invented scenario or an actual situation it's a sordid tale, love for another man, a deceitful woman and betrayal between them all. Besides sonnet sequences are old-fashioned now. He should keep to writing plays, it would have been better as a play."

Knowing Alfonso as well as I did I was sure he didn't suspect me, he had no guile. He wasn't a great lover of poetry and had obviously only glanced at the book and relied on what others had said. But I took the copy from him with trepidation. Afraid of losing him in espionage activities I had managed to persuade him out of Cecil's clutches, and now a greater danger loomed to threaten our closeness as my past came back to haunt me. I began to read, but with growing dismay, not able to believe what I was reading. They were all there - the poems he had read aloud to me in the attic room in Gracechurch street, the poem he had given me when I had played the virginals at Lord Burghley's and which was still in my ivory box, the poems he had said were not for publication but only for his own satisfaction. There were also many more, over a hundred in total - some beautiful love poems, some philosophical musings on the brevity of time, but others about me that were bitter and vicious. I thought back to all the times in the past when I had longed for a great poet to write verses about me and now that my wish had come true I experienced the same disillusion as Tithonus when he realised he had not been specific enough about his request, asking for long life but not the youth to go with it. I had wanted a poet to make me immortal, but by his worship and love, not by hate and degredation. I felt deeply betrayed that Will had made public for all men to read such a travesty of what I had believed to be true love. It was a fact that no names were mentioned and some people might consider the sequence a poetic invention for art's sake as Alfonso had suggested. But there were also those who knew more about the circumstances and might one day reveal information to provide the scandal-hungry public with a possible interpretation. My physical description was accurate enough and there were people in the theatre world who had suspected a liaison between us. Had Will thought about this or did he not care so long as his verse was admired for the poetic excellence it obviously showed.

For days I was in despair, torn between bitter disillusion and shame. I had been deluded in his love for me but I had known that for some time. Uppermost in my thoughts was the shame I felt that people should read such a representation of me, perhaps for years to come. This was the spark that lit my smouldering uncertainty about trying to get my own work published. I came to a decision finally because I wanted my name to be remembered for something more than William Shakespeare's whore in his sonnets.

"I know women don't publish books," I admitted to Alfonso. "This is why I need your help."

"And what can I do?" he asked in perplexity.

"I'm asking for your support. I shall need your acknowledged approval to be able to do this - your declaration, on the title page perhaps, that I am acting with your permission. I hate to have to humble myself in this way, you know what my beliefs are about the equality of women with men, especially in the artistic sphere. However I am not so naive not to realise that in this country, in this age, I must have your authorisation before anyone would even consider publishing the book."

His expression was surprised but sympathetic as he said, "I understand how much you hate to do this, how you have always rebelled against any conjugal authority I tried to impose." A slight smile hovered on his lips as I couldn't deny it. "But make no mistake about it I would be honoured to help you in any way I can, indeed you don't know how happy I am to be needed by you at last, to be able to do something for you at last."

"Think about it carefully because it is no small thing I am asking you, my dear husband" I said deliberately. "What I am planning to do will offend a lot of people. I shall be criticized, maligned, called immodest, unwomanly, and much of this condemnation will fall also on you, especially when it is seen that I have had your support."

"I'm no stranger to controversy, love," he smiled ruefully. "I will take your part wholeheartedly. You have surprised me but I see no reason why women shouldn't write as well as men, and I know most of our friends and kin in the music world will think the same."

"You don't know what I've written yet," I ventured mischievously. "I think you should hear some of it.

What about this -

> *Our mother Eve who tasted of the tree,*
> *Giving to Adam what she held most dear,*
> *Was simply good and had no power to see,*
> *The after-coming harm did not appear.*
> *But surely Adam cannot be excused,*
> *Her fault though great, yet he was most to blame,*
> *What weakness offered, strength might have refused,*
> *Being Lord of all the greater was his shame.*

And then to lay the fault on Patience back,
That we (poor women) must endure it all.
We know right well he did discretion lack,
Being not persuaded thereunto at all,
If Eve did err it was for knowledge sake,
The fruit being fair persuaded him to fall,
No subtle serpent's falsehood did betray him,
If he would eat it who had power to stay him?"

Alfonso remained silent for a moment then he threw his head back and began to laugh. "Santo cielo, Aemilia, this is dangerous ground. How much more is there of this? What's this poem about?"

"It's actually a religious poem because religion is the only subject that would have a remote chance of being allowed in print if written by a woman. The book does include other verses I must admit but the central premise is the Passion of Christ. However the Countess of Cumberland suggested I wrote it from the women's point of view so it does have some, er, feminine sentiments."

"Anti-male sentiments?" he prompted.

"No, not really. Just an appeal for us to be treated more fairly, more equally.

Then let us have our liberty again,
And challenge to yourselves no Sovereignty,
You came not in the world without our pain,
Make that a bar against your cruelty.
Your faults being greater, why should you disdain
Our being your equals, free from tyranny?
If one weak woman simply did offend,
This sin of yours has no excuse nor end."

"God's bones, Aemilia, and I'm supposed to give my consent to this?"

"I did warn you. But it isn't all like this. There are verses about women betrayed by men - Cleopatra, Fair Rosamund, Matilda – and homage to distinguished women of today like Lady Clifford and the Countess of Pembroke, and there is a poem about Cookham in the style of a classical eclogue. But the central work is a religious poem about Christ's passion and though my first intention was to use it as an excuse to get my work published, I became genuinely absorbed after the pictures in Venice gave me ideas for colour and imagery and drama."

Alfonso was silent for a while, ruffling his fingers through his hair, then he said, "Do you know how often I have been humiliated because of you Aemilia. First it was common talk that I had accepted money from Lord Hunsdon to marry you and that the child was not mine; then you couldn't bear me children so there were doubts about my virility; whispers were always reaching my ears about your being unfaithful and some of my companions were less than kind; then finally you turned me out of the house. Now what do you think people are going to say when I allow you to publish a book, nay give my approval to it, more especially a book with some controversial material that will offend many men. Don't you think I will be seen as less than a man, a man with no control over his wife."

It was my turn to be silent as for the first time I really understood the implications for him. I was expecting difficulties for myself but I had no right to foist such embarrassment upon him. I realised that in my self-indulgence I had not thoroughly considered his point of view and what it would mean to him. "Very well," I said regretfully, "I understand your reasoning and accept it. I have no right to ask so much of you. You must renounce it, tell everyone it is against your wishes. I know the accusations against you are not true, it was my fault we couldn't have children, you have been a true father to Henry, and you fought bravely in the Azores and the Irish campaign as your companions know. I wouldn't want to bring shame on you Alfonso because I think you are the most complete man I have ever known."

He left his chair and came to stand behind me with his arms around me and his head resting on mine. "What you think about me, my love, matters more to me than anyone else's opinion. If you need me then I'm here for you and I'm happy that you've asked for my help." I felt the warmth of his nearness and doubted that any of the men I had known would have made the same sacrifice for me.

"I'm proud of you, proud of what you have accomplished, proud to have you as my wife. I love you because you are different. I love your individuality - and your courage."

"And I love yours," I said simply, realising it was true. He had always had courage, albeit disguised by a nonchalant indifference. "When your name goes in my book I would have liked it to be Alfonso Lanier, Royal musician. But I think it should be Captain Alfonso Lanier as a tribute to your courage."

"It would also carry more weight. Cecil, Egerton, Bishop Bancroft and others all know me as a soldier. And sadly I'm not a musician at present."

"Then if you agree it will be poems written by Aemilia Lanier, wife to Captain Alfonso Lanier. I can't begin to tell you how grateful I am because words aren't enough. I just hope and trust you can read my heart."

He kissed me gently. "We must look around for a publisher and printer."

"I thought I might approach Valentine Simmes, he's known to take risks."

"I'll come with you. We'll see this through together, love, if this is what you want."

"Yes I do want it, despite what the consequences might be," I affirmed. "And you're a man in a million, Alfonso Lanier."

"And as a man with a very insubordinate wife who thinks men are good only for one thing, do you know what I want now?"

"Well judging by the way the candle's burnt down I guess it must be time for bed."

Now that I had definitely decided to publish my verses all my spare time was spent in correcting and thinking about the final form. Unlike male writers I needed justification for everything that I had written. I wrote because I felt I had a gift and I believed women should have the same opportunity to write as men did, but I had to use cunning to disguise my intentions in a more acceptable form. My verses to Margaret Clifford were a means of transferring onto her the responsibility for undertaking the work and implying her approval of me, as was the poem I had written in praise of Cookham. I had included amongst the poems a dream sequence, which had always been a poetic device used as licence to cover a wide range of subjects. I had addressed this to the Countess of Pembroke, Philip Sidney's sister, because she had herself written a pastoral romance and though it had not been intended for publication I was hoping that the implied association with an approved woman author would work in my favour. The main composition, the Passion of Christ, should be acceptable even from the pen of a woman though I was aware that some of the sentiments expressed might cause offence. As yet I had no title for the complete book and of necessity this must be a religious phrase to satisfy the public that it was a devotional work. Then one day I remembered how in a dream during those anxious days of the Spanish Armada many years ago the words Salve Deus Rex Judaeorum had been unaccountably imprinted on my mind. Looking back now it seemed that destiny had decreed I should write this work and I decided that this would be my title.

Now I had to choose some important people to dedicate it to and present them with a complimentary copy. Although my professional ambitions would be satisfied by any financial reimbursement, the expected gift of two or three pounds from a dedicatee was nonetheless not my first consideration. More important to me was official approval for what I had done. Alfonso had offered to approach some of the important personages he was acquainted with like Cecil, Sir Thomas Egerton and Archbishop Bancroft, but though grateful to him I had already decided that all my dedicatees must be women. Fully aware that I was undertaking a unique enterprise I was looking for solidarity amongst the female sex in the hope that they would appreciate my speaking for them and give me their support. The obvious choice was the Queen herself but though Queen Anne was young and pleasant and with her general amiability found favour with Londoners, she was neither intellectual nor religious, and I thought how much easier it would have been with Queen Elizabeth who had herself composed verses. Then on a visit to Richard Boniar, the publisher we had found willing, I noticed that amongst his most recent publications was the 'Masque of Queens', a masque we had recently watched at the Banqueting House through the offices of Robert Cecil, and this gave me an idea. Ben Jonson had again been the author, Inigo Jones responsible for the stage effects and scenery, while

Alfonso Ferrabosco was once more the composer. This time the Queen and her ladies were chief amongst the masquers, making their entrance as the queens of ancient civilisations seated upon a pyramid from which they descended into chariots drawn by eagles, griffins and lions. I realised I could address her in the language of the masque, portray her in the guise of all the goddesses she loved to impersonate. The underlying irony would rescue me from base flattery yet the comparison with the masques she so delighted in should encourage her to look with favour on my book. The other royal lady, the Princess Elizabeth, was only fourteen years old, but I had heard that she was both serious minded and kindly disposed so I would include her. The poem itself centred on Margaret Clifford but unfortunately she was far away in Westmorland and her expected approval could do me little good here in London. However her young sister-in-law, Lucy Countess of Bedford, was one of the Queen's favourite ladies-in-waiting, and as a Puritan and a known patron of authors, including Ben Jonson, Samuel Daniel and John Donne, could serve as a link between the Countess of Cumberland and the Court. I would include Anne Clifford who knew me well, and I wanted also to make a dedication to Arbella Stuart, not in the slightest hope that in her straightened circumstances she would be able to reward me but in the genuine belief that she would appreciate my work. I thought longingly of Penelope Rich, now Blount, whom I knew would be generous, but though she was now feted and honoured at King James's Court together with her husband and children, in view of her past history I did not think her endorsement would help in this particular case. The high-minded ladies I had chosen would be more suitable to grace this work while Penelope would always be remembered as the star

of a book of love poems. Instead I thought of my old
mentor Lady Wingfield. Perhaps she might be pleased
to see that her tuition had at last borne fruit. These were
the women I would dedicate the book to and send them
complimentary copies. I had done as much as I could
and sent my verses to Valentine Simmes the printer.
"Bocc'al lupo," Alfonso said, using a phrase that had
been popular with my father - into the wolf's mouth!

I thought of this now as I sat beside him. The book had not
been a success. Some copies had been sold and Samuel
Daniel had bought a copy and sent me a note of
compliment. I heard on the grapevine that Ben Jonson
and John Donne had also done so, as had all my musician
friends. Alfonso had presented copies to important
acquaintances like Sir Thomas Egerton, Richard Bancroft
now elevated to Archbishop of Canterbury, and Thomas
Jones Archbishop of Dublin whom he had known in
Ireland. I wondered if perhaps Will Shakespeare, still
writing plays but living back in Stratford now with his
family, had perhaps bought one. I was sure if he had seen
it in the booksellers on one of his visits to London he
would have done so and I pictured him reading it,
wondering what he thought of it.

The Queen had acknowledged her gift with a polite
impersonal note by the hand of one of her secretaries,
together with a small sum of money. So had Lady Anne
Clifford, wrapped up in the whirl of Court festivities her
marriage to the Earl of Dorset had brought and
preoccupied with the fact that her father had willed
away her hereditary lands not believing her competent,
as a woman, to administer them. The Princess Elizabeth
had written in her own hand a warm note of thanks
together with a more generous gift, as had the Countess
of Bedford. Lady Margaret Clifford had written from

Appleby, a long letter saying that her health was increasingly poor and that she was not long for this world but expressing her satisfaction with the way I had obeyed her command and certain that in such a work of faith I would consider any financial reimbursement unwelcome. There had been a letter from the Countess of Pembroke stating that she did not believe in the temerity of women to publish for personal vanity and financial gain and that she would request the removal of her name in any subsequent editions. My old tutor Susan Lady Wingfield also wrote that although she admired the learning displayed in the book she did not consider it in accord with a woman's modesty to put herself on a level with men and encroach on their prerogatives. There was no reply from Arbella Stuart for the simple reason that she was imprisoned in the Tower. Against the King's express command she had married young William Seymour secretly and after little more than a week of happiness the marriage had been discovered and they had been sent to the Tower, King James fearing the union of two people so close to the throne. Many years previously Seymour's grandmother Lady Catherine Grey had died there for the same offence. Poor Arbella, imprisoned in the splendour of a great house for much of her life by her martinet grandmother and now imprisoned for the rest of her life in the Tower by her cousin. My own misfortunes seemed small in comparison to hers and I wondered why I had ever envied the nobility. At least my book had been published and I was proud of that. It had brought criticism and anger from some narrow-minded people imprisoned by conventions of class and sex, but I had never subscribed to their opinions. I had entered, if only partially, the professional artistic life that was exclusive to men and my ambitions had been realised at least in this respect. And I had known love for much of my life instead of the fourteen meagre days afforded to Arbella Stuart. I was soon to be deprived of my husband but we had been granted longer than that, even if some years had been lost and at forty he was too young to die, especially when most of the Laniers and Bassanos were long-lived.

He opened his eyes and I kissed his cheek, gently so as not to hurt him. My hand rested on his as lightly as a cobweb so that no pressure might cause him distress. On the other side of the bed sat Henry, every so often a tear dropping gently on his father's other hand in company with the raindrops plopping from the eaves. Alfonso's breath was coming in great rattling gasps as he tried to form the words, "I love you, so proud of you."

"I love you too and I would give everything I possess, everything I have ever wanted, for you not to leave us," I said, meaning every word and praying they would register with him. I was weeping now, though I had tried so hard to control myself, not wanting to distress him.

There was a slight pressure on my hand and a faint smile touched his lips. Then this was followed by a grimace of pain as he summoned all his strength to say in ragged gasps, "I have known more happiness than many men have known in twice my years." The effort exhausted him and I suffered with him as he fought for breath, fearing each gasp would be his last. Then his breathing calmed and he turned to Henry, "Make my music for me and I shall always be with you."

Henry nodded. Everything between them had been said while there was still time. Alfonso closed his eyes again satisfied and appeared to sleep. We sat quietly, lost in our own thoughts. He had been encouraging about my book. "Times might change. Sometimes it takes years before a book is really appreciated. I'm privileged to have seen it and played my part." It was a book about women's independence of men but I had come to realise that equality with love was what I really desired. My sensual nature had always betrayed me in my dealings with men but celibacy was not a condition bequeathed to me. My experience had taught me that men and women needed each other but in an equal exchange of opportunities and respect. I believed that women's nature was to love and be loved, but only within a partnership of equal minds and hearts, not to be used or bought and then excluded from the large part of life that men considered their own sphere. Men had to realise this. And not only men but women too who were partly responsible for blocking their own advancement by fear, false modesty, subservience to authority that was man-made and male-dominated, and antagonism to other women who tried to break the mould. But my appeals to women to recognise this had fallen largely on deaf ears.

Suddenly both Henry and I felt a slight pressure on our hands and Alfonso's eyes opened again. His chest rose and fell, his breath expelled in a great effort, and I feared he was going to lapse into agonizing convulsions again. But instead he smiled and our eyes met and it seemed as if all the happiness we had ever known was distilled in those moments of contact. I do not know when I became aware that his breathing had stopped. Henry looked at me in alarm and I nodded, not able to voice the words. Then I reached over to gently close his eyes, my tears falling on his face. For a long time neither of us moved, not wanting to leave him and tell his family who, after making their own farewells, had left the final hour to us but were all waiting in the parlour below.

Then Henry spoke. "Someone at Court once said to me, 'Your father was Baron Hunsdon, the Lord

Chamberlain'. But I said to him, 'You are mistaken, my father is Alfonso Lanier the musician.' He said, 'But are you not proud to be the son of a great nobleman, kinsman to Queen Elizabeth?' 'What is nobility?' I replied. 'Being born into a family where someone once, hundreds of years ago, fought well on the battlefield and since then they have lived on that reputation, a life of ease and money, not earning their living or serving mankind in any useful way. On the contrary my father's music has enriched the lives of many, made them happy, soothed their cares, brought them a little nearer to Heaven. I am proud to be the son of such a man." His voice broke and he stood up.

I looked up at him, this handsome young man of eighteen who shared so many of my own beliefs. I had at first envied the nobility and wanted to be part of their world, then I had resented their privileges, until I had finally come to realise that exclusion from this class of society need not, and must not, be a bar to achievement. Henry could have grown up resentful of the life he had lost but instead he had valued the life he had been given. I hadn't welcomed him at first, been willing to give him away because he threatened the life I thought I wanted, and he could have been a constant reminder of what I had lost. Instead he had brought me so much unexpected joy. In him was the continuity of the life I had shared with my father and, not Lord Hunsdon, but Alfonso. When my father had died Alfonso had taken over his position as a recorder player in the consort of the Queen's Musick. In time Henry would take Alfonso's place. I was proud of my son, of Alfonso's son, our legacy to the world of music.

And I was proud of my book. In the end it mattered little whether it was successful or not. The fact remained that I had written it and published it, a feat few women had achieved. For the moment it might lie neglected on the booksellers' shelves but in the future it might inspire other women to write and publish, works of unlimited scope, and help forge their acceptance into the artistic world of men. I had recently had delivered to me by an anonymous hand a brief note with a single word "Bravo" and a scrawled signature that I knew well. Did he understand the reasons I had published it?

I took my last leave of Alfonso. I had believed in the past that I had loved and been loved by others, but it was the man who had been thrust unwillingly upon me who had finally gained my love, who had accepted me as I was, who had stood by me and supported me at great cost to himself. I now had to find the strength to live without him. I knew that I would have help from the family and the musicians, and Henry would be a constant feature in my life. But I wanted to make an independent life for myself also. I would see if I could get the Earl of Southampton's patent re-registered in my name, I would do some teaching again and perhaps open a little school of my own, and I would continue to write. I followed Henry downstairs to tell the family that my husband Alfonso Lanier, Court musician, was dead, and a sudden recollection came to me of when my father's body had lain in this same house and I had said, "He's gone to play his music with the angels."

HISTORICAL POSTSCRIPT

Aemilia Bassano Lanier lived for another thirty two years. She never remarried. She died in 1645 in the middle of the Civil War age seventy six. There are no extant contemporary references to her book 'Salve Deus Rex Judeaorum', though seven copies remain.

Her son Henry was a musician for James I and Charles I. He married and fathered two children.

The Bassano family and Alfonso's brothers continued as Court musicians throughout the reign of Charles I and the Protectorate, Clement only dying at the Restoration. Alfonso's nephew Nicholas Lanier (son of his brother John) became chief musician to Charles I but is also famous as an art collector for the King, responsible for acquiring for him the Duke of Mantua's collection of Italian masterpieces.

William Shakespeare died in Stratford in 1616 age 52. The first collected edition of his plays (the first folio) was printed and published in 1623 by his fellow actors John Hemminges and Henry Condell with an appreciation by Ben Jonson who later became Poet Laureate. His sonnets were never reprinted.

Henry Wriothesley, Earl of Southampton, helped to finance trade and exploration including an expedition to Virginia, where he was interested in establishing silk manufacture, and one to find the North West passage. He was a member of the East Indian Company and presented a collection of books for the new library at Cambridge. He died in 1624 leaving a son and 3 daughters.

Young Robert Devereux, 3rd Earl of Essex, was divorced from his wife Frances Howard. He became the commander of the army of Parliament opposed to King Charles I in the Civil War.

Penelope's son, the 2nd Earl of Warwick, was in command of the Parliament Navy.

Arbella Stuart was kept in the Tower until her death in 1615 age 40.

Walter Raleigh was executed in 1618, King James sacrificing him to the wishes of Spain.